WHILE GODS SLEEP

Book One of Perilous Gods

L.D. COLTER

Tam Lin Publishing
First Edition
Copyright © Liz Colter 2018 [L. D. Colter]

Cover Art Copyright © 2018 Trevor Smith
Interior Design and Formatting by

E.M.
TIPPETTS
BOOK DESIGNS

www.emtippettsbookdesigns.com

To Greg, for everything...

ACKNOWLEDGEMENTS

Many thanks go out to all the people who helped me along the way to seeing this book published, only some of whom are mentioned here. To Trevor for the fabulous artwork, and to the many who gave aid, feedback, and support as I wrote this, including the good friends and fine writers in the Glenwood Springs critique group and Codex novel competition, as well as Andrea, Terry, Amanda, and Stewart. Most of all, my gratitude to Natalia Theodoridou for being beta reader, teacher, and advisor, especially concerning all things Greek. Any inaccuracies that are not intentional fabrication are entirely my own errors.

L. D. Colter
July, 2018

PART ONE

Surface Tension

1

The Piper's Price

Ty lifted his throwing cup for the final toss of the bones. The clamor of the spectators quieted. He ignored the scattered cheers and taunts, the cigarette smoke and coughs of the twenty people crammed into the back room of Nikos' small market. With his opponent watching from the other side of the table, Ty rattled the cup and tossed the five small goat pasterns across the green felt. Nine points would tie the game; anything more and he'd win the championship. Life could return to normal. He'd settle his debts and quit gambling.

He'd live to see his thirtieth birthday.

The bones bounced and rolled. The first two landed on their flat, lowest-scoring sides; the third bounced to a stop for two points. The fourth bone rolled briefly up onto the convex bulge worth six points, but momentum carried it over for three. The final bone pirouetted on a corner. It toppled and landed on its flattest side. One point.

The game official, standing at the side of the table in his dark suit, intoned the scores formally, using Ty's given name. "The final throw for

Eutychios Kleisos totals eight points." The man's face, thin as a starving child's, held neither joy for the winner nor sympathy for the loser. "His final score stands at one hundred and two. Yannis Zaros' final score stands at one hundred and three. Yannis Zaros wins."

Shouts of joy mingled with a loud chorus of moans and curses. Simultaneous conversations began as the spectators settled their side bets. Ty heard it only dimly beneath a growing hum in his ears. His fog of single-minded obsession and cosmic certainty that he'd win the championship burned off now like morning mist, and the enormity of a debt he couldn't repay struck him with the force of one of the city's lumbering trams. Sweat dotted his forehead and palms. It ran down the insides of his dress shirt. He hoped his legs would hold him as he moved around the table to shake the hand his opponent proffered.

Memories ghosted to him of old tracks and backrooms in Athina— Athens, as the European tourists called his city—where his father had taken him as a small child, places where he'd been left untended among the shouting men with their changeable moods. He could no longer remember the chain of rationalizations that six months ago had hauled him back into this world he'd professed to hate.

"I'm sorry," Nikos said, patting him on the back. Friends from childhood, Nikos knew that in this one night, Ty had lost roughly what it would take him two years to earn in his job as a locksmith. Ty wasn't about to share with him that the game remained in play, the stakes raised now to life and death. He nodded in vague acknowledgement and tried to envision a scenario where Nikos wouldn't learn the depth of his stupidity these past months. He couldn't.

Others brushed past, offering condolences. He barely saw them as he searched the knot of spectators. His money-lender's stature made Kairos difficult to spot until the crowd shifted and he saw a flash of gaudy yellow, waist-high among the dark suits. Like butter in a churn, the press of people continued to move and Kairos flowed from the middle to the front, headed for Ty. Two black-coated men flanked him.

"I might not make it back to the hospital tonight," Ty said to Nikos. "Would you check on my mother for me? Tell her I'll be there as soon as I can?"

"Of course," Nikos said, not noticing the approaching trio. He gripped Ty's shoulder and pushed through the dark curtain that divided the back room from the store front. Ty wished he could follow him, run out of the store and out of the city. One look at the black-coated men told him he wouldn't get far.

His money-lender stopped in front of him and the two men placed themselves at Ty's shoulders. Kairos' head came only to Ty's stomach and he looked up, studying him with wide, dark eyes that perched above his pocked ball of a drinker's nose. His lemon-chiffon suit practically glowed in the room's shadows and made queasy contrast to his shock of rust-red hair. People standing nearby turned, sensing tension like sharks smelling blood.

Ty gave Kairos the only thing he had left: the truth. "I don't have it. Another lender sent men by today to collect on some other debts I owed." They'd tracked him down at the hospital. His mother had woken when they came in and had looked confused and worried as they escorted him out of the room. "I had all my stakes for tonight right up until today. They made me give them everything. It's why I borrowed the money."

"And you thought borrowing a better option than forfeiting?"

He'd been heading out of his apartment to do just that when the conviction that he would win tonight overpowered his common sense.

The justifications that had resonated so strongly earlier today felt paper-thin now, in light of the evening's catastrophic loss.

He didn't answer and Kairos continued. "The contract you signed stipulates you'll pay the money back tonight out of your winnings, plus twenty percent."

He'd tracked Kairos down and convinced him to draw up the contract, but the memory felt hazy and unreal, as if he'd been drunk. The obvious issue of how he would come up with the money in the event of a loss hadn't been Kairos' problem, and Ty wondered again at the man's motivation for agreeing to such a deal. He guessed he was about to find out.

Not for the first time, a niggling concern told him he'd been conned. He thought back over the past few months looking for proof, starting with the unexpected invitation from one of his locksmith clients to play in the big money bones games. Ty had ended up playing not just once but the entire season, from the first day of fall to tonight's spring equinox. He'd made new friends who had encouraged him to bet on horse and dog races, wrestling—pretty much everything—all of them venues where his losses outweighed his consistent winnings at bones.

He wanted to believe he'd been conspired against, manipulated, but it seemed impossible. The decisions, however uncharacteristic, had been his own.

"Take him to the warehouse," Kairos said to the two men. Now everyone in the room watched.

Kairos' men were hard and silent. They wore identical black trench coats, and both had hair as black as Ty's own, but instead of his blue eyes, theirs were obsidian. Despite the fact that one looked to be in his twenties and the other in his fifties, there seemed something about their similarities that made them feel like they belonged together.

The men patted him down. He'd never carried weapons in his life and hadn't been about to start today. Satisfied, they grabbed him by the shoulders of his suit jacket and herded him past the curtain and into the store, along cramped shelves of packaged goods and bins of bulk items. Nikos sat behind the counter pricing boxes of Paximathia biscuits. He looked up in surprise as they hauled Ty to the door. "What's going on?" he said.

"Tell my mother I'll come see her soon," Ty said. "Nothing else, all right?"

The little bell over the shop door jingled as they pushed him out of the store.

Outside, the streets of Athina hummed. It had been thirteen years since the end of World War II and eight since the bloody Civil War that had followed. Commerce in Ellada—Greece to their English speaking allies—had finally begun to revive. Restaurants, shops, and the ancient sites saw an increase in tourism each year. Cars flowed like stately yachts through the bustle, competing for space with pedestrians and trams.

Kairos' men led him into a more residential quarter of the neighborhood, home for all twenty-nine years of his life, where ancient white-washed homes squatted stubbornly among the new brick buildings looming over them. The oldest homes listed dizzily. Some sported patchwork stone, cobbling them to adjoining structures and forming shops with attached living quarters. Pillars and foundations from eons past sprouted like gray teeth, jutting between rows of apartments stacked four and five stories above the newer shops and department stores. Phone wires and lines carrying electricity crisscrossed overhead with the tram cables stretching between the tall buildings, like the intricate rigging of a ship. As if the old city might hoist her sails someday and sail away to the nearby ocean.

On the front porch of a squat house sandwiched between two larger buildings, the widow Savina wielded a rug beater with the vigor of an athlete. Six months ago she would have stopped to ask him who he was with, what he was doing, if he wanted to come in for a bit of supper as he had no wife at home. Tonight she stared at him and continued swinging. He didn't doubt that her cataract-clouded eyes judged his escorts and weighed his downfall accurately.

It was the widow who had sent a boy to the races to tell Ty that his mother had been found in bed, too weak from pneumonia to feed herself. He wanted to shout across the street to the woman that his mother had never called him for help. The excuses lodged in his throat. If he hadn't stopped visiting to keep her from learning about his gambling, he could have prevented her illness from progressing. Staying away had been a useless folly in the end; if the widow had known to send the boy to the racetrack, his mother had surely heard the rumors as well. He wished now he'd worked up the nerve to tell her everything as he sat with her at the hospital over the past few days, listening to her wet cough and labored breathing.

"Where are we going?" he asked.

"Somewhere we can talk privately," Kairos said, giving him no answer at all.

"If I could just..."

Kairos walked on as if he hadn't spoken, but the dark-coated men swiveled their heads and gave him a look that silenced him.

Lights popped on, countering the deepening twilight. Music drifted through open windows on twenty-year-old wooden cathedral radios and shiny new box radios. The newly revived rebetika, strains from

Hadjidakis' compositions, and Sofia Vempo's contralto followed them through the streets, lively tunes playing in sharp counterpoint to Ty's mood. In a few more blocks they came to a faded-pink tin warehouse. One of the dark-coated men opened the door. The threshold loomed over Ty like a point of no return, and dread filled him as he stepped over the boundary. His body felt remote, as if he watched through another person's eyes as he entered the building.

He expected a smelting factory or maybe a meat-packing plant— somewhere Kairos could kill him and dispose of his body without leaving any evidence. He wasn't expecting a beauty academy. The two men escorted him down a cavernous room dotted with stylists' chairs, sinks, and side-tables filled with scissors, combs, brushes and bottles. A strong smell of ammonia hung in the air, giving the impression that students had been here just minutes before. One of the men opened the door to an office on the left. Ty was pushed into a wooden chair while Kairos took a seat behind the desk.

Kairos hadn't appeared at the games until this past season, according to the long-time gamblers. Ty knew nothing about him except that he'd made himself visible and word had spread that he was a reputable money lender. Judging by the shortened legs on the desk and the chair that fit him perfectly, this had to be his office.

"You've cheated me, Ty," he said. "I can't abide a cheater." He nodded to the older man on Ty's right.

The man leaned in and wrapped the long, thin fingers of one hand over Ty's wrist and the arm of the chair. Some trick of the light made the trench-coated shoulders look like the humps of folded wings. His eyes flashed, small and beady, the whites invisible for a moment. Ty jerked his arm back but didn't manage to pull free. The man on his left grabbed his other wrist, and Ty's heart pounded against his ribs.

The top button of Ty's shirt was undone, as always, his tie knotted well below the old, ropy scar across the front of his throat. With one finger, the man on his right nudged his shirt collar and T-shirt to the side. He pinched above his collarbone and Ty flinched. Nails that looked like ordinary fingernails and felt like claws pierced his skin. The man pulled. To Ty's horror, he felt the flesh tear. His pulse hammered in his throat as he tried to twist free.

A paper-thin strip of flesh peeled loose, pulling away more easily than skin should separate from the layers below. Pain burned along the two inch path of the wound. Ty cried out, more in horror than agony. With a jerk, the man plucked the skin free and dangled it in front of Ty's face, a slender strip, pale on one side, bloody on the other. He tipped his head back, dropped the flesh into his mouth, and swallowed convulsively, bird-like, without chewing. Ty fought down a sudden, violent nausea.

"Your life isn't worth what you owe me," Kairos continued, "so what am I to do now?"

The younger man pushed two fingers into the bloody wound and placed his thumb on the other side of Ty's collarbone. He tugged very slightly, and the bone loosened and shifted. It threatened to pluck free of Ty's body as easily as the skin had done; as easily as carrion birds might pick apart the rotted carcass of an animal at the side of the road. The man pulled a fraction harder. Pain lanced through the ligaments securing Ty's collarbone to his sternum. Fear unbalanced his heart, sending it tripping into unfamiliar rhythms, hammering so violently it ached.

"I'll pay you back," he panted. "I swear it. Give me a week."

"A week?" Kairos said. The tension on the bone eased. "Well, how could I not trust that coming from someone who promised to pay the money back tonight? No. I think I'll take my payment now." He picked a large silver coin off his desk and spun it on end, watching Ty as it rattled to stillness. The faces of the nation's queens stared out, twins conjoined back-to-back, one head facing Kairos, one facing Ty. "What would you be willing to do to repay me?"

The joint at Ty's sternum throbbed. "Anything," he answered too quickly. He hoped that he hadn't just promised to murder someone or pledged to become Kairos' bed-boy.

Kairos nodded and the black-coated men released him. "I need you to get something for me. Something from Erebus." He watched Ty with his dark eyes, gauging his reaction.

Ty's mother had raised him in the Hellenistic religion that she and a tiny minority in Ellada held to—that the myths and fables of poets like Hesiod and Homer weren't mythology at all; the stories and the gods were real. As a teenager, he'd rejected the outdated, polytheist belief, but he'd never filled the void with the Catholicism that had supplanted the old religion in his country centuries ago.

Ty glanced at the strange men to either side, then to Kairos. His wound burned. Blood seeped into his white shirt. He'd experienced visions of the gods twice as a child, and for the last half of his life he'd believed in nothing but what he could see. Now he didn't know what to believe.

"Are humans allowed there?" Ty wasn't ready to accept that Erebus was real, but it seemed a good idea to humor the man who held his life in his hands.

"Of course humans are allowed," Kairos said. "It just hasn't been done before."

Ty had been taught that Erebus was a dark mid-world, adjacent to Tartarus and other underworlds. A place where monsters and offspring of the gods had been sent to dwell once the gods no longer walked the earth.

He'd thought Kairos odd the times he'd seen him at the games—his rust hair and his eyes that seemed older than his face, his fashion sense that bordered on the bizarre. Now he factored in the strange henchmen and the erratic bounces the bones had sometimes taken. Ty hadn't lost a game all season until the championship, yet his unlikely string of losses in every other venue had landed him deeply in debt.

Details that had seemed unrelated a few hours ago drew together like a chemical bond, individual elements combining to make something entirely new. Perhaps Kairos had played a part in his patterns of luck and loss, or some spell had influenced the murky quality of his decision-making these past few months. He forced the train of thought to a halt, dismissing it as ravings from a fear-saturated brain. Even the strange impressions of the thugs had most likely stemmed from adrenaline. If anyone was crazy here, he needed to believe it was the man across from him.

"Why me?" he said, trying to tack with the winds of his captor. "There must be a thousand men in the city who'd love the challenge. If I went to Erebus, I'd probably get killed in the first few minutes." He lifted his hands as much as the restraint allowed; a let's-be-reasonable gesture. "Let me pay you back, the full amount plus twenty percent. I don't need a week. I'll get it today." He didn't know how, but he'd find a way. "You can use the cash to hire someone else."

"If you're worried about going to Erebus, what do you think your chances are of surviving the day if you say no?" Kairos tapped the coin on the desk, letting the question hang in the air. "However, the quicker the thing is done, the better for all. Besides, the sooner you're back, the sooner you can see your mother again, right?"

Ty felt as if he'd been doused in ice water. He'd been a fool to mention her in front of Kairos.

"All right," he said, his attempt at negotiation crushed. "Whatever you want. You want me to go to Erebus, I'll go." A tension he hadn't previously noticed ebbed from the man's shoulders.

"You're a locksmith, is that right?" Ty nodded, though Kairos seemed to already know this for a certainty. "I'll want you to take a set of your tools with you, something discreet, but you have a stop to make before you go home to get them." He addressed his two men. "Take him to Kalyptra's."

The name was one Ty felt certain he hadn't heard before. He wished he had. It might have given him some hint of what lay in store.

2

A Marked Man

Full dark had descended by the time Kairos' men escorted Ty the few blocks from the warehouse and up three flights of stairs of an apartment building. The older man knocked on an unmarked door. When it opened, Kalyptra turned out to be a woman, younger than Ty, though hard for him to tell by how much.

She had light brown hair that came to just below her shoulders and she might've been stunning if she hadn't been so obscured by tattoos. Her entire face was dark green, patterned with black whorls and symbols. Her neck was heart-attack red with blue writing in a stick-figure script. The rest of her—what he could see from the man's work shirt she wore unbuttoned to her braless breasts and baggy fisherman's pants rolled to the knees—was the yellowish color of rawhide lampshades.

He couldn't guess the original color of her skin or if the pale yellow had been tattooed on or dyed into her body some other way. The "skin" was broken by large, black, stitches colored in irregular rectangles, making her look as if she'd been pieced together by some rough and untalented creator. He wondered how she moved about in the city without being arrested as a lunatic and how he hadn't heard of her living here so close to his neighborhood.

"Kairos sent him," the older man said, his speech oddly clipped. He indicated Ty with a nod.

She opened the door wider and stood back. One of the men shoved Ty, and he stumbled inside. The apartment was small and more or less tidy, though suffused with a musty odor. Kalyptra turned, waggled a finger over her shoulder, and padded ahead, barefoot. The men took up a position by the door.

Ty followed her to the only other room in the apartment, her bedroom apparently. She crossed to a large dresser and rummaged in the top drawer. "Take off your clothes," she said.

She was as strange as Kairos and his lackeys, but what she wanted from him he couldn't begin to guess. It didn't really matter. With Kairos' men in the other room, he wasn't about to put up any resistance unless left with no choice.

"Can I ask why?" he said, as he slipped off his jacket. He could, but apparently she wasn't going to answer.

He pulled his narrow, black tie free, then sat on the bed to remove his socks and shoes. His reserves faltered and he sat there a moment longer before he unbuttoned his shirt with a mixture of anxiety and resentment. He lifted the cloth gingerly from the congealing wound at his right shoulder and pulled it off, followed by his undershirt. The resentment increased as he stood and unbuckled his belt, but he didn't see any alternative. He stripped to his undershorts. She turned her head and made a perfunctory gesture for him to remove those as well.

A refusal flitted across his tongue unvoiced. Questions he wanted answered did the same. More than either of those things, he wanted to live long enough to see his mother again. Now that he was thinking straight for the first time in months he could apologize, explain what little he could, assure her he'd never gamble again. He couldn't imagine the hurt he'd caused her when she realized he'd followed in the footsteps of his father, the man who'd gambled away the family money and then abandoned her and Ty to poverty.

Kalyptra continued to sift the contents of the drawer, occasionally placing an item on top of the dresser. Feeling his exposure on multiple levels, he removed the rest of his clothing.

He covered himself with his hands and waited. Wedging his tongue between his teeth, he made a soft clicking noise. It took him a moment to catch the nervous habit that had come to his attention once he started gambling. Kalyptra still had her back to him, but he'd have to be on his guard if he hoped to live through this. She turned and faced him, a few small jars in her hands.

Women had appraised him before without finding anything that warranted pointing or laughter so he endured her inspection with what he hoped was a confident expression. Being nearly six feet tall and relatively fit, maybe he had whatever it was she was looking for. If not, his black hair and blue eyes usually won him more favors than he deserved. Her examination seemed a tad clinical, however, and her expression gave him no clues.

"Lie down," she said, indicating the bed. He did.

She sat on the side of the bed and set the jars next to him. Lifting a finger to his throat, she traced the scar there. The interest with which she touched it made him wonder if she felt his old death in the coarse tissue.

He'd died twice as a child, both accidents, each one leaving him with no heartbeat or breath for a few minutes. The first time he'd been five-years-old. He'd drowned and been revived by some older boys. The second time, two years later, he'd died by hanging and been revived by his mother. The thick, red smile across his throat was a memento from the hanging. He'd always believed that his third death would be the final one.

After fingering the scar, Kalyptra ran both hands down Ty's chest, pausing over his heart. Kairos had told Ty he would send him to Erebus; he didn't say in what condition. Ty tried to prepare himself for anything from intercourse to an elaborate execution. Sex wasn't necessarily the preferable option, based on tales he'd heard of jealous gods or some of their offspring who took after their promiscuous appetites and homicidal tendencies. Whether these people were playing at being something more than human, or truly were, the result would likely be the same for him either way.

Kalyptra opened a nightstand drawer and removed three objects. One was an item he'd never seen before, about the size and shape of a calligraphy pen. The second was a straight-bladed shaving razor. The third item made his palms break out in a sweat—a small knife with an edge so shiny it put the razor to shame.

She set the knife on the nightstand. Ty imagined lunging for it and holding her off while he grabbed a handful of his clothes. It would still leave Kairos' men out there, though, and he hadn't been lying when he'd told Kairos he'd likely die if confronted with anything resembling mortal combat.

She opened one of the jars. The liquid within was dark blue, but the scent of honey laced with sulfur smelled nothing like ink or paint. She picked up the pen-shaped thing. Instead of a nib, it terminated in a small bundle of sharp needles. She dipped the needles into the liquid, bent over him, and pressed them hard into the skin below his right collarbone. It burned like hell and kept on burning as she moved down, tattooing him as she went, though it seemed to go faster than he would have expected.

"What's this for?" he asked, trying to sound conversational. He'd never had a tattoo—few people got them except for mariners and dock workers and such. He wondered what made them want the damn things if they hurt this much.

Kalyptra made no reply, her expression as emotionless as if she hadn't heard. She held her face close to his body as she worked, her breath the light, rhythmic brush of a feather. Her hair tickled his skin like ants dancing erratic patterns on his chest, but the fiery, nerve-searing pain of the needles and ink more than counteracted anything that might have been sensual. He grunted and sweated and gritted his teeth as her work progressed down his body; his only breaks came when she changed nibs on the end of the tool as she changed colors.

He tried to think of something other than fear or pain, but it was hard to force his mind far from either. He tried to imagine Erebus and remembered the visions he'd had as a child. He'd always suspected that telling his mother about seeing the gods when he drowned had been the catalyst for her religious fervor. He couldn't remember how devout she'd been before that. The visions had frightened him, but his mother had frightened him more when she told him that the gods had chosen to show themselves to him, like the heroes of old. She'd thought it wonderful. The second time he died, he told his mother he hadn't seen anything.

Kalyptra used the straight razor to clear a swath as she worked, scraping through the middling amount of hair that ran across the center of his chest and in a thin line down to his navel. Pride made him struggle not to groan when she began with the needles again, but he didn't succeed for long. He couldn't see the design she drew, but the pattern swirled as she extended it from his collarbone toward his sternum, around his right nipple, and down the right side of his chest and abdomen to the top of his hip. By the time she was done the entire right side of his chest was on fire, even areas she hadn't colored.

"Lung for luck," she said, when she finished that side. "The pain is necessary, but this should help." She dipped her fingers in a jar of powder and stroked softly down the length of the tattoo. The pain abated slightly and muscles he didn't know he held tense relaxed.

He hoped the worst was over, but she shifted on the bed and began on his left side. The new pattern took a similar course, though when she finished she said, "Heart for love." Again, she stroked powder into the serpentine and again the pain eased somewhat.

She pulled his left arm to the side, about to start a new area, and he wondered how much of his body she planned to tattoo.

"I need a break," he said.

Her focus on her work was so intent that she looked at him as if he'd spoken gibberish.

"I need some water," he elaborated. "I need to use the bathroom."

She sat up and nodded toward an open door off her bedroom.

In the bathroom he went first to the single window. He peered down at the three-story drop and a fire escape ladder too far to the right of the window to do any good. Pulling back from the window, he saw his ghostly reflection framed against the black night sky. He no longer saw the body he had known all his life. Kalyptra had indelibly changed him, decorating his skin with a pair of inch-wide patterns in red, black, blue, and yellow. Tiny pinpricks of blood spotted the lighter colors. The tattoos glared back in the reflection, a lasting reminder of the person he'd become these past six months.

When he came back, she pointed to the bed and began the work on his arm. Though the powder eased the pain when she finished, the process was still excruciating. He thought it couldn't get any worse until she started on the soles of his feet. He gripped the covers and begged her to stop.

She glanced up from her work, then studied him with a long, assessing gaze. She murmured something he couldn't catch in a language he thought might be ancient Greek. The next thing he was aware of, she'd finished with his feet and was telling him to turn over.

Pain seared across his body in waves, and lying on his stomach was its own torture. He tried to focus on thoughts of his motorcycle, riding it out into the countryside, taking curves too fast in the rain. The 200cc engine growling, the leather saddle bouncing on its spring over the rough highway. Despite his hours of nudity in front of this woman, his face burned when she instructed him to roll over again and started on the inside of one thigh.

When she set the pen-thing down a final time, torso patterns twined down both sides of his chest, and smaller designs decorated the inside of his left arm above the elbow, the hip bone above his right buttock, the inside of his left thigh, and most of the bottoms of both feet.

She picked up the third item. He'd forgotten about the knife. He wondered if all that had gone before was just ritual—Ty as the sacrificial cow, lovingly readied for slaughter with his paint and his garland of tattoos. Maybe Kairos asking for Ty's consent to go to Erebus had been nothing more than a comedy of innocence. For the third or fourth time this night, he genuinely feared he was about to die.

Kalyptra gripped his left wrist and adrenaline ripped through him. He jerked his arm back but she had already cut him, four slices in all, so quick that he didn't feel the pain until some seconds later. She salted the wounds, forcing a groan from him, then powdered the cuts with a sickly-sweet-smelling white substance that stopped the bleeding immediately. She repeated the process over his right wrist. He inspected both sets of cuts when she finished and was shocked to see mature scars where fresh wounds should have been.

She opened her nightstand drawer and tossed the bloody tools inside. Ty dared to hope it was over, but she pulled out a length of black ribbon. Slipping it behind his neck, she tied a half-knot over the scar on his throat. Speaking again in a language that sounded only distantly connected to his own, she slowly drew the ribbon tight.

The pressure on the sensitive cartilage that lay under his scar detonated a panic more deeply primal than all his other fears that night. His shoulders came off the bed and he thrashed as he tried to slip his fingers under the ribbon, but the strip of material proved too thin and tight. He struck at her with all his repressed anger and resentment. She tilted her head out of the way. Unable to swallow or take a full breath, he grabbed both of her wrists. She was stronger than she looked. Stronger than he was.

White stars floated in front of his eyes before Kalyptra relaxed and allowed the ribbon to loosen. In his native language she said, "The tie that binds."

Ty gasped for air and his eyes teared with relief. He coughed and wheezed. He waited for his hammering heart to slow.

She bent over him and pressed her chest to his. Her lips touched his skin under his right collarbone. Ty heard her murmuring softly in that strange language as she moved down his body, her breath stroking his skin like warm snowflakes as she impressed her words into the patterns. In this way, she traced the entire path of all the tattoos and scars she had given him. Another place, another time, another woman, it would have been maddeningly arousing; with Kalyptra, he ground his teeth and waited for it to end. Last of all was his throat, where she had tied the ribbon.

Dawn was filtering in through her dirty window when she pushed herself off the bed and looked down at him. Impassive Kalyptra had returned. "You can dress now."

Ty pulled his clothes on over sore and swollen skin.

She escorted him to the front room where Kairos' men stood by the door, awake and alert. He wondered if they'd been standing there all night. They took him by the arms, as if he had any choice but to go with them. Kalyptra never said a word as they hustled him out of the apartment.

3

Crossing Over

The men escorted Ty to his apartment where, as Kairos had instructed, he picked out a small pocket-set from his locksmith tools. He'd hoped the black-coated men might let him eat something and maybe change out of his rumpled suit and bloody shirt before returning to the warehouse, or that they might allow him to stop by the hospital. Kairos' men made it clear they didn't give a rat's ass about his wants.

Back at the beauty academy, Kairos locked the building and they all walked to the train station, the two behind still wearing their trench coats despite the rapidly warming day. Ty's feet burned like hellfire on the walk; his clothes rubbed painfully at his newly colored skin and the wound above his collarbone. At the station, Kairos purchased tickets to Lake Marathon. He pointed Ty to an empty compartment for the two of them. His lackeys sat separately. Ty eased onto the bench seat, the tattoos on his lower back and thigh sending a jolt of fresh pain across his skin. The train began to move, and still Kairos hadn't spoken.

Ty watched the poorer neighborhoods of the nation's capital city slide by the window; cluttered streets, newsstands on the corners, trash piled up against the chain-link fence along the tracks, and people hunched against a cool, spring wind. Mount Lycabettus rose from the city like a wishful scale model of Mount Olimbos, which spread ten times its height and fifty peaks wider beyond sight to the northeast.

He leaned forward to look back at his city for what might be the last time. The Acropolis loomed over the town from its outcrop, its dead bones seeming fuller and whiter in the noonday sun, more imposing than he remembered. He hoped Nikos might go see his mother again today, and wondered what she would think of her son not coming to visit. The doctor had warned him that she remained in danger, that the advanced care and penicillin therapy might have come too late. She'd made it through those first questionable days, though. Perhaps she'd even be home by the time he returned. If he returned.

The urban outskirts condensed into the congestion of downtown, then back to outskirts before slowly opening onto suburbs, country farms, and finally, rolling hills of scrub. The train chugged on into the countryside before Ty broke the silence.

"So, are you going to tell me what it is I'm going to Erebus to fetch or am I just supposed to guess when I get there?"

"Someone there has a thing I need," Kairos said. "Her name is Naia. The item is small, no longer than my hand." He reached into an inside jacket pocket and produced a small piece of thick paper, which he handed to Ty. "That should be about life-sized," he said.

The drawing was sophisticated and detailed. The rectangular object depicted a gryphon in profile, sitting on its haunches: the top, the head; the shaft, the folded wings over the body; the flared base, the taloned front feet. It appeared to be flat on both sides, about the thickness of a letter opener, and only an inch or two wide. The colors were the same as those patterning Ty's body: red, gold, blue, and black. The gray edges that bordered the shiny colors gave the impression the item was made of painted metal.

"Are you going with me?" Ty asked.

"No."

"So how do I find this person? Is there a map or something? I mean, the less I wander around asking 'Can you tell me where Naia is?' the longer I'll live, right?"

"There aren't any maps of Erebus. It would be like trying to map the clouds. Erebus is... changeable." Kairos picked at a pimple on the side of his nose. "I've given you what advantages I can," he said, nodding his head in the direction of Ty's newly tattooed body. "Beyond that, instinct will serve you there better than anything else." He paused. "We'd better both hope you have good instincts."

Not lately, Ty felt, but usually he did. Right now he felt like a man just waking up, struggling out of a vivid dream. "So what's to stop me from turning around after you drop me off, hightailing it for someplace neither of us has ever heard of?" Ty wasn't exactly playing his hand. He knew Kairos would have a contingency plan, and he might as well know what it was.

Kairos reached into his jacket pocket and pulled a length of black ribbon from the depths. It looked disturbingly familiar. Holding it in his lap, he tied a loose knot in the middle and slowly pulled on the two ends.

Ty gagged. Then he choked.

The tighter Kairos pulled, the less air Ty was able to suck in past a constriction that felt like fingers wrapped around his neck at the level of his scar. His hands clawed at his throat, as if he could tear away the pressure.

Kairos untied the knot. Ty slid from the bench to his knees, gasping like a beached fish. He remained that way long after he'd recovered, his composure slower to return than his breath. At last, he climbed awkwardly back onto his seat.

Kairos said nothing more and they spent the next hour in silence as the train trundled on, making fewer and fewer stops on the way to Lake Marathon, the last point on the line. When the train finally squealed to a stop, a couple of families with picnic baskets and blankets were all that exited with them. Kairos pointed to a bench outside the station and the two black-coated men sauntered over and took a seat. After Kairos' little trick with the ribbon, Ty had to admit that they were a bit superfluous.

He followed Kairos down a rough boardwalk that led from the train station to the lake where the shallow waters were dotted with children screaming and squealing as they played, enjoying the rebirth of spring, the promise of warmer weather and water more than the actuality. The boardwalk terminated at a pier, and on either side of the pier were a dozen or more boats, mostly small crafts: wooden canoes, rowboats, a handful of dinghies with canvas sails neatly folded. A couple of larger sailboats bobbed at the far end.

Kairos unlocked the chain from one of the rowboats. The ladder down gave him no trouble, but the long step from the ladder to the boat looked to be a challenge for his short legs. Ty wouldn't have minded seeing him go for a swim, and was disappointed when Kairos managed the gap with an awkward but practiced leap.

Ty didn't care for deep water. His first death, by drowning, had been the summer he'd turned five, shortly after he'd been allowed to join the older boys playing at the quarry pond. On a day like any other, bored with the endless squirting games and diving for stones games and chicken fights, he'd decided to swim across the pond, despite the fact that he'd never learned to swim. He tiptoed along the underwater boulders that divided the shallow water from the deep. With the invincible faith of a child, he stepped off the rocks and dogpaddled just far enough to cramp up over a section of water deep and black as a night sky. His legs sank like columns of stone.

Drowning hadn't been the frantic, screaming thing people always seemed to imagine. It was a quiet death. He'd been unable to wave his arms because instinct kept them horizontal, pushing down on the water to lift himself up. He hadn't yelled as, unable to kick, his head was never above the surface long enough to both breathe in and yell out. Breathing trumped yelling.

He bobbed in silence a few feet from where his friends were playing for maybe a minute or two, frightened, but not yet terrified, his mouth intermittently at, and then below, the waterline. When he sank beneath the surface for the final time his drowning was still quiet, but that's when it got ugly.

He saw the old gods while he was down there—after the panic, after the struggle and the inevitable burning lungful of water. They were in some dark enclosure that was everywhere or nowhere. He could still remember their faces, all lined up on biers, as if they too were dead: Morpheus, Hestia, Thanatos, Hypnos, Eros, Hemera and more, stretching back into the shadows. The room vibrated with quiescent power. He was a child in the company of gods, and dead or not, real or not, they had terrified him.

The next thing he'd seen had been the rough rock of a boulder. Nikos and another, older, boy had him face-down, pounding on his back and pumping his arms while his lungs vomited pond water and his heart began to beat once more.

Kairos took up the oars and Ty climbed into the boat. His memory of drowning haunted him more vividly than it had in years. Remembering the gods, the turbulence of power in that room, he wondered how he had ever pushed aside his faith. Maybe he'd just wanted to put distance between himself and the gods after twice being pulled into their presence. He stared out over the lake as if he could see Erebus in the distance.

Kairos backed the boat and rowed with strong, sure strokes well out across the lake. They passed boaters and fishermen, and still he kept rowing. The shore diminished.

Ty watched as little islands he didn't remember seeing before appeared around a curve on the lake. "Mind telling me where we're going now?" he asked Kairos.

"Erebus," Kairos said. He'd been rowing about twenty minutes but didn't seem winded from his exertions.

Ty didn't know how to get there, but he felt pretty sure this wasn't it. "I thought Erebus was down," he said.

"We are going down."

Ty stared at Kairos, but said nothing.

They passed a tiny island covered in a dozen or so pine trees, and a bank of fog met them on the other side. Somewhere ahead loomed the reservoir's dam. Kairos rowed onward into the dense, gray mist. Perhaps five minutes inside the fog, the little man boated his oars. The rowboat rested on the water as it might on a cushion. Ty's senses told him it wasn't rocking with the waves or drifting in any direction, though the fog may have deceived him.

"You'll have to go on your own from here," Kairos said. "I can't go any farther."

Ty saw nothing but gray fog over gray water in all directions. "What do you mean?"

"Swim. That way." Kairos thrust a stubby finger toward the bow.

"Beg pardon?" Ty said.

Ty's friends had taught him to swim after he drowned, but it wasn't something with which he'd ever been comfortable. Being dumped out of a boat in the middle of a lake was decidedly uncomfortable, especially coupled with the ambiguity of the directions.

"Swim," Kairos repeated. "That way."

"How far?"

"Not sure," Kairos answered. "Distance is as variable as everything else in Erebus. Just head that direction. You'll figure it out."

Maybe there really was no Erebus. Maybe this was some inventive plan that Kairos had come up with to kill him. Plop him in the water, tie his little ribbon in a knot, and that would be the end of Ty Kleisos. He gripped the edges of the metal rowboat so hard it creased his palms. He tried to talk himself down, rationalizing that Kairos could've killed him a dozen ways easier than this.

Ty looked around for alternatives. He could dump the boat, club Kairos with an oar, steal the black ribbon, right the boat, row back to shore and try to evade the two flesh-eating men at the station. Ironically, he had to admit that swimming away from the boat seemed the better option; at least he'd get away from this wretched man and his thugs. Ultimately, now that Kairos and his men knew that Ty's mother could be used for leverage, it made no difference what Ty did or didn't want to do.

He removed his jacket, tie, socks, and shoes. The tie he left in the bottom of the boat. The socks and shoes he placed in the middle of the jacket, then spun it by the sleeves in an attempt to trap some air. He tied the arms tight around his waist, but knew that he'd be struggling before long with the weight of his wet clothes no matter what he did.

Still hoping this was a joke, he looked back at Kairos once more but the man sat waiting. Ty grabbed on to the gunwale and slipped over the side, taking no special care to keep the boat righted. In defiance of the laws of physics as he knew them, the boat and Kairos remained stable. Ty let go.

The water was cold this time of year, more so this far from shore, and he gasped when it soaked his skin. His pants, his shirt, and the bundle at his waist saturated immediately. The cold soothed his burning tattoos but, as soon as he struck out, the motion of swimming and the agitation of his clothes countered any relief the water offered. He swam into the fog, hoping that whatever was going to happen would be over with as quickly as possible.

Swimming fully clothed was more awkward than he had expected. From the waist down the lake embraced him, pulling him toward her silty belly like a mother trying to take a child back into the womb. He briefly considered discarding his clothing, but the thought of navigating Erebus was disturbing enough without thinking of navigating it in nothing but his underwear.

Within the first dozen strokes his legs listed at an ever steeper angle, like a sinking ship with a bilge full of water. Another couple of dozen strokes and the muscles of his upper arms burned. Panic tickled the edges of his nerves. He was tempted to turn and swim back to the island they'd rowed past, but it had been tiny, only a few lengths of the rowboat, and he might miss it altogether in the fog. That, and Kairos might still be drifting nearby.

He splashed forward a few yards more, his freestyle crawl increasingly inefficient against the weight of his clothes. His arms burned like fire and his kick became progressively less effective. He shipped some water that his gag-reflex didn't catch and swallowed a fraction of the lake. Worse than making him cough, it told him he was no longer keeping his head above the surface on each breath.

Ty didn't care anymore about showing up in Erebus with no clothes. He stopped stroking with his arms and tried to scissor-kick while fumbling with the knot in the sleeves of his jacket. As soon as his arms were still, his head dipped underwater. He splashed to the surface with strokes that were too wild, too energy-wasting. He knew he was in trouble.

Ty jerked his arms in a strong breaststroke, trying to lift his upper body out of the water. Gasping, he gulped air and blinked water from his eyes, searching for any hint of land. The fog and his waterline-perspective allowed him to only see a dozen feet any direction, and now he'd lost his forward momentum. His legs sank to vertical from the weight of his pants and the bundle at his waist. An all too familiar sensation.

"Kairos!" he yelled. Or tried to yell.

One of the small, rapid waves hit him in the face and washed to the back of his throat. He coughed and choked, trying to breathe in and out at the same time. Water snorted up his nostrils and ran down the back of his throat. The half-forgotten details of his first drowning came back sharp as a knife. Being underwater. The panic of suffocation. The pain and horror of breathing water into his lungs. His clothes dragged him under again even as he tore at the knot at his waist. His head sank beneath the waves and this time he didn't resurface. Too late, he realized he'd submerged with almost no air in his lungs.

The murky water turned darker as he sank. Terror fired through him like sparks from a severed power line. Reduced to instinct, he thrashed uselessly. By pure coincidence he produced a strong scissor-kick at the same time he stroked down with his right arm. His internal gyroscope told him he had moved up. He tried to repeat the motion. Slapping down with both arms, he kicked as hard as he could. His head struck something.

Surprised by the sharp, unexpected blow, he felt above him and touched rock. The shock of encountering something other than water engaged his brain, crank-starting it. With a fresh wash of panic, he wondered if he was upside down, his head against the bottom of the lake. He let out a single bubble of precious air and felt it tickle along his cheek and up past his eyes, confirming that his orientation hadn't changed. Pressing his hands against the rock, he moved himself through the water. He'd somehow sunk between underwater rocks he couldn't see in the murk. He searched for the hole he must have come through, as if he'd fallen through a frozen pond. Air hunger tunneled his vision. He fought the compulsion to inhale against his will. A synesthesia of fear, blue and magenta, danced in his retinas.

One hand suddenly felt nothing above him. Ty pulled himself to the gap and bobbed upward. His head broke the surface of the water. Gasping, he grabbed at the knobby protrusions in the rock to stay afloat while he sucked in great lungfuls of air.

For awhile, he did nothing but breathe and cough and breathe some more. When he finally blinked the water from his eyes his world was still dark. He explored it with his hands and found he was in an air bubble trapped somehow beneath a shelf of rock. He felt certain this wasn't Erebus and couldn't think of any explanation except that he must have sunk deeper than he'd realized and drifted up under the rocky outcrop of an island, though he came up with no explanation for the air pocket.

The rock around him extended below the water's surface farther than he could reach with his feet, and spanned a little wider than both arms stretched out. He could just brush the highest point of the roof with the tips of his fingers. His clothes still dragged at him, but the friction of his hands against the stone kept him afloat. He kept his lungs fuller than he needed to, breathing out in tiny puffs, sipping air back in immediately.

He pulled himself along by the protrusions in the wall. The ceiling lifted, and something told him he'd entered a much larger space. One foot scraped a flat surface. He felt a burst of renewed hope and pulled himself along more quickly until he could touch the bottom easily with both feet.

The water dropped to chest-level as he limped through the blackness, the rock scraping the aching undersides of his bare, tattooed feet. His clothes tugged behind him through the water with the drag of an open parachute. Defying natural laws, the water level continued to drop as he walked, though the cave sloped downward. Eventually the water fell to his hips and then to his knees. His fear of drowning began to recede. The cool water and colder air chilled him, and he rubbed at his arms. He walked out of the lake and stood on damp rock in pitch blackness. Kairos had said he would find what he was looking for, and this was what he'd found.

The walls were wider than arm's reach and the smooth floor continued to slope downward at a gentle angle, inviting Ty deeper. He put on his soaking wet socks, shoes and jacket and started off again, trailing his hand along the right wall, unable to shake the feeling that at any moment the lake would come rushing down upon him. He found no openings where his hand brushed the wall, though there was no way to know if he was missing any on the other side.

The air felt thick and heavy with moisture, and the only sounds that carried through it were his shoes squish-clicking on the rock, his loud breath in the dark, and the drip of water pooling on the ceiling and succumbing to gravity with loud plops. His clothes and hair were still wet, and he shivered in the cold. He inched forward for what felt like half an hour, increasingly jumpy. Fears born of his blindness compounded: that he'd hit his head, get lost, fall in an unseen crevice.

Without warning, the wall he'd been following dead-ended. He turned and traced his way along the back wall. When he felt the bulk of the left side looming, he put his hands out and discovered a narrow gap, about shoulder-wide where the left wall and the back wall met. He didn't want to push into the tight space, but wasn't about to turn around and swim that lake again. Something told him he probably couldn't anyway.

Again, he descended. The cold in the cave continued to intensify the lower he went, and involuntary shivers traced random courses through his arms, legs, and chest. The rock scratched at his shoulders. He made a mental note to add confined spaces to his list of things he didn't like: things tight around his throat, water more than chest deep, cramped spaces.

The ceiling lowered until he walked in a crouch and then a crawl. He no longer had room to turn around; to get out, he'd have to back up the slope. His knees bruised on the hard, uneven floor. He was blind as a whitefish and cold as death.

Suddenly, the rock opened up. He stood tentatively in a small, rectangular space. The rock on the far wall felt different from the rest of the cave, flatter, with evenly spaced horizontal and vertical indentations. Not quite brick. Rougher, like a stone and mortar wall. He examined every inch with his fingers, bottom to top, left to right, looking for any kind of door, gap, or latch.

On the first pass he found nothing. On the second pass he found a small, irregular hole about waist-high near the left-hand side. It was smaller than his smallest finger, larger at the top than the bottom, and surrounded by smooth metal. A keyhole.

Ty dropped to his knees and fished in the inside pocket of his jacket. He realized with a start that he hadn't checked for his locksmith tools since his swim, and huffed a breath of relief when he encountered the small, leather case. The wet zipper peeled open grudgingly.

The keyhole indicated a simple lock, like one a skeleton key might open. Finding two items by feel—the specific rake he sought and a tension wrench—he removed both. Trying to control his shivering, he slipped the wrench into the keyhole and slid the rake in next to it. He applied rotational tension. A few scrubs of the rake later, the lock snicked open. A heavy section of wall swung silently inward.

Ty replaced his tools and stepped through into a dim light. He didn't notice the door closing until he heard the lock catch again. He looked at the place where the keyhole should've been and found none.

Wherever he was, there was no going back.

4

Erebus

The light in the chamber seemed to originate through an opening not far ahead. It shone with the muted brightness of early twilight or late dawn, yet had an artificial quality that left Ty unable to guess the source.

His shoes clacked on the stone floor and he walked on the balls of his feet to silence them. After thirty meters or so, he came in sight of a stone arch signaling the tunnel's end. His stomach rumbled, reminding him that he hadn't eaten since sometime yesterday. The loud protestation made him freeze. When nothing came to investigate, he edged onward to the opening.

The cloudless, sunless, gray-blue sky above seemed to be the source of the crepuscular light. Below, he expected to see the green meadows of Elysium, the ghostly fields of Asphodel, or some dark realm of torment. Instead, Erebus appeared to be no more than a city, much like the one he had left this morning. Ty wondered what else the theologians had gotten wrong.

He stood near the top of one of many rolling hills surrounding the urban sprawl of the city below. He'd hoped for a vegetated landscape; something that would have provided cover. Instead, dry, brown dirt covered the hills. There were no trees, scrub, bushes, or vines in sight. No heather. Not even weeds. He hesitated, reluctant to leave the shelter of the passageway.

Making it this far should have felt like a victory, but the city below teemed with unknowns. He wanted to shout a "fuck it all" from his hilltop and turn around, but the memory of Kairos tightening the knot in his black ribbon was still far too vivid, as was the man's reminder that the sooner Ty accomplished his goal, the sooner he'd see his mother. He started down the hill.

Ty studied the city as he descended. It reminded him strongly of Athina—whitewashed buildings flinched beneath tall, modern constructions of pale pinks, light browns and grays. Knots of homes and businesses stood shoulder-to-shoulder, so close that a blade of grass wouldn't fit between them. The structures were surrounded by narrow paved streets, which weaved chaotically around buildings that must have pre-dated the roads. Cramped developments clustered where disintegrating neighborhoods had succumbed to entropy.

The more he studied the city, the more familiar it looked. With a start he realized why. There on the fringe to his left was the peaked courthouse building and squat city hall of his own city; to his right, the Parliament building bordered the dense verdure of the National Garden which covered about twenty city blocks.

He felt certain now it must be Athina below him, but it looked as if it had been turned inside out and stirred. What should have been on one side was on the other, what should have been nearest to him was farthest away, what should have been in the city's center was on the perimeter. The Acropolis was nowhere in sight, and neither was Mount Lycabettus, but a massive peak with the familiar outline of Mt. Olimbos framed the horizon beyond the city. From his current vantage he saw no sign of the sea.

Another reason he hadn't recognized Athina more quickly was the lack of outlying suburbs and farms. It was as if the city had been truncated at some random degree of urban density. Below him lay not a population of over two million, but perhaps 50,000. Where Athina spread out all directions, here the crush of urban congestion ended abruptly, morphing into a rolling landscape with tiny clusters of homes. He wondered if this was one city out of many or if what he saw comprised all of Erebus.

He searched the perimeter of downtown again and located what he thought might be his apartment building. With no idea how to begin his quest for Naia and the object he sought, his best option might be to start there. Maybe it would offer a measure of refuge while he figured out what to do next. Also, the building stood close to the perimeter nearest him. The walk would be short, his risk of traveling through the city reduced proportionally. His decision made, he descended quickly, conscious of his exposure on the hill, and neared the city sooner than he'd expected.

Ty soon approached the sharp border of buildings and stepped from the skirt of the hills into the city, like an artist stepping into a painting in a single stride. At the end of the alley he'd entered he saw people but no vehicles. He merged into the smattering of pedestrians without the faintest idea what to expect. Pointing. Stares. Full-scale attack. To his surprise, none of those things happened.

The first few people he passed were dressed much like people in Athina, right down to current fashions. More surprising, no one seemed to take the slightest notice of him. He walked a couple of blocks, finding nothing much out of the ordinary except the placement of the buildings. A laugh built somewhere deep in his chest, a euphoric discharge likely to morph into hysteria if it broke free. He suppressed a smile of victory. He was walking through Erebus.

A clattering sound neared from ahead and to his left, but the recognition was distant, a second- or third-level processing: animals, hooves on stone, possibly horses. He turned a corner, watching for the front of the building to come into view, hoping to find some pattern in the out of order landmarks. A blow struck his left shoulder and knocked him from the nightmarish sight he glimpsed into an awkward bicycling stumble backward. He came up hard against the stucco wall of the building.

Four creatures passed by. The head of the one that had struck him registered first. An oversized and elongated human head on an unnaturally large neck, which appeared grafted to the body of a horse. Ty's stomach twisted at the perversion. All four elongated faces and necks sported silver piercings through cheeks, necks, and ears. The teeth that showed as they conversed were large and flat and intimidating. Small, human-sized arms with thick, knobby elbow joints flapped at the base of the necks, slapping the upper legs of the horse bodies with limp hands. The centaurs were far from the elegant imaginings of artists he'd seen, and the thought of having touched one of the things sent a wave of nausea through him.

They walked past, two on the sidewalk and two in the street, one pair in front of the other, both sets carrying on conversation. He recognized nothing in the human-sounding vowels and consonants, punctuated occasionally with rumbling grunts and sharp snorts. Their oddly-shaped faces and the broad, muscled, equine chests gave no clue to their gender, though the milk bags of the first two and genitals of the pair behind did.

The female he'd run into never lost a step, not surprising as she was probably five times his weight, though her large head turned back in mild surprise. When her round, heavy-lidded eyes didn't find him, she resumed her conversation. Ty remained pressed against the wall until they crossed to the next block.

"Ti skatá," he swore on a shaky breath, pushing off the building. He rubbed his shoulder and found muscles so tense that a twitch pulsed in his deltoid.

His knees felt unsteady for nearly a block and his heart rate increased whenever he passed someone, though they all seemed ordinary-looking and still appeared not to notice him.

Two streets later he looked ahead to see a woman walking toward him. She moved unevenly, in a limping gait. Her head swung side-to-side, as if searching or scenting something. He stood a little straighter, hoping he might catch her eye. He reminded himself that he was trying to go unnoticed here, but her beauty stole his breath. He ignored the tightening in his belly as they drew closer, and he kept wishing she would look straight ahead.

They were less than fifty meters apart when he felt a burning sting high on his left thigh. He looked down, confused, and when he looked up again he noticed for the first time that what he had assumed to be red hair was actually living fire, and that her odd gait came from walking on one leg of bronze with the other terminating in the foot of a donkey. Her oddities did nothing to diminish her beauty.

Childhood teachings struggled to surface, as if fighting up through sticky cobwebs. Empousa. The name came to him suddenly. A creature who fed on unwary male travelers. He wondered if chance only had brought her toward him. Adrenaline burned through his thighs, screaming at him to run. Had he not recognized her for what she was, he would have walked straight into her trap.

He didn't run, he studied his shoes as he crossed to the other side of the street, chanting a silent mantra now that she *wouldn't* notice him. As they passed, he risked a glance to the side. Still swinging her head, searching, her gaze never quite rested on him. He turned quickly down a side street. A block later, he slipped into an alley to avoid a creature that was mostly lion, with the head of the goat protruding from its back and a tail that ended in a live snake's head.

As a child he'd imagined the monstrosities dwelling in Erebus, but seeing them in the flesh made him feel lightheaded and disoriented. He tried to draw on the confidence he'd felt when he first realized he could pass unnoticed here, but found it buried too deeply beneath an avalanche of sensory inputs. Telling himself to keep moving, he managed to force himself from the shadow of the alley.

Staring back at yet another creature a block later, he looked ahead just in time to avoid running headlong into a man wearing a robe of burnt orange. The man sported a white beard that hung to the top of his sternum, and he walked with a wooden staff, though he looked fit. He mumbled some curse or apology at Ty, then stopped and stared at him, actually seeming to see him. Unnerved by the attention, Ty hurried on, glancing back once over his shoulder. The man continued to stare.

Ty put distance as quickly as he could between himself and the old man, but was hampered by the constant need to reassess his location. He felt as if he was trying to navigate from inside a broken mirror, walking on the wrong side of the street along buildings that were in reverse order. When he recognized an entire block of buildings, he began to hope. If the neighborhood didn't turn 180 degrees in the next couple of blocks, he should be approaching his apartment. To his relief, the familiar brown building soon appeared.

Going in what should have been the back door, he took the stairs two at a time and reached the fourth floor without encountering anyone. The hallway was empty. He looked on the wrong side of the hall for the first few steps before finding his apartment—on the left side and in the first third of the hallway rather than the last. He tried the door handle, but it was locked. Feeling along the top of the doorjamb for his spare key, he turned up nothing but dust. He reached into the inside pocket of his jacket and pulled out his toolkit, but froze when he heard a scuffling, grunting noise inside the apartment.

In his single-minded focus to reach his destination, it had never occurred to him that someone else might be living in this apartment. He slipped his tools back inside his jacket, wondering what he should do, when the scuffling came closer and the door opened.

The first things to emerge were a T-shirted belly and the glowing end of a long cigar followed immediately by the head, shoulders and feet of a large, round-faced man. Ty held his ground as the door opened wider. There was little else he could do. The man stepped forward, peering into the hall as if near-sighted. He nearly brushed Ty's shoulder before seeming to realize he was there.

"Ho, what have we here?" he boomed, peering into Ty's face. "A visitor from above, isn't it? An interloper? A monster-slaying hero? A thrill seeker?"

The big man's face bristled with a heavy five o'clock shadow. His faded blue shirt sported food stains: a yellow spot that looked like egg yolk and a grease spot as large as his two meaty thumbs. His baggy, brown pants were in little better shape.

"Sorry," Ty said, wishing he'd run before the door had opened, whether the man would have seen him or not. "I must have the wrong apartment."

"And whose apartment were you looking for?"

He had to say something. Besides, he didn't know how in the hell he was going to find the person he was looking for without asking. "I was trying to find someone named Naia. For a mutual friend," he added.

"I see. I see. And you are...?"

"Ty," he said, not elaborating further.

"Ty." The big man rolled the name in his mouth like he tasting a new food, his cigar bobbing as he spoke. "Unusual name." He puffed and removed the cigar. "Well met, Ty. I'm Momus." He extended a thick hand into which Ty's vanished when they shook. "Come in." Momus swung the door wide and stood back. Ty entered.

The layout was the same as his own apartment, though the furnishings were different and in rougher shape. A well-worn recliner covered in a cheap, chocolate-colored fabric occupied the center of the room, while a faded red sofa took up the wall to the left and held a couple of shirts wadded into one corner. A small, plain table with two metal chairs stood to the right. On the surface of the table, a pottery dish, crusted with the remains of a meal, shared the surface with an assortment of cups and mugs. The small kitchen was laid out like Ty's own, though a few days' worth of dirty dishes poked above the rim of the kitchen sink. The door to the only bedroom stood open, centered in the wall in front of him, showing an unmade bed and small hills of clothes on the floor.

Momus gestured to the sofa and plopped down in the recliner. He put his feet up on the scratched and chipped coffee table between them, pushing an ashtray that brimmed with cigar stubs out of the way. His shoes were enormous. He puffed on his cigar, creating a plume of smoke that momentarily obscured his face. Ty mentally added a shiny red ball on his nose and a bit of makeup, and decided Momus could have passed for a grungy, off-duty circus clown.

"I didn't mean to disturb you."

"No bother. No bother at all," Momus said expansively. "I'm quite intrigued, really."

Intrigued. Not the word Ty wanted to inspire here. He kept his face relaxed and unconcerned. "It's nothing, really. Just a quick trip on behalf of a friend who couldn't come."

"Banished, eh?"

"Pardon?"

"Your friend, one of the banished? Kicked out? Evicted from Erebus?" Momus puffed another gout of smoke and tapped the ash onto the floor. Ty could see that a multitude of gray smudges encircled the recliner. "It happens. Not often. Have to go live above then, poor fools."

Ty thought of Kalyptra and Kairos. How many others? He wanted to ask what would get someone banished, but it didn't seem politic.

The little gerbil in his brain climbed onto its wheel. The wheel felt rusty, not used in too many months, but it turned enough for him to realize that Momus had handed him a cover story.

"Yes. Right. It's a misunderstanding, though. He's trying to get it straightened out and asked if I could come down on his behalf. It looks like I've gotten his directions wrong. Do you know where I can find Naia?"

Asking this question meant that if he ever did find her, did find the object, did manage to steal it and got it back to his world alive, he was practically announcing himself as the thief. One problem at a time, though.

"Sure, sure," Momus replied. His repetitions were apparently an idiosyncrasy that wasn't about to stop. "I can help you find her. Not doing anything anyway." He shoved his cigar between his teeth and gestured with both hands, indicating the otherwise empty apartment. "I suppose you want to get on with it then?" He quirked an eyebrow in question.

Ty nodded, unsure what the man meant.

Momus pushed himself out of the recliner, grabbed three extra cigars from a box on the coffee table, and waited expectantly. Ty realized that Momus intended to accompany him. The gerbil in his brain ran faster, trying to decide if he was better off alone or with a guide he didn't know and wasn't sure he could trust. He remembered the monstrosities he'd seen outside, and decided to accept.

"If it's no trouble."

"No, no. Quite fun, in fact. Don't usually get to converse with mortals, you know."

The last time Ty had relieved himself had been early morning when Kairos' men had taken him by his real apartment. "May I use your bathroom first?" Momus waved vaguely toward the door.

The bathroom held a cramped toilet, sink, and claw-foot tub, as did Ty's own. Rinsing his hands, he noticed with a start that the scars on his wrists had vanished. He removed his jacket, unbuttoned his shirt partway and pulled it and his undershirt to the side. The fabric stuck to the wound above his collarbone and he peeled it gently away. Red pinpricks of fresh blood oozed where he'd disturbed the clotting. Raw flesh glared back, puckered at the edges and dotted already with a granular, yellow crust of early healing. Below the collarbone, though, there was no tattoo. None on the other side either, though his chest, feet and the other tattooed areas still burned.

He ran a finger down the right side of his chest. His skin felt raw and puffy, though it looked as smooth and pale as it had a week ago. The scar at his throat was unchanged, the same weal he'd had since childhood, a thick, ropy smile that looked and felt like the skin had melted. Ty bent to the sink, rinsed the blood as best he could from his shirt and dabbed at it with a towel, before putting his jacket back on. When he left the bathroom Momus was standing at the door, ready to usher him out.

They left the building and headed in the direction Ty might have called north, though Momus said Naia lived Oldside from his apartment. The buildings grew grander as they walked through the backward city. It relieved him to find that, even in the company of Momus, the people and occasional creatures they met on the street continued to ignore him.

They passed familiar buildings in unfamiliar order, though the store fronts were different than the ones in his Athina. A scent of warm bread, garlic and olive oil emanating from a corner eatery caused Ty's stomach to rumble loudly again.

"Hungry?" Momus asked.

Ty nodded and Momus fished in the voluminous pockets of his baggy pants, coming up with what might have been a piece of bread folded over a sausage. Ty was more than hungry, he was famished. Yet he hesitated on a number of grounds, surprisingly the least of which was that the thing had just come out of Momus' pocket.

He'd grown up on stories of warning, like the one of Persephone in Haides that cautioned against taking food or drink in otherworldly places. On the other hand, how long could he go without eating? It wasn't likely he'd waltz in to Naia's home, see the item he'd been sent for lying out in the open, pilfer it, and be home by dinner. He accepted the food. It tasted a fair bit like it looked, but he was hungry enough not to care.

The direction that should have taken them downtown continued to look more and more like the smart neighborhood of Kolonaki, normally to the east of downtown. Ty had spent more than a little time in this area of his own world, fitting deadbolts on doors to protect elegant belongings and jimmying doors to shiny, new cars that held the keys locked inside.

"Is Naia wealthy?" he said, as a roundabout way of asking if she was powerful.

"Wealthy? Well. Hard to say. That's more of a surface concept, I think. She's a demi-goddess, you know, so that sort of says it all." Ty must not have covered his shock well. "You didn't know? Well, not surprised, not surprised." Momus slapped his shoulder in friendly camaraderie. "Most of the population here is like me, the great-great-great, and so on, grandchildren of the demigods. Some are the gods' punishments or follies, or descendants of those." Momus waved a large hand in the direction of a creature with three snake heads across the street. "There's only a handful of the real thing, you know. The actual children of gods, gotten on some consort. Naia is one of those."

Ty suppressed a wave of nausea that might have been the sausage or might have been the scale to which he was finding himself embroiled in this mess. "Whose daughter is she?"

"One of the oldest. Other than the Titans, of course. Eros' daughter. His and some nymph he fancied."

"Ti skatá," Ty muttered.

The tall building Momus led him into was one of the most elegant he'd seen on their walk. On his way down the hill from the tunnel, Ty had planned a story that he was a locksmith sent to do whatever job seemed fitting for wherever he found this Naia. With Momus at his side, he was stuck with the story he'd already started. Just as well, probably. Momus had pegged him as mortal on first sight. Maybe he could say he was here on behalf of a friend, but imply he was also a thrill-seeker, as Momus had guessed.

In the center of the enormous and deserted lobby, Momus rang the buzzer for the elevator. A clank above them announced the message had been received and a little, gold cage descended. When it rattled into view of the lobby, Ty saw an elderly man at the controls. He wore a bellhop cap that looked incongruous over the thin white hair which stuck out beneath it like the remnants of dandelion down following a windstorm. His shriveled arms and legs, stick-like in the red uniform, brought to mind spider legs. The old man pulled the folding metal lattice of the door open with one arm, surprising Ty that he had the strength to perform the task.

Momus stepped in and said, "Penthouse." He held the door for Ty who wondered just how long and how closely Momus planned to stay by him. The little man pushed the top button of the panel and it lit up with an orange glow. The elevator jerked into motion. Ty watched the polished marble floor of the lobby recede below them.

The elevator rose to the penthouse without interruption and bounced to a stop. The old man hauled the door back for them to exit. Ahead lay a wide expanse of marble foyer with ornate columns spaced in two rows. Beyond them, centered on the far wall, was a white marble arch and, within the arch, a white door.

Ty's heart was beating so hard he was surprised it didn't echo through the foyer. He'd tried sketching a more detailed plan on the way up of what he might say to Naia, elaborating on the thrill-seeker angle, but now found himself doubting everything. He wished he'd taken more time to come up with a better story. Momus stubbed out his cigar on the sole of his shoe and dropped the remainder of the stogie into his T-shirt pocket. He reached out and rapped gently on the door with his large knuckles. Remembering the blood on his shirt, Ty straightened his collar and adjusted his jacket.

A woman in a long, white summer dress answered the door. She had dark brown hair that fell to her hips, a complexion darker than Ty's own, a long, bold nose that gave her an aristocratic yet serious bearing, and emerald green eyes.

"I've brought a visitor from above," Momus said, before Ty could speak. "He'd like to talk with Naia."

The woman looked Momus over. Momus slapped a heavy hand on Ty's shoulder and she focused on him then, a cross and suspicious cast tightening her eyes. She flowed away without a word into another room. Ty heard her accented voice when she spoke, though he couldn't make out the words or the accent. It had been stupid of him to think that someone living in a place like this would be answering her own door, and he couldn't afford to be stupid here. A moment later, another woman appeared.

He had only thought the first woman beautiful.

Naia had hair as black as night that stopped mid-back, and eyes so dark it was hard to make out the pupils. Her skin was olive, tanned slightly, and she had an oval face, perfectly formed. She wore shorts rolled at the hem over long, tanned legs and a close-fitting, short-sleeved, button-down shirt. She was barefoot.

Not only did Naia notice Ty, but—unlike most others here—she *saw* him without difficulty. Her dark eyes absorbed him, pulling him in the same way they seemed to drink in the light that touched them. Ty wondered what her black eyes read within the ice blue of his own.

Momus broke the spell. "I apologize for bothering you, but Ty here has come to Erebus looking for you on behalf of a friend of his."

"Is that so?" she asked.

Ty wondered how one addressed a demigod. "Yes, ma'am." He scrapped his concocted story on the spot. He felt absurd that he'd even thought about lying to this woman. What came out instead was the truth, as far as he could tell it.

"Someone from Erebus holds my life in his hands," he began. "I owe him money. A lot of money. To pay my debt, he told me to come down here on his behalf."

And that was it, as far as the truth took him. "I think he hopes that you'll help lift his banishment somehow," he continued, winging it. "But in the meantime, he sent me here to serve you, in whatever way I can."

"And who is this person seeking my favor?" she asked.

"I'm not at liberty to tell you. At least, not yet. If I accomplish what he hopes, I suspect he'll make himself known. If not, then you send me back to the upper world and he'll kill me."

"Don't trust him," said the woman at her shoulder, in her cold, accented voice.

Naia ignored her. "Come in."

She stepped back, allowing Ty and Momus to enter. It seemed too easy, and Ty wondered if the markings on his body were somehow in play. He and Momus followed her into the open living room, where she took a seat on a plush sofa. "And you," she said to Momus, "what is your part in this?"

"Ty here showed up at my door, my lady. I offered to bring him to meet you, is all. Piqued my interest, if you know what I mean, being mortal and all that."

"Yes," she said slowly, "I do know what you mean." Her eyes returned to Ty. He felt like an ant under a magnifying glass, burned by the heat of her examination. "And what is it you propose to do for me, Ty?"

"Whatever I can, ma'am. My lady," he amended in imitation of Momus. "I'm indentured to you, if you'll have me. If you won't, then I'm a dead man."

"Intriguing," she said. There was that word again. "Tell me your full name."

"Eutychios Eperitus Kleisos," he said.

Eutychios was common enough, though he guessed his gambler father had named him for good fortune more for himself than for his son. His mother and her love of the old stories had added the middle name. At least she'd taken it from a hero's disguise and not the ostentatious name of the hero himself.

"Why Ty?" With Ty not a proper Greek name and Eutychios pronounced 'eftEEcheeos' it was something he'd often been asked.

"My father gave me the nickname. He was friends with an American called that. Tyler, I think was the man's proper name. I never knew him."

"Well, Eutychios Eperitus Kleisos," a strange tingling ran from his chest to the crest of his hips along the disappeared lines that Kalyptra had painted into him, "I suppose we can find something around here for you to do. I'd hate to condemn you to death without even giving you a chance." She turned to Momus. "Thank you for escorting him here. I'll see that Lamia gives you something for your trouble."

"Oh, no trouble. No trouble at all," Momus said, though he didn't move.

The handmaiden, or whatever she was, crossed the room to a broad, polished wooden desk. She lifted the lid of a little box and took something out then walked past Momus to the door, opening it for him. Momus followed her like a dog after a bone and she pressed a large bronze coin into his palm. Ty saw the flash of it as it disappeared into his shirt pocket.

Momus retrieved the butt of his cigar from the same pocket and jammed it into his broad, grinning mouth. "See you around," he said to Ty. The door closed behind him with a snick that plainly said Ty was on his own.

5

Lies and Other Truths

"*Lady...*" Lamia said, returning from the door, heavily investing the single word with distress. Ty wondered if she would hand him a coin, too, and shove him out the door behind Momus.

Naia lifted one palm toward the other woman. She continued to study Ty, but her words were directed to Lamia. "He's mortal, I don't doubt that. And I think I'm well enough protected to risk one mortal near me." She smiled. "Besides, there's something about him, an enigma that begs solving." She shifted on the couch, tucking her feet beside her hip, and addressed him directly.

"So, Ty, what makes you special enough for this person to send you on his behalf?"

"Nothing," he said honestly, and shrugged.

She shook her head uncertainly. "I wouldn't be so sure."

Guilt at his deceptions, intended and otherwise, crawled up from his stomach and flushed his cheeks.

"Maybe I'm wrong," she said lightly, misinterpreting his blush and trying to reassure him. "Maybe it's something simpler." She flashed a smile, little-girl-like. "Do you sing, by chance? I love singing."

Despite his tension, Ty coughed a short laugh. "I'd be killed for sure if I sang for you."

"Recite poetry, then?"

He shook his head.

"Act?"

Again, no.

He doubted that any of his leisure activities would interest her. Bouzoukia clubs, American movies, riding his motorcycle.

"Paint?" She sounded less hopeful.

"I've dabbled with it," he admitted.

It had been years since he'd thought about his art. He hadn't sketched or painted anything in six years, not since the day he threw his ex-fiancé's framed portrait into the trash. It had been a surprise to go with the engagement ring he planned to give her. Instead, he'd been the one surprised when he went by a friend's house to tell him, and had found Anna there as well.

"I've done more drawing than painting," he said. "Nothing I've ever really shown anyone."

She clapped her hands, delighted. "Do you work in charcoal? Could you do a portrait of Lamia?"

He studied the woman standing possessively at Naia's shoulder. "I could try."

"Fetch what he needs, Lamia. You can sit for him."

The woman's plump mouth drew tight and sour. She left the room and Ty heard the rustle and clatter of things being roughly searched.

"Don't take it personally," Naia said, "She doesn't warm up easily to anyone." She gestured to a thickly padded chair.

Lamia returned with a large sheet of fine-textured paper, a smooth wooden board, and a small clay jar that held thick charcoal sticks of various lengths. Ty received the things from her with a smile. Her stony expression never changed, and he accepted the challenge she set to win her over.

Naia asked Lamia to lie back on a reclining couch at the right side of the room. It was narrow and white, all of one piece, with a raised back and long seat. The sort of couch where one might be fed grapes or fanned with a palm leaf. Lamia settled, her white dress melting into the white couch. She arranged herself in a relaxed pose, one at odds with the contempt and suspicion that narrowed her eyes.

Using a corner of the charcoal stick, Ty outlined the back of the couch then sketched in a few lines, framing Lamia's head and shoulders. He slowed, carefully delineating the shape of her face and general features. Naia came to stand behind him.

"Who did you learn from?" she asked, as he continued to draw.

"No one, really. I spent a lot of time on my own as a kid. My mother used to give me a sketch pad and pencils to keep me busy while she worked."

Thoughts of his mother stirred a snake pit of emotions in his belly. If he died down here, she'd never know what had happened to him. And if *she* died before he could return...

"What did she do?"

"She cleaned houses for folks."

"No brothers or sisters?"

With swifter, surer strokes, he drew the long lines of the dress. "Just me. Dad left when I was four, and my mother never remarried. I don't think she had the heart to try again."

He slammed the doors shut on the plethora of emotions he'd stirred to life, past and present: the hurts Anna and his father had carved onto his heart, and worse, the pain he'd caused his mother when he'd forsaken the one person he'd sworn never to hurt. If he dwelled on it now, he'd be lost. He had to stay sharp here to stay alive. He'd deal with it later, when this was all over. And with Kairos, if he could, for any part he may have played in these past months.

Naia moved from behind Ty to perch on the arm of his chair. "It's a shame you never apprenticed," she said. "You have talent."

She sat far enough behind his elbow not to interfere, but her presence was like a tiger at his shoulder, something that couldn't be ignored. Her upper arm brushed his back, her breath tickled his hair, her words tumbled onto the nape of his neck. The skin on the right side of his body prickled into goose bumps, as if pulling toward her magnetically.

He tried to focus on the sketch, alternately drawing with the charcoal and blending and shading with his fingers. She stayed quiet as he leaned closer to the sketch pad to detail Lamia's hands and face. It surprised Ty how easily his discarded skill returned, as if he'd never stopped, and how much it pleased him to rediscover the craft of it. Finished with Lamia's face, he began smudging shadows into the folds of her dress where it cascaded over the edge of the couch.

"Do you have a wife or children?" Naia asked.

He shook his head.

Chances at the 'real thing' had probably come and gone more than once since Anna. He was self-aware enough to realize his father's abandonment had likely made him overly sensitive to Anna's betrayal, but since then he'd gotten used to the safety of distance. It felt easier than fixing whatever had broken in him.

Lately, he'd been seeing the women who lived at the fringes where the serious gamblers dwelled, drifting by like seagulls hoping for tasty scraps. They fed off the excitement, riding the crest of the waves and flying away before the troughs came along. He'd dated a couple of them briefly, finding their inconsistent and capricious natures exciting, though now he remembered it all with a kind-of morning-after hangover perspective.

He put a couple of final touches on the sketch—the window on the far wall for depth, some finishing details to the hair and eyes—then tossed the piece of charcoal up and grabbed it from the air. A completion habit he'd formed as a teen. He smiled.

"It's lovely," Naia said, and sounded sincerely impressed. She took the sketch pad from him, studied it a moment and crossed to Lamia. Lamia swung her legs off the couch and Naia sat next to her, holding the sketch for her to see.

Side-by-side, both Naia and Lamia were beautiful. They looked to be of a similar age, perhaps mid- or late twenties, but the contrast between them became evident as they sat close together. Naia in shirt-sleeves and shorts and Lamia in her flowing dress, yet it was Naia who wore power like an aura.

The taut lines around Lamia's eyes and mouth relaxed as she examined the final product. "It *is* lovely," she agreed. Ty thought he heard the ice between them breaking just a little. Naia left the sketch with Lamia and moved to the large picture window on the far wall.

"Do you ever work with oils or watercolors?"

"I've played with them a little," he said.

"Perhaps while you're here, you could paint a landscape for me."

"Sure—I mean, yes, lady—I could try. Something in particular?"

"Whatever you like," she said. "There's plenty to choose from." She was staring out the window as she spoke.

"You mean the city?" he asked, pretty sure she didn't mean the distant mountain.

She turned to Ty. "You see a city?" She indicated the window with a flip of one finger. "Odd. Well, we may have to do a little experimenting to find a landscape for you. In the meantime, perhaps you'd let one or two of my friends sit for you."

He shrugged, not sure what she meant by her landscape remark. "Of course, if you like."

His last word was interrupted by a knock at the door.

Lamia's face went hard again as she crossed the room and opened the door. Ty could only see a slice of the man beyond, but felt a jolt of recognition. He stood to more clearly see over Lamia's shoulder. It was the old man in the orange robes he'd run into in the street. The man stared at him. His eyes, hooded and sharp, nailed Ty in place like a bug pinned by a needle.

Naia approached and stood next to Lamia, blocking the robed man from Ty's line of sight. "What is it, old friend?"

"They've started." His voice was deep and resonant, like a stage actor's. "We have word of a play in motion. A meeting has been called."

"I'll be there directly," Naia said.

The man nodded once. He craned around her and stared at Ty one last time, then turned and left.

"Lamia, you'll need to stay with our guest," Naia said.

Lamia opened her mouth to protest, but shot a withering glance in Ty's direction instead. Naia went out the door, barefoot and empty-handed. Lamia paced to the window and looked down, as if Naia might already be outside. She looked for only a second then crossed back to the closed door and turned the deadbolt.

The old man coming to Naia's might have been coincidence and nothing to do with Ty, but it might not. Either way, he might not get an opportunity like this again. Whatever intuition or powers demigoddesses possessed, Ty didn't want Naia around while he attempted to steal from her, and the sooner this thing was done, the better.

"Is there a place I can wash up?" he asked, proffering hands covered in charcoal.

Lamia glared at him as if he'd just uttered a string of profanities. To the left of the living room was an open kitchen and on the right a hallway leading to the bedrooms. She waved absently toward the hallway then moved back to the window and stared out again, arms tightly crossed.

Glad that she had indicated the hall instead of the kitchen, Ty went exploring. The door to the master bedroom was open, allowing him an unobstructed view of the simple yet luxurious room: a large bed draped in white linens and soft pillows, a gold-veined, white marble floor, a balcony, and an archway opening into an enormous bathing room containing what looked to be a large sunken pool.

The middle room at the end of the hall must have been Lamia's. Smaller yet still stylish, done in shades of brown except for the marble floor that ran through the entire apartment. What he could see of it from the middle of the hall showed it to be spare in decorations and tidy as a naval officer's quarters, but with subtle signs of occupation: a book on the nightstand, a silver brush and comb on the dresser. The door to the third room, on the right side of the hallway, also stood open. The bedroom within appeared to be the guest room. Entering and taking a good look around, he saw the room was less austere than Lamia's, beautifully attired in pale yellow and green linens and draperies. Pastoral paintings in matching colors adorned the walls. An ancient work of pottery enhanced a beautifully crafted wooden nightstand, and a sculpture of a charging lion adorned the writing desk opposite the foot of the bed. Like the other bedrooms, it had its own bathroom.

Ty could hear the gentle rustle of Lamia's dress as she fidgeted in the living room. He stood at the door, alert for any sign Lamia might be coming to check on him. He barely recognized his own life—gambling, lying, stealing. If not for his need to get back to the hospital in one piece, he wondered if he would have just said the hell with it and left, the consequences be damned. His right wrist itched. He rubbed his new scars absently and listened to Lamia's nails tapping on the living room window sill. Drawing a steadying breath, he stepped across the hall to the master bedroom.

He felt a twisting in his guts, similar to the day he'd ridden his motorcycle down from the lake, hurrying before a light rain turned heavy. He'd taken one corner too many at his normal speed and hit a light slick of oily water on the road. For a heart-pounding few seconds the steering and brakes were as useless as they would have been if he'd ridden over a waterfall. Entering Naia's bedroom felt much the same.

Ty scanned the ceiling and walls, looking for any indication of a hidden safe. The marble pretty much ruled out a floor vault, but there were framed paintings covering portions of the plaster walls; something to investigate later. The unpleasant possibility that the item wasn't in the apartment was something he didn't care to consider.

Encouraged by the ease with which things had worked out for him in Erebus so far, he continued into the bathroom. The bathing pool was large enough to hold a dozen people. Beyond a plaster wall divider stood what amounted to an extremely elegant pit latrine. Opposite the bath, a marble counter sported a polished granite basin, a pitcher of delicate pottery and a bar of creamy-looking soap. The pitcher and the bath were full, though he saw no evidence of running water.

Planning to play dumb if caught, he smudged the pale blue handle with charcoal as he poured water from the pitcher into the basin. While he lathered his hands with the bar of soap he examined the ceiling, walls and every inch of the bedroom that he could see through the archway. The bedding hung low, but bending down he could see most of the floor under the bed. There was a desk against one wall that would certainly warrant rifling through at some point. He rinsed his arms nearly to the elbows then dried with a hand towel. Looking at the charcoal on the handle of the pitcher, he lathered that and poured water into his other hand to rinse the handle.

"Get out!"

He jumped and the pitcher slipped from his hands, exploding into shards and powder on the hard floor. Adrenaline pumped through him, his voice sounded unsteady and unconvincing. "I was washing my hands," he said to Lamia. He held his wet hands up for her to see. He hoped the pitcher hadn't been valuable.

Lamia launched at him. One moment she was standing in the hall doorway, her face twisted in rage, and the next she leaped into the air. She didn't come down again. Instead, she dissolved until she was nothing but gray feathery shadows, as insubstantial as the rendition of her that he'd drawn.

Her body elongated into a trailing, wafting cloud, while her face sharpened and stretched into terrifying angles. A skull with the merest hint of flesh covering it. Her face was longer than any human's, with a mouth stretching into a wide, gaping hole. A pit that could swallow Ty whole. White wisps of hair flowed back as she streaked up the left side of the bedroom. Not wanting to be trapped, he ran, but she cut him off as he tried to reach the door. Fingers like talons stretched toward him. An unearthly scream emitted from her bony jaws, loud enough to shake the air.

Ty clapped his hands over his ears. He fell to his knees. The thing that had been Lamia angled down toward his face. He rolled away from her, onto his back, still holding his ears. Her hands touched him, her nails clawed the skin of his neck and shoulders. She lowered her face to within inches of his. The gaping mouth opened wider, flaunting rows of sharp pointed teeth.

He screamed.

The human form of Lamia returned, solidifying from the boneless thing she had been. Kneeling beside him, she let her sharp, human nails dig in slightly, her face still nearly touching his. Her eyes were glassy with restrained violence.

"Never," she hissed into his ear. "Never enter my lady's room."

"No," he said in a quavering voice. "Never again."

She released him and stood. Anger pulled the muscles of her face tight, and she stared at Ty wide-eyed and unblinking. He remained on his back, afraid to move. She stepped backward two slow steps and he breathed a little deeper. His muscles had dissolved to the consistency of water, leaving him unable for the moment to lever up off the floor.

He sighed a deep shuddering breath and let his head drop back, trying to gather his wits and slow his heart. His eyes rolled upward, away from the sight of Lamia, or maybe just in relief. Or perhaps from providence.

His head was only inches from the bedroom desk, giving him a clear view of the underside. In the middle, bordering the back edge, were faint lines indicating a small compartment with a recessed lock. It lay between the wooden struts supporting the desk, making it something that he never would have found by feel, and never would've seen except from this angle.

6

Theft

Ty sat up, doing his best to hide his reaction. If Lamia had been ready to kill him for entering Naia's room, he couldn't imagine what she would do if she realized he'd discovered her mistress's secret—though perhaps she wasn't aware of the hidden drawer.

He pushed to his feet, testing his knees for strength, and indicated the broken pottery. "I'll clean this up," he said, his voice still unsteady.

"Leave this room. Now." Her lack of intonation invested the words with a cold ultimatum. Ty gave her a wide berth as he skirted past, back out to the living room.

He returned to the chair where he'd done Lamia's sketch and sat like a child being punished. He didn't even pick up one of the old books on art or poetry from the coffee table, just listened to the shards of pottery scraping against the marble floor as Lamia cleaned. When she returned to the living room, she crossed to the window without glancing his way.

They stayed in their relative corners for about a quarter of an hour, until Lamia suddenly hurried to the door. She opened it a moment before Ty heard the rattle of the elevator.

"What news?" Lamia asked once Naia was inside.

"Rumors of activity. Nothing solid." Naia studied Ty's contrite posture and looked back to Lamia's stern face. "What happened?" she asked.

"I discovered him in your bedroom."

Naia turned a weighing gaze his way. Even barefoot and wearing cutoffs, she intimidated him more than Lamia. He'd never stolen anything except a toy sword from Giorgos Condos when they were kids. Giorgos' mother must have noticed the tip sticking out of the coat he'd wrapped it in as he left their house. She'd insisted he put his jacket on to walk home and Ty had been mortified when it fell out. The humiliation had cured him of ever wanting to steal again—a tenet that served him well in his profession as a locksmith.

"I was just washing the charcoal off my hands." The lie burned his throat.

Her thoughtful silence filled the room. He heard the clicking noise he made with his tongue and stopped.

"Perhaps we should talk," Naia said. Her face was unreadable.

She crossed the room and opened the door to the balcony. He followed her out. Lamia glared as he passed.

The clear blue sky outside glowed with the same diffuse light, a radiance perhaps equal to a cloudy summer day on the surface. With no sun in the sky there was no uncomfortable glare from the white marble of the balcony. Naia took a seat at the far side of the balcony, sitting sideways on one of the three chaise lounges. He remained standing.

Ty owed her his full attention, but the view of the city hijacked it. It appeared to have shifted since he last saw it. When he first arrived, her apartment had looked over the majority of the urban jumble to the towering mountain beyond. It still looked over most of the city, but now faced the hills he had descended when he arrived, as if the building had not only rotated but had slid silently across the metropolis. He searched for any sign of the cave mouth at the crests of the hills and saw no evidence of it.

"Why do I still want to trust you, Ty?"

He twitched minutely as her voice jolted him back to more immediate concerns. "I don't know, my lady," he answered, trying not to think of Kalyptra whispering into the marks on his body.

She weighed him in silence a moment. "Have you heard of the New Order?"

"No, lady," he replied.

"What do you know of the gods?"

He shrugged, surprised by the turn of the conversation. "A few people perform devotions to one or all of the old gods, but most don't these days. There are some who think they're dead and some who believe they never existed. Most have adopted the Christian God, others are agnostic."

"And what do you believe, Ty?"

"I really don't know," he said, honestly. "This is real," he waved a hand at the city beyond the balcony, "so I suppose I believe what I always have deep down, that the gods were more than just stories. Whether they still live... " He shrugged.

The image from his death visions came to him as vividly as if he were a child again, standing in that vast, cold room. Two torches burned at opposite ends, dimly lighting the enormous space and the heavy, gray stone walls. The musty smell of the earthen floor and stale air wafted to him. He saw the figures lying on their biers, looking for all the world as if they were dead. Immense loss and an impression of ancient deaths haunted that cavern, though the air around him thrummed with vital power.

Naia leaned one shoulder against the high back of the chaise, hands pressed between her knees. He felt odd standing above her and lowered himself onto the edge of a wrought iron chair.

"It's not surprising that people think they died. When humanity started placing more faith in machines than in the gods, the gods withdrew. They stayed entirely in Aether, above their mountain, but they watched and sometimes helped or guided. Or punished. Twenty-five years ago, by your reckoning, everything changed. A spell was placed on the gods, one that stripped their memories from them."

"Who could spell the gods?"

"It was one of the Graeae, the three sisters. She stole the gods' memories in the first step of a larger power-play to kill them all and become the one and only deity in Ellada."

He'd learned of the Graeae in his youth, three very old witches who shared a tooth and an eye or something. "What happened to the gods?"

Naia stood and paced. "Most panicked when their memories were stolen. Some wanted to fight, some hid and plotted. My father, though, was the first of all the gods. His love begat creation." Naia crossed her arms and looked over her shoulder at the city, or whatever it was she saw. "He knew no more about who he was or what had happened than the others did, but he tried to lead them, advocating calmness and logic. Prometheus also tried to keep the peace, as did one or two others." She met his eyes again. "It soon became obvious that many would leave Aether to seek answers. They possessed their magic, but no knowledge of how to use it. Some tapped it subconsciously. Fear and anger began to manifest in spontaneous violence. The gods, if not the world, stood on the brink of catastrophe, so Prometheus and my father lied to the others; they announced that they had discovered a cure. Not everyone believed them, but they all came to hear what they had to say."

She shifted again to a chair, the story seeming to make her restless. "The wine pitchers had been drugged. Before long, all but my father, Prometheus, and Ares slept. Ares had either only pretended to drink or his strength overcame the drug. Either way, he fought them and managed to escape. Prometheus went after him. My father waited, and when neither of them returned he reached out, imagining a place of safety. He moved all the gods, taking a portion of the drugged wine with him for himself. Even he didn't know where they would end up. Somewhere safe, he hoped, where they could sleep until someone found a way to reverse the spell of amnesia."

The memory of the nowhere place of Ty's visions suddenly took on new perspective. He wondered if it could have been real. Not only the vision, but him actually being there, in that room, surrounded by sleeping gods. He relived the terror he'd felt as a child. The memory of the room came back to him so strongly it seemed he could almost identify the location. Almost.

"Why didn't the other two Graeae just reverse the spell?"

"Apparently they couldn't. They tried to force their sister, but she was beyond reason. She fought them and the other two killed her. And the gods have slept ever since."

Naia stood and returned to the balcony, leaning her back against it. He twisted in his chair to face her.

"If the gods had amnesia, how do you know Ares escaped, or that Prometheus helped? How do you know any of this at all?"

My father wrote all of this down. He corked it in a bottle and set it in a river. The note asked whoever found the message to locate someone he loved. He included a detailed description of himself in hopes that someone might connect the description with news of those missing and identify him. Whether he knew it or not, his magic must have been in play, as the message made it safely to a trustworthy friend. That friend climbed to Aether and searched for the gods, finding them already gone. He saw Prometheus' body as he ascended Olimbos; he'd been dashed on the rocks of the mountain. The messenger came to me next. Between my father's description of the god who escaped and the fact he was able to kill Prometheus, the messenger and I both agreed that the escaped god was Ares."

Ty asked his final question, the one nagging most at him. "Why tell me all of this?"

Naia studied him a long moment. "I asked if you were aware of The New Order," she said, at last. "They're a faction here that seeks to find and wake the amnesiac gods. They believe if they wake the gods, they can control them, teaching them only what they want them to know. They plan to place binding spells on the gods and force them to wipe out the entire world as we know it, then remake it with the New Order in charge.

"In response to the New Order, another group formed: the Revisionists. They're trying to find and kill the gods to prevent widespread destruction from either the New Order or the gods. And then there are the Preservationists, of which I am one. We live in hope of finding a way to wake the gods and cure them of their amnesia. My father trusted that if his message reached a loved one, help would come eventually. I've searched for a cure ever since."

She turned and placed her hands on the railing, silent for a long moment. Emotion tightened her beautiful profile and he thought he understood her restless tension now—guilt, sorrow, self-incrimination at twenty-five years of failure to save her father and the other gods.

She looked back over her shoulder. "So, Ty. I need to know. Are you affiliated with a faction?"

He stood and moved to her side, meeting her question without flinching. "I was aware of none of this until you told me just now," he said. He didn't mention his suspicion that Kairos almost certainly was involved.

She turned sideways, bringing them face-to-face. The breeze carried the clean scent of her to him, like a breath of air off a mountain lake with a hint of distant pines and autumn leaves. Her black eyes were deep enough to drown in. He couldn't help the leap his mind made, wondering what it would be like to make love to the daughter of Eros.

"Why do I feel such importance surrounding you, then?" she asked. She seemed to expect no answer. Reaching out, she brushed the left side of his chest with her fingertips.

"*Heart for love,*" Ty remembered Kalyptra saying when she'd finished tattooing that side. *Whose love?* he wondered.

He stepped forward into the touch. Everything about her attracted him. The curve of her neck where it met her shoulder, the hollow of her throat, her scent, her eyes. His fears shed like a chrysalis: his fear of trusting again gone, of giving himself over to someone, of his purpose here, fear of Erebus. For the moment, anything seemed possible.

Lamia opened the balcony door and Naia dropped her hand, as if suddenly aware of the intimacy of her gesture.

"My lady," Lamia said, "I thought perhaps a bath would help you relax from the stress of the day. I have everything ready." The interruption was as easy to see through as a bridal veil, but Naia nodded.

"A bath sounds welcome." She followed Lamia inside without a backward glance to him.

Ty started to follow them into the living room but Lamia closed the door in his face, as if he were as invisible as his tattoos. He returned to the wrought iron chair and sat, considering the day's events.

The trust Naia spoke of went both ways, and it perplexed Ty as well. He felt at ease near her. More than that, he recognized a growing desire for her, though he'd known her less than a day. But what chance would any man stand against the daughter of the God of Love?

His mind played over the centuries of depictions of Eros. The early ones focused on his power and beauty, but many of the later ones showed him shooting arrows at unsuspecting victims. He pictured Naia with a drawn bow, aiming at him right now from her bedroom balcony. He pictured it so strongly that, feeling foolish, he turned to look. The other balcony was empty.

It unnerved him to think back on her touch and realize how infatuated he'd been in her presence, or of the guilt he'd felt when Lamia told Naia that he'd been in her room. Letting someone close enough to hurt him again disturbed him more. But if he wanted to live, wanted to see his mother again, he had to finish his task here and get back to the surface as soon as possible. Whether Naia was intentionally seducing him—for reasons he couldn't begin to guess—or whether he felt the pull of his own accord, he wasn't going to be hanging around Erebus. A passing fancy for a demi-goddess was as ridiculous as it was unsafe.

He needed to figure out how to find the item he'd been sent to steal, get it, and get the hell out of here.

Daylight winked out like a doused fire, replaced a moment later with the faint glow of a rising full moon to his left. He wondered why there would be a moon here but no sun. A single light appeared inside the living room, multiplying as Lamia moved about, touching a small flame to the elegant oil lamps affixed to the walls. Naia was nowhere in sight.

Ty opened the balcony door cautiously, not certain if he was welcome inside yet. Lamia turned from lighting the last lamp and glared at him. She stalked to the kitchen, picked up a tray of food and gestured with her chin for him to follow. She led him past Naia's closed door to the guest room, where she had apparently been instructed to see him settled. She set the tray on the desk.

"Thank you," he said.

She left without a word and closed his door harder than necessary.

Taking a seat at the desk, he found a smaller meal than he'd hoped for—fruit, cheese, and bread. He dived into it, finishing it too soon. Hunger somewhat sated, he moved to the window. The full moon rode above the horizon now, not shedding quite enough light for him to tell if the landscape below it had shifted again. He wasn't sure, but thought that at home, in the real sky, the moon had been a narrow sliver only a couple of nights ago.

He paced from the window, prowling the small room, examining the artwork and books. Finally succumbing to exhaustion, he got ready for bed. He entered the bathroom and wistfully considered the inviting tub, a smaller version of Naia's sunken bath. It offered the chance to bathe the wound above his collarbone and the opportunity to rinse out his clothes, but he felt too edgy to indulge. Having swum the lake in his clothes would have to suffice.

In fact, not only Lamia, but all the creatures that lurked outside this building and Erebus in general, were enough to make him want to sleep fully dressed. If he'd been wearing something other than his suit, he would have.

Still trying to wrap his mind around the fact that he was really in Erebus and the uneasy guest of a demi-goddess, he climbed into the soft bed in his underclothes. He lay awake a long time before a fitful sleep filled with troubled dreams finally took him.

The next morning, Lamia watched him like a falcon tracking a mouse through tall grass, as if patiently waiting for him to reveal himself so she could strike. Thankfully, Naia sent her out mid-morning to invite two friends over so he could do portraits in charcoal of both. While they were there, Lamia reluctantly left again and returned with, among other things, a box containing a palette of watercolor paints for their eventual field trip to find a landscape.

In the afternoon, he lay in his room and read a play from an old, hand-bound book, hoping he might nap after his rough night. The story followed a standard premise of ancient writings: a man committed an act of hubris and was brought low by the events that followed. Apropos, Ty thought. The paper was on vellum so fine that he turned the pages carefully, afraid of damaging it, and wondered how ancient the thing really was. For that matter, he wondered how ancient Naia might be.

Through the walls, he heard a knock at the front door, followed by the purposeful stride of Lamia crossing the living room. A man's deep

voice—the old man from the other day, Ty thought—asked for Naia.
Ty stood and slipped to the bedroom door to listen.

"Their oracles have been talking," the man said, his resonant voice
easily overheard. "It has set the New Order to buzzing. I believe change
is in the wind."

"Even if that's true, Enyalius, speculation will avail them little,"
Naia said, her tone calm and her words more difficult to make out.

"I would you told that to the others," he answered.

"I'll be along shortly," she replied. The door closed.

Lamia spoke urgently, sotto voce, even harder for Ty to hear. "...
could be a ruse. You *must* let me come... you."

"You know I can't," Naia said.

"How long do you plan to indulge this mortal?" Lamia's voice was
louder now, and she invested the last word with such venom that Ty
didn't have to see her to know she was almost certainly waving a hand
his direction. "Why is he even here?"

"I don't know, Lamia, and that's *why* he's still here. It's important I
figure it out. I have to go now, but I'll be back soon."

Naia left. Footsteps swished past Ty's room and Lamia's bedroom
door closed with a bang. Ty's slim hope that they would come to trust
him enough to leave him alone at some point seemed foolish. He
couldn't wait on a 'someday' opportunity; his mystery and his mediocre
artistic talent wouldn't keep Naia entertained for long.

With the fright Lamia had given him the last time she discovered
him in Naia's bedroom, maybe she would suspect him least when she
was left to guard him. Before he could over-think things, Ty reached
into his jacket where it hung over the chair at his desk, pulled his toolkit
out, and slipped it into his pants pocket. He eased the door open and
cat-walked across the marble hallway. Naia's door had remained closed

since his last foray into her room. He held his breath, pushed the handle down slowly, and opened the door with one finger, listening all the while for Lamia.

His heart pounded below the prominent cartilage of his throat, as if constricted by his scar. Moving as fast as he dared, he made a beeline for the desk, lay down, and scootched on his back until his head was just below the small compartment on the underside. He pushed up to see if the catch would release. It was locked, as he had expected.

He lifted and turned his head, trying to see the lock. His stomach muscles trembled with the awkward position. Hoping there was no alarm system, either mundane or supernatural, he removed two tools and slipped a tension wrench in, followed by a rake. He scrubbed at the pins. Nothing happened. He couldn't afford the time to try different rakes. Choosing a hook pick by feel, he began picking each pin individually.

Footsteps echoed from the room next door. He froze. Lamia was pacing. Considering her stress when Naia was absent, she could easily leave her room and pace to the living room window at any moment. Ty eased his shoulders back onto the floor and held his breath, listening. A drop of sweat ran across his forehead and into his hair. Lamia's door remained closed.

He began again, trying not to rush. His abdominal muscles screamed at him. He felt the last pin slide down and tried pushing up again. The compartment snicked softly and tipped open toward the front, apparently hinged at the back. No alarms sounded—at least, none that he could hear.

Unable to see inside, he felt around blindly. Almost immediately he discovered a flat, metallic object. He pulled it forward with one finger, palmed it, and pushed the compartment closed again.

Ty slid out from under the desk with all the urgency of the guilty thief that he was, and hurried across the room. He listened at the door and heard nothing. His hand was on the latch when Lamia's door suddenly opened. He'd pushed Naia's door nearly but not quite closed. He prayed Lamia wouldn't notice. Quick footsteps strode past and down the hall and he laid his head against the doorframe with relief. Ty heard someone—Naia he assumed, as there was no knock—enter the apartment. He wondered how Lamia knew when Naia was near.

The two women talked in low murmurs.

Ty couldn't care less what they were saying; all he cared about was how he was going to get out of this bedroom. The hallway could only be seen from the far side of the living room, away from the front door. Taking a bigger chance than he dared stop and think about, he silently pulled the door open an inch. Putting one eye to the crack, he watched the end of the hall as best he could for movement. He didn't know which had the better chance of success, getting out now or waiting, as either course could prove disastrous. His decision was as rash as it was random; he chose the former.

7

Landscapes

Opening the door no wider than the depth of his body, Ty slipped around it and into the hall, closing it behind him as quickly and quietly as possible. He took one long stride across the hall reaching for the handle to his room. Footsteps pounded toward him from the living room. Lamia marched into the hall.

He depressed the handle to his room and pivoted toward the hall as she appeared. He tugged his door so that it clicked shut again, as if he had just exited. Shoving both hands deep into his pants pockets he let go of the metal object and hoped neither Naia nor Lamia had a connection to the object similar to what Lamia had to Naia.

He kept his breathing even and his muscles relaxed, hoping his face wouldn't flush and that sweat wouldn't spring from every pore. Lamia glared at him with an expression of deep suspicion, but not certainty.

"That was quick," he said casually, sliding past her to the living room. In fact, it had been bizarrely quick. If Naia had actually gone to a meeting and returned, then time in Erebus was as random as its cartography. He wondered if time on the surface passed at a different pace. Slower, he hoped.

"Long enough to accomplish what I needed," Naia said. "By the way, I think I found a place where you could sketch some landscape."

"Sure," he said, "whenever you like."

"Why don't we go now?"

He forced a smile. "I'll get my jacket."

He opened his bedroom door and Lamia moved into the doorway behind him, looking around suspiciously. Her narrow-eyed gaze flicked from the neatly made up bed, to the book on the bed, then scanned the rest of the unremarkable room.

Ty wasn't sure if he would have stashed the item somewhere or kept it in his pocket if he'd been alone. No choice now. He took his jacket from the chair and smiled at Lamia as he slipped it on. When she stepped back into the hallway, he moved his toolkit to the inside pocket of his jacket.

Lamia stuffed the watercolors, a canvas, and some food into a small picnic basket. Ty followed her into the kitchen to offer his help, but her surly look changed his mind. He went back to the living room and sat. The irregular edges of the item he'd stolen poked into his leg. He struggled to ignore the sharp reminder and keep his expression neutral.

Ty felt as unsure about the real purpose of this outing as he did about everything in Erebus. The timing seemed odd, considering Naia had received unsettling news and been called to urgent meetings twice in the two days he'd been here. She paced to the window more than once before Lamia had everything ready to go. He hadn't known her long, but her restlessness seemed uncharacteristic.

The same ancient elevator and its ancient operator clattered into view at their call. Ty followed the women inside. When the gold bars closed in front of his face, the impression of being on the wrong side of a cage was difficult to dispel, and he wondered again what Naia had planned for him. More, he suspected, than just painting a landscape. He touched a finger lightly to his leg as they clanked down six or seven floors, reassuring himself the item was secure and hoping this trip might provide him with an opportunity to escape. They reached the lobby and exited. The little elevator rattled its way up again and out of sight, answering another distant buzzer. Ty wondered if the old man ever left his confines.

He stuck close to Naia and Lamia as they made their way out onto the city streets. It seemed he was still largely ignored by the people and things they passed, and the tension in his shoulders loosened minutely the farther they walked.

Where he might have seen panhandlers outside shops and stores in his own city, here he saw golden men or women. Quite literally golden—skin the color of a bar of gold. They sang the accolades of the services or products within in sirenesque fashion. Naia glanced at Ty as he passed the first of them, a stunning young man with curly hair a shade or two lighter than his skin. Though most other residents of Erebus moved past the singer without a glance, Ty found it hard to look away, transfixed by the beauty of both the man and his voice. He craned his head after they passed the singer until he bumped a knee into the basket Lamia carried, earning him a sharp glare from her.

Disregarding the golden people became easier with each one he encountered, until by the third or fourth he barely noticed them. Naia and Lamia shared a look, and Ty wondered if he'd just passed some test. Or maybe failed one.

Trying to orient himself to the inside-out city, he realized suddenly where they were headed. "Are you taking us to the National Garden?"

She didn't seem to recognize the name. "We're headed for the park," Naia replied. "I thought it might be a place where we could both see the same thing."

A couple of blocks later the park came into sight and it did, indeed, seem much like the National Garden he knew. Other than the landmarks appearing in random order, it had the same hundreds of species of grass, flowers, shrubs, and trees, all planted along winding paths, though less groomed than in his own park. This place felt wilder, more alive. He saw no statues here, though they did pass a sundial pedestal he recognized. It took him a moment to realize the other nagging difference: there were none of the songbirds that were so common on the surface. In fact, he'd seen no birds or small animals at all since arriving in Erebus.

Naia led them down paths, through a series of twists and turns, under a living arch of tree branches, and deep into the park. They came to a wide, grassy spot bordered on the far side by a small creek. The National Garden had ponds, but Ty couldn't remember if it had any streams or not. Naia stopped in an open area of grass.

"This is one of my favorite spots," she said, and indicated Lamia should set down the basket and the watercolors. "Do you think it might serve as inspiration?"

Ty surveyed his subject. The creek in front of him was perhaps five or six strides across. It curved into sight serenely from his left and curved out of sight again not far to his right, where he thought he saw the edge of a railing to a small bridge. Cypress, pine, oak, and palm trees had grown tall and lush bordering the water, and the undergrowth grew thick in myriad shades of green. Rocks bordered the creek and dotted its depths, ranging from small pebbles to stones larger than Ty could have lifted and spanning a palette of colors more varied than his skills would be able to duplicate.

"I'll give it my best," he said.

Naia gestured to the basket and Lamia pulled a thin blanket from within, spread it, and set out the picnic items. Ty shrugged out of his jacket and hung it on a tree branch, shifting into the long-dormant practice of framing in his mind's eye what he planned to paint. It surprised him how much he looked forward to the challenge. He studied the colors Lamia had brought, the scenery, and the size of the rough-framed canvas. He felt incongruously lighthearted. Nearly forgotten parts of him seemed to be reawakening: the person he'd been before starting to gamble, when he'd smiled more easily, spent more time on his motorcycle and less in windowless back rooms.

Leaning against the trunk of the tree, looking from the canvas back to the creek, he slipped a hand into his pants pocket out of habit. The stolen item rested there in the depths. Reflexive guilt made him look up quickly.

Naia stood watching him. Her calm expression never changed. She turned, as if not to disturb him, and walked to the bank of the little brook. Squatting, she dipped her fingers into the water. Ty couldn't be sure, but he thought he heard her speaking.

She plucked a leaf from a nearby bush, as green and healthy as the exemplary representative of spring itself. She set it on the surface of the water that murmured its way through the park. The leaf floated to the center of the brook and bobbed along, never submerging and never drifting to one side or the other to catch in the shallows. Ty could see the bright green of it clearly as it made the turn in the creek and floated out of sight.

He looked back to Naia. She still squatted like a child on the bank, dangling her fingers in the water and humming a small tune. After a moment more, she stood and walked back to him.

"Do you have everything you need?" She indicated the canvas still in his hand.

If she wasn't going to mention her strange actions, neither was he. "I think so."

"Will it bother you if I watch?"

She stood close to him, wearing the same cutoffs as yesterday, with expensive looking sandals and a thin, loose fitting, long-sleeved white shirt. "No," he said, "you won't bother me." He hoped he sounded convincing.

Naia picked an apple from the basket and cut a small wedge of white cheese. She looked over her shoulder to Ty, who shook his head at the unspoken offer. He dipped some water from the creek into a clay pot, opened the paint jars, and settled to begin. She sat cross-legged near him.

"Do you mind if I talk while you work?" she asked.

Her voice was a casual sing-song, almost as sirenesque to him as the golden youths on the streets.

"No, that's fine."

He chose a large brush and began to whitewash the canvas. She seated herself close enough to him that he inhaled her with every breath. Except for her nearness and warmth, her scent was nearly indistinguishable from the rainwater fragrance of the brook and the earthy greenness of new growth around him.

She sliced the apple and lifted a piece to her mouth between the knife and her thumb, and followed it with a thin slice of cheese. "May I ask how you came by that scar?"

Ty thought first of the scars on his wrists before realizing she was looking at his throat. As usual, his top button was undone. He was used to the question, and glad she hadn't asked about the pink bloodstain at the shoulder of his shirt instead.

As a child, he used to tell other children that a gang of pirates had tried to hang him before he heroically escaped. These days he'd sometimes tell people that a girlfriend stuffed another woman's bra in his mouth when she'd found it in his bedroom, and he'd performed an emergency tracheotomy on himself with a pen knife. They'd usually laugh and ask why he didn't just pull the bra out of his mouth and then leave off questioning him about it. To Naia, he told the truth, if somewhat sheepishly. "I sort of hanged myself."

She quirked an eyebrow.

"When I was born, the country was between monarchs. King George had been deposed a few years before, and the government seemed to change hands every few months. When I was five, the Queen began her reign. World War I and the Asia Minor Campaign were in the past, WWII hadn't yet begun. It was one of the few quiet times I remember as a child."

He fanned the canvas to dry the thin coat of whitewash. She watched him curiously, probably thinking he was avoiding the question, but he wasn't. "American movies started coming to our cinema for the first time. I was seven when my mother took me to see 'The Arizona Raiders.'" As he'd expected, Naia showed no sign of recognition. "It was a Buster Crabbe western. In the opening scene, some men are wrongly trying to hang the hero and he escapes on his horse with the rope still around his neck. When the rope catches on things, he ends up nearly hanging himself before he finally gets loose."

He tested the whitewash, then dipped a thin brush in brown paint and made a few long strokes to outline the trunk of the largest tree on the opposite bank before continuing. "My mother sent me off to bed when we got back from the movie, but I was so wound up I couldn't sleep. I got up, climbed onto the bench of my bay window, and played a stupid hangman game with a lace curtain. I twisted it at the back like a noose and jumped to the floor, but I underestimated by about six inches. My body weight tightened the twist in the curtain so it couldn't unravel, and I wasn't able to reach the end behind my back to unwind it. If my mother hadn't come back in to check on me when she did, I would have been too far gone to revive."

He concentrated on swishing the brush in water and outlining the creek. She looked away from his throat and changed the subject.

"Have your queens ruled Ellada well?"

"I guess so. The anti-monarchists have been pretty quiet about them since they repelled the invasions in WWII. The queen doesn't seem too concerned about the political divisions between the left and the monarchists, but when things nearly erupted into civil war when I was about fifteen or sixteen she must have stepped in somehow."

"Shouldn't that be 'queens'?"

"Probably. They go by one name, though, 'Enoméni.' I'm not sure if they took the name "United" for their conjoined status or their goal to unify the country. Maybe both. I don't even know what their real names are or where they came from. I don't know if anyone does. Some small village is all I've heard. Anyway, it's probably why people tend to refer to the twins in the plural and the queen in the singular." He outlined more details of the bank on the far side.

"It surprises me they were accepted so well, when there had only been kings before them."

He'd thought she was going to say because of their conjoined nature. "I think when King George got deposed and the country went through years of upheaval, everyone was ready for a change. The people chose to believe in something new." He painted a single leaf floating in the brook.

Naia took a breath as if to comment, but said nothing. She watched him as he alternated between studying the landscape and sketching lines of color on the canvas. "I'm glad they've ruled well," she said finally. He turned to her, wondering what more she'd been about to say.

Her legs were tucked to her side and she was braced on one arm, leaning toward him. A playful breeze carried a whiff of lavender from her blue-black hair. He made the mistake of looking directly into her face, at her skin, smooth as carved ivory, and her dark eyes, which drew him in like a deadly whirlpool. He looked away.

"Is there anything you can tell me about your world, my lady?" he said, correcting the informality into which he'd lapsed.

She shifted her weight to sit cross-legged. Whether by accident or design, her knee almost but not quite touched his hip. He could feel the minute distance between their bodies without looking. "What would you like to know?"

"If all the gods are asleep, who rules here?"

"No one rules, per se, but factions occasionally vie for power in certain matters, like they do now over the fate of the gods. The strongest or most invested group wins. Currently my faction, the Preservationists, is strongest, but times are uncertain right now."

Erebus didn't sound so different from his own politically divided world. Civil war had been prevented, but polarizations that pre-dated the war and had worsened during it still resonated strongly. Not so much with him, or many his age, but the older generations chewed the bitter seeds of it still.

Lamia sat apart from them, near the picnic basket. Ty could see her clearly over Naia's shoulder. She was following every word, her eyes sharp as the tips on a hawk's nails. When he looked at her, Lamia turned away. Ty thought she was pretending not to listen until he saw her smiling at something in the distance. Naia turned as well and both she and Lamia stood. A woman was walking toward them, coming through the trees and underbrush rather than along the path by which they had arrived.

"Aletheia," Naia greeted the woman when she drew near. The two exchanged kisses on each cheek. Lamia dipped her head to the woman in a cordial hello.

The newcomer, Aletheia, wore a gown as green as the leaf Ty had seen floating down the creek. She was an older woman, with white hair piled on her head and skin as delicate as a moth's wings.

"Aletheia, allow me to introduce you to a guest of mine, Eutychios Eperitus Kleisos."

"Just Ty," he said.

He left off any honorific. It wasn't that he minded showing deference to anyone here—he felt as insignificant in Erebus as an ant on a city sidewalk—he just wasn't sure if calling her "lady" would put her on equal footing with Naia, and whether or not that would be appropriate.

He expected the woman to peer nearsightedly at him, perhaps touch him to bring him into focus, but she apparently had no difficulty seeing him. A small smile played at her lips. "And how did you come to be here, Ty?" she asked.

"I was sent down here by one of the banished living above."

"Well, that's... unique." Her words rose at the end with the intonation of a question, and hung in the air, waiting for an explanation.

He looked to Naia, but she did nothing to assist. In fact, she and Lamia were watching him with interest, though he'd already related his story to them. Turning back to Aletheia, Ty felt as if soft, feathered wings were beating at the stronghold of his fortress. Though the moat was deep and the walls were solid, the sensation was all around him, urging him to truth, but he was as immune to the urging as stone would be to feathers.

"I don't know much about him except that I was in his debt, and that he'd been exiled for some infraction. He sent me here on his behalf." Ty tried hard to say as little as possible. The intensity of her focus disturbed and distracted him.

Both Naia and Lamia looked to Aletheia. It was obvious that painting a landscape for Naia had not been the real purpose of this outing. He hoped he was passing whatever new test he was taking.

"Curious," Aletheia said, mildly. She smiled at the other women as if this were nothing more than an intriguing conversation. "Do I know him?"

"Ty says he is sworn not to reveal the name," Naia replied.

"I see." She turned back to Ty. "And what is it you have been sent here to do on his behalf, then?"

And there was the crux of it.

Ty reminded himself that he'd been gambling for months, he *could* do this. He *could* keep from flushing or sweating. He *could* look her straight in the eye and tell bold-faced lies. He controlled his impulse to suck at his teeth with his tongue.

"Entertain the Lady Naia, I suppose. Make her favorable to his goal." Ty gave a small shrug. "As I say, I'm in his debt. I got few instructions and asked few questions."

The dishonesty prodded at him sharp as a knife pricking his skin, but there was not the slightest hesitancy in his voice. In a whiplash reaction to his insecurity of a moment ago, confidence filled him.

Aletheia reached out and took his left arm just above the elbow. "How very brave of you." Her thumb massaged lightly on the inside of his arm, right over one of Kalyptra's tattoos. His confidence smashed to dust. He struggled to keep his face calm. He tried on a smile.

The look Aletheia gave Naia was unreadable. Lamia's was not. Anger tightened the corners of her mouth.

Aletheia removed her hand from Ty's arm and laid it gently along Naia's cheek. "I wish I could have been of more help." She turned back to Ty. "It was most interesting meeting you, Eutychios Eperitus Kleisos." And with that, she left the way she had come.

"Perhaps we should pack up for the day," Naia said. Subdued, or perhaps disappointed, she turned and wandered back toward the creek, leaving Lamia to ready their things.

"No," Lamia said loudly. "He's hiding something." Naia kept walking, but Lamia spun toward Ty. "Take off your shirt," she demanded.

"What?"

"Take it off," she grated. "*Now.*" Small wisps of vapor trailed from her upper arms. There was a flash of skeletal fangs, a superimposed image on her face, gone again in an eye blink.

Ty's heart lurched with remembered fear and he looked to Naia for help. She had stopped and looked back at him, but said nothing.

"Why?" he managed to ask Lamia, assuming it a reasonable question.

"Aletheia sensed something." She pointed to his arm. "I want to know what."

Praying his marks were still invisible, he unbuttoned his shirt, cuffs first. Removing it, he tossed it to the ground. She gestured to his undershirt, and he removed that as well.

Lamia grabbed his left hand and stared where Aletheia had rubbed his arm, then examined him up one side and down the other. Her anger increased as she looked harder, evidently seeing nothing more unusual than the wound above his collarbone.

Naia returned, and Lamia stepped back. Ty thought she might chastise Lamia, but instead she had a look for herself. She examined the inside of his arm, then touched his chest, first on the left and then on the right, where the hair was no more than prickly nubs of regrowth directly over his invisible serpentines. Her touch sent a shiver through him and his nipples hardened.

"We really should be going now," she said, not meeting his eyes.

Ty put his undershirt and shirt back on. He pulled on his jacket, his mind working furiously and his nerves tense enough to make muscles in his jaw twitch. Going back to Naia's apartment would be insanity. He had the item that he'd come for in his pocket. He needed a way out of here. Right now.

"My lady, obviously I'm not accomplishing what I was sent to do," he said, though, actually, he'd very much accomplished his goal. "Perhaps I should go back. Above."

She did meet his eyes then. "To your death? I must have been a poor hostess indeed if that's preferable to being a guest in my home."

"Ah..." he mumbled, "You've been very gracious. I just thought maybe, well, that this is getting a little awkward all the way around. Maybe my debtor will be willing to negotiate a new contract."

"I'm sorry Lamia asked you to disrobe. I'm sorry I felt the need to check for myself. Unusual things are afoot right now; your appearance here and your story seem more than just coincidence coming at this time. Things are waxing more dangerous by the day, and you're a mystery, in more ways than one." She began walking down the path, back the way they had come. Lamia was still gathering the canvas and paints. Ty had no choice but to walk with Naia.

"I tell you more than I should, Ty, and I'm not sure why. I enjoy your company, even though it seems unwise. And I'm not generally foolish."

He enjoyed her company, too. And he was absolutely damn sure it was unwise on his part.

Lamia quickly caught up to them and walked behind. Once they emerged from the trees, the city and surrounding bare hills sprang back into view, though the hills were now in front of him rather than to the right. Ty scanned the crests but still saw no sign of the tunnel.

The city had turned itself inside-out once more while they were in the park. It was as if a great hand was reaching into soft putty, pulling up from the middle, and redistributing it helter-skelter. If it didn't change again while they walked, Ty felt he could find his way around eventually, but right now his sense of direction was as muddled as when he first arrived. Not exactly fortuitous when one was trying to plan an escape.

Naia made small talk as they walked and Ty was glad of it. He'd had enough intensity for one day. Besides, he needed to think. He couldn't just break and run, or Lamia would be on him like a hunting dog. He wished he could fade out of their sight, the way he seemed to with every other person and creature they passed, but Naia—like her friends Enyalius and Aletheia—had never had trouble seeing him. And Lamia certainly hadn't since he'd first entered the apartment.

Ty began to get his bearings as they skirted the downtown high-rises. Wealthy apartment buildings and homes began to appear more frequently and the sidewalks became more crowded. Desperation welled up. He felt increasingly sure that he wasn't going to get away from Naia and Lamia before reaching her apartment. He shoved his hands in his pockets as he walked, feeling the rectangle of cold metal against the fingers of his right hand.

Whatever the thing was, it had been well hidden and was important to at least Naia and Kairos. He may not know Naia well, but he was very certain that what she'd said about not generally being foolish was true. With political angst on the rise and a stranger staying in her home, it was almost certain that Naia would be checking that the item remained where it should, in the secret compartment of her desk. Ty looked around again for any chance of escape. One found him instead.

They were within sight of Naia's building when the attack came.

8

Out of the Frying Pan

Two forms rushed from the shadows of an alley. Ty, who'd been looking down, lost in thought, flinched back at the size and speed of the attackers in his peripheral vision. Lamia shifted instantly into wraith form before Ty had even processed that one of the creatures coming at them was a giant, a male, nearly twice as tall as himself, and the other was a centaur. Also, that they were, indeed, coming at him—or more precisely, at Naia, on the other side of him.

Lamia launched without hesitation. The giant bellowed and lunged, swinging an arm as thick as Ty's waist toward her. His hand closed on mist. Lamia re-formed in mid-air, claws streaking for the eyes beneath his heavy brow.

The centaur shouldered Ty out of her way, hardly seeming to notice him. He landed sprawled on the sidewalk as the creature closed with Naia, using her small human arms to try and throw a black cloth bag over Naia's head. Naia twisted out from under it. Ty tucked into a ball as the centaur spun on her hind feet, trying to cut Naia off from the alley. Hooves flashed over his head and landed with a sharp clatter near his elbow.

The giant's roar, Lamia's screech, and the ensuing fight had the effect of a ringmaster's whistle signaling the clown act to commence. The busy street around them erupted in chaos. Pushing to his knees, Ty saw prey running and predators snarling everywhere. Fights broke out spontaneously, some fighting to escape and some who looked to be fighting for the hell of it.

Two human-looking forms dissolved into air and gusted in dusty whirlwinds past Ty. A cacophony of non-human hoots, shrieks, and brays echoed between the tall buildings on either side as monsters and various get of the gods reacted to the attack. A heavily-muscled woman carrying a spear and shield and wearing an ancient-styled, knee-length chiton ran across the street to Naia's aid. Seconds passed like minutes while Ty's mind grappled with the violence around him. There seemed no direction he could move that would be safe.

The warrior threw her spear at the centaur. The centaur partially deflected the weapon with one of her human arms, but the head of the spear grazed her equine shoulder and she gave a roar of pain. She reared and knocked the shield from the woman's hand, throwing the warrior onto her back, next to Ty. The centaur reared again, her long, overly large face twisted in rage. Ty pushed to his feet and ran as the slashing hooves descended.

The warrior only had time to bring her arms partway to her face before the front hooves struck, backed by half a ton of muscle. Ty ran for the alley on the opposite side of the street. Looking back, he saw the centaur pound at the warrior until she was reduced to little more than a puddle of gore and blood spreading on the sidewalk.

Ty dodged past fangs, talons, and claws. Behind him, the giant roared again. The sound conveyed such immense anger and pain, it made Ty turn to see the huge man holding his palms to his eyes while he continued to bellow. Blood trickled down both cheeks. He swept blindly at Lamia with one hand, then the other, moving with lethal strength, striking nothing but air. The centaur, her forelegs splashed to the knees with blood and bits of flesh, lunged forward to assist the giant against Lamia. Ty looked desperately for Naia in the melee and saw no sign of her. He froze in the middle of the street.

His attraction to her was moot, nothing he could ever act on even if circumstances were different, but leaving her in danger felt wrong. He'd figured Lamia and a couple of the other creatures who'd thrown in with the warrior would be a match for the centaur and the now blinded giant. But not seeing Naia meant he couldn't feel assured that she was all right.

Every fiber of him pulled toward where he'd last seen her. Unable to leave her and unwilling to lose this opportunity to escape he stood, surrounded by chaos, searching. *Heart for love*, he thought again, wondering what really kept him here; was it his abhorrence at the thought of more abandonment, or something else? The item he'd been sent to steal dragged at his pocket. If staying led to his death then he'd never see his mother again, never have the chance to apologize or explain.

He ran.

At the far side of the street, he dodged around the body of one of the golden boys who lay torn and bleeding outside a fabric shop, his blood vivid red against his gold skin. Ty made it to the mouth of the alley and peered in, checking to see if it held more combatants. To his relief, it was empty.

He took one step toward the shadowed opening before three or four hundred pounds of muscle, fur, claws and feathers struck his left shoulder and upper chest. There was no time to parse the situation beyond the facts that a creature had launched into him—or, more likely, considering the ungainly angle, had *been* launched into him—and that he was falling too fast and too hard to protect his skull. He wrapped one arm tightly around the animal's back and grabbed a handful of mane. Pressing his face close to the incongruous beak, he smelled its warm, meaty breath.

One outstretched forepaw of the animal broke their fall. Instead of crushing Ty's chest, the creature's momentum caused it to somersault over him. Ty hit the sidewalk hip first. His shoulder then his head struck the paving bricks, hard enough to stun him, but not hard enough to do real damage. He looked between his feet. A bull—the adversary that must have head-butted the other creature—stood a few yards away. He tipped his head back. The creature that had struck him—a gryphon he saw—rolled to its feet facing the bull. It leaped. The first lunge brought its front feet either side of Ty's hips. Its hind feet planted on his shoulders and pushed off again, eagle's beak lunging for the bull's throat.

The bull charged to meet it. One hoof trampled the inside of Ty's right calf and he cried out as the flesh compressed and tore. He rolled to his knees, head under the gryphon's belly, and tried to crawl toward the street, stubbornly refusing to die here, all odds to the contrary.

Hands grabbed his shoulders from behind, pulling him upright. Ty thrashed and tried to slide his arms out of his jacket but was hauled backward into the mouth of the alley. When he found his feet, he turned with a wild roundhouse punch. The man stepped back from the punch and Ty found himself face-to-face with Momus.

He wore the same stained clothes, the same clown-sized shoes. A cigar gripped between his teeth glowed red through the black ash as he took a big puff. "Well, well. Ty, my friend. It looks like we should get you out of here."

Blood leaked down Ty's legs under his torn pants. He cradled his left arm where the gryphon had crashed into the front of his shoulder, the back of his shoulder had struck the paving stones, and the beast had trampled him. His hip ached, but seemed to have fared better than his shoulder or calf.

Momus moved with more determination than in their previous encounter. Ty struggled to keep up until the man grabbed him by the back of his collar, propelling him stumbling along at the speed of his great lumbering strides.

"Best to stay away from spats like that, I say," Momus said, as they hurried along. "Yes, indeed. Best to stay away from those."

Momus guided Ty a few streets away from the fray, zigzagging between alleys and streets. The squall of battle was dying down behind them and the outburst seemed to have cleared the nearby, smaller streets entirely. Without warning, they popped out from between two large buildings. Brown, denuded hills rose up before Ty.

"I need to get back to the surface," Ty said, the sight of the hills sparking new intensity, "to my own world."

"Well, you won't get there that way," Momus said, slinging a heavy arm over Ty's sore shoulder and guiding him down the narrow track between the hills and the city.

"No," Ty said, pulling back. "I need to go that way." He pointed uphill. "That's where I came in."

Momus took a great puff on his cigar. "Really?" he said, the cloud of resulting smoke flowing out with the word.

"The lake to the cave, then out the tunnel and down the hill." Ty glanced over his shoulder to make sure no creatures were pursuing them.

"Well friend, I don't think that's going to work today. No caves up there. No siree. We'd better go the way I know." He started forward again.

A sudden, cold doubt washed through Ty. He didn't follow.

Momus looked back. His expression turned quizzical, almost comical, on his grungy clown face. "You want to go above, right?"

He was being paranoid, Ty thought. Momus had already helped him twice. And he needed out of here fast. "Sure. We'll go your way," he said.

Momus took him along the edge of town, where the city looked as if someone had taken scissors to a photograph of it and laid it in the center of a brown and bare field. No buildings were cut in half, but the demarcation was so abrupt it almost seemed some should've been. This outer edge was quiet, though, with no one in sight except a few residents glimpsed through open windows.

At what looked to be a random spot in the perimeter, Momus angled toward the rear of an old, tan brick building and disappeared down a narrow concrete staircase. Ty paused, searching for another option, but he found none. He followed Momus.

The staircase didn't end at a basement door but continued down into complete blackness, zigzagging deeper and deeper. The only thing that lay below Erebus was Tartarus, and childhood fears snagged at his resolve. "You're taking me up to the surface world, right?"

"Of course, of course," Momus said, but he said no more. Ty's suspicions returned doubled.

He'd gone only a few steps beyond the last dim, gray light into darkness and was about to protest going any further, when a match flared to brightness ahead of him. Momus held it to the end of a fresh cigar, then held the still burning match aloft, shedding a small, murky pool of light.

Ty decided he would continue to a count of fifty, no more, and turn around if he still felt doubtful. At forty-two, Momus had gone through five matches, during which time Ty had become increasingly disoriented. They continued to walk down the stairs according to his visual senses, but proprioception told him he was on level ground. It felt as if he walked on an escalator where each step was only one inch lower than the previous before it slid backward to the original height. At fifty-one, the bobbing matches said he was now going up, but his thigh muscles performed the eccentric contractions of a long, steep descent and his bruised and bloodied calf muscle agreed. Another count of thirty-eight, and Momus pushed a loud, squeaky metal door open. Ty followed him out into morning sunlight muted by low, coastal clouds.

They were standing on a rooftop. Ty walked to the edge and carefully looked down. The metal sign "Cineak," outlined in light bulbs, dropped vertically below him. The building was home to the Kotopouli Theatre, attached to and part of the Rex Theatre in downtown Athina. Ty felt like laughing. "You did it." He turned, grinning, to Momus, still standing in the doorway of the stairwell. "You brought me back."

"Well, sure. Sure I did. We needed to get you out of that pickle back there, didn't we?"

Ty walked back across the roof to him. "So what now? Are you going to stay on the surface a bit?"

"Me? Oh, no. No. It's not for me up here, you know. I'll just be heading back down now." He didn't move.

"I... uh, I'm afraid I don't have anything to thank you properly." Ty's pockets were empty but for his tool kit and the stolen item. He put out his hand.

Momus shrugged, shoved his cigar in his mouth, grinned around it, and took Ty's hand. "You take care of yourself from here on out," Momus said. The big man turned and vanished down the stairwell.

Ty looked around the roof, wondering if there was any way down other than the stairs. The manual hydraulic hinge had nearly closed the door when he thrust his fingers in the narrowing wedge. With his sleeve pulled up, he noticed the scars on his left wrist. They stood out white and clear. Hauling the door open again, he peered down. The stairwell looked normal. Unlike the darkness of a moment ago, it was lit by sodium lights in small metal cages. There was no hint of Momus.

Fervently hoping he wouldn't end up back in Erebus, Ty stepped into the stairwell. The roof door closed behind him with a clunk. Nails of anxiety clawed at his belly as he started down.

Nothing untoward happened during his descent down the four flights of the stairwell, except that his calf hurt like a bitch. Ty pushed a door open on the main level and found himself behind the stage of the empty theatre. He hurried across the stage, down the steps, and up a side isle between the seats. The front ticket office and lobby proved as empty as the hall, and he pushed at the bar of a heavy door, emerging

onto Panepistimiou Avenue. He grinned to see his own, stable city—
traffic, tourists, and all.

As much as he ached to check on his mother, his first priority
had to be getting them both out of danger by handing this thing off
to Kairos. He headed for the warehouse. The fourteen block walk was
the first chance to reflect on anything since Naia took him to the park,
what seemed like days ago, though it had only been this morning.

He hoped she was okay. He even hoped Lamia was. The fear that
Naia might have died in that fight wrapped around his chest like a
python and squeezed. He'd had nothing to do with the attack, of course,
nothing to feel guilty about. It would've happened whether he'd been
there or not, and he'd been lucky to get out alive. It's not like he could've
done anything to help them fight off a giant and a centaur. Running
had been the smartest thing he'd done in days. The rationalizations did
nothing to soothe the sick feeling in his guts.

Ty reached the warehouse and, for the first time, noticed the
lettering centered on the industrial metal door "Mesógeios Acadimía
Omorfiás." Mediterranean Beauty Academy would be the obvious
interpretation, though it could also be read as Midland Beauty
Academy, an intentional double meaning, no doubt. He tried the door
and found it locked. He knocked. After a full minute of knocking and
waiting, Ty had to admit no one was going to answer.

The building was joined to its neighbor on one side, but Ty circled
it the other direction as far as possible. He discovered two small
windows, possibly bathrooms, both locked. Giving up, he headed for
his apartment, deciding he'd better change and clean up before going
to the hospital.

The first thing he did upon arriving at his flat was to lock the door
behind him. The second was to call Nikos. The game had been held the

evening of March 20th. According to a newspaper he'd seen on the walk home, today was the 24th, though he seemed to have lost only twenty-four hours while in Erebus. At least years hadn't gone by in the normal world. Long enough, though, that his mother might be home by now instead of in the hospital.

Being mid-morning on a Monday, he called the store. Nikos answered.

"Nikos, it's Ty."

"Where have you been?" he said. "What happened to you?"

"It's a long story. I owed Kairos money and had to get that taken care of. I'll tell you about it later." He had no idea what he'd tell Nikos, or anyone else, but he could find out how much people knew already and go from there. That could wait, though. "How's my mother? Have you seen her since the night of the game?"

There was silence at the other end of the line. Ty gripped the earpiece tighter. "Nikos, is my mother home yet? Is she doing all right?"

"Ty, I'm so sorry." His blood ran cold. He didn't want to hear more, but he kept the phone to his ear. "She died. I went to see her that night, like you asked, and they told me she'd taken a turn for the worse during the day and had died a few hours before I got there."

Before the game even took place.

All his concern that Kairos might harm her if he didn't go to Erebus, his worry about how she was doing while he was gone, and she'd died before he even left. If he'd forfeited the game when his other money lender took all his cash, he could have gone back to the hospital and been with her. She'd worked all his life to give him everything she could. He hadn't even put her first when she was dying.

His hand holding the phone dropped to his side. "Ty?" he heard through the earpiece he still gripped. "I tried to find you, fi le mou. I looked everywhere. Her friends and neighbors held a service yesterday."

Ty placed the earpiece in the cradle, disconnecting the call. She'd been fifty-four. He felt numb, as adrift as a cork in the ocean. He walked into the bathroom and sat on the edge of the tub. The sculpted metal edges of the item in his pocket pricked his leg. He removed the thing and took a good look at it for the first time.

It was beautiful. Finely crafted, heavy for its size. It fit in his outstretched hand, not much thicker than one of his lock picking wrenches. The metal—iron, he thought—was covered in vivid red, blue, yellow, and black paint. Three of the colors strongly evoked the celestial: an indigo sky, the soft and shimmering yellow of a full moon low on the horizon, the black of a starless night sky, but the red was the dark, rich ochre of fresh blood. It was all the colors of his tattoos.

Maybe he'd force Kairos to admit how he'd manipulated Ty before turning it over to him. Or maybe he wouldn't turn it over. Maybe he'd charter a boat and drop the damnable thing in the ocean. Maybe he'd follow it down to the sea floor, and rob Kairos of the pleasure of killing him. He turned the water on to draw a bath, wondering when the tears would come.

While he waited for the bath to fill, he looked again at the thing in his hand. The condition of the metal was like new, but the unpainted back and the style of the art was more like something out of one of his school texts on the ancients. He still had no clue what it might be, but the head was beautifully outlined in profile, the wings folded over the shaft made it feel somehow right in his grip, and the flared tail formed a good stop. He remembered seeing a gryphon in the flesh not an hour or two ago, and his head swam dizzily at the impossible reality of Erebus.

Ty shut the water off and closed the bathroom door to keep in the heat. He opened the medicine cabinet, removed his shaving supplies, adhesive bandages, aspirin and other sundries and put them all in the sink, then he removed all three shelves. At the point where the middle shelf attached, a small lock lay exposed.

He'd thrown the key away years before, right after installing the lock. Ty removed his toolkit from his jacket pocket and opened the small lock. The cabinet swung free of the wall exposing the hidden space behind, his poor man's safe. It was empty except for the ten silver queens he'd hidden long ago from his first winnings of the season. He placed the letter opener, or whatever the metal item was, inside the safe and restored the medicine cabinet to normal, replacing all the items on the shelves. He'd made enough rash decisions lately; he could decide what to do with it later, when he could think straight.

He stripped for his bath and studied his tattoos in the mirror. The inked patterns were made up of geometric designs, the same as decorated the metal gryphon, but out of order and repeated over and over. All his tattoos had returned: the serpentines, the one on his back above his hip, the inside of his thigh, the soles of his feet, and the inside of his left arm—the one in which Aletheia had seemed particularly interested. The dried skin over them was peeling. The scars shone pale against his olive wrists. He'd hoped that once his task was completed, the marks might disappear. Anger at Kalyptra welled in him again. Anger at all of them.

Trying to focus on the fact that he was home and alive, he inventoried the wounds he'd received since he'd last left his apartment. His left shoulder and hip moved well enough, though the bruising on the shoulder, front and back, would be impressive once it matured. The laceration on his calf was less deep than he'd feared but would need a thorough cleaning in the bath. Worse than the cut was the trampling his leg had taken, the swelling already too sore to touch. The torn flesh above his collarbone seemed to be knitting without infection. Ty crawled into the steaming tub and lay against the curved back.

He tried to push away thoughts of his mother to deal with later, when he felt stronger. He couldn't, and the tears finally came. Ty cried for the poverty of her childhood, her hopes when his lout of a father charmed her away from her family with his lies and ephemeral money. For how hard she'd worked to raise a son alone. For gambling being the means Kairos had used to force his hand, and the hurt it must have caused his mother. For doing worse by her in the end than his father had ever done.

The bath water had cooled by the time his tears ran out. He was wondering if he would ever find motivation for anything again when the bathroom door opened and Naia walked in.

9

Exposure

Ty sat up with a start.

Naia closed the door and crossed the small bathroom. She leaned against the sink, which nearly touched the tub. Her vantage gave her a unobstructed view of him. His towel hung on a rack by her head, and he had not so much as a washcloth at hand.

"Is that how you did it?" From under her crossed arms, she flicked a finger at the tattoos running down his chest.

He looked down and gave a listless shrug. "I didn't do this. It was done *to* me." It made him sound too much the victim. She deserved better than excuses from him. "I'm sorry I stole from you. I didn't know what else to do." He paused, not sure if he had the right to say more. He did anyway. "I'm glad to see you're all right, though."

Saying it made him realize just how much he meant it, as if some cog in his chest had loosened on seeing her safe, allowing him to breathe easier.

"*Friends* came to my aid."

"Ah." He deserved that. "How did you find me?"

"You're not the only one with secrets." She relaxed slightly, uncrossing her arms and resting her hands on the lip of the sink behind her. "Ty, do you have any understanding of what it is you've taken from me?"

"I don't have the slightest understanding of anything that's happened for the last few days. Maybe the last few months." He wanted to get out of the bath, but he wasn't ready to stand up in front of her. Silly as it was, he felt less exposed under the water.

"Then why steal it?"

He looked at his toes and sighed before meeting her eyes again, his will to resist any of this drained from him by bigger events. "Most of what I told you was true. I staked a game, a big one, with a loan I couldn't cover. I lost. The man—demi-god, whatever he is—that loaned me the money is the one who sent me to Erebus and told me what to get. I have no idea what the thing is."

"What was his name?"

Someone was going to kill him over this whole mess. It might as well be someone he didn't like. "Kairos."

He saw she recognized the name.

"I suppose he has it already."

Instead of answering, Ty said, "Now you know why you kept feeling I had a role to play."

She pursed her lips, her black eyes searching his as if unsure. "Do you remember what I told you about the factions?"

"Some in Erebus want to wake and control the gods, some want to kill them, and your faction wants to cure them."

"That's right. And do you know what prevents the factions that want to wake them or kill them from taking action?"

He waited.

"Even if they eventually find them, they don't have the key to open their resting place."

The implications hit him in the face like a giant's punch. A key. How could a locksmith look straight at a key and not see it for what it was? The flared tail for the bow, the wings fashioned the shaft, and the profile of the flattened gryphon's head was the bit.

"You begin to understand," Naia said. She moved from the sink to sit with one hip on the rim of the bathtub. "The key was in the bottle with my father's message. The friend who brought me the message also brought me the key. If the New Order comes into possession of the key, it could mean the end of everything: life on the surface, in Erebus, even below Erebus, in Tartarus. Kairos belongs to the New Order."

It confirmed the suspicion Ty had formed when Naia first told him about the factions in Erebus. "Is he the leader?"

She shook her head. "No. A minor player. A bastard son of Plutus with some small talents at influencing chance, especially where money is involved. He was banished about a century ago. I imagine he bartered his help in exchange for some deal to lift his banishment."

Ty hunched forward and hooked his elbows over his knees. "I'm sorry. I really am. I told you the truth when I said my life was on the line, but I know that doesn't excuse anything."

"You were a pawn," she said. The forgiveness in her voice hurt as much as her resentment earlier had. "You're not the first play they've made for the key. Just the most successful."

Feeling like he was about to expose not just his body, but all he was, Ty stood. Water sluiced off him. "Do you know what these marks are?" he asked, spreading his arms. "Are they going to be able to keep using me?"

Naia stood as well. She examined him slowly, lightly brushing the scar at his throat, touching first one serpentine and then the other, as she had unknowingly done in the park, then the tattoo on his arm and the scars at his wrists.

Ty shed the last of his modesty and showed her the one on his inner thigh, then turned for her to examine the one on his right hip bone. He lifted each foot in turn, hooking it over the edge of the tub, exposing the soles of his feet.

When she'd finished touching each—tracing some and stroking one or all fingers across others—he reached over her head, grabbed his bath towel, and gratefully wrapped it about his waist as he stepped out.

"They're cunningly done," she said. "A master's work. I might know someone who could decipher them but I can't, not beyond the obvious. I would guess they were how you could come and go from Erebus and how you were able to lie to Aletheia in the park today, when no one should be able to tell her a falsehood. Why I felt... " She stopped. Some deep emotion crossed her face. Like a surrealist painting it was many things at once.

With a modicum of equilibrium returning, he remembered the feel of her touch and wondered what she'd been about to say. "I have something for you," he said. "I'll bring it out."

A faint spark of hope lit her dark eyes.

She glanced around the bathroom, looking twice at the small window. He didn't blame her for not trusting him, but something in his eyes must have convinced her. She left the bathroom and closed the door behind her.

He'd lied and stolen, but to sacrifice everyone in two or more worlds to save his own skin was way out of his league. To be honest, he didn't really care what happened to him anymore. He removed everything from the medicine cabinet again, opened the lock, and took the painted key from its hiding place.

Leaving the bathroom, he dressed in clean clothes: a pair of jeans, a plain navy T-shirt, and boots. If he was going to get killed, he might as well be comfortable. Picking up his toolkit from the bathroom sink, he slipped it into his back pocket. It had come in handy too often lately to leave behind.

He found Lamia and Naia in his kitchen. Lamia looked a little worse for the wear, sporting deep scratches on her face, throat, and arms. The injuries appeared half-healed already, but her sour expression on seeing him was the same as ever. Ty handed the key to Naia.

Her slender fingers closed around it and then blanched as she squeezed it tight. Her breath became shallow, as if afraid that moving too much might cause it to disappear again.

"Thank you, Ty," she said. She stretched up to give him a long, gentle kiss on the cheek. It did interesting things to the rest of him.

"Why thank me? I've done nothing but return what was yours."

Lamia looked as if she couldn't agree more.

"Then thank you for making up for doing the wrong thing by doing the right thing." Naia looked to Lamia. "We need to get this back as quickly as possible and find a new place to hide it."

Ty walked them to the door.

She placed a hand on his forearm as he reached for the handle. "You may be safer back in Erebus than here, now that you don't have the key to give to Kairos. I'll take you with me if you want."

What she said was true, but he decided he'd rather fight his battles on familiar ground, even though it meant he'd never see Naia again. The thought wrapped like a fist around his solar plexus. "It'll be okay. I'll leave town. Go somewhere they won't find me."

She gave his forearm a brief squeeze and he opened the door for them. On the other side of the door stood Momus, cigar glowing, one ham-sized fist raised to knock.

"Oh," he said, "my lady. And Miss Lamia. Well, fancy meeting you here. I just thought since I was in the neighborhood, maybe I'd stay up top after all and visit my new friend, Ty."

Lamia stepped in front of Naia. Bits of her skin frayed into mist.

That Momus could find the apartment was no surprise, but the coincidence of the man appearing here at the same time Naia retrieved the key stretched credulity. "Come on in, Momus," he said, buying time for Naia and Lamia. "They were just leaving."

The big man stepped back out of the way with a small bow and an attempt at a courtly wave. Lamia squeezed through the doorway side-by-side with Naia, inserting herself between Momus and her mistress. When they were out, Ty gave Momus' sleeve a gentle tug to redirect the man's attention from the women. Truncating any chance he or Naia had to say goodbye, he pushed the door closed almost before Momus was fully inside.

"I thought you didn't like being above," Ty said. He struggled for a way he could rid himself of his visitor quickly, while still giving Naia and Lamia plenty of time to get below. It would take some finesse, too. The man might look like a big, dumb clown but he was still the great, great-whatever of whomever. Ty didn't want him changing into a Cyclops or hundred-armed monster if he pissed him off.

"Well, never say never, and all that. You never know until you try, right? You just never know." Momus looked around the apartment appreciatively. "I like what you've done with the place."

"Thanks. So, what are your plans? I was actually just headed…"

Momus grabbed Ty by the collar and lifted him off the ground.

Ty shouted in surprise.

Momus opened the door and hauled him out the front door of the apartment. Ty jabbed an elbow at his big belly to no effect. He tried a backwards head-butt, hoping to break Momus' nose, but only slammed his skull against the man's much harder head.

Momus dragged him down the hallway. Ty's neighbor, Mister Rokos, was leaving his apartment across the hall, but froze in the doorway at the sight of Momus manhandling Ty toward the staircase. "Official business," Momus boomed. He looked far from official but the man disappeared back inside. They reached the fire exit and he bellowed down the stairs, "Do you have the others?" There was no answer. Ty could hear scuffling noises far below. "I'm bringing the mortal down," he shouted.

Ty tried squirming out of his shirt as Momus shoved him into the stairwell, but the man shifted his grip to include a handful of hair. Next he tried shoving a foot through the railing, anything that might slow or trip Momus, but he only succeeded in losing his own balance and viciously twisting his ankle before pulling free. Between being held by his hair and the momentum of the big man, Ty could only get his feet under him every few steps. Twisting and struggling, he suddenly remembered that the pressure against his ass was the toolkit he'd stuffed in his right pocket. He slipped his hand to his back pocket. Momus, intent on reaching the bottom, didn't seem to notice. The toolkit was still unzipped. To the left of the picks—no, to the right if the zipper was to the outside—there should be a pointed steel rasp. He knew he'd found it when being yanked down the next step caused him to prick his finger on the tip.

They rounded a corner of the stairs and Momus jerked him again. He lost his grip on the tool and swung his arm for balance. One corner later he was able to get two fingers back into the pouch.

A piercing screech came from below, a sound like nothing human could make. The sounds of struggle came louder. Momus began to run, still dragging Ty like a rag doll. Ty lost his footing again but managed to work the rasp partway out of the kit just as they reached the tiny landing in front of the emergency fire exit.

"We don't need him," Kairos said. "She has it."

Momus heaved Ty off the last step and sideways into the stairwell wall. Ty rolled awkwardly to his hands and knees, trying to take everything in at once. Kairos, dressed in a suit so bright red it was shiny, had Naia trapped against the same wall. He wasn't touching her, but was mumbling a chant in a tongue Ty didn't recognize. Naia stood with one arm extended, as if daring Kairos to close with her.

The screech had come from the opposite side. Lamia faced both of Kairos' two black-coated thugs. Ty's palms grew sweaty at the sight of them. His unsettled dreams of the night before returned suddenly to him: nearly drowning in an ocean, the tides washing his limp body ashore, carrion crows picking at his flesh while he still lived.

Lamia had assumed her wraith form, but the men stood with both their arms outspread like wings, as if they were containing her in some way. They darted in alternately, plucking at her. Each time they snatched at a bit of misty flesh, she screamed. She slashed at them whenever they moved, but they seemed to be preventing her somehow from either flying up or around them.

Ty pushed to his feet, too unimportant to merit anyone's notice as the one mortal amid all the forces in play. He glanced up the layers of empty stairs, but knew he couldn't leave Naia in danger again. Pulling his rasp free of his toolkit he faced Kairos. The man might not have caused his mother's death, and he may or may not have precipitated the events that kept Ty from his mother's side, but he had, unequivocally, endangered Ty by sending him to Erebus and threatened the entire surface world when he forced him to steal the key from Naia. He brandished his rasp, trying to plan an attack that stood even a slight chance of success.

Momus shoved Kairos roughly to the side and stepped in front of Naia. "She can't get us both, can she? She's not so fast as that. No, not so fast are you, my lady?" With his longer arms he reached for her left hand, which was clenched around something hard. He twisted his chest away from her outstretched free arm.

"It's mine," shouted Kairos. He gave Momus a great shove, trying to force him to collide with Naia's open hand. "And you," Kairos kept his eyes on Naia, but Ty realized he was being addressed. "You stay back." Kairos fished in the right pocket of his bright suit and removed enough of the length of black ribbon for Ty to have no doubt what he held.

Ty reassessed his odds. The thought of what that ribbon could do terrified him, but he felt sure Kairos had too many things going on to follow through on the threat at this moment. Momus was closest to Ty, but far larger and stronger. Ty waved his pointed rasp, trying to decide which one to stab. He already knew the answer: neither one. Lamia was their best bet for survival, though attacking the black-coated men probably equated to suicide. He'd rather face the gryphon and bull again any day than the two black-coated men.

He delved for all the anger he could muster at Kairos' men for the torture and fear they had inflicted on him. Lamia was quick enough and dangerous enough that they couldn't afford to take their eyes off her. He searched for a good target. The collars of their coats protected the backs of their necks, and nothing but the luckiest of stabs would slip between vertebrae anyway. Taking his best shot, he leaped.

The stairwell landing was so small it only took him one jump to reach the younger thug nearest him. Without pausing, he plunged the pointed tool as hard as he could into the right shoulder blade beneath the trench coat. Not a killing blow, certainly, but disabling those outspread arms seemed imperative.

With a loud cawing noise, the man whirled faster than Ty would have believed, the rasp still buried in his shoulder. The second his arms lowered, Lamia's wispy form flashed into motion. Her fangs had no difficulty finding the man's neck and Ty heard the tearing of flesh and crunch of bone as she bit down. Blood ran from between her teeth.

The older man struck at her, pulling a great wisp free from one of her arms. Lamia turned on him and he hopped nimbly back. The younger one lay lifeless and bleeding on the floor. Ty kicked him over onto his stomach and pulled his rasp free of the shoulder, tugging against the resistance of the bone before it let go. He turned to Naia.

Probably less than thirty seconds had passed since he'd jumped into the fray. In that short time, she'd lost ground to the dual attack of Momus and Kairos. Momus had her by her left wrist, squeezing as if he would break the bones to open her grip, though still avoiding the touch of her fingers. Kairos held her right sleeve, but seemed unwilling to risk her touch to reach across to her other hand. He continued to chant but it seemed directed now at Momus. The big man sported beads of sweat on his forehead.

The emergency exit alarm blared. Momus and Kairos flashed quick glances toward the door. The older thug ran outside and into a blaze of sunlight, his coat shredded and soaked with blood. Ty was certain he caught a glimpse of a multi-colored woman just outside the door. Fire engine red, dark green, and lampshade yellow.

The door swung shut and Ty jerked his thoughts back to more immediate problems than Kalyptra. Lamia flew at Kairos, whose chanting cut off with a sudden scream. He wrapped his arms tightly around his head. Wearing his red suit and covering his face, he looked like a freshly painted fire hydrant.

Kairos may have posed the greater threat to Naia, but Ty wished Lamia had tackled the larger man instead. With Kairos no longer chanting his spell, Momus squeezed Naia's wrist harder and shook her closed hand. *Ti skatá*, Ty thought, as he launched at Momus and plunged his rasp into the back of the man's hand. Momus let go with a roar.

Lamia clawed viciously at Kairos. He tightened his arms around his head while she raked at him. Naia, free of both men, reached forward and touched Kairos' chest. At the same time, she slapped her other hand into Ty's. Just as her palm met his, Momus struck Ty across the face with a backhand—the rasp still protruding between the tendons. Ty's fingers reflexively closed around the key Naia passed to him just as Momus' blow sent him flying. He landed hard, and the key skittered across the concrete and under the staircase. He hardly felt the impact of his landing on his sore shoulder and hip for the adrenaline crashing through his bloodstream like ocean waves.

"Go!" he heard Lamia screech. He rolled up to his knees, braced to fend off an angry mountain of Momus. Instead, he saw Naia disintegrate into a shower of water that rained down onto the floor. He froze in shocked surprise at the transformation, only then remembering that Momus had said her mother was some sort of water nymph. The puddle flowed toward the thin line of light at the bottom of the exit door.

Lamia disengaged instantly from Kairos. The man did nothing but drop his bloodied arms and stand, looking stupidly at the puddle of water. The introverted, stunned expression that painted the man's face made no sense to Ty.

Momus' response to Naia's disappearance was quite different. He stomped furiously at the wandering puddle of water, dispersing it. Like mercury beads, the fragments dribbled together, trying to rejoin the whole. Ty didn't know if the man was having a tantrum or if between being stabbed and the noise of Lamia's screams, he'd missed the fact that she'd already passed off the key.

Momus' stomping elicited an even more bizarre reaction from Kairos. He roared like a sow bear protecting cubs and lunged at the bigger man's midsection, appearing too frenzied to consider a more sensible attack. Lamia was more effective. She wound the smoky tendrils of her body tightly around Momus' face.

Ty's ears were ringing, perhaps from Lamia's incessant screeching or perhaps from his impact with the floor. He turned his back to the fight and crawled toward the key. He found it with his fingertips in the farthest corner under the stairs and finger-walked it into his grasp.

Forced to crawl backward from under the staircase, his spine tingled with vulnerability. His head emerged just in time to see Momus grab Kairos, despite Lamia still wrapped around his face and throat. He took the small man's neck in his large hands and squeezed. Kairos struggled weakly until Momus smashed his head into the concrete wall. He let go and Kairos fell bonelessly to the floor.

Free of Kairos' attack and losing air, Momus tore at the wisps of Lamia. His cigar fell from his lips to the floor, right through Lamia's midsection. Ty watched the water that had soaked the leather of Momus' great shoes suck back out of the material to join the puddle at the door, leaving his shoes dry.

Momus thrashed with increasing desperation but seemed unable to gain purchase on Lamia as Kairos' men had done. Apparently, though, she was corporeal enough for her task. Gagging, choking noises came from Momus as he tried to suck in air and breathed in only wraith. Ty cringed inwardly at the desperate sounds of suffocation. Momus lost consciousness and fell with a thud.

"Do you have the key?" Lamia snapped, spiriting free as the big man fell. She crossed the small space and stood, partially solidified, in front of Ty.

He held out his open palm in answer. The colors of the key glinted in the low sodium lamps of the stairwell.

Wordlessly, she grabbed him by one arm and dragged him with as much force as Momus had toward the exit. "Wait!" Ty shouted. Sticking out of Kairos' jacket pocket was an inch of black ribbon.

Lamia ignored him, pulling him forward. She reached for the exit bar of the door. Ty jerked back with such desperation that he broke free of her grip and landed on one knee near Kairos. He grabbed at the ribbon. She gave a shriek of frustration and clamped onto his arm again, yanking him to his feet. The ribbon slipped from his hand. He dived sideways but she held tight. He fumbled at the tiny scrap and felt it between his first and second fingertips. Pinching frantically, he trapped the cloth. It slithered out of Kairos' pocket as Lamia pulled him away and plunged out the exit door. He looked up as he stumbled out onto the sidewalk but neither Kalyptra nor the second thug were anywhere in sight.

"Look for the nearest manhole," Lamia snapped. Her form was still shifting back to flesh and her voice, somewhere between normal and wraith-scream, scraped at him like nails on a chalkboard.

She was looking to the right so he looked left. There was a manhole cover not fifty feet from him. Her hand still gripped his upper arm like a vice, so when he tugged she moved with him. He was limping on his injured right ankle but it was nothing to the deep and terrible injuries appearing on Lamia's body as her torn flesh solidified.

"What now?" he said when they stood in front of the iron cover. He looked for any sign of wetness from water that might have drained down it, but saw none.

His neighborhood wasn't as busy as the downtown area, but there were still plenty of people around. Men and women shied to the far side of the sidewalk, away from the white-robed woman whose head drifted from mist to flesh and back again and whose clothes sported ragged, bloodied rents. Mothers turned prams or grabbed small children by the hand and ran. Ty heard the squeal of brakes followed by the deep clunk of one large, chrome bumper hitting another.

Lamia took no notice. With her hands still wispy gray talons, she bent and hooked her great nails into two opposite holes in the heavy metal. She lifted the cover and pushed it aside. Ty saw a ladder on the far side of the hole.

"Go!" Lamia said.

Before he could take a step toward the ladder, she pushed him. A strangled yell escaped as he fell into the darkness, unsure how far he would drop. He landed a couple of meters later with stiff knees and ankles in water about thigh-deep. The water broke some of the force, but pain lanced up from his bad ankle. He gripped the ribbon harder, grateful he hadn't dropped it as he fell. He tucked it deep into the pocket of his jeans.

The stink told Ty more than he wanted to know about where he had landed—a sewer main, channeling everything from bath water, to street runoff, to raw sewage. Lamia was a shadow across the opening as she launched onto the ladder. She descended far enough to pull the cover back in place, then dropped the rest of the way into the water. Murky darkness enveloped them all, broken only by light from the street drains. Lamia's white gown floated, ghostly, at her hips.

"Naia?" she called softly.

"Here," came a voice not far from them. Ty felt a wash of relief. He couldn't see Lamia's face, but he sensed the tightness in her relax. There came a soft splashing as Naia approached.

"Do you have the key?" she asked Lamia, her voice tight.

"I have it," Ty answered.

"Thank the gods." She sighed the words on a strong exhale. "Leaving that behind was the most frightening thing I've ever done."

"You should have left sooner," Lamia snapped. "You risked too much."

"I had to be sure you had the upper hand. Ty, thank you for your help."

"Why? He was only saving his own skin," Lamia said.

"I'll carry the key," Naia said, ignoring Lamia's comment. Ty handed it to her.

"Hurry, my lady" Lamia said. "We may be followed."

Even in the dim light of the sewer, a quick inventory of Lamia's wounds made Ty wince. He wondered how she remained upright, much less so in control. Her arms were ragged strips where the flesh-eaters had plucked at them. The barely-healed lacerations on her face and throat had re-opened. Like fish gills, they flapped to reveal tissue pink with capillary oozing when she moved. Her jaw was swollen. Through a tear in the back of her dress, he could see a fist-sized area of darkened skin. Two of her fingers were missing, bloody stumps all that remained. He'd witnessed her powers of regeneration, but thought these wounds might be beyond repair.

The tunnels were tall enough for them all to move upright as Lamia took the lead, splashing through the filth. Ty's ankle gave out on his first step after the short rest and his left shoulder and hip burned like fire, but school-boy competition with Lamia—combined with the thought of whomever or whatever might be coming after them—spurred him to keep up.

The smell in the enclosed space made him gag, and he tried to ignore the bits of solid matter bumping into his legs as he waded forward, imagining them all to be sticks rather than bodies of dead rats, or sewage, or creatures from Erebus swimming these waters. Lamia moved quickly despite her grotesque injuries, making turns at the myriad junctions without hesitation, sewer water dripping from the great gouges in her arms.

The splish-splash of their progress seemed noisy enough that asking Naia what she had done to Kairos didn't feel unreasonable. "What..." he began in a low tone.

Lamia turned back sharply. "Quiet!" she hissed, louder than he had spoken.

Falling silent, he pondered the facts for himself. When Kairos and Momus had dodged Naia's hands, he'd assumed they were trying to avoid falling under a love spell. Daughter of Eros and all. Kairos' trance-like state after she touched him reinforced his conviction.

Ty remembered her hand on his own chest during their conversation on her balcony, his rapidly growing feelings for her after that. But in the fight, he'd seen her turn to water. Perhaps Kairos and Momus were trying to avoid being liquefied. Perhaps Kairos was in some in-between state when Momus knocked him unconscious. More important to him, perhaps Naia had inherited only her mother's talents for water. If so, then his feelings for her were genuine. They certainly felt genuine.

They made another turn and the water decreased to knee-high then ankle-high as they progressed up a slight incline. In a few more steps they were walking on dry metal, their footsteps echoing. Ty checked his pocket; the soaking wet ribbon lay bunched at the bottom.

Another hundred meters or so and a familiar dim, blue light outlined the inside of the pipe and illuminated his companions. One more curve of the pipe and Lamia pushed on a rusty metal grate. It squeaked open, admitting them to nighttime in Erebus, on the outskirts of the city.

PART 2

Erebus Rising

10

Raising the Stakes

"The key has surfaced at last," the figure in the shadows said.

Aello cocked her head, bird-like. Though her face and torso were human, it was a habit she had whenever listening with her full attention. He paced. It was unlike him, and the fact that he was anxious made her anxious. She kept silent, letting him say what he had come to tell her.

"Things are coming to a head. So long a wait and now everything moving so fast."

Aello hopped from the floor of the cave and flapped heavily to the highest limb of the branch that she had dragged inside for a sleeping perch. She still couldn't see him. She never could when he appeared here; he remained in deep shadow at the back of her lair, hidden, even from her.

A small bone crunched underfoot as he paced. She shat while she waited, adding to the layers of droppings covering the cavern floor. They ranged from old and dry and small as one of her dark eyes, to the fresh droppings—as large as an egg cracked open and plopped, white and green and gelatinous, like the one that now lay splattered on the ground beneath her tail feathers.

He stopped and gave a snort of indecision, as uncharacteristic as his pacing. "I suppose you'll need to be able to recognize it," he said, talking more to himself than to her. She heard him scuff at the dirt. A small puff of dust drifted from his feet into the murky corona between the deep shadows and the light outside. Gray against the black, he bent to lift something. He moved one hand to his side, to a pocket perhaps, and she watched his silhouetted arm wave over the object he'd picked up. There was a long moment of silence.

"Here," he said. "Eat this. You'll know the key when you see it and should feel it if you're close enough."

Hard and fast, he launched something at her head. She lifted one wing and caught the thing with the skinny arm she normally held tucked beneath her wing. It was a piece of bone as large and long as two of her fingers together. The top edge was splintered where she had gnawed the flesh long ago. It glinted dully with colors the bone couldn't have held a moment ago: blue, yellow, black, and red. It would hurt to swallow—if she could. She placed it in her mouth and tried to break it with her teeth, but a tooth broke instead. She worked a little moisture to her tongue and attempted to swallow bone and tooth together. The bone stuck just above the tracheal cartilage of her throat. It cut at the soft tissue, sawing its way slowly down as she swallowed convulsively.

"Spread the word to all in the New Order," he said. "Naia and her companions must be captured quickly, before it disappears again. We *must* get that key."

She continued to work the bone down bit by painful bit. A triangle of cloth peeked out from the deep shadows as he paced, and she glimpsed a patch of pale skin within a voluminous sleeve. The sleeve and the arm within it vanished again in the gloom.

"Find it," he said, "and I will see your greatest wish fulfilled. You will be restored to your former beauty."

Aello's eyes widened. She dipped her head in excitement. The motion caused the jagged end of the bone to press deeper into the sensitive tissue of her throat. Her obeisance, somewhere between a nod and a bow, created a domino effect of sagging flesh in motion. The skin beneath her eyes rolled against the loose flesh at her jowls, which compressed the flaps of reddish skin hanging to either side of her throat. Her pendulous and wrinkled naked breasts swayed forward. The few sparse and scraggly feathers on her bald head waggled. "As you say," she croaked.

Selia waited at the appointed meeting place for her officers. She had arrived early, to think in peace. Her fingertips brushed the great oaks one-by-one as she passed them, lost in thought.

The key had been revealed. She could feel it as the gold of its pattern had been made with moon dust. Her connection to the moon—though not the same magnitude as her mother's—was sufficient enough that she had long ago forged a link to alert her should the key ever surface. The attempt to capture it today had been botched, though. She had rushed, and sending her centaur and giant to attack in broad daylight had been an error. Night had always been her element.

Selia stood in a river of moonlight as it flowed between the trees. She looked up at the moon, full and heavy and low in the sky as it rose, shining silver and gold onto the silver and gold of her gown.

Helios had no children here, so there was no "little sun" in Erebus, but Selia's moon rose nightly, always full, almost low enough to touch as it rode the sky devoid of stars. The little moon was entirely hers, but like her mother's moon in the real heavens, it could strengthen spells of healing, increase wisdom, or incite madness.

She squatted and touched the ground at a division of light and dark, gathering a handful of moonlight and a handful of moon shadow. Caressing them, she melded and molded until she fashioned them into a new thing, a thing that would answer to her. An agent to slide through the night and seek out its secrets, to find the key again.

She shooed her servant of light and shadow off to its duty as a rustle of footsteps announced her first officers arriving. When the full dozen had gathered, in human forms and creature forms, she nodded to Cyrene, her chief lieutenant.

"The meeting of the Revisionists will come to order," the woman intoned. "All attend Selia."

11

The Truth Shall Set You Free

"We mustn't go back to the apartment, lady," Lamia said as they emerged into Erebus.

"I don't plan to," Naia replied. She turned to Ty, who'd fallen behind again due to his ankle and calf. "Can you make it to the park?"

He looked up from examining his wrists and left arm where the tattoo and scars seemed to have disappeared again. He couldn't guess how far away the park might be, but nodded his assurance anyway. At least the soles of his feet burned less now that the tattoos had faded. Good thing, considering the friction of walking in wet boots.

"You go to Aletheia?" Lamia asked.

Naia nodded.

Under the light of the full moon they progressed block after block through a residential part of the city, an area unfamiliar to Ty even in its surface equivalent. Lamia tried to watch everything at once and Naia seemed lost in her own thoughts. He limped along behind them reflecting on the irony that Naia had been right. For the moment, at least, he probably was safer in Erebus than in his own world.

Without transition, they left the darkened, cobbled streets and stepped into the National Garden, as if the park had crept up on the neighborhood during the night. Maybe it had, Ty thought as they turned onto the small, wooded path. He heard rustlings and occasional animal noises in the bushes as they walked, but thankfully the paths they took were empty but for the three of them. He emerged from a heavily wooded section to see a small wooden bridge spanning the brook ahead. Across the water and to his right, the full moon shone on the grassy expanse where he'd started his watercolor this morning.

"Wait here," Naia said. Instead of mounting the arched bridge for vantage, as he'd expected, she waded calf-deep into the flowing water. Wondering if she would summon Aletheia with a leaf again, he was watching closely when her skin suddenly shimmered to translucence, shifting from olive to gray to silver. A shaft of moonlight glinted on the surface of the brook, and Naia took on the same reflective sparkle. Her features blurred. From one instant to the next, she became a sheet of water, a waterfall suspended in mid-air, before breaking into thousands of drops. With a sound like heavy rain, she merged into the brook and was gone.

Ty stared at the air over the water, waiting for the process to reverse. When it didn't, he assumed they would have a welcome rest break until Naia returned. He glanced over his shoulder to Lamia, concerned about the grievous wounds she'd suffered, and opened his mouth to ask how she fared. The words never came out. She drifted above the ground, half-way through changing to her wraith form. Alarmed, Ty checked all directions, braced for an impending attack, but she shifted back a moment later, her gown dry again and white as snow.

Ty's muscles unwound. He spent a futile wish that she could do something similar for his own clothes. She couldn't, of course, but he decided the nighttime air in Erebus was warm and he was already soaked enough that he had nothing to lose by getting wetter. He walked to the creek, knelt in the middle, and rinsed the stink of the sewers from his clothes and hair. Climbing back onto the bank, jeans and T-shirt clinging to his skin, he sat and inspected the swelling in his ankle. Puffy, but not too bad. He lay back on the bank, exhausted. Lamia stood as erect and alert as always. He didn't doubt she still had the strength to defend them from any ordinary monsters that might happen by. Defend herself and Naia, at any rate.

Naia returned about ten minutes later. She flowed up out of the water, appearing bit by bit, as if walking up to shore from a great depth. Both she and her clothes were dry.

"Where do your clothes go when you do that?" he asked before thinking.

Lamia flashed him a hard look.

"We really should have someone see to your eyes while you're here," Naia said, with no hint of sarcasm.

"Or see to his mouth," Lamia said.

"We need to go," Naia said. "She's waiting for us."

They crossed the bridge and headed left, past benches, more open areas, and sections of thick trees and undergrowth, veering onto side paths whenever someone approached. The ground began to rise on their right forming a small bluff. Centered in the bluff was a cave-like opening with lamplight shining from the interior. Naia crossed to it and entered without hesitation.

The same gray-haired woman Ty had met this morning waited for them near the entrance. She greeted Naia with kisses on either cheek.

"Thank you for the asylum, Aletheia," Naia said. "I know you risk much, but I don't think we were seen coming here."

"Nothing is too much for your sake." Aletheia replied, gesturing them all inside. Ty felt self-conscious of his wet clothes as they entered the large front room of the cave, though he seemed to no longer be dripping as much.

Ty found the rustic feel of the cave surprising for such an aristocratic woman. A heavy table of rough wood stood in the middle of the room. Benches of wooden slats lined the sides, with a couple of extra benches along the walls. A cookfire pit, recessed into one wall, glowed with low flames and he moved to stand in front of it, hoping it would dry his clothes more quickly. Lamia stood at the edge of the room, nearest the entrance. In the light, Ty could see that even the deepest of Lamia's wounds were healing.

"What happened since I last saw you?" Aletheia asked Naia.

"Two more opponents have surfaced. Do you know either Momus or Kairos?"

Aletheia shook her head. "I don't personally know either, though I've heard of Kairos. I remember his banishment about a century ago."

Aletheia studied Ty as a cat might watch a pet mouse in a cage, her expression one more of fascination than ill-intent. "Your new friend is still with you," she observed.

"Ty helped us retrieve the key today."

There was a derisive snort from Lamia's direction. "After he stole it."

"I saw his protections," Naia continued. "He's been cleverly marked by someone."

"Her name was Kalyptra," he said. "I think I saw her today, standing outside during the fight."

Naia looked to Aletheia, who indicated she didn't know the name. "Doubtless she's also with the New Order," Naia said. "The marks are how he was able to avoid telling you the truth. I can't decipher all of what they do, but perhaps there is some way to make them work to our advantage as well."

Aletheia crossed to Ty and examined his arm again. "Here?"

He nodded. "That's one of them." He resisted squirming under her inspection.

"I'm sorry," Aletheia said to Naia. "Even knowing the mark is there, I'm unable to detect it. Perhaps Enyalius could help you decipher them."

Enyalius. Ty remembered that name. The old man who'd come to Naia's apartment on two occasions. "Old friend," she had called him.

"You may be able to help us in another way, then," Naia said. "It appears Ty has difficulty seeing Erebus for what it is. He might be safer if he could."

"If I can't make him speak truth, I may not be able to make him see it either." She looked back at him. "Did Kairos or Momus do anything to your eyes?" Aletheia asked Ty.

"Not that I know of," he said, suddenly apprehensive.

"Then the problem must be your own mortal limitations." She motioned for him to take a seat on one of the benches and knelt in front of him.

"Open your eyes wide," she instructed.

He looked to Naia, who nodded.

"Keep this one open," Aletheia instructed, centering her index finger in front of his left eye. "Don't let it close." Laying a firm hand behind his head, she touched the surface of his eyeball. He jerked back and tried to blink, but her hand held his head in place and his eyelid couldn't close for her finger. He panicked and tried to stand.

"Be easy, Ty." It was Naia, standing next to him now, voice, calm and reassuring. She laid one hand on his shoulder. "She means you no harm."

He steeled himself and remained seated. Aletheia exerted no pressure, but her fingertip pulled the moisture from the surface of his eye, leaving it burning and scratchy. His eye watered profusely.

Aletheia sang in a low voice, soothing and lullaby-like. He felt again those distant soft wings that he had experienced this morning in the park. Aletheia pinched the bottom edge of his eyeball and he jerked back again, but she maintained her grip on the back of his head.

Tugging, she peeled something up from the bottom of his eye, like one might pull the skin from a shelled egg. A yell built in his throat, but before he could loose more than a croak, she was done. She held the opaque, wrinkled layer of skin up for him to see, then tossed it aside and moved to his other eye.

When she'd finished with his right eye, Ty blinked hard and repeatedly, trying to rid himself of the sensation of having his eyes peeled. After a moment, his blurry sight cleared. He looked around.

The room had changed entirely, to something palatial and elegant. Nature had been generously used in the design, utilizing stone walls, living trees, plants, and even a waterfall, but it looked as far from a cave as a museum painting from a child's drawing. The furniture was beautifully handcrafted hardwood. Ornate decorations of carved onyx, crystal, marble, and turquoise accented the large, open rooms. He narrowed his eyes in surprise and received an even bigger shock when he suddenly saw the wooden benches and rock walls in his city park on the surface, a quiet curve he knew well, with a natural, rocky outcrop sheltering a shallow cave. The surface image seemed overlaid on the room, so that he saw both at once. The double image disoriented him, making him dizzy.

"What do you see now?" Aletheia asked.

"Both worlds, I think." Ty looked down at his left arm and his wrists. If he squinted, he could see the shadows of his markings and scars. He stood and walked to the archway of the next room. The images changed with him as he moved, as if he walked simultaneously through the park above and Aletheia's home in Erebus. He turned, and the dual viewpoints shifted with him. It left him slightly nauseous. He relaxed his eyes and saw only the elegant home.

"I hadn't anticipated that," Aletheia told Naia.

"You let him see the truth," Naia said, with a small shrug. "His truth is both worlds."

"The double vision is permanent?" he said, alarmed. "Will I have it above, too?"

"I don't know," Aletheia said. "I only know that what you'll see is real."

"Thank you, Aletheia," Naia said.

He wasn't at all sure it was something for which to be grateful. He moved back to the fire to dry off some more while Aletheia set out a light meal for them of unleavened crackers, fruit, cheese, and wine.

"What will you do with the key?" Aletheia asked when the three of them were seated. Lamia had been invited, but chose to maintain her post at the entrance.

"I'm not sure," Naia admitted. "Though even if I knew, I wouldn't say. I've endangered you enough already. In fact, I'd feel better if you left your home for a little while. Maybe visit your children."

"Things are that bad?"

"We were attacked today on our way home from the park, and again just a few hours ago on the surface."

Aletheia's face hardened into a mask of concern. "Who discovered you have the key?"

"Everyone, apparently. Selia must have felt it once it had been removed from its hiding place, even though it was daytime. I didn't recognize the giant, but the centaur is an agent of hers. The second attack came from the New Order."

Images from the two fights came back to Ty, and he took a large swig of the strong, red wine.

"Kairos always seemed to be at the center of one trouble or another before his banishment," Naia continued, "but what I don't understand is how he found out I held the key. It must have been a recent discovery, or they would've made a play for it earlier."

"If things are escalating," Aletheia said, "maybe new information will finally surface that could help us rescue the gods. As long as the others don't know the whereabouts of their hiding place, even stealing the key would do them no good. Hide the key again, and it's almost impossible for either order to wake or kill the gods."

"But if both groups have discovered I hold the key, I worry they may have learned other things as well."

Ty was following the conversation, but was also looking around the large room, playing with his new vision. He lifted and dropped his head to see if it changed his perspective, but the vision didn't appear to be positional. The table existed now as a beautiful hardwood furnishing, and when he squinted, as a picnic bench superimposed on the real table. Lamia, of course, was doubled, wearing both her human form and her wraith form. Naia and Aletheia had no counterpart doubles, not even a watery nymph for Naia. The only tangible difference seemed to be in her clothing—her present day outfit overlaid by an ancient-style gown—but it was a less pedestrian difference that struck him. In his true vision, she was even more beautiful. He felt almost hypnotized if he looked at her for too long.

He distracted himself by examining other items scattered about the rooms, learning which had counterparts and which didn't: a dish of soft cheese and roughly-broken flatbread crackers held an after-image of a square of factory-processed cheese and a stack of identically stamped round crackers, while the pears and apples were the same no matter how he looked at them.

He was trying to focus on the afterimage of one of the tapestry rugs by the front door when his attention was snagged by something moving along the floor. He stared hard to determine if it was a thing, a thing with a shadow double, or just a shadow. It was a thing, he realized. A spider. A big one, carrying no double image. He'd never seen a tarantula before, but a spider larger than his palm with a segmented head and body, long, bristly gray and black hair, and eight, long hairy legs couldn't be much else. He'd always been a bit arachnophobic; apparently his distaste increased proportionally with the size of the spider.

"Excuse me," he said, interrupting their conversation, "but is that yours?"

Aletheia and Naia leaned out from the table to look down where he pointed. Lamia turned from where she had stationed herself between the front room and dining room.

The spider crossed the front room and hovered uncertainly in the archway to the dining room.

"No, she isn't," Aletheia said. "I get the occasional visitor wandering in from the park." She stood and shooed the creature gently back toward the entrance.

The spider moved quickly, but Lamia snatched it up as it scurried past. She stared into its multi-faceted eyes for a long moment, her habitually suspicious expression tightening her face. Apparently she discerned nothing out of the ordinary. She carried it outside and tossed it into the grass.

Ty examined the rest of the floor carefully.

Naia and Aletheia resumed their conversation about the factions and the best course of action for the Preservationists. Aletheia offered some general suggestions for hiding the key. Half an hour later, having reached no solutions to any of their problems, Naia arose.

"We've stayed here too long, my friend. We should go."

"Wait until morning, Naia. You'll be safer in the daylight. Nighttime is Selia's strength."

"At least we know that enemy. Knowing her, I know how best to avoid her. It's the head of the New Order I'd love to discover." She took Aletheia by the hand. "We need to leave, and you should too. There are few who know of our friendship, but I'm under more scrutiny than ever now. We'll go to Enyalius. I think you're right that he may be the most likely to decipher Ty's markings. Maybe that will help me decide what to do next."

The tarantula stayed at the front entrance. Her eight eyes did little to help her see clearly, but the hairs on her front section, legs and head, quivered with the conversation inside, while the hairs on her hind legs and abdominal section sensed the vibrations behind her. She felt the wind, the gurgle of the brook, and most of all, the furtive, jerky movements of a small mouse hunting bugs in the grass. If not for the importance of this assignment, the mouse would have captured her full attention.

Suddenly there was a new disturbance. Her hairs quaked from her hind legs all the way up the dorsal surface of her abdominal segment and over her cephalothorax. She sidestepped quickly, marching her legs around like clock gears, until she'd turned to face the source. Large wings beat the air as the harpy braked to land.

"You found them?" Aello rasped, keeping her voice quiet.

The tarantula waved two forelegs in affirmation.

"Good. Good. Then you'll get the master's reward." Aello reached forward and lifted the tarantula to her mouth. "Listen closely," she said. She bit the tarantula in half. Little legs beat against her lips with headless-chicken-like reflexes. She chewed slowly and popped the other half in her mouth.

That taken care of, Aello assessed the situation inside. There were four of them, but one was a human. She knew both demi-gods, and neither were children of war; they possessed no battle talents. She wouldn't need help for this, which was a good thing as they seemed to be preparing to leave. The wraith was the only real concern. As if reading her thoughts, the wraith turned her direction, scanning the darkness. Aello shrank further into the shadows and waited.

"Where will you go?" the white-haired one asked Eros' daughter.

"I'll get word to Enyalius. If anyone can come up with answers, it'll be him. Promise me you'll leave as well."

"I promise."

The group moved toward the door, saying their farewells. Good. The white-haired one was not leaving with them. Aello would come back and take care of that one later. Her master always insisted she be thorough.

She primed herself as the group neared. She would go for Eros' child first if she could, and secure the key, then deal with the wraith. The mortal would pose no more threat than the tarantula. She faded back into the brush as her quarry left.

A palm-sized patch of moonlight and shadow broke free of the lintel above the entrance. The harpy didn't notice its subtle quality of independent movement. Indistinguishable from other patches of light and dark, it followed her.

Ty brought up the rear as Lamia led them into the park. He stared back in wonder at the entrance to Aletheia's home. The cave mouth was still there in the shadowy background of his second sight, but far more prominent was the impressive, stone-fronted façade. It looked as elegant as a temple, with carved columns and frescoes, and its tall, wooden, double doors remained open to the night after they left, showing the soft glow of lamplight from within. Turning to watch where he was going, he squinted to compare the park in Erebus with his own. The park here seemed similar, though it still retained a far wilder and more natural look compared to Athina's cultivated city park.

Suddenly remembering the tarantula, Ty checked the ground all around his feet. It didn't seem to be in his immediate vicinity. The chances of seeing it in the grass in the dark were small, but the queasy feeling it might be coming up behind him made him look back. Instead of the spider, he saw something else entirely. Above a rhododendron bush to the right of the door, a pale head and torso contrasted the dark foliage. It seemed to be the disembodied top half of a naked, old woman. He opened his mouth to point the thing out to Naia, when it suddenly launched into the air.

"Look out!" he yelled.

The creature flapped its great wings, gaining altitude. Skinny arms and flabby breasts dangled toward the ground. For as large and ungainly as it looked, it flew quickly. Lamia changed form even as she turned to see what he warned against, and still she was barely quick enough to insert herself between the thing and Naia. The two creatures clashed in midair. Lamia's scream overlaid with the bird-woman's screech nearly deafened him. Ty had thought until now that little could be a match for Lamia. He realized he might be wrong.

Naia looked back toward the cave and shouted, "Aletheia, run!" Ty thought the sound of the two combatants screeching would have been warning enough.

Lamia attempted to wrap around the thing, trapping its wings, but the bird-woman threw her off with a shrug and a strong kick from her taloned feet. Where Kairos' men had shown caution, darting in when they saw an opening, this new enemy attacked viciously and confidently. She latched to Lamia with talons as long as Ty's hands. Like Kairos' crows, she had no trouble penetrating Lamia's insubstantiality. The nails dug deeply in a line down Lamia's chest and abdomen, with the rear toe of each foot piercing her back.

Ty could see the bird-woman's powerful muscle contractions as she buried the long nails deeper into Lamia's ethereal body. Lamia screamed and bent nearly in half, then bit at one leathery ankle with her great fangs. She gripped the pale, wrinkled skin of the thing with her own nails. Though wingless, Lamia seemed to propel herself through the air at will. Ty saw her struggle now to turn, to dive—anything to free herself. The bird-woman hung on. She beat the air hard with her long wings and kept them both aloft, like a falcon, hovering in one spot. Her skinny arms reached out and grabbed Lamia by the throat, hands sinking into the wraith's misty form. Naia grabbed Ty by the hand and squeezed. She seemed anxious to flee, but remained unmoving, her eyes locked on the battle.

Fragile as it looked, the bird-woman's skin must have been tough as iron. Lamia's nails seemed to have little effect, while the other's claws dug ever deeper. The creature shifted her hands to the wraith's head, and curled in the air to bring them face-to-face. She opened her mouth and bit Lamia's right eye.

Lamia's boneless gray mouth stretched even wider, wide enough to swallow a man's head whole. Her fangs flashed helplessly as the bird-woman moved to her other eye. Red blood dripped down the wraith's ghostly face. Ty's heart pumped ice. Unimaginable as it seemed, Lamia was losing.

Naia screamed a heart-breaking cry of anguish. Ty gripped her hand and jerked her into a run. He glanced back as he ran. The bird-woman had fluttered to the ground, still gripping Lamia's wraith-form. She tore at her face with her human mouth. Lamia was fading back to human form, but otherwise didn't move.

Naia looked back as well, causing her to stumble. She gave a wrenching moan of horror. Ty helped her keep her feet, and pulled her onward. He couldn't resist one final look back. Lamia's face had been shredded of nearly half its flesh.

Certain she was dead, Ty jerked in horror when Lamia's hand shot out and grabbed the bird-woman by the throat. In the now-quiet darkness, he heard the thing gurgle in surprise. It pulled back but Lamia's grip was strong. He had no illusions that Lamia would live through this, but with the last of her strength she bought them time to escape. He made sure they didn't waste the gift.

Ty's ankle turned and a stab of pain made the joint give. He fell to his knees. Grabbing the branches of a bush, he hauled himself to his feet. "Go," he said to Naia. "Don't wait for me. Change to water if you need to."

Naia ran as if she would never stop.

Ty remembered how fast the bird-woman had flown. He ignored his ankle and began running again. Bursting through a gap in the undergrowth, he emerged into a grassy area and recognized the spot where he had painted the landscape. The brook flowed serenely, oblivious to the violence around it. Naia stood at the edge of the water.

"We have to keep going," Ty said, limping heavily as he caught up to her. The dried tracks of her tears striped her cheeks in the moonlight. "Come on," he said, more gently.

He took her hand, but she pulled back in unspoken resistance. He looked where she stared at the water and saw nothing. And then he did.

The creek grew more active. It bubbled and gurgled. In the moonlight, Ty saw small whitecaps forming, rapids of a much larger river, though the creek itself hadn't changed dimensions. The water flowed faster, stronger. Naia reached into her pocket and removed the key. She tossed it into the teeming waves. Ty watched the glimmer of gold crest a wave and then disappear, rushing downstream.

"We need to hide," she murmured through lips that sounded numb.

He grabbed her hand again and jogged toward a tall clump of vegetation, only to discover they were caper bushes, laced with sharp barbs. The heavy beat of wings approached and Ty looked about desperately, not wanting to cross the open grass or the wide main path ahead. The whooshing whistle of feathers moving through air neared and then retreated as the creature turned and followed the brook downstream. It had sensed or seen the key, he realized, and followed it instead of them. If the creature failed to find the key, it would return. Naia seemed uncertain whether to run or hide. Ty decided for them.

While the prominent landscape in his vision remained that of Erebus, he now had the ability to see the surface-world parallels also. Searching across the street, he saw the shrubbery of the more overgrown park here, but also the paved sidewalks that bordered the main road through the park above. Squinting, he spotted a gutter drain. If some parallel existed in this world, the opening could be a close fit, but it might widen lower down like the sewer tunnels Lamia had led them through earlier.

He yanked Naia's arm hard enough to elicit a grunt from her. Feeling their exposure, he hurried them across the open ground and stopped where the opposite side of the dirt path was bordered with large lavender plants and broom bushes. Ripping a couple of low growing branches aside he found what he had hoped for, a dark hole in the dirt. It had the look of a large animal den, a fox or badger hole if the fox or badger were the size of a wolfhound. Hopefully the den was long abandoned.

"Can you fit?" he whispered.

"I think so, but not if it gets smaller farther down."

"I don't think it will. Go feet first. Watch out for a drop."

She squirmed into the hole. As her hands disappeared, Ty heard the heavy beat of wings behind him. If the bird-woman-thing had come back for them, it seemed likely it hadn't found the key. Ty scrunched further into the hedge. The creature circled overhead. When it began a long, sweeping turn, he squeezed into the small opening.

He had to hold his arms above his head, and even with that, his hips stuck. He squirmed as the wings beat closer. The image of the thing biting out Lamia's eyes came vividly to him and he twisted harder. He worked his hips beneath the opening and stopped when his chest and shoulders stuck fast.

There came a snotty sound of the bird-woman sniffing the air loudly. He heard her flutter to the ground on the opposite side of the hedge and begin pushing branches aside. He was going to die, trapped like a kid at the beach buried to the neck in sand. The creature would feast on him at her leisure. Lamia's ravaged face returned to his mind's eye.

There was a strong tug on his feet, but he only budged an inch or two. A moment later, the soil at his chest felt damp, then muddy. He struggled violently and the wet soil loosened and gave. He plopped below the surface just as the bushes above him were pulled aside.

12

---◈---

Down the Rabbit Hole

Ty kept his arms over his head to make himself as narrow as possible, and worked his way deeper into the hole. The dampness descended side-by-side with him, drying behind him. When he'd dropped a little over a body length, the hole widened slightly. The moisture rolled ahead of him and he fell the last couple of feet to land on the ground. He balled himself into a tight squat and felt ahead for the top of the tunnel, discovering it lower than he'd hoped. Naia resumed her human form in front of him, filling the small space.

They both stayed scrunched and unmoving, listening. Violent scrabbling sounded above them. In the moon shadow, above the deeper darkness of the burrow, the pale form of the hideous bird-woman's head hung inside the hole, her scraggy feathers drooping down toward him. She thrashed against the opening, too small for the extra width of her wings, then retreated, scratched at the lip of the hole some more with her fingers, and tried again.

Naia tapped him on the arm and crawled forward. Dirt rained down on Ty as the thing above him turned and tried digging with the strong talons of her toes. He crawled quickly forward as soon as Naia had progressed far enough in front of him. The anticipation of hearing the creature drop into the hole behind him pebbled his arms with gooseflesh.

He'd been right about the tunnel being wider than the opening, though it was still small enough that they were forced to crawl forward on elbows and toes. It brought back unpleasant memories of the confinement in the lower part of the cave that first led him to Erebus, except that this burrow had the additional disagreeable quality of possessing a hideous smell, a stench like rotten meat and decomposing fungus. The thought that something might have died down here disturbed him less than the thought that it might still live.

He went only a short way before he paused to listen again. With Naia crawling forward he couldn't be positive, but he thought he heard a few last scraping, digging sounds from the surface, and then nothing.

Over the next couple of minutes, the fear of the monstrosity behind him faded and a new fear of what might have made these tunnels took over. Naia could always do her water trick, but there'd be little he could do in this cramped space if some resident—or residents—suddenly appeared. He wanted to ask if she knew what might have made these tunnels but, afraid to make more noise than absolutely necessary, he followed her instead in silent apprehension.

"There's a branch ahead of me," Naia said. She whispered, but the suppressed grief and horror of the night's trauma still choked her voice. He resisted an impulse to reach out and touch her. "Do you know which way to go?" she asked.

His double-vision was no help in the darkness. Even with light it probably wouldn't have done them much good, as the parallel for his vision here would be the inside of the drain system in his world. He knew that place no better than this.

"Go right," he said. He regretted it even as she followed his advice. What had made him think his instincts were better than a demi-goddess'?

The new tunnel they took dipped downward after a few feet and Naia stopped.

"I think it keeps going down," she whispered. "Go back."

He began the laborious process of trying to crawl backward while still unable to get to his hands and knees. He'd gone only a couple of feet when the hairs on the back of his neck stood on end. A sound he'd believed before to be entirely from the hiss and slide of Naia's movement continued. He heard it distantly, somewhere behind him.

"Go forward," he said. The urgency in his voice needed no elaboration. Naia crawled quickly onward, deeper and lower into the tunnel. He hurried after her.

The smell pervading the burrows grew stronger, overtaking Ty in waves, as the sound of movement came closer. The ground leveled out and Ty watched with increasing desperation for a branching tunnel that would take them up, but they passed no openings at all.

"Heebedy, heebedy, beebedy."

Ty froze. The set of nonsense syllables had come from far too close behind him. Maybe a tunnel away. Maybe not. The acoustics of the underground burrows were confusing, but the speech of the thing sounded human, though lisping.

He didn't want to picture the possibilities. Digging in hard with his elbows, one after the other, he dragged himself forward, rubbing his skin raw. He very nearly stopped in surprise a moment later when he realized that he'd been going slightly uphill for the last few meters. Naia must surely be having a harder time with her long dress, especially uphill where it would work down under her knees.

The sound of motion behind him was louder, though Ty still couldn't pin it to any specific distance or location in the warren.

Another couple of scootches forward and he bumped into Naia's feet. Ty stopped crawling and braced his hands against the soles of her slippers, giving her a boost up the rapidly increasing incline of the hole.

"Hibbity, bibbity, boo."

It was definitely closer. This tunnel for sure, and not far behind him. Ty thought he heard a soft whimper from Naia, though it might have been a grunt of effort.

The consonants the thing behind him chose shouldn't have been sibilant, but somehow they were. And unlike the dragging, scuffling sounds of his own movements, the motion behind him had the scratchy whisper of something gliding smoothly over the dirt. Something heavy.

Ty re-doubled his efforts, boosting Naia higher every couple of crawl cycles. Glancing up to check on her, he saw lighter shadows of open air and moonlight not far above her head.

"Higgety, diggety, do."

The thing suddenly stopped its chanting babble and began a low, nasal humming. Ty halted to listen more closely. He felt sure that words were buried in the droning sound. If he listened just a moment longer, he'd be able to make them out. The hidden words were important, he felt certain, something crucial he needed to decipher before he moved onward.

"Ty," Naia's voice drifted to him from above. "Hurry!"

He looked up again, though his head felt odd on his shoulders when he moved, like it had doubled in weight. His head bobbled in the same way a baby's might as he tried to see her. She was out of the hole and reaching down toward him.

"Ty!" She stretched farther. "Take my hand."

He would in a moment. A second or two more and he'd catch the words. Then he'd go.

"Ty," she said. Her voice was louder, but paced. Reasonable. "Look behind you."

His head moved like a doll's head torn off and perched on a narrow stick, but he did as she said.

Whatever was behind him filled the tunnel. It moved steadily upward, faster than he could crawl. The face was vaguely masculine and vaguely human, though triangular in shape and slanting back toward the body. Its enormous mouth was open, and the humming came from the back of its soft, pink throat. The sound was multi-tonal, as if multiple voices chanted one song in many keys. He looked deep into the mouth, to where those amazing sounds originated.

The tattoo over Ty's left inner thigh burned suddenly, as if hot spices had been scoured into the skin. The fierce burning snapped him out of the spell. As if they had only just appeared, he registered the great fangs spiking down from the upper jaw, almost touching the thin lower lip. The pointed ends of the teeth, thick as the tips of his little fingers, dripped viscous fluid. The breath that wafted from that mouth enveloped him in a stench of mossy rot and sour vomit.

Completely free of the hypnosis, Ty scrabbled with all his strength up the last few feet and extended his hand, stretching toward Naia. The thing slid up behind him, still gaining. Naia hung down into the hole to close the last few inches. His fingers hooked at the tips with hers.

Freed from the haze of the spell, he heard the words beneath the humming that he'd been trying so hard to catch. "Boodily, boodily, bop. Tipity, tapity, doe."

Naia pulled and Ty kicked with his toes and knees against the steeper slope of the exit. He emerged, falling half on top of her, then rolled off and away from the hole. Naia pushed to a sitting position. He grabbed her by the arm and jerked her across the ground to him. He heard the quick, hissing movement of a strike and anticipated the bite of the stake-sized fangs in his ankle so strongly that he felt a momentary phantom twinge of pain.

The creature's head broke the surface of the hole for an instant, rising to half Ty's height and lunging toward them. It missed by a handspan and Ty crabbed backward before realizing that the thickest part of the body was wedged at the top of the hole. He took in the full horror of the thing in the moonlight before it slithered back down below the opening again. The thing must have outgrown its ability to leave its den—at least until it went hungry long enough.

He pushed upright, finding his knees unreliable and shaky and helped Naia to her feet. Still holding hands, they hurried on through the park. He didn't even think to look for the bird-woman until they were well out of the bushes. Remembering, at last, the creature they'd originally been trying to escape, he stopped and searched the skies and tree branches. The silence of the Erebus night, full of furtive hunters and hunted, enveloped them. Naia gave his hand a squeeze of shared experience, part apprehension, part reassurance. Nothing appeared to be stalking them for the moment.

Ty tried to slow his breathing. "How did you know that getting me to look at that thing would break the spell?"

"I didn't. I thought you were lost. The only thing I could think might help was seeing it with the true vision Aletheia gave you."

Ty suspected that wasn't what had saved him. At least, it hadn't been solely responsible. His tattooed thigh still burned faintly.

Naia's dress was as covered in dirt as his still-damp T-shirt and jeans. Her hair was mussed, her face drawn. Her voice held less strength than usual. Seeing her reduced to such vulnerability filled him with emotion so deep it took his breath away. He wanted to wrap his arms around her. To carry her somewhere safe and watch over her while she slept. To heal her many hurts. He hadn't let himself feel love for such a long time that he wasn't even sure it was the right name for this wash of feelings.

"You got your dress dirty," was all he managed.

She brushed at it absently and his hands twitched, trying to reach out to her of their own volition.

Something small rustled in a nearby tree. "We should keep moving," she said, and started mechanically forward. He followed.

"Do you think the bird-woman is still looking for us?"

"The harpy? Probably," she said. Her voice sounded tired, monotone.

So that's what the creature had been. He listened for the heavy flap of wings and heard nothing. Naia seemed to intentionally stay a step or two ahead of him.

He felt the pain of his own recent grief as sharp as a sword, and thought of his mother dying without him ever saying anything of importance to her. He stopped under the cover of a tall tree. "Naia."

She looked back with weary impatience. "I'm sorry about Lamia."

Her mask crumbled.

"She should never have tried to fight it." The moonlight glittered on the tears brimming in her eyes.

"You couldn't have stopped her."

He closed the distance to her and laid his hands on her shoulders. She folded into him. He felt the wetness of her tears soak into his shirt. Despite the hundred other things he should be feeling right now, the electricity of their embrace burned into him. The other thing he felt surprised him even more: an emotional bond every bit as intimate as their physical proximity. He tipped his head toward her. Her mouth was so close to his that he felt her breath. He inhaled its sweetness into his lungs. He wanted to kiss her.

"It wasn't your fault," he said. "It was mine. None of this would have happened if I hadn't taken the key."

"It would have come to this eventually." She pulled away gently. "They've long suspected me of hiding it. If I'm going to start blaming, then the blame goes all the way back to the Graeae sister who took the gods' memories."

She turned her back and stepped away, as if what she had to say was too painful to face him. "I never asked for her service," she said, apparently returning to thoughts of Lamia. "I never bound her in any way."

He hadn't asked for an explanation but the pain in her voice said that she needed to give one.

"She was a queen once, until her children were killed as punishment for some act of hubris on her part. She was headed down a terrible path of self-destruction and revenge. I was the only one, I think, to show her any love. It pulled her back from the edge. I wasn't in time to keep her from becoming a wraith of herself, or to save all the children, but it stopped her from harming any more. She swore her service to me, as if I had saved her. I did nothing; she saved herself with her strength of spirit. Whatever she thought she owed me, I never saw it that way. She didn't *serve* me, she was my *friend*."

"I could see she knew that," he said. "She died saving you, like you saved her. I'm sure that's what she would have wanted, but I know it doesn't make it any easier."

She remained silent a moment before looking up again into the trees. "We should keep moving," she said.

"Don't we need to go back for the key?" Ty asked, brushing more muddy dirt from his shirt and jeans.

"No. It's safer hidden for now," Naia said, though the tightness in her face and voice told him how much it pained her to be separated from it.

A patch of light and shadow slid through the trees and came to rest at Selia's feet. She gathered the folds of her gold and silver gown with one hand and bent to scoop the mottled moonlight to her face. Molding it in her palms, she formed it into a globe, softly glowing with pale golden hues and swirling patches of night. She gazed deep into the orb, between the dark bits that moved like clouds across the moon, and saw there all that her servant had observed. Naia, leader of the Preservationists, and a mortal man on the run.

"Aello," she whispered, when the harpy attacked Lamia.

The events of the evening spun on within the little sphere. When she saw Naia remove something from her pocket and toss it into the creek, Selia clenched the globe so hard that dark blotches spread like ink in water, blocking her view.

She relaxed her grip and the globe cleared. The creek rose and tumbled violently, floodwaters suddenly crashing into the calm. The item, the thing that held the element of moon dust, which must surely be the key, was swept away out of sight.

Her servant continued to follow Naia and the human until they vanished down a hole. When it tried to follow, the globe turned entirely to shadow. She set the darkened sphere on the ground and was pondering what to do next, when the globe suddenly lit again. Squatting down she watched as it back-tracked out of the hole and retraced its steps to the place where the harpy and the wraith had fought.

"Good," she said stroking the top of the sphere. Golden light followed her thumb like a kitten pressing into a hand.

Lamia lay broken and bloodied on the ground in her human form. Her death had not been easy. Aello was an agent of Haides, expert at torture. It was probably no coincidence that the injuries she inflicted would have caused a slow and painful death.

Shimmering through the treetops, Selia's servant had found the harpy again and followed it. Aello moved with strong wing beats, flying Oldside, scanning the ground as she went. Suddenly, she tucked her wings and dived at an angle so steep her breasts fell forward nearly to her shoulders.

Selia drew closer to the globe, watching with keen interest. She had used her moon shadow magic on a number of occasions, but her enemies had always been hidden, furtive. The key was bringing them all out into the open.

Aello came to a two-story building that formed a square around a large courtyard. The foundation was stone, the walls common whitewash and sun-dried brick. A number of doors were visible, meaning many residents. Aello landed in the courtyard, oriented, and fluttered up to a second-story balcony railing. She shat onto the flagstones below and hopped down to knock at one of the doors.

A large man emerged, wearing dark baggy breaches and loose shirt over a great belly. He took a live coal from a little box in one of his pockets and lit a fat cigar.

"The master told me to contact you if ever I needed to reach him," Aello said.

"I see. I see," the man replied, smoke puffing from his mouth with his words.

And then the man led Aello to the head of the New Order.

13

And Into the Jaws of the Tiger

"Are we going to Enyalius?" Ty asked.

"He's my most knowledgeable ally. If we can make it to him, he can help us." They were near the margin of the park, though the demarcation between the park and the residential area no longer seemed abrupt. "Keep watch for the harpy," she said, "or anything else unusual. That tarantula, for instance. It was naïve of me not to have suspected it." At the mention of the tarantula, Ty searched the ground around his feet as if it might be preparing to climb his pants leg that moment.

Not seeing the spider, he looked around to try and get his bearings. By the light of the full moon and the glow of lamps burning in windows, he made out the shapes of buildings clustered tightly together. It looked like a business district. They passed various workshops and markets, though the lettering in ancient Greek made them nearly impossible for him to identify. Few of the buildings were more than two stories, and the road was hard-packed dirt with no sidewalk. Squinting to use his second sight, he was startled to see the tall, clustered buildings of downtown Athina.

The streets of Erebus rose and fell with the same hilly undulations as Athina's streets. Topping a particularly tall hill, Ty and Naia came to an open area paved with stone. The tall columns surrounding it gave it the appearance of an agora from ancient times, only the construction didn't look ancient as far as he could tell. He looked back over the city from his new vantage. The moonlight, bright enough to throw shadows, showed the outlines of a far less populated settlement than the one he'd seen from the hillside when he'd first entered Erebus. He looked ahead again at dots of lights grouped in the distance, marking other villages. Erebus, in its true form, appeared to be a series of villages separated by rolling hills and pastoral country blanketed in tall, dry grass, much like the old depictions he'd seen of his country. Distance was difficult to judge in the dark, but he guessed the next nearest village lay no more than a couple of kilometers ahead. Naia's community, apparently, equated only to the central part of Athina.

Ty stood so the park they'd just come from lay on his left, and the distant villages on his right. He squinted and thought the villages slid closer together, but it was hard to tell at the limits of his peripheral vision. Giving up on trying reconciling distance or anything else in this place, he followed Naia as she started down the hill and out into the countryside.

She moved purposefully, though he noticed her flinch at unexpected shadows and sounds, as if her thoughts drifted only to be pulled back abruptly to the fact they remained in danger. Ty had little trouble keeping up with her. The laceration on his calf burned with each step, but his ankle seemed to be improving with the steady walking. The repetitive motion had decreased the swelling and stiffness, and the ankle gave him less pain now than it had in the stairwell, sewer drains, running through the park, or scooting through the monster's burrows.

They closed on the next village sooner than he expected. Topping another small hill, he thought it looked familiar. His own neighborhood, he thought, narrowing his eyes, but partially hidden as it was by the rolling land, he couldn't be sure. He wondered again how he had perceived a contiguous set of districts while walking from Momus' apartment to Naia's. Perhaps his visual perceptions alone had kept him from feeling the uneven ground and the grass against his legs.

Rounding one more hill, another small village came into view just in front of them. A suburb farther from downtown than his own, he thought, one he only knew superficially. He followed Naia as she circumnavigated the main cluster of houses and stopped before a modest single-story home on the right-hand edge of town. The home looked to be made of whitewashed mud bricks, like most of the structures, with straight lines and square design, devoid of embellishment or a courtyard. Naia crossed to the door and knocked.

The old, orange-robed and white-bearded man Ty had seen twice before answered.

"Enyalius," Naia said, warmly.

"My lady." He sounded surprised. "What are you doing in these parts? Please, come in." He stepped back and opened the door wide, giving Ty a weighing look as he followed Naia inside.

Naia had called him a powerful ally, but based on his home, Ty guessed she didn't mean powerful in the same way Aletheia and she were. His house was as modest inside as out—spare furnishings with only the bare essentials in evidence: one couch, one wooden chair, one table that looked to double as writing desk, one bedroom open to the main room with a sleeping pallet on the floor. It was clean and tidy, though, and tastefully but minimally decorated with colorful rugs and wall hangings of dyed cloth. An ancient-looking spear hung by the front door. Enyalius' one indulgence seemed to be books. They were everywhere, filling bookshelves, stacked on every surface, and piled in the corners.

"I'm sorry to intrude on your privacy," Naia said. "I know you value it, but things have come to a head."

He gestured for them to sit on the couch while he took the narrow chair for himself.

"Tell me," he said.

Naia filled him in on the events of the day, listing the players in both attacks as well as the tarantula. Apparently, she knew the harpy by name, calling her Aello. Enyalius' face went darker with concern at the mention of her.

"We must find you a safe place to stay, somewhere suitable to your station," he said when she finished. "You are of course most welcome to my room in the meantime." He looked from Naia to Ty and back again. Ty realized the man was wondering if they would be sharing a bed.

"I'll be fine on the floor here, if that's all right," Ty said.

Enyalius stood and gathered a plain wool blanket from the back of the chair and another from behind the couch. "Do you know why they chose today to move against you?" he asked Naia, holding the blankets to his chest.

"Someone from the New Order who lived above discovered the location of the key and blackmailed Ty into retrieving it."

Enyalius shot Ty a hard look.

"Does he have it still?" His question was addressed to Naia, his face grave with concern. "If so, I could hide it for you." He lifted his hands to indicate the house around them. "I would not be suspected, and I have the means to mask it."

"No," she said. "We don't have it with us."

"I see," he paused. "Well, as long as it's safe. At least now the key has been found, it brings us one step closer to our goal." Ty realized with surprise that, apparently, even her trusted friend hadn't known she'd been keeping it.

Enyalius set the two blankets on the arm of the couch and went into the bedroom. He opened a chest at the foot of his bed, removed another blanket from the chest, and spread it on the bed. "It is safe, isn't it?" he said, returning to the front room.

Naia changed the subject. "We're out of time, Enyalius. We *must* find a cure for the gods."

"We've looked for nearly three decades, my lady."

"If anyone can find it, you can." She gestured to the stacks of books lying everywhere. "You're the most learned man I know. Please, if there's anything you haven't tried, try it now. Any resource you need, only ask. Many times I've offered to be your patron, to make you more comfortable, as well as give you access to things you might need. I make the offer again."

"Your patronage would've made no difference. I have my books, and I'm happy as I am. But I'll do what I can for you, lady, as always. Believe me when I say I want the gods back every bit as much as you do." He sat again in the hard chair. "That the New Order sent Aello doesn't surprise me, but it's interesting that Selia attacked you in the open as she did. She has always been one for shadows."

"Not as much as some. At least we know she leads the Revisionists. We know many followers of the New Order, but the leaders have been surprisingly elusive."

"True," he said. He turned to Ty. "Who else does Kairos work with, do you know?"

"Momus," Ty answered. "And Kalyptra. She's the one who did my markings."

"Kalyptra has always been too clever by half," Enyalius said to Naia. "Hard to imagine her behind this, though. She keeps to the surface world and has never been one to ally with any group." He addressed Ty directly again. "These markings you mention, where are they? I thought I detected shadows on you."

"They're visible on the surface world," Naia said, "Scars at his inner wrists and tattoos in the colors of the key in many places on his body. Here they are unseen."

"You've seen them, though?" She nodded. "How interesting. May I investigate them?" He, again, addressed Naia.

"Sure," Ty answered. If this man had any clues as to what had been done to him, he wanted to hear them.

"Show me, then." Enyalius stood.

Ty took off his boots and socks. He pulled his T-shirt over his head and dropped it on the couch.

"Lie down on the floor," Enyalius instructed.

Ty did as he said, and twisted his head to watch as the man retrieved a volume from a stack in the far corner near the table, nearly at the bottom of the pile. He wondered how he could remember one book out of so many.

Enyalius flipped through the pages. "Here," he said, apparently to himself. He went to the far end of the room where shelves lined the walls above a small hearth. He took down a glass jar filled with a bright yellow powder that sat next to a small, wooden statue—female, holding sheaves of grain. Hestia.

Returning, he knelt beside Ty, set the book aside, and dumped a small amount of powder into one hand. "Where?"

Ty knew each one without needing to call on his second-sight. He indicated the two serpentines, his inner left arm, both wrists and the soles of his feet. "There are a couple of others, too."

Enyalius spread the powder over the snaking lines down his chest, and smeared what remained in his palm above Ty's left elbow. Ty tipped his head to watch, and saw the tattoos appear in full and vivid color.

"Fascinating," Enyalius said.

"Well?" Naia prompted.

Enyalius pointed to Ty's right side. "Lung," he said. "A powerful protection of luck. I don't see it aimed at any one goal, which makes sense if they didn't know what obstacles he might encounter. It's no guarantee of succeeding at what he attempts, of course—no luck is—but it bestows a strong advantage." He drew his finger down Ty's left side. "And this is love. Also very powerful, though this one seems aimed." He looked up significantly at Naia. "At you, I would say."

She blanched and her mouth drew into a tight line.

"I didn't know," Ty said feebly.

Taking Ty's left arm, Enyalius said, "This one keeps secrets hidden."

Naia nodded and muttered, "Why Aletheia couldn't make you tell the truth, no doubt."

Enyalius dusted Ty's feet and examined them for some time. "The right is to help him find his way through unfamiliar territory. The left is to help him find what he seeks."

"Isn't that the same thing?" Ty said.

"Not exactly, one is more a map and the other more a compass. You said there were others?"

"Two more," Ty stood and turned his back to the man. He unbuckled his belt, unzipped the top of his jeans, and pulled his pants down off his right hip. He pointed to his back and felt Enyalius dusting the area. Looking down, he saw that the tattoos on his chest were already fading.

"This keeps him from notice," Enyalius said, touching his back.

So *that* was what made him all but invisible down here. Ty turned, pulling his jeans down to his knees. At least he was wearing skivvies this time for showing this tattoo. He pulled up one leg of his underwear, realizing for the first time since the park that the burning there had abated.

"This is the last." He held out one hand to brush the powder on himself, but Enyalius didn't notice. He dusted Ty's inner thigh with the clinical detachment of a doctor.

"This one wields a protective spell, I believe."

"Aren't they all protective spells?" Ty asked.

"Not necessarily. The marks on you belong to the ones who convinced Kalyptra to make them, therefore they are for the benefit of those people more than for you. This one protects your person, though."

Ty thought of his near drowning in the lake, bruised shoulder and hip from the gryphon, lacerated calf, and sprained ankle, not to mention the pain of being tattooed. He wished it'd been a more effective spell, but at least he hadn't died in the burrows of that last monster or had his face eaten off by the harpy.

Before Ty could put his T-shirt back on, Enyalius took his wrists. He tried the powder to no effect. He consulted two more books and experimented with three more herbs. When none of them worked, Ty saw anger flash across his face. It rippled over his features, transforming them, momentarily making the old scholar something that frightened Ty more than the tarantula and the harpy together. The effect was so fleeting Ty wasn't sure he'd really seen it, and he glanced back at Naia for confirmation. She was looking down at her knees, deep in thought. The sadness in her expression tugged at his heart.

"I'm sorry, my lady," Enyalius said, sounding the composed and elderly scholar again. "If there are marks at his wrists, they must remain a mystery for now. I'm most curious, though. I assure you I will investigate." His eyes met Ty's with such promise that Ty looked away.

"We have kept you up late, old friend," Naia said, rising from the couch. "And I need to rest now, and think." She kissed Enyalius on one cheek. "It might be best if we all rise before the sun and talk more. Plans need to be made, but they're not ones to rush into lightly."

"Of course, my lady."

She left them both without another word. Ty wasn't sure if her mood was more due to the events of the day catching up with her or if she was thinking of Lamia again. He hoped it wasn't something else— something to do with him or the tattoo over his heart.

He picked up one of the blankets and a cushion. "You take the couch," he said to Enyalius. "I'll be fine here." Ty spread the blanket on the floor, glad to see it was wide enough to cover him as the window cut-outs in the walls had only shutters, no glass. He lay down.

Enyalius extinguished the lamps. In the darkness and silence, Ty felt the loss of his mother loom large. The ordeals of the day had pushed his grief aside, but now sadness and exhaustion overwhelmed him.

Ty heard the couch creak. In the light that the full moon cast through the windows, he could see the old man sitting upright, unmoving.

Ty came awake suddenly, what seemed moments later. He lay still, retrieving the memory of what had woken him. A sound. A cry. Naia.

He was up in an instant, moving toward the bedroom. The old man wasn't on the couch. Looking around, he caught a silhouette of him standing in front of the unshuttered window near the table.

Ty paused in the open archway of the bedroom. Soft scents filled of humid night air filled the room. Naia slept on her side facing the door. Her hair was loose, and shadows emphasized her closed eyes, her aquiline nose, her full lips. She moaned again.

Ty knelt by the pallet, reaching out gently to touch her arm, hoping to soothe her without waking her. Gods knew she needed her sleep. Her eyes opened instantly, and she gave a small gasp that might have been either startlement or a sob. She grabbed his hand, gripping it hard, and then just as quickly let go. "I was dreaming about Lamia," she said.

"About the attack?"

"A centaur was trampling her to death."

Ty shifted to sit cross-legged. Her pain shattered him. It broke something inside him to see her on the run, sleeping on a pallet on the floor, and without the companion who had guarded her for who knew how long. And what could he do to help her against her powerful enemies? Run away, like he had before?

He should console her, he knew, or at least puff up with some manly desire to protect her. All he could think about was kissing her.

"I wish I could take the pain away," he said. "I wish I could turn back the clock and make everything okay."

"You'd have to turn it back a very long way."

He smiled. "I'd try."

She stayed quiet. Her eyes didn't meet his, they focused lower.

"Has all my trust in you only been because of these?" She brushed her fingers lightly over the left side of his chest. Gooseflesh raised on his arms at her touch.

"I don't know. I hope not."

"Considering the strength and skill in these markings, I suspect it must have been."

Her words cut him like a knife. "Maybe we can start again," he said. "Build a new trust. Unless you've done the same to me." He mimicked grabbing at an arrow striking him in the heart, and smiled. He thought it a good lead-in to telling her how much he'd come to care for her, but she rolled onto her back and turned her face from him. His grin faded.

"You didn't, did you? Place a love spell on me?"

He thought of her sitting at his elbow as he sketched Lamia days ago, of their conversation on her balcony when she'd laid her hand on his chest, of holding her after their escape from the monster's den—all the times he'd felt overwhelmed by her closeness. Had it all been nothing more than a conjurer's trick? Had she treated him no differently than her enemies had done, marking and manipulating him in the same way they had?

"At least now I know how it feels," she said.

He felt blood drain from his face at the confirmation. "Why?" He choked the word out.

She sighed, and faced him again. "Fear. I've been caught in a deadly game, Ty, and I didn't want to die. You were an unknown."

"When did you do it? That first day?"

She nodded in the dark. "On the balcony. After Lamia found you in my room, I needed a way to feel safe. I know this doesn't help, but it's not a talent I use often or lightly."

"Is that how you stopped Kairos, in the stairwell?"

She nodded again. He thought of the man, staring vacantly at the puddle of water she'd become. Charging Momus with no thought of his own safety.

"Can you undo it?" he asked.

"No more than you can." Her bare shoulders lifted in a shrug. "It seems not to have mattered anyway. You seem unaffected. You even turned my own trick back on me."

He wasn't about to tell her how deeply her arrow had struck despite his protections.

"I've told you before that I didn't do any of this," he said, gesturing to himself, suddenly angry. "It was done *to* me. And at least I *would* have undone it if I could have." Ty pushed himself off the floor and left the room.

Enyalius was still standing in the next room. He couldn't have helped but overhear everything. Ty lay down heavily on his blanket.

He should have trusted his instincts. Kept his distance. Maybe it had all been a ruse: her vulnerability, her tears, her touch. People looked out for themselves. He should have learned that well enough from his father, from his old girlfriend's betrayal and the friend who had cuckolded him. They pulled your heartstrings when they wanted to and they left when it suited them. How had he let those lessons lose their impact? He knew exactly how. He hadn't been given a choice.

A sharp knock on the front door made Enyalius turn in surprise. Through the bedroom doorway, Ty saw Naia throw back the blanket and step quietly into the archway. He got up as well. He'd noted earlier that there was no back door, but the window by the table was easily large enough to climb through. He eased toward the table.

Enyalius lit a lamp, though Ty didn't see flint or match. He opened the front door with a look more of irritation than hesitation, which seemed odd considering his age and the fact that he was hiding a demi-goddess. Ty braced for anything—except for what he saw.

Momus stood in the open doorway.

"I have a message for you," Momus started, but cut off when he saw they weren't alone. "Well, well. Hullo again, my lady." He squinted despite the lamplight, apparently having trouble seeing Ty clearly after their separation. "Hullo, Ty."

14

To Touch the Moon

"Well, here we are. Here we all are," Ty heard Momus say. "I just stopped by to give you a message. Is this a bad time?"

Naia glanced from Momus to Enyalius to Ty, assessing them all with equal suspicion.

"As good as any, I suppose," Enyalius said, letting the big man in.

Momus hesitated at the anger in the old man's voice. He stubbed his cigar out on the bottom of his enormous shoe before entering.

Enyalius gestured to the door as Momus pushed it closed. "Take that blanket from the floor and put it along the gap at the bottom. We don't want her flowing out of here."

Ty watched as Momus obeyed, cutting off the only egress for Naia if she changed to water.

"Enyalius," Naia said, sadly. "Even you?"

"I'm a philosopher, my lady, and, unlike you, practical enough to see beyond mere emotion."

Naia moved to stand near Ty. He tried to ignore the cramping in his belly, the worry for her safety above his own. It was artificial, he reminded himself, part of her spell on him. He took a small step back from them all.

"Don't even consider it," Enyalius said, evidently noting Ty's small moves toward the window. He busied himself lighting another lamp. "I know the charms you carry, therefore I know how to circumvent them. Have a seat there, both of you lovebirds." He gestured to the couch. "My lady, I'd suggest keeping your talents to yourself. I can override anything you do to Momus, and your love spells won't work on me. And if you change to water, you'll be set on fire until you evaporate."

"So, all the vermin are indeed emerging from the shadows," Naia said.

"Yes, so it would seem." Enyalius turned to Momus. "You had a message for me?"

"Hmm, well, it may be a bit moot now, you know. All this, and all." Momus nodded to Ty and Naia on the couch. "A, uh, a friend of yours sent her apologies that she didn't accomplish her task."

"Aello?" Naia said sweetly to Enyalius. "Whom you sent to kill me?"

"Ah," Momus gave a belly-laugh that brought a residual wisp of smoke from his lungs. "No secrets among us, then, eh?"

"Only one," Enyalius said. He moved closer to Naia and loomed over her. "Where is the key?"

"Even if I knew, I'd see you rot in Haides before I told you."

He struck her hard across the face. Ty started to his feet, hand balled into a fist. Enyalius pushed him roughly back down. Like seemingly everyone here, the man was stronger than he looked.

Naia laid a hand on Ty's leg, silently imploring him to stay seated. The skin near her mouth reddened, and she wiped at a thin trickle of blood. "Whose son are you?" she asked.

"Perhaps I'm not a demi-god at all. Would that rankle if I were just some old philosopher who had fooled you all these years?"

"One need not be wise to be a liar."

"It does, however," he said lightly, "take a measure of cleverness to do it well. But never mind that. The key was marked with the power of Prometheus during its making. It's not as if it would go unnoticed by those of us with skills."

"Why never steal it before this, then?"

"Your property has been searched, of course." Enyalius shook his head in mock disappointment. "You were so naïve at first, sending heroes off with instructions to seek a place that would open with a key. All your enemies knew what to look for. What we didn't know was where you kept it."

Naia turned her head from his gloating. A tear leaked from one eye.

"You learned, though," Enyalius said. "The first ones to search your home were clumsy, and by the time we moved, you had hidden or warded it well. We'd given up hope that you kept it near you. And then Kairos approached me. His suggestion was unique; have Kalyptra spell a human and tackle the problem from a new perspective. If it worked, I would see to getting his banishment lifted."

"Why didn't you just take it from me once I had it? Ty asked Momus. "Why bother leading me back to the surface?"

Enyalius answered for him. "So that Naia would follow you there, where few would have been willing or able to rescue her. We hoped to take our time making certain she didn't know the location of the gods as well. But we know how that worked out, and as Momus so eloquently put it, 'here we all are.'" He turned back to Naia. "So, lady, let's start with where you've stashed the key this time. Should I have Momus summon Aello to convince you to talk, or will you tell me what I want to know?"

"You said you know what to look for. Go find it yourself."

"I would like to very much, but it seems you've managed to hide it again."

Naia made no reply.

"Fine, then. Your lover was with you. Perhaps he knows." Enyalius motioned to Momus.

"Anything special?" Momus asked.

"Something quick."

Momus stuck the cold stub of his cigar in his mouth and reached deep into his pants pocket and pulled out a small, stone box, which he popped open with one thumb. He removed a pair of tweezers from the lid of the box. They were nearly too delicate for his fat fingers to manipulate, but he managed to lift a live coal from inside. In his second sight Ty saw the coal as the burning match it had appeared to be when Momus escorted him to the surface.

Momus grabbed him by the throat with his free hand, and blew on the little coal until it glowed red. He held it just under Ty's left eye. Ty barely noticed the coal with Momus' hand around his throat. His old panic of suffocation detonated, overshadowing any fear of being burned. When the coal came close enough to singe Ty's lower eyelashes, the two fears competed for priority. He grabbed Momus' wrist with both hands. Unable to budge Momus' grip, he squeezed his eyelids closed. The coal hadn't yet touched him, and already the heat penetrated the lid and warmed his eye.

"I'm sorry, Ty," Naia whispered. He heard tears in her voice and he knew she had no means to help him.

Ty didn't think of himself as a brave man, but stupid bravado had always been his strong suit. "Give Kairos a kiss for me when you see him," he rasped against Momus' grip.

Momus chuckled around his cigar. "Oh, won't none of us be seeing that pocked little bastard again. I took care of that before I left above. Squeezed his head like one of his damn pimples. It popped just like them. Yessiree. Now hold still." Momus fingered Ty's eyelid open. Ty screamed, but it came out as a wheeze. He heard a sobbing gasp from Naia. Her hand gripped his knee like a vise.

Ty shook his head so violently, Momus momentarily lost his hold on his throat.

"Well, this shouldn't take long," Momus said, apparently speaking to Enyalius. He roughly pried Ty's eye open again and lowered the coal to it. "Come on. Come on now. Don't roll your eye up like that."

The harder Ty fought the more he choked. He tried to cough but couldn't. Momus could have killed him in the first minute, but torturing him into talking meant the man had to temper the pressure and pain. Maybe he could tip the scales. Steeling himself against his terror of suffocation, Ty twisted to force Momus to grip harder while he leaned forward into the pressure. His heart pounded, his muscles warred with his willpower. He prayed that he would pass out. With luck, they'd leave him alone if he was unconscious. If not, at least he wouldn't be aware of what they did to him next. Or to Naia.

"Where is the key?" Enyalius said again, sounding bored. The heat intensified.

The front door burst open and Momus jerked back, letting go of Ty's throat.

Ty lurched up off the couch, gasping and coughing. More than a dozen intruders poured into the house, mostly women dressed in leather and bristling with weapons, aided by a few creatures of various sizes and shapes. Momus half-turned toward the door. Ty punched the big man on his stubbly jaw for every ounce of fear and anger the man had engendered.

Momus fell back into a centaur as it hurtled through the doorway, taking the creature to its knees as he fell. Through Ty's good eye—the one not watering like a river—he saw Enyalius strike two of the women, one after the other. One slammed into a wall, the other dropped to the floor. Both lay still.

A woman with adders wrapped around both forearms reached for Enyalius as a thing that looked part scorpion and part giant mantis crawled toward his leg. Momus and the centaur had both regained their feet and wrestled like two titans.

Ty yanked Naia to the open window. He wanted nothing more than to leap out and be done with them all. He stood back, instead and motioned hurriedly for Naia to go first.

Enyalius reached the wall and grabbed the spear hanging there. He brought the butt end down on the scorpomantis, crushing it, then turned the point on the woman swinging her open-mouthed adders at him. A deep strum and heavy thunk occurred nearly simultaneously. A sound of finality. Of death.

A strikingly beautiful woman in silver and gold robes stood in the doorway. She held her bow vertical, her elbow still at her ear, though the shaft had flown. The arrow protruded from the center of Enyalius' upper left chest. The shaft's diameter looked thicker than ordinary arrows, and it had sunk more than half its length. It was black as night and decorated intricately in gold and silver. The end of the shaft was fletched in golden feathers. Naia straddled the window frame, as transfixed by the turn of events as Ty. He pushed at her to go.

The old man kept his feet a few seconds more before he fell to his back but, to Ty's astonishment, a moment later he rolled over and began to crawl on hands and knees toward a small side table that rested against the wall, below where the spear had been. Two creatures clawed at his back and an adder dangled by its fangs from one of his arms. The woman in the doorway strung another arrow but Momus and the centaur crashed into the doorframe beside her.

Naia landed on her feet on the ground below the window. Ty threw one leg over the sill and then the other, but he couldn't resist another look back. Enyalius hauled himself to his feet and grabbed a jar from the side table. Wrenching the lid open, he scattered a handful of powder in a wide arc. The resulting blast threw Ty from the windowsill to the ground. The house shook. As if through wads of cotton in his ears, he heard the front of the house crumble and collapse. He thought of the archer in the doorway, and all of those along the arc of the powder.

Naia helped him to his feet.

"Turn to water," he hissed. He couldn't hear his own words for the ringing in his ears. "Get out of here. Now."

"What of you?"

He read her lips more than heard her faint words. "I'll take care of myself," he said.

Enyalius stood amid the dead and dying. The butt of the arrow protruded from his chest but the arrow head had been forced back into his thorax when he fell. The point of it rubbed across a rib in his back when he moved and stabbed at the exit hole. He ripped the front of his robe from the arrow shaft up to the neck, and peeled the bloody rag down to his waist, exposing the strong arms and smoothly muscled chest he generally kept hidden. Gripping the shaft with both hands, he pushed. Slowly, the head re-emerged from his back, slicing a larger opening as it cut a new path. He clenched his jaw but made no sound. One of the first things he'd realized about himself after forgetting all else was that he endured pain well.

Adjusting his grip on the remainder of the shaft still emerging from his chest, he applied opposing pressure. It should have snapped in two, but it didn't. The bitch had used one of her mother's arrows. Grimacing, he increased the pressure, feeling the shaft pressing against tissues in his chest cavity. His lung felt heavy on the left. His breath frothed, wet and bloody. Finally the shaft snapped. He pulled the butt-half free and threw it onto the floor, then grappled to pull the rest of the arrow from his back.

Something stirred near his feet. One of the virgin-goddess-wannabe followers of Selia seemed not quite dead. She had lost most of one arm but gripped a long-bladed knife in her remaining hand. Unable to lift herself from the floor, she brought the knife down in a shallow arc, narrowly missing one of his sandaled feet. The blade chinked into the stone floor.

Enyalius stepped on the knife, breaking the blade. He squatted and placed the bloodied arrowhead still in his hand against her back, over the heart. Slowly, he pushed the razor sharp tip home. He jerked it free again.

One or two other injured Revisionists watched him or tried to rise as he threaded through the room. He could see the incongruity of his strong body with his old face and white beard perplexed them. Let it.

They would get no answers from him. The disguise had served him a long time, as had the name he'd been using.

He executed others as he worked his way to the front door. Momus lay in the doorway, entangled with the long legs of the centaur he had killed. A red crescent on his forehead showed where at least one hoof had landed. Enyalius kicked Momus hard in the side. The large man gave a soft grunt but remained unconscious. Enyalius stepped over him and out the door.

Selia was nowhere to be seen. Damn her. And neither were Naia or her mortal consort.

The contenders were indeed emerging from the shadows. They had discovered his identity and attempted to kill him. This called for serious counter-measures.

Enyalius tore off the rest of his robe and returned to the bedroom, naked but for his sandals. His wound was troubling him less already; breath came easier, and the bleeding had nearly stopped. The charms he had learned and woven around himself years ago must still be working, though he had never had occasion to test them this far.

He dressed in a fresh robe and left his house for the final time, stepping over the bodies of his enemies. The moon was high in the sky, night only half done. The timing should be about right. He began walking Mountainside across Erebus.

Nothing challenged him on his way to the mountain. Nothing dared. His anger was terrible. He hated the fog in his mind that came with such anger. Violence had always stirred a deep and terrible response within him. It pushed away the trappings of a learned man and opened him to a chaos that seemed distantly familiar. The source was forgotten though, like so much else. He often thought on the coincidence of his confusion and the fact that Deino had stolen the memories of the gods, but looking back to the wellspring of his condition was like looking into a mirror pointed at the sun; too hard, too blinding, too painful. It didn't matter anyway. If he had been a god at one time, he was one no longer. And if he wasn't, at least he aspired to the next best thing.

His wound pained him, but his breathing continued to improve. He walked strongly with a ground-covering stride. Distance, like everything else in Erebus, was a matter of perception more than actuality. Well before morning he reached the Mountainside perimeter of Erebus, where the rolling hills met Erebus' image of Mount Olimbos. Had he skirted the mountain and kept going, he would have found himself at the opposite edge of the land again. Instead, he began climbing, not slowing his pace.

The balmy night air followed him nearly a third of the way up the rocky trail. The middle third became sharply steeper and cool winds tugged at his robes. On the upper reaches of the mountain he walked through snow, though he never felt it against his sandaled feet. He climbed until there was no mountain left, and he stood on the summit with all of Erebus spread out below him.

The summit was familiar, though when he'd come here before he'd been seeking something different than tonight. As before, he looked up, hoping to see Aether, a realm none but the gods themselves could perceive. If he said just the right word, did just the right thing, maybe it would open to him. The feeling was strong, the impression of a world above him acute. If it existed, though, it still refused to reveal itself to him.

The moon had nearly finished its journey through the sky. He waited patiently while it covered the last of the distance to the top of the mountain. He felt not the least fatigued by his journey now, and

seemed fully recovered from his injury. His anger had cooled as well—
the burning fury that fueled the spell of explosion, fury so consuming it
bordered on joy, had been contained once more. His desire for revenge
on Selia, however, had not lessened in the slightest. Her warriors may
have been decimated, but he would see her pay in a more personal way.

He was glad again for his discovery of the powders. During those
early days when he'd wandered, knowing no more than a child, he'd
quickly realized his talent for magic—erratic and unpredictable though
it had been. Years of study had led him to an otherwise unreliable text
that hinted at various powders to channel magic, a technique he'd
refined far beyond the scope of the material in the book.

The moon sailed closer to the mountain, mindlessly prepared to
drift over the top and vanish until its appointed time to rise again.
Unlike the corporeal moon in the real heavens, Selia's replica grew no
larger as it neared. The circumference of it fit within the circle of his
arms now, just as it appeared it would have when across the sky from
him. Close up, the shadows and craters drew a face that seemed to
study him. Illusion, though. He knew the little replica was as inanimate
and unintelligent as a brick.

It cleared the rocky precipice of the mountain by only the smallest
margin—little enough that it might sweep him from his perch if he
couldn't stop it. The moon drifted nearer, head-high. Enyalius reached
into a pocket of his robe and tossed a sprinkle of fennel powder onto
its surface to increase his strength against it. He channeled his spells
through the powder and wrapped his arms around the moon. Selia's
moon might have the circumference of a large ball, but it still possessed
the mass and orbital pull of a celestial body.

The little moon strove to complete its assigned tracing across the
sky. Enyalius held it in place. He leaned into the struggle, grunting

with effort, wrestling it with all his magically enhanced strength. Sweat appeared on his brow and dripped down his temples. Still the moon pushed forward. Like a wind-up toy against a wall, the pale golden orb persisted, unconscious of the impediment.

Enyalius increased his effort. He focused on the enspelled fennel dusting it. He strained again. A creaking, groaning noise filled the air around him.

The moon pushed mindlessly forward and Enyalius pushed back with muscle and will. The friction between them rubbed burns into his chest and the side of his face. It tore open the newly healed wound over his heart. The little moon drew its power of motion and light from the real moon. So, too, it reflected the moon's other powers: the magic that made a spell cast in moonlight stronger, that incited madness and howling and fear. These powers pounded at his mind, trying to push through him to the other side. It shattered bits of his mind; the few bits that he had painstakingly pieced together. The creaking noises intensified in the air above his head, loud as huge plates of rock shifting in an earthquake.

With a last heave, he tore the moon from the sky.

He felt his mind rip free at the same time, as the moon claimed a steep and unexpected price for his success. With a grunt, he tossed the little globe over the far side of the mountain. It tumbled and bounced down the steep cliffs. It didn't shatter as he had hoped it would. It remained undiminished in size as it rolled away from him, landing at last in a deep cleft.

He wiped the dripping sweat from his face and turned a full circle, wondering how he had come to this place. It hardly mattered. There was only one direction he could move from here. He began the long descent, listening to the voices of the new companions in his head.

Selia lay in a patch of moonlight not far from Enyalius' house. Her hearing remained muffled from the explosion, as if rabbit tails were stuffed in her ears. The moonlight had shifted throughout the night and she had crawled to stay within it, healing in its soft glow. By the time moonset neared she felt stronger. She hoped she had recovered enough to make it to safety.

When she pushed herself to a standing position, her head felt like a melon that had been split with an axe. She didn't want to leave without checking for other survivors, but she couldn't risk returning to her enemy's house. Not even for Cyrene. Going back was sure to amount to no more than a body count, and might mean the death of her where the explosion had failed. If Cyrene had survived, they would find each other. Moving with the support of trees and rocks when she could, and crawling when she couldn't, she made her way up a small hill. She needed to be at the right angle when the moon set, and that was coming soon.

If she'd had to reach the moon to be home, like her mother—even her own small, close moon—she never would have made it. Fortunately, she needed only to achieve the path. Her home lay along that shimmering road, along a trail no other could follow.

The moon reached Olimbos and skimmed the top. The mountain looked as though it had tipped back its rocky head and blown a great, golden bubble. Selia knew she had only minutes left. She crawled as fast as she could, head pounding, ears ringing, breath strained. She crested the hill. Her chest burned with each inhalation, but she made it in time.

The angle of the moonbeams continued to change. Another moment and a shaft would appear, one unlike the others. One visible only to her, and only in those last seconds before the moon finished its course for the night. Wide. Substantial. Inviting. She could step—or crawl, if she must—onto the road that would take her home.

Always she felt the road unfurling a second before she saw it. She felt the expansion in the air before her and waited. Suddenly, a tremendous tugging in her chest yanked her forward. Her heart felt as if it was tearing out through her intact flesh. She fell prone with a cry of surprise.

With an effort, she turned her head to look up. Her moon rocked in the sky, as if a great celestial wind buffeted it. A circle inside her mirrored the motion, throat to abdomen and side to side. It felt as if her ribs and flesh had been sawed through, and now someone tried to tug the disk of flesh and bone free of her body. Her ribs spread painfully to accommodate the formless moon-sized mass being torn from her. She screamed. The little moon jerked from its place over the mountain and fell over the far side.

Choking and retching, Selia fell unconscious.

15

---◈---

Nikos, Can You Hear Me?

One minute Ty was holding Naia's hand and the next she rained across his skin. She turned to a rivulet of water and vanished down a narrow drainage track where the gravel around Enyalius' house ended and dirt began.

A high-pitched ringing persisted in his ears from the explosion, but he could hear well enough to realize that the tumult of battle had ceased abruptly. Only one person still moved about inside the house. He knew which person that would be, and knew he needed to get as far from here as fast as he could. Skipping and stumbling down the small slope where Naia had vanished, he ran from the house the best his ankle and calf allowed. He stopped at the bottom, realizing he had no idea where to go next.

He supposed he could return to The National Garden. The place was at least somewhat familiar, and maybe Aletheia wouldn't have left her home yet and could help him when he got there. Most compelling, though, he'd come into Erebus this last time through a grate in the city, not far from the outskirts of the park. He doubted he could find the staircase that Momus had taken him down, but using both his current vision and his second sight, he might be able to find the sewer grate.

He shoved aside the thought that Naia would probably head to the park as well since she'd tossed the key in the brook there, and told himself that had nothing to do with his choice. His feelings for her were no more than a spell on him. If he never saw her again, then all the better. Now that Kairos was dead, he planned to get the hell out of Erebus and stay gone.

The moon had been in front of them when they walked to Enyalius' home and had passed the middle of the sky since. If the landscape hadn't all turned inside out again, he hoped that keeping the moon before him would get him to his goal. He could look for the small grouping of homes they'd passed on the way here to be sure he went the right direction.

Once clear of the village, he saw the shadowy but familiar contours of the shallow valley, and moved ahead with more confidence. He'd gone not quite half the distance he thought he needed to when he heard soft scurrying noises and the crunch of heavier tread in the tall grass behind him. He turned, heart beating hard, but saw nothing. A short distance later it happened again.

A sound of dry grass breaking crackled directly behind him, almost on his heel. He spun, arms lifted to defend against his unknown foe, but the moonlit grasslands behind him were empty. He stared into the deceptive shadows cast by the moon, sure that he saw something sliding away. Overactive imagination he told himself, but he increased his pace nonetheless.

With relief, he neared a small hill he'd been aiming for, hoping it might be one of the two he and Naia had passed on their way to

Enyalius' home. He debated the worsening pain in his calf from all the walking tonight against the vantage he'd have from the hilltop to check his progress. Vantage won. The hill stood perhaps thirty meters tall, and the incline made him wince as the laceration and bruised tissue of his calf stretched and the stress on his ankle increased.

Feeling as exposed on the crest of the hill as if spotlighted, he dropped to a martial crouch. Below and in front lay the small village he'd noticed when coming this way with Naia. He felt a mild surprise to find himself this close to it. Things had either shifted slightly or he'd drifted one hill further right than he'd intended. Still, it relieved him to have found the landmark he'd sought. Squinting, Ty looked at the village with his second sight and realized that not only had he been right before about this being his neighborhood, but if he entered here he'd be close to his apartment building. Momus' apartment building.

A grunting noise snuffled not far behind him. This time he had no doubt something was out there, and he didn't have so much as a tree or bush to hide behind. Thoughts of Enyalius chasing him down or Momus taking this same path to their shared apartment made him hurry down the hill and head for the cover of the buildings.

He planned to avoid the apartment at all costs, and scanned the buildings with his second-sight as he looked for another option. He spotted the front of the widow Savina's home, where a woven rug hung from an open window to air. An owl, larger than any had a right to be, perched on top of the rug, peering out into the darkness. Ty's glance landed next on a butcher shop he recognized, but thoughts of the Erebus version of a butcher shop quickly dissuaded him from going there. The butcher shop lay only a block from Nikos' market, though he knew he wouldn't find his childhood friend there. In fact, he might not like what he found there at all. But he wanted away from whatever followed him through the valley, and it seemed the best of his limited options.

He passed stores that looked familiar if he squinted and foreign if he didn't, as he wove his way past outlying buildings and into the village proper. Looking up at the moon, he figured it must be around midnight. The stillness of the night gave him little comfort, though. Erebus had its share of nocturnal denizens. Maybe a third of the structures here had lamps lit, proving his point. A scorpion the size of his foot scuttled out from between two buildings and across his path, reminding him that not everything here needed lamps.

Thinking about his apartment not far from here made him wonder if everything about Momus had been a set up. It certainly hadn't been chance that the man knew and worked with Kairos. Maybe the apartment had been empty and they'd planted Momus there when Kairos sent Ty to Erebus. Maybe Kairos' men had killed the real tenant. Then again, having seen another side of Momus tonight, maybe Kairos wouldn't have needed to send his thugs.

The building-that-was-not-Nikos' market was one of the shops with a light burning. Ty's second sight showed a typical market display behind a large window. Here, though, it seemed to be some kind of apothecary. He relaxed his eyes and peered through the wide open front door at wood shelves lined with jars. One held a live cobalt-blue snake within its glass confines; another was filled entirely with tiny webbed feet. Most of the rest he could see contained various leaves and powders, much like he'd seen on Enyalius' shelves.

A figure moved near the back of the store, a woman. Dark brown, curly hair, full figure. His heart beat a little faster and he debated his options. A swish-hiss of something large moving though the grass near the hill behind him made up his mind. He opened the front door and stepped inside. A little bell jangled over his head.

"I'm sorry to intrude," he said.

The woman behind the counter turned. She looked young and utterly human, and wore a simple, sleeveless gown of pale yellow that tied at the waist. Her heart-shaped face framed dark eyes, and she smiled at him with an expression of mild curiosity. She walked toward him behind the long counter, which was similar to the one in Nikos' shop. Her expression never changed, but the squint to her eyes told him she was having trouble making him out.

"Who has come to visit me this night?" she said.

He passed a jar at the end of a shelf containing what looked like human fingers. One twitched at him as he walked by and he suppressed an oath of surprise and revulsion.

"My name is Ty. I saw your light on and wondered if you were open." He was winging it, but winging it was pretty much where he lived these days.

She leaned both arms on the counter, a habit very much Nikos'. "My name is Mara. You're mortal?" Either being close enough or talking to him must have brought him into focus.

"Uh, yes. Just visiting." He glanced out the store window but, even with the light of the full moon, the lamplight inside made it impossible to see if anyone had followed him here.

"How intriguing."

He really wished people would stop saying that.

She lifted a hinged board and came around to his side of the counter. Leaning her back against it, she crossed her arms. "There must be a story in this. I'd love to hear it."

He narrowed his eyes briefly and saw her in a simple, short-sleeved dress, a yellow and tan print, belted at the waist. Her features might have seemed ordinary on another woman, but her smile crinkled the corners of her eyes and bridge of her nose in a way that made him smile back. Her manner was reassuring and open. She made sense to him, where so many here hadn't.

Maybe his luck had turned. Maybe she really was Nikos' equivalent. If so, then it stood to reason she would be friendly in an easy-going, no-pressure sort of way. After the night he'd had, he couldn't have wished for anything more. His tension ratcheted down one small click.

"It's not really much of a story. I met one of the banished above and he asked me to come down here and deliver a message for him. I'm just trying to help get his name cleared."

"And who would that be? Maybe I know him."

"I'm not really at liberty to say. Nothing personal, you know." The oft repeated cover story slid easily off his tongue.

She pushed away from the counter and reached past his shoulder to grab a jar that was only one-third full. He caught a scent of soap and cold cream on her skin. "You must have quite an adventurer's spirit," she said. Returning behind the counter, she bent, pulled out a small sack, and began filling the jar. "What do you do above? No, wait," she said, flashing her smile again. "Let me guess." She recapped the jar, her lips pursed in concentration. "Explorer? Cartographer?"

He laughed. "No. Not hardly."

"Scientist?"

"No."

"Gambler?" she ventured.

Her strike jarred him. "I'm just a locksmith," he said.

"Ooh. An unlocker of secrets. Well, that makes sense, I guess." She returned the jar to the shelf. "So, you came down here to speak on someone's behalf—very brave and noble, by the way—but it doesn't explain why you're in my shop. Do you need a potion to help deliver your message?"

He wanted to say yes. It would be as good an excuse as any, but then she'd ask what he needed and he wouldn't have a clue.

"No. I delivered my message earlier this evening. I'd hoped to stay there tonight, but my host had other company show up. It seemed polite to leave. I was just sort of killing time until daylight."

"Are you tired?"

With the battle and the explosion and the running, he hadn't had time to think about it. Now that she mentioned it, exhaustion weighed on his shoulders like a heavy cloak.

"Actually, yes. I thought I might head to the park."

She looked surprised, maybe a bit alarmed. "That might not be the best idea for a mortal. Well, for anyone, really. A lot of things are afoot there at night. I have a bed here, if you like."

"Oh, I didn't mean... "

"No, really, it's all right. I work at night and sleep in the day anyway. And Erebus is no place for the likes of you to be running around after dark. You could get some rest and be on your way in the morning." Before he had a chance to protest further, she waved him to follow her. "Come have a look. Then you can decide."

A warning jolt sprang up in his head like a mailbox flag. His heart beat faster, imagining what might await him in the back. He followed her, keeping a fair distance between them. Not much else he could do except run outside into more unknowns.

A curtain divided the shop, just like in Nikos' store. Here, the back room held a small work desk and boxes of inventory and supplies piled high. Ty held his breath as she opened another door, the one that in Nikos' store would have led to a storage room. Visions of an elaborate torture chamber played on his mental movie screen and vague fears danced under his skin. In fact, the door led to a neat and very ordinary room with a narrow bed, simple and ancient in style, wash bowl and water pitcher, and a storage trunk.

"It's yours to use for a few hours if you like," she said. She held the lamp aloft for him to see into all the corners. "I'd hope it's a nicer option than the park, but it's up to you."

Her manner was not in the least tense or hopeful. He was sure he could say no and leave. One more look at the bed, though, and he felt incapable of turning the offer down.

"Thank you. You're sure it's no trouble?"

"I'm certain. In fact, I'd feel guilty sending you back out into the night."

She smiled. He thought he saw a friendly wink in the shadows of the lamplight. Then she turned and closed the door before the fact that they were standing next to her bed had a chance to seem weird.

Within a minute he had his shoes off. He lay under one blanket and on top of the other, finding the thin mattress over the wood frame more comfortable than he'd expected. He gave the wretched Kalyptra a mental nod of thanks for the tattoo that helped him find what he sought. Mara hadn't left a lamp, but there was a small, high window that let in ample moonlight, and the warm blanket and soft pillow conspired to lull him to sleep immediately.

He dreamed a hodgepodge of monsters, chases, and betting games with outrageous stakes. The last variant found him at the back of the cave on Lake Marathon, dicing with two giants. If Ty lost they would suck the marrow from his bones while he still lived. He was nine-tenths of the way to losing a best-of-ten game when Naia came in from some adjacent tunnel and told him to stop playing and come to bed. Ty promised to continue the game another night and the giants went home.

He walked down the same tunnel where Naia had vanished, and came to a comfortable bedchamber. Though they were deep inside the cave, moonlight entered the chamber from somewhere above. He'd been right behind her, but she was somehow already abed when he got there. Judging from her bare shoulders, she wore nothing beneath the thick blankets. He undressed to his T-shirt and skivvies and she scooted over to accommodate him.

He lay down on his back, exhausted. Naia ran a finger across the scar at his throat, then leaned over and kissed the scar. Then she kissed the hollow of his throat. He wanted to sleep, but she kept moving down his body tracing the pattern of his tattoos, placing kisses against his skin rather than words as Kalyptra had done.

Her kisses inflamed him and he wanted to kiss her back, but he drifted off instead. He floated in that uncomfortable place between waking and sleeping, where the mind is aware, but the body doesn't obey. When she breathed a soft kiss against the tattoo at his inner thigh he became fully aroused, but no more wakeful.

She pulled at his T-shirt. He felt too tired to help her, and she had to tug it under his back to pull it off. She pushed down on his underwear. Her hands felt sharp on his skin. They were too narrow by half, more like claws, and scratched his hips. It felt as if she used progressive sets of limbs to push his shorts down—one set moving them off his waist, another down his thighs, another set to push them over his knees and off his feet. In his half-dream he couldn't remember if Naia normally had two sets of extremities or four. All he knew was that she wasn't what she had seemed. She'd fooled him into trusting her and now he'd pay for it. Panic sparked through the synapses in his brain, setting the alarms clanging, even as he tried to tell himself it was only a dream.

She straddled his hips and lifted his hands to her waist, but his arms fell back to the bed. Yes, she definitely had four sets of narrow limbs, like the tarantula he'd seen. The tarantula. He felt a jolt of adrenaline at the thought, but even that failed to wake him.

An upward pressure pulled against his navel, as if she were pulling loose some essential part of him from deep inside, sucking it out through his umbilicus. His heart pounded in strong, painful contractions as his panic increased.

Weakness and lassitude suddenly compounded his paralysis, in the way that shock and blood loss might drain away the horror of a deadly accident. His panic flowed out of him like his lifeblood. If Naia wanted something inside him so badly, she could have it, he thought. All he wanted was to sleep. He didn't care anymore whether he woke again or not.

A guttural cry that was no part of his dreams snapped him truly awake, leaving him disoriented. He was in a narrow bed in a darkened room. The back of the cave. No, the bedroom behind the apothecary.

He suddenly became aware of another presence in the room and looked down. The blanket had been pushed to his feet and a human-sized creature crouched above him, hunched over his belly. Its sucker-like mouth was wet. He felt a cold certainty its rubbery lips had just lifted from his navel.

The creature stared at the small window above him and cried out again. Ty echoed the cry, fully awake now. He scrambled back crabwise on the bed and pressed into the corner of the wall. The cold stone against his skin made him aware of his nakedness.

"The moon," the creature wailed.

The dark creature on the bed was thick-skinned and wore a sleeveless, yellow gown. The gown bulged in odd places, as if large tumors covered the body beneath. It seemed transfixed by something happening outside.

Ty pushed to his feet and jumped off the bed. The creature seemed not to notice. He grabbed his clothes from the floor and ran, not caring he was naked or if anyone lay in wait for him outside. He looked back once but Mara, or whatever she was, remained crouched on the bed, staring at the high window.

His ankle and calf had stiffened again with sleep, and his tattooed feet slowed him without the protection of his shoes. He ignored the pain and ran out the front door and right out of the village, gritting his teeth as he transitioned from paving stones to rocks and dried grass. He glanced once at the sky as he ran. The moon rested at the peak of the mountain, where it vibrated like the branches of a tree in a gale.

Ty made it to a large bush and ducked behind it. Hearing no sound of pursuit he looked up to the sky again, holding his clothes clutched to his chest. The shaking of the moon stopped. With a distant, grinding noise it jerked radically to the right. It fell from the sky and disappeared behind the mountain.

It didn't look natural, but he'd never witnessed moonset here. For all he knew, this was how it set every night. Judging by the lamps of the villagers who had been drawn outside by some instinct or impulse to stare at the sky, he guessed not.

With no moon, the night was as black as the cave at the lake. He dressed hurriedly, relieved to find that he'd gathered and held onto all of his clothes. His locksmith toolkit was a tight fit in his back pocket and had remained in place. Suddenly remembering the ribbon, he checked his front pocket in panic and found it undisturbed. He thought about burying the thing out here, but suspected there were creatures that could sense magic on an item. He wasn't letting anyone get a hold of that ribbon.

Once dressed, he started out again, moving as quickly as he could in what seemed the right direction for the village that held downtown and the park.

16

Queen Takes Pawn

The fresh stiffness in Ty's ankle and calf loosened again as he walked, but he made poor time. Fear of re-injuring his ankle in the inky darkness, or worse, losing his way, slowed him till he wondered if he should even continue trying. He looked back over his shoulder for the umpteenth time, though in the black shadows of the now moonless night he'd never see Mara or any other monster until they were on him. What he saw instead was the flash-bang of dawn in this world—the sky suddenly transforming from dark to light. He felt like a cockroach caught in the act of exploring when the kitchen light gets turned on for a midnight snack.

In the blue light of day, he saw the village nearer than he'd expected. Now he had a new problem—no cover as he approached. Mara had strained to see him until he talked to her, so he assumed Enyalius' powder had done nothing to negate his protections. He hoped so, anyway, but he didn't dare rely too heavily on them. Aletheia and

Enyalius had seen him easily enough despite his tattoos; others might too.

It took him little time to reach Naia's village. He climbed another small rise to get a better look and plan a route to the park. The sight Aletheia had given him did nothing to sort out the constant shifting of the landscape. Apparently, the fluidity here was more than just his human perceptions at work.

Seeing Erebus as the residents must see it, he found that, as he'd suspected last night, the buildings were all done in ancient style; columns, white marble and stone, statues, fountains, courtyards, and wells. Unlike the centuries-old historic buildings and temples in Athina, though, the entire village looked occupied and in good repair. At the center, there appeared to be a town square.

He scanned the village looking for the park. It took a minute to find as he hadn't expected to see it running up the shoulder of a small hill. The new location might help him, though, as he should easily be able to spot it from nearly anywhere, provided it didn't move again. Another advantage was that the village looked far more manageable than the whole city squished together that he previously saw—it looked to be only a few blocks between the edge of the village and the start of the park. He still didn't understand the physics of walking between villages when looking at Erebus one way, and dealing with one large city when looked at another, but then, it was only one of many things he didn't understand here.

Ty sighed deeply and descended the ridge. As he entered the village, he felt his mortality ringing as loud as a klaxon bell. He might have said a quick prayer if he hadn't known the gods slept. Maybe he should anyway—maybe one of the gods could dream him to safety.

He looked up often to make sure the park hadn't moved, but otherwise kept his eyes down, trying hard not to catch the attention of anyone or anything he passed. He was only a block from the nearest entrance to the park when he saw Enyalius coming down the dirt street toward him. The man wore a clean robe of pale blue and moved with no sign of injury from the arrow. He swung his head oddly from side to side, like an elephant swaying in stress.

The color of the robe had kept Ty from noticing the man until he was nearly on him. Ty hurried into a narrow gap between a merchant's cottage and a home, but what had looked like a gap turned out to be a dead end when the two buildings joined after only a few feet. Ty pressed against the wall, as if he could push himself into the stone, and held his breath.

Enyalius appeared at the opening. Level with him now, the man's head swung to the left and he looked directly at Ty. His eyes were as pale gold as two coins and Ty wondered if he'd developed some issue with his sight, maybe from the explosion. He tried seeing Enyalius with his native vision, but in the busy sidewalk of his own world's downtown the man disappeared altogether. Enyalius' lips moved and Ty heard indistinct words, muttered like the ravings some old men above spouted, lost in some past no one else saw.

He crept from his hiding place, staring at the man's retreating back. Small spots of red dotted the dirt where he walked, as if his feet bled. Ty suspected he could've stood right in the man's path and still not have been noticed.

Impressions rose like bile: the coal held to his eye last night, the choking, the explosion, Mara, Kairos' thugs. Relief at not being recaptured made his knees feel weak. He should be running, should be hiding—but he could only stand and watch Enyalius walking away.

When other pedestrians blocked Ty's view he finally began to move again, first at a walk, then a run.

He didn't stop until he was well into the park. Zigzagging from one landmark to another as he recognized them, he found the brook and followed it downstream until he saw the bluff. He cut toward Aletheia's home and edged his way to it, trying to stay as hidden as possible by the denser sections of foliage. Her tall, stately front doors stood open. There was no light from within, but in daytime none was needed. He crept into the entry hall of the high-ceilinged home. The house had an abandoned feel, as if that could be a tangible thing, and there was no sound except his footsteps on stone. Reaching the elegant living room, he saw couches overturned, and crystal and onyx decorations shattered against the floor. Peering into the dining room, he saw more broken items, but no bloodstains or bodies. The skin between his shoulder blades tingled. Whoever had vandalized the home could be watching it even now.

Ty left quickly and headed back to the brook. He searched the stream for any sign of the key, unsure what he'd do if he found it. Take it to the surface? Get a message to Naia? Not that he owed her anything, he reminded himself. She may have placed a love spell on him out of fear, but his actions had been the result of an immediate threat of death. If she had feelings for him because of his tattoos, it wasn't his doing. And if a love spell *had* been in his power to cast, he wouldn't have, not even for his own safety.

Realizing he was nearing the edge of the park he stopped and looked around. He hadn't passed the grassy area, the bridge, or Naia. He headed back the other way, certain he'd missed the bridge by cutting through the park from Aletheia's. If he could find the bridge, he might find the grate to the sewers. The surface might be no safer than Erebus if the New Order got the upper hand, but at least he'd be back in his own world and out of this insanity. The thought of abandoning Naia, alone and hunted, made him queasy, but anger at her manipulation followed quickly. He wondered if the spell was permanent or if it would fade in time.

Rounding a bend of the river, he came to the grassy area where he'd started the painting, though he felt certain he couldn't have missed this on his previous pass. Halfway across the lawn he heard a commotion on the dirt path to his right, a clattering and thudding coming closer. Whatever made the noise hadn't emerged into view yet. He didn't feel sure he could make it across the broad lawn or over brook into the trees beyond in time. He turned toward the path. The sound came from his right. To his left, dense bushes lined this side of the path. He hurried to the hedge only to remember they were spiny spurge and thorny caper bushes.

The sound grew louder; he had no time left. He crouched and pushed against the vegetation. From his vantage, he could see only a small swath of the path. He strained to see with his second sight, but saw only shadows of daytime traffic approaching and passing like images in a flickering zoetrope. The noise became more distinct: a clatter of wheels, a soft pounding of running animals, a stomping of booted feet.

He felt a sting of adrenaline in his thighs, hands, and jaw as four male lions appeared, two running down the road and one to either side, bounding through the park. All four moved oddly but he wasn't about to take time to analyze it. He pushed his shoulder and hip further into the thorn bushes. Tips pricked through his jeans and into his skin. Behind the lions, a regiment of perhaps twenty uniformed soldiers came into view, and behind them a large, ornate carriage drawn by eight harnessed creatures that looked for all the world like living gargoyles.

It didn't matter if anything else was coming. He'd seen enough. Ty pushed head-first into the needle-sharp undergrowth. Rough branches and sharp thorns snagged his clothes and caught his skin with long, hooked points. He held his hands and arms in front of his face, letting them take the worst punishment. One barb escaped to whip across the side of his cheek and he felt a drop of blood slide down his face like the brush of a finger.

He strained to hear the progress of the lions, but their softly padded loping vanished beneath the clatter of the oncoming procession. A strong whiff of animal drifted to him, a mingled scent of warm cornmeal, salt, and dank fur. He hunkered lower. He imagined himself another branch—unmoving, camouflaged, silent. No breath. No heartbeat.

The animal smell came from the swath of grass behind him, toward the brook, where he was most exposed. By the sound of things, the carriage was drawing near. The lions must be even closer.

The bushes parted violently. He had time for one panicked thought, wondering if his human scent had given him away, or the smell of blood from his scratches, or maybe some minute noise, before a tawny head twice the size of his own rammed through the branches nearest him. He twisted to face the lion and shoved back into the thorns only to find himself blocked by the trunk of the plant. Huge jaws snapped around his bruised left shoulder and tore him from his hiding place. The thorns clung to his skin, hooking and holding, but the pain went almost unnoticed next to the feel of enormous teeth pressing into his flesh.

Once out of the bushes, the beast stood on its hind legs. It walked upright, the middle joint bending forward, like a human's knees rather than backward, and its height left Ty's feet dangling off the ground. It hugged him to its furred chest with front paws as large as Ty's face, still holding his shoulder in its mouth. Numb with fear, he couldn't distinguish the pressure against his skin from punctures. The lion strode out to the path, Ty swinging from its mouth like a rag doll. The carriage had pulled to a halt opposite them.

Warm saliva soaked Ty's T-shirt and a thin trickle of moisture ran down his arm—whether saliva or blood, he didn't know. The animal's strange joints gave it a lumbering, bouncing stride, causing the teeth to gouge painfully into his flesh with each step. Ty gasped and grunted. He might have yelled. His pulse pounded in his ears and fear blunted his ability to think clearly, but his brain stubbornly cataloged every detail, looking for any element that might save his life.

The lion carried him past the guards. They were male and female, judging by body shape, dressed alike in livery of maroon and gold, all on average perhaps a head shorter than Ty. Each wore snow-white gloves and a white porcelain mask that covered their faces from hairline to chin.

The masks gave them a disturbing sameness and a sinister anonymity, but it was worse when the lion passed near one and Ty saw into the eyeholes of the mask; nothing lay beyond. Infinite nothingness stretched out forever in the pits where eyes should have been. More than shadow, more than darkness, more even than emptiness. It seemed as if the blackness beyond the porcelain mask didn't end at the back of the skull, but began there, a thought so horrifying Ty thought his bladder might release.

Beyond the lines of guards stood four double rows of gargoyles. Where the guards were smaller than Ty, the gargoyles were both taller and broader, eye to eye with him as the lion jounced past. Their skin had the appearance of gray-green leather, thick and tough. They were identical to the last detail, naked with long, thin tails. They lacked genitalia, but had male facial features and bare, muscular chests. Great fangs the color of their skin protruded onto their lower lips. Their harnesses were made of thick, black leather straps, and at the back of each was a length of chain that hooked into yokes attached to the tongue of the carriage. There were no lines to steer them and no driver sat on the carriage seat.

The elegance of the carriage, deep maroon with gold inlays, exceeded anything Ty had yet seen in Erebus. The lion carried him to the side door. The window had no curtain, but whatever waited inside did so behind a gauzy veil of red and gold. A cold suspicion contracted his stomach.

One soldier stood at either side of the carriage, and the one closest to Ty opened the door as the lion approached. Ty doubted Enyalius was rich or powerful enough to be behind this but whoever was in that carriage, foe or not, he didn't want to be in there with them. He kicked at the side with one foot and clawed with a hand at the doorjamb. The lion easily shoved harder and Ty's joints strained. Forced to choose between broken bones or giving up his resistance, he let himself be roughly shoved inside.

The guard pushed the door closed behind him and Ty stumbled forward. Afraid of pitching into the material that tented down from ceiling to floor—and more afraid of landing on what lay behind it—he threw his weight backward, half-falling against the door. He righted himself. There were no benches he could see, only the red and gold gauze veiling the majority of the interior. Free now of the lion, he probed at his left shoulder. His hand came away bloody.

"Kneel." The voice came from behind the gauze. In stereo. Feminine.

Ty dropped to his knees, his suspicion confirmed. Still, the fact that the queen was in Erebus and traveling with such a bizarre entourage made his mind reel. A slim hand pulled the gauze aside. A bench, padded in rich velvet, ran down the center of the carriage, though it stopped short of touching either end. Sitting on the bench, facing him, was one half of his conjoined queen. The other, by necessity, faced away.

She gazed at him from a face sharp as an icicle and beautiful as a snowflake, her features finely sculpted. He'd never seen her in person as she seldom left her residence, but he knew her two faces were identical, though only one looked directly at him. He'd never heard the queen's age and couldn't guess—perhaps older than her youthful complexion, or younger than her bearing. Her pale skin seemed almost paper-white compared to the olive shade normal in Ellada.

The sisters wore a single gown of gold brocade, fitted to accommodate their wide torso and four arms. At the queen's throat hung a shiny strip of copper-colored metal. He couldn't tell from here if the other side of her single neck sported a similar adornment for the other sister. On their fused heads—which divided only slightly at the crown—short, circular diadems balanced. To the inside of each coronet rested a separate narrow circlet of gold. Half a dozen thin, gold rods arced up from the circlets and then curved down over each of the twin's foreheads, like an ant-beetle's multiple antennae, ending in stunningly crafted starbursts of varying sizes. Set within the starbursts of the backward facing sister, Ty saw small mirrors. And in those mirrors, he saw his own awe-struck reflection.

He bowed as best he could from his knees.

"Show me your arms."

He looked up in confusion and lifted his arms out to his sides. The sister facing him gave a slight "come-here" wave of her fingers. He extended his arms toward her, palms up. With her two hands she took both his wrists. Fused to her sister at skull, neck, back and hip, she was unable to tip her head forward; instead she raised his arms and lowered her eyes to examine what she held.

The scars were still invisible here in Erebus, and only shadows in his second vision. He squinted while the queen studied his wrists. He saw no second sight of her, which made sense if the twins looked the same on the surface as here. He wondered to which world they truly belonged.

"Yes. We have found you." Her words, spoken from two mouths in one voice, explained why the queen was usually referred to in the singular. He wondered what she saw there on his wrists, in the marks that even Enyalius had been unable to discern.

"What do you know of the moon?" she asked.

Of all the questions she could have asked, this was the last he expected.

"I...uh... Nothing, your Majesty."

"Were you there when it was pulled from the sky?"

"I saw it fall, but I was in the countryside. I have no idea what happened." It sounded too silly to say he'd been unsure at the time if it had been a normal moonset.

"Who was responsible?"

"I have no idea," he said. "Majesty," he added belatedly.

"You are mortal," her voices said. She spoke so coolly there was little inflection to any of her words. "And yet you were here when this unprecedented thing happened. We see a connection."

As if everything he'd been embroiled in already wasn't enough, now the queen suspected him of destroying the moon?

"I swear on my life, I don't know anything about it."

"Where is the Daughter of Love?"

Phrased more vaguely, Ty might have denied knowing Naia. Obviously the queen knew more about his recent doings than he wished.

"I don't know. I really don't. We were separated last night."

"Will you see her again?"

He'd been trying to leave Erebus when the lion grabbed him. He could say what he wanted to say, bluster about his resolve that he would never see her again. Over the past few days, though, his hubris and his defenses had been beaten, trampled, and intimidated right out of him. He didn't know if escaping Naia's love spell was even possible. The way his gut twisted when he thought of her, he suspected it wasn't. And even if he could, even as angry as he was at her, could he really have abandoned her, left her to her enemies?

He gave the queen his honest answer. "I don't know."

"Then we must summon her."

She touched the copper strip at her throat. As she ran her finger lengthwise down it, the metal produced a chime as loud and shivering as if she'd run a wet finger around a crystal glass. The carriage door opened immediately, the soldier alert, as if expecting danger. Seeing nothing amiss, the porcelain-faced guard bowed.

"Send a lion to find the Daughter of Love, then take us to the palace."

Momus became dully aware of a repetitive thumping against his ribs. His head rocked side to side with each impact. Slowly, he comprehended that the thumps were kicks to his body. His eyes opened. It was daylight. He lay on a floor. A memory of battle returned, and he grabbed the kicking foot hard with one hand.

"Finally," someone said. It sounded like Enyalius, though the patient arrogance was gone from his voice, replaced with an uncharacteristic petulance. "Get up," he said. "We have work to do."

Momus rolled to his side and pushed to his knees, where he stayed a long moment until the bells in his head silenced and the world stopped rotating many times faster than it should. He recognized Enyalius' home, though noticed it was now missing two walls. He lumbered to his feet and saw that more than Enyalius' home had been altered; the man looked younger, his facial features almost those of a different man. Stranger still were his eyes, they'd turned almost entirely gold. The color looked even more prominent when the light caught them at a certain angle.

"What's happened?" he asked carefully.

"Nothing. Everything," Enyalius said. "The dancer danced, the player played and the moon fell out of the sky." He said it with angry impatience, as if Momus should have known these things.

While grappling with the centaur last night—Momus assumed it had been last night—he had seen Enyalius shot with an arrow. The rapid healing didn't surprise him. Demi-gods—or whatever the man might be—had varied talents after all, but Selia may have tipped the arrow with poison. Perhaps that's what had caused the golden sheen in Enyalius' eyes.

"Oh, well, so you say. So you say," he answered mildly, wondering how best to proceed.

If Enyalius was mad, Momus would be next in line to take his place as head of the New Order, but it had never been his way to be conspicuous. He carried nearly as much power and far less risk as the right-hand man. It seemed in his best interests to try and piece the broken egg-shells of the man's mind back together. As soon as possible, too, before anyone else saw him like this.

Momus rubbed the left side of his forehead. A hoof-shaped indentation depressed the skin there, and possibly the skull beneath. His pounding headache made it hard to concentrate. He fished in the breast pocket of his T-shirt and came up with the flattened stub of a cigar. Checking his pants pockets, he was unable to find his coal with which to light it. He pushed the thinned end of the cigar between his teeth anyway, bits of tobacco falling onto his tongue through the splits in the wrapping.

"Perhaps you should come to my apartment for a while," he suggested, talking around the cigar. "It got a bit wild here last night, eh? Maybe let things cool off a bit."

Enyalius seemed malleable to suggestion at the moment, which was good. The man looked around his home as if not recognizing it, the gold reflection in his eyes glinting as his head swiveled. He was dangerous enough when he had all his wits; Momus was going to have to be very careful now. But, then, he was always careful.

His ties to powerful ancestors were so far removed he might as well be mortal. Few in Erebus could have risen so high without impressive bloodlines behind them. But it was that, if anything, that pushed him.

He had spun a small but strong web, and he had caught himself a fat fly. One whose opinion of himself was so lofty that he barely listened when Momus spoke; yet Momus' words floated like pollen, dusting everything. And if Momus' plans for the New Order bore fruit, his bloodlines would never matter again. Maybe the man's madness could even work to his advantage.

"Come on then," he said, motioning for Enyalius to follow. "It isn't very far. Ol' Momus will take good care of you."

17

The Space Between the Stars

The carriage started forward without the slightest lurch, and the queen pulled the curtain around herself. The sisters sat bolt upright within the gauzy tent, visible to Ty only in outline, the front-facing sister seeming to stare straight at him. Ty had been told to kneel and never instructed otherwise. Hoping he wasn't committing some major infraction of protocol, he finally shifted around on his knees and watched the progression of their passage out the carriage window.

The soldier standing on the sideboard composed most of what he could see. She stared eyelessly in at him as he stared out. The carriage moved with astounding speed, the land passing by in a blur, but he caught glimpses of the gargoyles occasionally when the road curved to the left. They ran upright in their harnesses, bony elbows swinging together, powerful leg muscles flexing and extending rapidly with unvarying rhythm, their long strides perfectly matched.

No one had chastised him for changing position, and there seemed no indication that they would arrive at their destination anytime soon.

He shifted to a cross-legged position, too low now to see anything but sky out the window.

They traveled on for what might have been an hour or so. Ty watched the queen's rigid, unmoving outline and wondered if she might be asleep or in some sort of trance. Looking at their unnatural stillness, he had the strange feeling the sisters might not be in their bodies anymore.

Out the window a mountain came into view, tall enough that he could see it while still seated on the floor, though he couldn't see the top of it. They circumvented it for so long that he thought it must be Olimbos.

The mountain dropped behind the window and the land flattened out again. A few minutes later a great, jarring bump sent the carriage flying. Ty braced his hands against the walls. Instead of the crash and roll of the hard landing he expected, there was nothing at all. No descent, no rumble of wheels. A glance at the queen showed she still hadn't moved. Ty cautiously relaxed his arms. He wanted to get to his knees for a better look outside, but decided facing the unnerving eyeholes of the guard on the sideboard was bad enough without also seeing why they seemed to have left the ground.

A moment later, the sky grew black. It remained dark outside and he wondered if night had suddenly fallen. He didn't want to think about the other option.

Over time the darkness and quiet, combined with little sleep the past few nights, conspired against his vigilance. He must have dozed, for he couldn't have said how much later he felt the gentle bump of wheels meeting the ground. Either the moon was still absent from the sky or they had come to a place beyond any moons. The vastness beyond the carriage window and a sky full of stars suggested the latter.

The vehicle rolled to a stop and the door opened. Ty stepped out between two rows of waiting soldiers and wondered if they were the same ones from the park and, if so, how they had traveled here. Above him, the night sky looked close enough to be a blanket of black velvet dotted with foil stars. It covered the sky in all directions, right down to the horizon. Those horizons, he realized, were horrifyingly close. He stood on a flat rock, perhaps the size of a few city blocks, floating in space. The air felt chill but not cold, and more importantly, despite all logic to the contrary, felt like air.

Ahead, at the end of a long rocky path, stood an enormous palace. He stared at it, trying to place what memory it evoked. Fireworks, he realized. The gold ones that showered down like fairy dust. The palace seemed to be made of thousands of those, so many that the walls— contoured as they were to towers and windows—seemed constantly drifting toward the ground. He tried narrowing his eyes but, again, found no parallel in his own world.

Globes of light the size of his palm bobbed in the air between him and the palace, bouncing slowly, almost as if restless with excitement or joy. There were hundreds of the little lamps, throwing their small pools of light. The stars, hanging so close overhead, looked like millions of globe children, floating along behind the lights like myriad goslings following their mothers.

A soldier fell in behind Ty, the female from the sideboard, he thought. He heard the whisper of the curtain and the creak of the carriage step, and looked back to see the queen stepping down. His guard pushed him roughly to the side and held him by one arm as the sisters swept past, one body walking forward and the other walking smoothly backwards in perfect synchronicity. The guard prodded Ty to follow.

The lights bobbed faster, swarming around and above the queen, shooting inside as she crossed the threshold. The light from the little lamps sparkled off the flowing gold walls. Ty glanced back through the door. The remaining lions were bounding off to some destination of their own. The gargoyles stood stoically in their traces, so motionless he wondered if they had de-animated into the stone they so strongly resembled.

Soldiers stationed themselves around the palace, though Ty couldn't imagine what threat could ever track the queen here. She swept onward, out of sight, followed by about a third of the guards and servants while others fanned out to various posts.

Three guards stayed with Ty, including the female from the sideboard who guided him to the right and up a set of stairs. His sprained ankle and bruised calf gave a sharp pang on the first step and he grabbed the stone banister. The downward motion of the walls as he ascended the stairs left him dizzy.

They topped the stairs and the guards led him to a room richly furnished with a large bed, a couch, and a few chairs. A handful of the little dancing globes followed him in and placed themselves strategically about the room. He'd heard no one but the queen speak, and it surprised him when the guard addressed him. Her voice, neither masculine nor feminine, boomed softly, as if coming to him from a great distance. "The queen will call for you when she's ready."

He sat in a chair near the window and watched the door. The palace was no warmer than the outside had been and his T-shirt, torn and tattered by the thorns and the lion, offered little protection. After sitting for only a few minutes, he wrapped himself in a comforter from the bed. He paced his confines, investigating the corners, windows, and alcoves, bookshelves and the attached bathing room.

He chose an old, leather-bound book from a bookshelf. Sitting back in a surprisingly comfortable padded chair, he began reading about the ancient political history of Ellada. A couple of hours later he paced again, ending up in the bathroom. It was similar to Naia's, with a sunken tub, though here, in the cold, the water steamed to the ceiling in great, white clouds. Cold drops dripped down into the pool like a soft, slow rain and he wondered what kept the water hot.

He used the facilities and found the same manner of pit toilet as at Naia's, though made of gold as well as marble. Again, he felt too vulnerable to bathe, but he pulled off his shirt and inspected his wounds as best he could with no mirror. He was unable to bend his neck far enough to see the torn flesh above his collarbone, where he'd been skinned by Kairos' men, but his fingers told him it was scabbing and not unusually swollen or warm.

He checked his right upper arm and left shoulder where the lion had bitten him. The skin had been punctured in two places, fortunately not deep enough that infection seemed likely. The new bruises were dark against the older, brightly colored purple and yellow where the gryphon had knocked him to the ground and used him as a launch pad. At least the swelling in his ankle was mostly gone. The laceration and bruising on his right calf from the bull was still the worst of his wounds, but he'd soaked and treated it in his bath at home. Using a towel and rough cut bar of soap from the side of the tub, he washed his new wounds and pulled his torn T-shirt back on.

Memories of his various attacks couldn't help but make him think of Naia. He wondered if she'd escaped safely last night. If the queen's lion had found her yet. If it would treat her as roughly as it had him. He tried to tell himself he didn't care.

Returning to the other room, he picked out another, far older looking book, titled *Discourses on the Soul: The Philosophy of Will Versus Fate*. He nodded off only a few pages into it and jumped when his door opened. One of the male guards appeared, not with a summons from the queen, but with a meal of unidentifiable meats and sauces and a fresh pitcher of water.

Left alone again, he ate the meal gratefully, finding the food delicious. Once he'd eaten, he looked around for something new to distract him. The rest of the books were as dry as the two he'd flipped through, so he tried Will vs. Fate again, but found himself unable to focus on the words. It must have been close to two days since he had slept more than an hour or two at a time. Still wrapped in the comforter, he lay down on the bed.

He woke later, unsure how much time had passed but suspecting it had been significant. Sitting up, confused and disoriented, he rubbed at eyes crusted with sleep. Someone had opened his door: the female guard, the same one from the carriage again, he thought, though they were all alike enough that he could easily be wrong.

"The queen will see you now," she said, in her echoing, androgynous voice.

Ty unwound himself from the bedspread and followed her out. The two guards standing outside his door trailed behind. He followed his porcelain-masked guard down the stairs and through a series of elaborate rooms and halls until she pushed open a wooden door hinged in some mystifying way to its flowing golden frame. She stood back to let him in. He felt suddenly self-conscious in his dirty and torn clothes, but it wasn't like he'd been given a choice. The door closed behind him. Apparently, the queen didn't require a guard.

The walls in this room were the same fairy-dust gold as the rest of the palace, but the furnishings and decorations were rich, deep blues, light sky-blue, and midnight black, all with a celestial theme. Anthropomorphized suns and moons had been embroidered into the upholstery, draperies, and carpets along with small silver stars. An elegant mobile of golden constellations hung from the center of the room and a grandfather clock showed the face of the sun with the hands ticking through midmorning. If the clock was right, he'd slept a full night and then some, though the landscape outside the windows remained as black as when he'd arrived. The queen was seated in the center of the room on a richly padded bench facing a couch.

Ty barely registered any of these details. Sitting on the deep blue couch, facing one half of the queen, was Naia. She rose to her feet when he entered, surprise lighting her face. He saw her in gown and sandals here, with no shadows of the contemporary clothes of his world.

His first impulse was to cross the room and grab her in a great bear hug, but he pushed the urge down, reminding himself of the artifice of her love spell on him.

"I'm glad to see you're okay," he said, walking to her.

The emotion that had changed her face on seeing him and made his heart beat a little faster faded. She matched his reserve. "Are you well?" she asked, looking first at the scratch on his face, then the bloodied shoulder of his shirt.

He nodded. "I'm okay. Where did you go last night?"

"I stayed water for much of the time. I was about to change when the moon was ripped out of the sky, so I flowed along the drainages and streams until Enyo and Pemphredo's envoy found me."

The lion, he assumed, and wondered how the lion had been able to locate her in her water form. She'd nodded toward the queen when she said the names, but he'd known the twins only as Queen Enoméni. Those names, though, Enyo and Pemphredo, tickled something from childhood memory. It slipped away before he could grab onto it. Abruptly aware of the queen watching them, he fell silent. Naia returned to her place on the sofa. He sat at the other end of the smallish couch.

Ty wondered what hierarchy existed between Naia and the queen. Naia was a demi-goddess, daughter of the oldest of all the gods. The queen, though, was obviously more than the human conjoined twins he had always believed them to be. They were impossible to read— their posture rigid by necessity, faces as implacable as ice. Naia sat with her hands folded in her lap, her bearing nearly as stiff as theirs. If he had to guess, he'd say Naia's manner indicated at least a measure of subservience. Or fear.

"The two of you have been in our visions," the queen said in her dual voice, "since the moon was stolen from the sky. We wish to know why."

Visions? Ty thought.

Naia answered for them both. "I cannot say, except that I had naught to do with the moon. If Ty says he had nothing to do with it either, then I believe him."

Ty noted her lack any honorific and reassessed their standing.

"He does say this, and we also believe him," the queen said. "No mortal could have accomplished such a feat. No half god, either, which leaves little doubt as to who could have done this thing, though even one of the gods would risk madness. We do not believe you are acting in concert with a rogue god, but you are connected somehow."

The scale of events seemed to keep outpacing Ty's ability to keep up with them. He tried harder to put everything together. *Enyo and Pemphredo.* The tickle wouldn't go away. Not goddesses, he was sure. He sorted through the other stories from childhood. The connection rushed in, like a tide suddenly turning. *Enyo, Pemphredo, and Deino.* His belief that his queen might ever have been human shattered. It shocked him into blurting it out. "You're the Graeae."

Naia had used their names, so it must not be a secret, but the tight apprehension that flashed across her face told him that what he had observed in her earlier had indeed been fear of these sisters. If Naia feared them, they moved immediately to the scariest end of the continuum of things that frightened him.

"We are the Graeae," his queen said.

They were two of the three, anyway. He remembered Naia telling him the third sister had been killed by these two when she went mad.

"When our sister spelled your gods," they continued, "we felt it our duty to oversee mankind on their behalf until they could be found and cured. It is why we came seeking the two of you. If someone in Erebus is strong enough and mad enough to destroy the moon, then we must intervene to ensure the protection of the mortals above. With whom have you had recent dealings?"

"Selia launched an attack last night on a man named Enyalius," Naia said. "We witnessed it."

"We are not familiar with this name," the Graeae said in their odd harmony.

"An alias, perhaps," Naia said. "One he gave me long ago, when he first pretended to be my ally. He recently proved himself false. He is the head of the New Order. Was. Selia killed him last night. I'd suspect the New Order of taking revenge on Selia's moon for his death, but I can't believe that they have revived and controlled one of the gods. If so, they would have already defeated us."

Ty noted that Naia made no mention of the key or her role as its guardian. He thought of the previous night, the strength of the old man after the arrow skewered his heart. Naia hadn't seen him stand again, but Ty had.

"Enyalius didn't die," Ty interjected. He glanced to Naia, unsure if he should have shared this in front of the sisters.

"Are you sure?" Naia asked.

He nodded. "I saw him near the park, just before I was brought here. The arrow should have killed him, but the only sign of injury I could see were that his feet were bleeding." He paused to let the next bit sink in. "He was raving like a madman."

Ty watched the implications come together for Naia. She had told him before that the only two gods unaccounted for were Ares and Prometheus, and her messenger had seen Prometheus' dead body on Olimbos.

"Ares," she whispered. She reached across the couch and gripped his hand in excitement, wanting him to confirm what she didn't dare believe.

"Prometheus' death was never established," the queen countered. "This Enyalius may be either Ares or Prometheus."

"Charon seemed certain of Prometheus' death when he delivered my father's message to me," Naia said. "The body was gone by the time he descended the mountain, but the marks where it had lain indicated it had been dragged away by predators."

The queen looked thoughtful. "Whatever his identity, it seems the one called Enyalius is the one we seek. If he is mad now as well as amnesic, then we must find him soon."

"To what end?" Naia said, sounding suddenly more afraid of the possibilities than of the Graeae. "You can't destroy one of the gods," her voice rose at the end, pleading. "He might be able to lead us to the other gods, or to the cure for their memories."

"Whether this is Ares or Prometheus, or whether some other god has woken and emerged, they are dangerous," the Graeae said. "We have sworn to protect humanity in the gods' stead. This we will do, however we must."

Naia slid from the couch onto her knees.

"Enyo, Pemphredo, I beg you. This is the closest we've come to finding the gods since their memories were taken. The two of you are the only ones I know powerful enough to help. Perhaps if you could examine Ares, you could divine the nature of the spell your sister cast. Perhaps he could help us find the others. It's a chance to make right all the wrong that Deino caused."

Ty saw both fear and determination in her face. He guessed that pushing the Graeae too far would be unwise on a scale he couldn't even imagine.

The queen considered for a long, silent moment. Ty wondered if the sisters were communing somehow with each other, or if they were searching the future and past for answers, as the Graeae were said to do.

"Will this Enyalius contact you again?" they said at last.

"I don't know." She reseated herself carefully at the edge of the couch. "Now that he's exposed himself as my enemy, it's hard to say what he may do. If he believes himself nothing more than the head of the New Order and me his chief opponent, I suspect that our paths will continue to cross. I also recently uncovered two of his agents. I might be able to find them again, if they don't come for me first."

If Enyalius' madness was permanent, then his next move was anyone's guess. If not, Ty was sure he'd never stop pursuing Naia until he had the key, though she still failed to mention that component to the Graeae.

"Very well," the sisters said. "Tell my guards all you know so they may aid in the search. We will summon the Daughter of the Moon to us and question her. You will start by seeking these allies you mentioned. If you find the god, bring him to us. We will avoid killing him if we can."

Find and capture a mad, amnesic god and bring him to the Graeae. "Gamoto," Ty swore under his breath, not caring who might be offended by the vulgarity.

The queen rose and paced to a window then paced back again without turning, smoothly alternating from one body leading to the other. Both lifted a finger to each mouth as she contemplated. "We may summon you again after we have spoken with the Daughter of the Moon. For now we will return you to Erebus."

Without waiting for an answer she stroked the metal at her throat. From this angle, Ty could see that both bodies performed the same action. The metal chimed and the door opened immediately. The forward facing queen pivoted them to look at Ty and Naia, while the other sister observed them through her mirrors. The Graeae addressed the guard. "Prepare the carriage."

Ty followed Naia from the celestial room while she related the account of the attack at Enyalius' home to the female guard. They were led from the palace out into the void of space, the little globe lights bobbing along beside them. The gargoyles and the carriage waited at the end of the walkway, and stars still winked in the vast black sky all around the speck of rock on which they stood. He tried to take in too much of the heavens at once and vertigo nearly stole his balance.

"Did they bring you here in their carriage?" Naia asked Ty.

"Yes. Why? How did you get here?"

"The lion brought me."

She didn't explain further. He tried to imagine her riding the lion through the stars and failed.

When the guard opened the carriage door Ty could see that the queen's bench had been removed, leaving nothing but an open floor of polished wood. He and Naia sat against the back wall. The guards took up their positions on the sideboards.

The wheels clattered over the gravel and rock of whatever made up this tiny island of substantiality. A moment later he felt the carriage leave the ground. He didn't envy the guards their vantage, with nothing but a narrow sideboard and a grip bar between them and the void.

Neither guard seemed to be taking notice of them, but Ty asked Naia none of his dozen questions. She stayed silent as well, looking as overwhelmed as he felt. He wanted to take her hand, but didn't.

They passed the length of the trip in silence.

The sisters sat alone in the celestial room—or as alone as they could ever be. Enyo raised her left hand and Pemphredo her right. Together, they unbuttoned their dress from neck to shoulder. The spell holding in Deino released in concert with the release of tension on the fabric.

Their sister's face emerged from the side of their joined neck. In their mirrors the dead, gray flesh ballooned out like a fungus growing in rapid sequence. Lumps and ridges resolved into the mold-gray features of forehead and cheekbones, nose and chin. A short neck protruded like a mushroom stalk. Deino's eyes were open and unseeing, her face forever reflecting the horror of her murder. Fully emerged, her head fell limply toward their shoulder.

"What if the rogue god has regained his memory and remembers we were the ones who spelled them all into forgetfulness?" Enyo said. She didn't need to speak out loud but she enjoyed the sound of her singular voice, something she never exercised in public. "What if he destroyed the moon to lure us into a trap?"

"If he'd recovered his memory, he would have come straight to us and not bothered with the moon," Pemphredo replied. "The fact that he sought retribution against Selia is proof he's unaware of his identity. He fights with the children of gods instead of his real enemies."

Pemphredo wished to stand, Enyo did not. Releasing Deino's corpse had eased the pressure on their neck, though, and Pemphredo contented herself with pulling their shoulders down and stretching their neck upward an inch or so, the slight stretch their only possible movement above the shoulders. Pemphredo continued.

"This is to our advantage. One god will be easy to kill, and he's given us the perfect excuse. When we absorb his power, we gain back some of what we lost from Deino. And with that we'll be more likely to find the rest. Once we find them and have the key, we can kill them in their sleep, one at a time."

Pemphredo relied on the certainties of the past. Enyo knew the restless ambiguity of the future. She would not rush into finding and killing this god without knowing more about his current state of mind. "Do you see anything new since meeting the mortal and Eros' daughter?"

Pemphredo was silent for a moment, sifting images she'd seen a thousand times. "No."

Neither of them were surprised. The information they had learned today was more likely to show a shift in time's future tide than to reveal more of the past.

Enyo closed her eyes and searched for new futures. Even before they had killed Deino, the gods had been difficult to see clearly. The dramatic diminishment of her and her sister's power following Deino's murder remained an unexpected and unfortunate frustration.

"I see only what led us to the demi-goddess and the mortal. A mortal pushes up against the underside of the world and all of the land heaves. A drop of water shines with a hundred refracted possibilities, meaning that the path of Love's daughter is not set. I cannot see if either of them will help or hinder us. And of the gods, only that it was indeed a star which pulled down the moon."

"Still, it is more than we had before. A gods' mask has slipped."

Pemphredo overrode her sister's wishes and stood. They sidestepped the bench and Pemphredo walked backward, as was her preference, until Enyo was at the window. Pemphredo studied the darkness outside. Despite what others thought, she could see perfectly well through her sister's eyes; the mirrors helped them both with peripheral vision only.

"And if this god is setting a trap for us?" Enyo said, coveting the infinity of universes surrounding them every bit as much as Pemphredo did. "Will Deino have been worth it for a mere quarter century?"

"I would rather a chance to rule all this than live in immortal obsolescence." Pemphredo gestured to the room but saw the stars. "And so would you. This is the first god to surface since our attack, and he has done nothing more potent than reveal himself to us. I still see the rest as a cluster of stars in the darkness. They are together, blind and lost, and no threat to us."

Enyo turned them both, moving away from the darkness outside. "And the marks on the mortal's wrists?"

Seeing the scars, Pemphredo had seen their making, though the maker had remained hidden to her. "The right is potential. A hole to be filled. Perhaps it pushes him to actions he might not otherwise undertake. The scars on the left are for the maker of the marks to track him. We now have a way to follow him as well. We must make certain to guide events so that any changes he sets in motion are the ones we seek."

18

Emergence

It had been a very long time since the god had last been to Erebus. Coming here was a risk, especially with the Graeae afoot, and it wouldn't have been done now for any reason but this one.

Knee-deep in the brook, fifteen or twenty fish of various sizes and colors bumped the slender ankles of his disguised body and nibbled at his delicate toes. At last, one answered the call that glowed in the god's eye like a lighthouse beacon. He reached into the water and lifted the slippery, scaly body out.

"Don't struggle little friend," he said gently, "this won't take long." The fish calmed, though its mouth and gills gaped, working to siphon water from a dry world. He held it by the tail, head down, and milked the soft, slimy belly with feminine hands until the fish vomited an achingly familiar object from its hard-lipped mouth. He placed the fish back into the brook to swim away, and plucked the item from beneath the water where it had fallen between two small rocks.

Strange that it was a key in more than one sense. No attempts at magic had restored his lost memories, no matter what he'd tried. Not until a dream had begun to repeat, a dream of constructing something, always with the same few elements. Finally, toying with them during waking hours, combining moon dust and midnight with deep ocean and blood, bits of memory had begun to surface. There had followed a strong urge to sketch using the colors of the elements; more and more often a gryphon emerged in the sketches. That had been nearly two years ago, and the start of the long road back.

He turned the key over and over with the delicate fingers of his stolen body, studying the still vivid colors, remembering the effort to make a thing that could never be copied, something worthy of safeguarding gods. A sense of wholeness beyond words suffused him at being reunited with the item. The work was not done, but with the key in hand once again, the goal was a god-sized stride closer. Genuine hope filled him for the first time in a long time that at last he might be on the path to waking and curing the others.

19

Reunion

The carriage touched down and Ty watched with relief as solid ground rumbled past. It was daytime in Erebus, and he soon picked out familiar landmarks. A short while later the carriage pulled to a stop in the park. The topography seemed to have flip-flopped again, this time in a mirror image, but he thought they were in the exact spot on the road where he'd been taken by the queen's guards.

He stepped out of the carriage, grateful to stand on his own world again, even if it was the changeable underworld of Erebus. Holding out a hand, he assisted Naia down. The porcelain-faced guard climbed back onto her sideboard, the gargoyles leapt into motion, and the carriage streaked away from them. Ty stared after it as it retreated into the distance. Of all the bizarre things that had happened in the past few days, his time with the queen had trumped everything.

"Is it safe to ask about them now?" he asked.

Naia gave an '*I don't know*' shrug. "I'd never feel certain of what the Graeae can or can't hear or see, but better here than anywhere near them or their guards."

She began walking and Ty felt content letting her choose the direction.

"So what are they? Witches?" Stories of three witchy sisters who possessed one tooth and one eye between them were all he'd ever heard of the Graeae. Apparently, the tales had been either metaphorical or patently wrong.

"What they truly are surpasses understanding, but they're much more than witches. They don't perform magic, as the gods do; they *personify* it. They may be a single entity or two or three. They're at least as old as the gods, and I'm not certain that the magic of the gods—or any magic—would exist without them, yet their magic is utterly different than our own." She brushed a tree they passed with her fingertips and he wondered if she was as glad to be back here as he was. "They seem able to do things most of the gods can't," she continued, "like seeing future and past, yet they aren't all powerful. Their magic may be the source of the gods' magic, but they can't replicate the magic of the gods. Or of each other, it seems."

"So even the Graeae can't find the gods to help them?"

She shook her head. "But if they can track Ares down, perhaps they could intuit something about their sister's spell, or my father's—or both."

The skin of his forearms raised in goosebumps at the memory of the nowhere room he'd seen twice as a child. The breath of the sleeping gods drifting in a chill draft across his young body, dressed once in swim trunks and once in pajamas. Feeling something vaster than gods sharing that space.

"So how could Eros send you a key that opens their hiding place if he didn't know where he and the sleeping gods would end up?"

"That's why Prometheus had to make it before they moved. He made a key that would open a thing—a concept of a place more than the place itself."

Ty struggled with the incongruity then let it go. His mind cycled back to the Graeae, unable to set aside the idea of having been on a rock floating in space, in a perpetually flowing castle, and in the presence of both his queen and the Graeae. They were approaching the brook and, despite the inverted landscape, Ty began to get his bearings. "Do you trust them?"

"I don't know," Naia said thoughtfully. "The Graeae have always been a law unto themselves. I respect the fact that Enyo and Pemphredo sacrificed their own sister to save the gods." She turned before they came to the water's edge and headed downstream, which now flowed the opposite direction. "I sent a message to them when they first took the form of your queens. I asked for their help, but I never received an answer. Meeting with them today could change everything. I doubt much is beyond their ability and I want very much to trust them, but I trusted Enyalius and was nearly killed for it. Right now I can't afford to trust anyone."

Ty wondered if that included him.

"Where are we headed?" he asked, seeing that Naia was angling for the little bridge.

"Too many forces are converging here. The safest thing would be for you to return to the surface. Kairos is dead, Momus is here in Erebus, and the other factions probably realize by now that you no longer hold the key."

Though he'd wanted to leave, the thought that she wanted him gone nettled him. Her loss then. He had advantages that could have helped her: his newfound luck, help in finding what he sought, a spell for going unnoticed. He might have stayed if she'd asked. Whatever. She was doing him a favor. If he hadn't discovered that she forced him to love her, he might never have found the willpower to leave her. His only regret was leaving without knowing if she hurt as well.

"Okay," was all he said. "Momus took me out by a staircase somewhere." He looked around. "It was on the edge of the town." He pointed. "That way, I think. At least, it was two days ago." The staircase had been disorienting and disturbing, but better than the lake or the sewers.

She nodded. "It won't be the same staircase, but I'll find one for you." She sounded subdued. Or maybe he only heard what he wanted to hear.

He followed her onto the bridge, neither of them saying more. Faced with leaving Erebus, Ty discovered a surprising appreciation for the odd place. The manicured park of his world had colors less vibrant, air less pure; it had traffic and dust and, well, a mundane quality by comparison.

He stopped in the middle of the bridge to absorb Erebus' shifting strangeness one last time, but what he thought about was Naia. Knowing he might never see her again, he wanted to apologize. For everything. He stared upstream instead, sliding a hand in his jeans pocket to check for the ribbon before he left.

It wasn't there. He looked in panic around his feet then in the water, though common sense told him it hadn't jumped out of his pocket that very moment. Maybe it had fallen out at the palace, or in the carriage. His blood ran cold at the thought of the Graeae holding it. He stared ahead, reviewing everywhere he'd been since last checking for it. He'd last seen it when getting dressed outside Mara's village. Maybe it had fallen out when the lion grabbed him. The thorny bushes weren't far from here.

He was about to tell Naia that he'd be right back when he noticed a woman standing in the middle of the water at the bend in the creek. At a glance she'd seemed tall enough to touch the sky, a giant, taller than the giant that attacked them the other day, huge enough to dwarf the tiny stream. When he focused on her, though, she seemed a normal size again.

He used both the sight Aletheia had given him and his background sight, but the impression of immensity didn't return and he wondered if he'd imagined it. The woman's back was to him and she seemed to be looking down at something in her hands. He ignored the shoulder-length, light brown hair and the men's clothing she wore, and focused on the skin below the rolled up pants. A chilly fear gripped Ty as he made out the black, patchwork stitches. The woman turned. Her fire-engine red neck nearly glowed in contrast to the dark green face that found him.

"Kalyptra," he breathed. Naia followed the direction of his gaze. "She's the one who tattooed me," he said in a hoarse whisper.

"Gods on high," Naia said. "She has the key." She bumped him into the railing as she ran past.

"Wait!" Ty shouted, grabbing for her arm. She slipped out of his reach. Ty ran after her. He hoped she remembered that everyone who had seen his tattoos said they had been inked and charmed by someone powerful.

Naia reached Kalyptra first, Ty only a few steps behind.

"That thing you hold, it is mine," Naia said, breathless. "I must have it back." She touched Kalyptra on the arm. It might have been a gesture of sincerity. Knowing what her touch could do, Ty suspected it wasn't.

Kalyptra laughed. A rich sound, utterly at odds with the cold woman Ty remembered. Naia grew very still. "Your little tricks won't work on me, Daughter of Love. Even your father's love spells wouldn't. Besides," Kalyptra lifted her closed fist, "this is not yours. It is mine."

"I was entrusted with that by the first of all gods." Naia no longer sounded calm, she sounded desperate. "You risk his wrath."

"His wrath sleeps as soundly as he does," Kalyptra said. "Be easy. It is safer with me."

"Who are you?" Naia asked, her voice a whisper.

Kalyptra looked up into the tree branches, or possibly above that, to the airy canopy that passed here for sky. The impression of her towering hugeness flickered again, so quickly there and gone that Ty couldn't have said if he saw it with real-world eyes or the ones Aletheia had given him.

"We shouldn't discuss this here," Kalyptra said. "My protections don't hide me as well in this world." She took them by one wrist each.

"Wait!" Ty tried to shout, thinking of the ribbon, but it was too late. The air swirled, turning as opaque as if they had fallen into the eye of a hurricane.

He felt enveloped, cradled; his senses spun, though he lacked any visual confirmation of movement. The world looked as immutably gray as it had on Lake Marathon, surrounded by fog. The utter lack of sound or smell added to his disorientation. He could no longer see either Naia or Kalyptra.

He wanted to call out to them, but he was too afraid his voice would make no sound. His fear grew as each passing moment failed to return him to any familiar world. There was no ground beneath his feet for him to gain purchase to run. His head felt like a gyroscope spinning with tremendous velocity while his body stayed upright and centered. A violent nausea assailed him.

His feet struck solid ground and he fell to his knees.

Aello flew above the park, her breasts and the folds of her skin dangling toward the ground below. As ordered, she had stayed close to the park—the last known location of the item her master sought—watching for anyone seeking to recover it.

Her eyes darted, trying to take in the myriad shrubs and trees and hiding places. She scanned the paths and the grassy stretches bordering the creek. Nothing. She flew downstream, a bit further. There. A woman she'd never seen before, fist closed tightly around a thing of power. Standing with her were Naia and the mortal.

Aello banked, excited. The thing the woman held was hidden from her, but she felt the resonance of it in her throat, where she had swallowed the bone for her master. She flapped her wings and extended her claws to strike.

In the blink of an eye they were gone. Aello cawed in surprised distress. Her eyes and ears were not those of other predators, they were human, and she glided anxiously on the breeze, straining to hear the slightest sound. She held her wings as far back as possible to see as much of the ground as she could. Her master had promised her the one thing she desired most in the world, if only she brought him the key. She had to find it. If she did, he would make her beautiful again, as beautiful as she and her long-dead sisters had been in their youth.

Having heard nothing, Aello stopped coasting and flapped frantically. She shat a green and white gob the size of a duck egg that splattered through the foliage below her, then zigzagged above the creek with increasing speed, unsure which direction to look next.

They had been there, right there. She had seen them for only the space of an eye blink but she knew Naia already, and the mortal as well. He was difficult to focus on but she had seen him before, and this time he'd been easier to make out. The other woman with them she committed to memory. Her bright colorations would make her easily identifiable. The trio didn't reappear, though Aello circled many passes. Her dreams crumbled to dust. Today was not the day she would regain her beauty.

Sadness morphed to anger. On earth, she had tormented kings and beggars equally and dispassionately; in Haides she discovered a knack for torture over torment, but never before had she felt such personal desire to inflict pain. Those three, who had vanished somehow before her eyes, stood between her and The Promise.

Anger bloated her. The pressure of it rose, and the bottom of her vision turned the same hazy red she knew sometimes colored her eyes. A loud cry croaked out from her ugly self with her ugly voice, and sent creatures of all sizes and lethal dangers scurrying for cover.

The bulbous weight of Aello's bird-shaped lower half tired her wings easily. She landed in a tree with a good view of the brook and the bridge. The branch bent and she flapped for balance until it stopped swaying, then settled in to wait.

She waited the rest of the day. Her vision cleared as the blood in her eyes ebbed away, but her sadness remained. As did her conviction to find the trio.

Moonless night appeared, smothering the light in an instant, but her eyes saw just as keenly in the dark. She doubted herself. Should she have waited here so long? Should she have searched farther afield? Should she have gotten word to her master immediately? And the biggest question of all: which choice would have brought the most praise from her master, and which the greatest wrath?

20

---◆---

Aether

Ty landed with an impact that took him to his knees. A rushing, roaring clamor surrounded him. His head stopped spinning so abruptly that he spewed up the remains of the meat stew he'd eaten at the queen's palace.

Unsure whether he'd vomit again, Ty didn't try to stand. He wiped his mouth and teary eyes, and straightened to look around while still on his knees. The world remained misty gray and he knelt on what felt like solid ground, but he appeared to be in the middle of a waterfall. It moved all around him, tumbling with enormous force from high above to farther below than he could guess. He couldn't tell if he fell and tumbled with it or not.

It seemed too enormous to be real, too dry, and too singular. He appeared to be within the stream of it, yet he felt no more than mist touch his skin. Things tumbled to either side of him—insubstantial things: shadows of fish and trees, people and celestial bodies, plants and livestock and ocean waves that raised gray tides through the vertical lines of the waterfall. Millions of images plummeted past each second in a watery Tree of Life, and though he'd never heard the theologians mention such a thing, there was only one place he could think of that this might be.

Ty wondered if the Moirai existed somewhere in this strange landscape that might or might not be Aether, weaving the fates and patterns of the myriad shadow things in the waterfall. Images crashed together occasionally, merging and forming a new thing. Others tumbled side-by-side in thick and complex patterns. The speed at which his brain processed the individual representations seemed impossible.

Turning finally from the images, he made out Naia standing not far from him. She seemed no less disconcerted than he felt. A figure stood on her other side; a well-muscled man of indeterminate age wearing nothing but a loincloth. He appeared alternately human-sized and enormous, as if he phased briefly into a reality that Ty could comprehend and back out again.

"Prometheus." Naia whispered the word, though Ty heard her clearly over the waterfall. "I thought you were dead."

Prometheus morphed back to a comprehensible magnitude and held the form of an unbearably beautiful man. "For a time I thought I was also," the god responded. His voice was deep and sophisticated, rich with untold centuries. "Perhaps I *was* dead for awhile on that mountainside, but it's no easy thing for an immortal to die, harder for one to remain dead."

Ty's head swam not only with vertigo, but with the mind-numbing fact that he was in the presence of a god. The only thing that kept him sane was that he'd been surrounded by monsters, and demi-gods ever since descending to Erebus—not to mention his trip to the palace of the Graeae, and the fact he'd probably chatted up Ares while believing him to be Enyalius. Moreover, the god before him was also Kalyptra, with whom he'd already conversed; Kalyptra who had laid hands on nearly every inch of his body. He took a chance on his stomach and pushed to his feet, trying to keep his knees steady.

"Where have you been?" Naia asked Prometheus. Her breath caught in her throat on the last word. Tears glinted in her eyes. One welled beyond the limits of surface tension and fell to join the droplets from the waterfall surrounding them.

"On the surface, in disguise."

"You have your memories back." she said. "How? Do any of the others?" She fired the questions at him in rapid succession.

Prometheus smiled at her discomposure. "Yes, I have my memories. No, the others do not. How is a longer story but, essentially, my memories returned because of this…" He held out the key then clasped his fist around it again. "I only regained my full memory within the past year."

"Now that you have the key, can you wake my father, restore his memory?" Ty heard the hope in her voice.

"Not yet. I must keep to the shadows for now. That's why I used one of the banished living above to gain the key instead of coming to Erebus myself."

Another piece fell into place and crawled through Ty's body. It moved through him like an illness, cramping his stomach, shortening his breath. "Why me?" Ty asked. "Why set Kairos on me?"

"You're a locksmith and a gambler's son. A useful combination," Prometheus said, without apology.

Useful. For that he'd endured changes to his body and torture by Kairos' men and Momus. He'd been sent to Erebus to risk his life because he was useful.

His voice caught when he spoke again. "You manipulated the games?"

"Kairos did. I picked him for his talent with altering the course of chance; the ability to trade it, deal it out, shift it. He also had considerable skill with persuasion, influencing others to act in ways they otherwise wouldn't."

Ty swallowed hard, trying not to vomit again. So much manipulation, so many levels. At least he knew now for certain that it hadn't been his fault; he hadn't followed in his father's footsteps, turning to obsessive gambling and abandoning his mother out of blind selfishness. Not that it helped him now. Or his mother.

Anger clutched at Ty's nerves, at his heart, trying to latch on. Waves of sorrow washed it away. His voice, when he could speak, felt remote. "My mother died because of my gambling. She needed me when she was ill and I wasn't there for her."

Naia turned to him, concerned surprise written in the tightening of her eyes and brows.

"Worlds were at stake," Prometheus said. He sounded genuinely sympathetic, if still not apologetic. "Your mother's illness was nothing I had anticipated. I think it likely, though, that her infection would have progressed the same regardless of anything you might have done. Her lungs were weak all her life."

Ty looked at the images in the waterfall, all that life and death endlessly cycling, imagining all the people who died unfairly every day. Just because Prometheus was a god, it didn't mean he could control everything within those tumbling waters. *Or could he?*

"Can you bring her back?" Ty said, suddenly hopeful.

Prometheus shook his head. "It's too late. Even if Thanatos had been here to bring her back the day she died, she would have come back with the sickness in her lungs and would have died again."

Ty wandered deeper into the dry waterfall. If one step took him plummeting over some unseen edge to fall with the millions of other life forms, so be it. He held out his hand, trying to touch some of them as they fell, but they passed through his flesh.

"Do you know where the others sleep?" Naia asked. Ty heard her voice only distantly, his mind still processing the surfeit of information and emotions assailing him.

"No, Eros couldn't tell me where he might end up. I've dreamed of them asleep, though, and know they are safe. And I'll know how to find them when the time comes."

"I may know a way to find them now," she said, catching Ty's attention at last. Naia spoke with the enthusiasm of a child able, for once, to inform a parent on a fact. "We've just spoken with the Graeae. If you could talk with them they might be able to decipher your dreams, or maybe see new clues in the present or past."

"Were I to expose my true identity to them, however briefly, I'm certain they would strike with lethal force."

Naia nearly glowed with excitement. "No. It was only Deino who plotted against you. Enyo and Pemphredo killed her after she took your memories. Deino's been dead for more than two decades, but the other two sisters had no part in plotting your destruction."

"Enyo and Pemphredo killed Deino, that much is true," Prometheus replied. "But my memories have returned to me. I know my enemies. It wasn't Deino who plotted against us, it was the other two who wanted our power and set in motion the plan to kill us. Deino opposed them.

She sent a warning to us moments before the other two Graeae struck. It wasn't enough to save us from the spell of amnesia, but while Enyo and Pemphredo negotiated with Deino and then planned her murder, your father and I had time to drug the other gods and get them to safety."

Naia's olive skin paled. Ty returned to her side as she absorbed the realization of yet another betrayal. And as she discovered new and even more powerful opponents. He felt the echo of it within himself. If Enyo and Pemphredo hadn't thought them potentially useful in trapping Ares, he and Naia might not have survived their trip to the palace.

Naia seemed unable to speak. Over the rushing sounds of the waterfall, Ty asked the question for her. "What now? You said you have a way to find the other gods. Will you wake them?"

"I can't do that yet. I must go to the Graeae first and learn the magic that took our memories."

Ty was so stunned by the idea that the objection tumbled from him before he thought about to whom he spoke.

"You can't. You just said if you went to them, they'd kill you." Naia had a god on her side. A Titan. Prometheus for fuck's sake. He couldn't just march off to the sisters who were trying to kill him.

"They don't know me in this body," Prometheus said. His form morphed like melting butter into the female Kalyptra, tattoos and all. "I can approach them as a confederate, as the person Kalyptra has always seemed to be—an independent agent who works with the New Order, but has no love for them."

"Why go to the Graeae instead of the other gods?" Naia asked.

"I have to learn the spell they used so that I can restore all the gods' memories at once, and quickly, once begun. Otherwise, I'd accomplish nothing but revealing my defenseless brothers and sisters to the Graeae. Even with only two-thirds of their original strength, the sisters could kill the entire pantheon if the gods don't know how to channel their power. It's why I must not learn their location before I can restore their memories. The Graeae could take it from me."

Prometheus opened his hand and looked at the key lying in his palm. "I planned to get the key first and the means to find the gods so I could move quickly once I contacted the Graeae, but I hadn't planned on Ares rousing the Graeae by attacking the little moon. I'm glad to know he lives, but I could wish he hadn't found such strength yet. He was always one to act on instinct and impulse. He must have found something that he believes directs his magic."

"He uses powders and grimoires," Naia said.

Prometheus smiled, no doubt appreciating the irony of a god believing a powder or old text held a magic he did not. "For me, it was painting. I rediscovered the symbols I'd used on the key. I didn't remember the key or what the symbols meant, but they became a conduit for my magic until I regained my memory."

"How can I help you?" Naia asked.

"Once I have learned the Graeae's spell, I'll restore Ares' memory first. If I succeed, our chances of rescuing the others will be doubled. My plan requires a number of steps to go well. Keep others from interfering while I carry them out. Keep enemies from my back. Don't engage Ares until I'm ready. And keep your lover safe. I may need him again. The marks I placed on him may come in useful."

Naia and Ty looked at each other.

"We're not lovers," Ty said, in a voice tight with discomfort.

"My love spell didn't bind him," Naia said on his heels. "Though the one you gave him for me found its mark." It was the first time Ty had heard her admit her feelings for him, and the closest to anger he'd ever heard her.

"The hell yours didn't," he shot back, matching her anger.

Prometheus laughed. A rich sound, rolling and tumbling with the waterfall around them. "Neither worked," he said. He turned to Ty. "Yours accomplished the initial interest and trust that I hoped it would. Enough to get you into her home. No more." And to Naia. "Yours was negated by his protections. If the two of you are unhappy at being in love, you have only yourselves to blame."

Prometheus gave them a wide, genuine smile. He looked around at the waterfall, at the millions of lives playing out around him. "It's good to remember the joy in life. It's been too long." He looked down at the key once more, his expression sobering. "I hope I live to see more of it."

"You go to the Graeae now?" Naia said, her voice anxious.

"I do," he said, gripping the key so tightly his knuckles blanched.

21

Judge Me By My Enemies

Eyes still closed, Selia slowly realized that she lay on her right side. Wool blankets covered her and her head rested on a thin pillow. She stirred. Her chest ached as if every rib had broken. Warm hands reached forward to brush strands of hair from her face.

Mustering the energy and will to open her eyes, Selia saw a blurry image of a woman leaning over her. Cyrene. Selia would have known her even if she were blind. "How long?" she asked. Her voice was as dry and broken as her lips.

"Two days," Cyrene said. "It took me a full day just to find you."

She remembered the events leading up to the attack and they felt now like a dream: Naia's handmaiden torn to pieces by Aello; the harpy flying to the apartment of the cigar smoking man; the man leading her to the head of the New Order, and her summoning of her warriors.

She had, again, been too sure of herself, the same as when she sent the giant and the centaur to attack Naia on the street. Only this time, instead of one giant being blinded, the cost had been in lives, nearly a dozen. She'd shot Enyalius in the heart with her mother's arrow. There was no doubt the aim had been true. She would never have believed he could stand after that, let alone wield magic so powerful that the explosion had ripped her followers to pieces and had nearly killed her as well. Cyrene lived, though. Selia tried to suppress what her heart told her, that having Cyrene safe was worth the lives of all the rest.

"I'm sorry I left you," she croaked.

"You were right to. I would have been angry if you hadn't."

"I tried to make it home, but the moon... " Selia shrank from the memory.

"I know." Cyrene stroked her hair again. "Drink," she said, holding a cup of cool water to her lips.

Selia tried to lift her head but couldn't. Cyrene lifted it for her, and she sipped awkwardly. Water ran from her lips onto the pillow. The last drops in her mouth dribbled toward her lungs with her next breath, and the pain of coughing nearly caused her to pass out again.

"How many others?" she asked when she could speak again.

Cyrene understood. Her face pulled into a mask of reluctance and pain. Tears flowed from the corners of Selia's eyes before Cyrene could say the words.

"None." She set the cup on a nightstand. "No one else survived. I was well inside the room when the explosion came. I lost consciousness and Enyalius must have thought me dead."

Selia tried to touch the bruises that covered Cyrene's face but she couldn't lift her arm. Tears dripped along her temples and into her hair. "My moon?"

Cyrene shook her head.

She wanted to ask if the bodies had been recovered, how Enyalius could have harmed her moon. Instead, the room faded.

She stood in the night sky, somewhere between the Earth and the real moon. She tried to ask her mother, Selene, if her little moon was well, but the moon in the true heavens didn't answer. It never did anymore. Perhaps it was why Selia could be so coldly pragmatic about eliminating the gods, now her mother was no longer numbered among them. There was nothing left of Selene but this rocky satellite and its magnetic orbit around Gaia's Earth; the mindless love affair of one celestial body with another.

Selia drifted from half dreams into something deeper. She stopped trying to talk to her mother and became her mother instead. As Selene, she looked down on the Earth from her silent travels through the heavens. She stepped down from the moon, knowing she was in her mother's past, a time when Selene had still indulged in enjoyment of something more than moving through the black sky.

She felt the Earth beneath her feet as she walked to the cave. There, on a blanket covering a bench of rock, lay the mortal who had caught her eye when out in the fields at night with his cattle. His beauty pulled her in the same way the Earth pulled the moon. Selia-Selene enjoyed the feel of the man beneath her hands as she explored him, the soft curls of his hair tangling in her fingers while he slept and dreamed of her.

She mounted him, and the feel of him inside her made her forget the silence of the heavens for a time. He moaned with pleasure, still sleeping, and she lived out his passionate dreams. Emotions renewed within her that had been steadily seeping away in her cold and lonely sky.

She went to him often after that. Until one day she went to him and he slept too deeply to rouse to her touch. An eternal sleep. His dreams of her had been too pleasurable. He had begged another one of the gods that his dreams should never end, and his prayer had been answered.

Selene's belly swelled during the months she mourned his loss. She birthed her final child at the next full moon, a half-mortal daughter that she named Selia and left with his family, and she stepped back into the heavens one final time.

Like her father had done, Selia slipped even deeper into sleep, and dreamed her mother's dreams no more.

A pounding at the door brought Selia wide awake. She didn't know if she'd dozed for a moment or a day. Fumbling with the blankets, she discovered herself still too weak to push them aside. She heard Cyrene moving in the other room, looking out a window, perhaps. The door, or maybe its frame, splintered with a loud crash. There came the soft smacking sound of a fist on flesh; a solidly weighted thump. The front door opened with the heavy scraping of something being pushed. Booted feet entered.

"Cyrene," Selia called in a dry whisper. She attempted to rise. On her second try, she fell from the bed to the floor. The booted feet came closer until one filled her vision.

"Take her," an unfamiliar voice said. The voice echoed, softly booming, as if from a great distance, neither male nor female in tenor. Selia tried to look up, but could see no higher than the crisp maroon material of the pants leg.

Hands reached down and lifted her; they were white-gloved, like the hands of maidens at a summer garden party. Strong arms pulled her to her feet but her legs refused to support her, and she dangled from the grip of her captors' hands like a life -sized doll. The pain in her chest, where the essence of the moon had torn free, was excruciating. Looking for the eyes of her abductors Selia found none, only holes leading into a blackness that extended deeper than the universe.

She must've lost consciousness again, for she woke to intense pain in her chest as she was dragged by her arms. Her muscles screamed, her head pounded in time with her heart, yet she could do nothing to free herself. She thought she might be paralyzed, but a twitch of her toes reassured her. She looked down at the wide floor over which she was being hauled, a floor longer and wider than Cyrene's house could contain. Walls flowing like molten gold surrounded her. She was laid, not ungently, on a couch in a room richly decorated in greens and golds. Skirts moved toward her, but the impression was wrong. The skirt seemed too wide, the footsteps had too many beats.

"So long and still not recovered?" Two voices spoke in perfect synchrony. "We hadn't known you drew so much power from your moon. Considering your mother's unique properties, perhaps it is not surprising."

Too weak to respond, Selia gazed up at the cold face of one of the two remaining Graeae. She remembered the dream where she had been her mother, and wondered if the Graeae had inspired it. Perhaps they had searched for her through her ties to her mother, the moon. In a haze of pain and injury, Selia wished she could do the same as her mother had done, drift into her moon until she became the thing herself. But her little moon was gone, and her human half anchored her to this physical life. Having been kidnapped and brought to the Graeae as helpless as a babe, she wondered how much longer that life might last.

The front-facing sister, likely to be Enyo, studied her no more than a moment. Heat flooded Selia, followed by vibrant energy. The sisters had uttered no spell and Enyo's face had reflected no hint of effort, yet the invisible damage along Selia's ribs and skin knitted whole again. Her weakness fell away from her like a cloak dropped to the floor. She sat up with no remnant of dizziness or pain.

The Graeae's demonstration of power terrified her even as it cured her. Selia could in no way have approached the ease of their magic, and Asclepius himself couldn't have equaled their healing. They spoke before she could marshal words to thank them.

"We have learned recently of someone named Enyalius," the sisters said in unison. "What do you know of him?"

Selia realized with cold certainty that her healing had been entirely for their own convenience. She would have been too sluggish to respond to them efficiently.

"Little," she confessed. "I only learned of him recently—a scholar, according to one of my followers who knew of him. He leads the New Order." Restored now and thinking clearly, she remembered the crash of the door, the guards hauling her away. Her thoughts flew to Cyrene. "Is Cyrene here? Is she all right?"

She knew immediately she had erred by interrupting their questions. Enyo grew still, her impassive face colder. Chances were they neither knew of nor cared about Cyrene. At least, they hadn't until now.

"What else do you know of this Enyalius?" they asked.

Ducking her head in apology, Selia continued. "I discovered him by following his servant, Aello, to one of his lieutenants' homes. I launched an attack on him, and pierced his heart with my mother's arrow, but he had strength enough before he died to injure me and kill my warriors."

"Your Revisionists have vowed to kill the gods, is that right?"

The harsh creed stated so boldly disturbed Selia.

"I act to preserve three worlds. The New Order would see us all destroyed, from the surface to Tartarus, if they were to wake and control the gods. As to the gods themselves, the Fates alone know what they might do if they awoke without their memories."

The sisters turned and moved away. Pemphredo watched Selia as she smoothly walked behind her sister to an open section of the room.

Selia knew little about the Graeae. For all the centuries the gods had been active, the sisters had remained separate, aloof and living among the stars. All she knew for certain was that the third sister had died. Even if that death had diminished their powers, they were still formidable.

They turned so that Enyo faced her, the reflection of Pemphredo staring at her now in the coin-sized mirrors. "The Preservationists are still your enemies, as are the New Order?"

The Graeae wouldn't care about the distinctions Selia drew between the two. The New Order's goals were abhorrent. Enyalius had killed her followers, people closer to her than family. Someone in the New Order had found a way to destroy her moon. The Preservationists, on the other hand, were merely naïve, their goal as risky as that of the New Order, whatever the difference in motives. Whether killing the gods distressed Selia or not, she knew that neither the New Order nor the Preservationists could be allowed to prevail.

"Yes," she said, giving the sisters the simplest answer.

"Good," the Graeae said.

Their coldness chilled Selia. Even the gods showed passion, she thought—even her mother had at one time—but not these sisters.

"Your strike did not kill Enyalius," they said. "We believe he is one of the gods. Possibly Prometheus. More likely, Ares."

It took Selia a moment to process this, though once she did, she realized she should have put the facts together sooner. The arrow would have instantly killed anyone but a god. And a god would surely have the means to pull her moon from the sky.

"His memory has returned?"

"No," they replied. "That is what makes him dangerous. Love's daughter also searches for him, but it is her wish to wake the gods. We do not trust her."

Selia nodded. "Naia was at his house when we attacked. Her and some mortal. Enyalius and his lieutenant had captured them and were interrogating the man."

"You were able to see the mortal?"

"Nothing can hide from the moon. My moon shadow revealed him to me previously, when he and Naia were on the run from Aello."

"Who is this lieutenant you mention?"

"I don't know his name, but I've seen where he lives," she said, recalling the moon shadow globe following Aello to the apartment of the cigar-smoking man.

"Can you find the god again?"

If Enyalius truly was Ares—if he was without memory and had destroyed her moon, if he was responsible for killing others—then everything Selia had feared was coming to pass. "I am willing to try."

"Good."

Selia's mind reached for her globe, conjuring it. It didn't come. Wherever she was, she was farther than moonbeams could travel.

The hairs on the back of her neck prickled at the thought. Enyo and Pemphredo gave no indication they had noticed Selia's miscarried attempt to conjure.

"I can go to his house," Selia said, "and the home of his lieutenant. I can also seek Aello. If I find Ares, though, I realize now that I don't possess the strength to kill him. My mother's arrows were my surest weapon, and they failed me already."

"We will aid you. Take this," an arrow with a shaft the deep color of dried blood materialized in Enyo's hand. "The arrow will be as true as your aim."

Selia took the offered weapon. It was more beautiful even than her mother's arrows. Gold leaf designs ran the length of the shaft, which was tipped with a head of red stone and tailed with feathers of iridescent red and black.

"I'll need my bow, and a few of my own arrows in case Ares is with others."

"We will see it done," the Graeae said in unison. "Go then. We will know when you have accomplished your goal. Love's daughter may help us draw Ares into the open. You are not to harm her yet, but the mortal you may kill at anytime. Later, we will help you eliminate all of the Preservationists, so they will pose no risk of waking the other gods."

22

Love's Daughter

The gray mist of Aether faded slowly into white. Ty wondered if he'd gone blind in some Erebus twist on total darkness until his surroundings cleared enough that he could make out a white reclining couch on a white marble floor veined with gold.

His eyes and stomach adjusted to the change as the room came into focus. Prometheus had sent them to Naia's home. He saw it for the first time as Naia must. If he didn't squint, the modern, uptown apartment disappeared altogether and he stood in an elegant home decorated simplistically in ancient style. Vases and pottery adorned small stands. The desk still stood against the wall, though heavier and less ornate than the counterpart he'd seen before Aletheia altered his eyesight. The furniture occupied the same spaces as before, but was covered now in roughly tanned and dyed leather or coarse linen. The kitchen held a large hearth, framed in a mosaic of small gold and blue tiles.

Naia stood at his elbow. "Good luck, Prometheus," she said softly, though she and Ty were alone.

A wooden door had replaced the glass patio door, so Ty went to one of the large windows and pushed the shutters open. Naia's home now sat on the crest of a hill overlooking rolling, dry grass. A wide river flowed lazily a couple of benches below him. The downtown he'd seen before—the large village he'd seen since—lay a couple of miles to his left. Newside, he supposed, from what he was picking up of the cardinal directions in Erebus: Newside, Oldside, and Mountainside so far. A few scattered villas dotted the hills near Naia's home, but between these and the larger community of "downtown" lay open land.

He turned at the sound of Naia's sandaled footsteps tapping down the hallway. Following, he found her standing in the arched doorway of Lamia's room. Ty didn't need to see her face to sense her sorrow; he could read it in the lines of her body. His own fresh grief channeled such empathy with Naia's that he felt her pain like a fist around his heart.

"You should leave Erebus as soon as you can," she said without turning. "I don't think I could stand it if you died too."

He moved closer and placed his hands on her shoulders, pulling her into him. She nestled her head against his throat. Unbound emotions overwhelmed him. Yes, she had tried to put a love spell on him, but knowing it hadn't worked changed everything. When he thought he'd been spelled, it had forced him to admit to being in love for the first time in years. To know those feelings were genuine now opened doors in his soul that he'd thought forever closed.

"And I don't think I could stand to leave you."

She turned into him, her face against his shoulder. Her arms slipped around his waist and he wrapped her in his embrace.

He'd built a strong palisade around his heart over the years: erecting it after his father's abandonment, bracing it after the disinterest of a first crush at school, fortifying it after his fiancé's betrayal. All of his protections burned to ash now in the fire of Naia's closeness, the heat of her body, the feel of her hands on him.

In a rush of sudden need, his fingers tangled through her hair. She looked up, bringing their faces close together. Passion radiated from her like heat from the sun. Desire ran both ways; he didn't doubt it anymore. He lowered his mouth to hers and felt her lips part. He kissed her deeply and slowly.

Her hands moved on his body, up the muscles of his back to his shoulders, then back down to his waist. The intensity of her touch was like nothing he'd ever known. All his past experience might as well have been nothing more than a series of performances; acts where he and the women with him had been living mannequins playing parts, convincing but emotionless. Holding her, the nerves in his chest and arms and legs felt as if they'd been electrified just beneath the skin, a web of synapses so charged with sensations that it seemed almost too much to bear.

The kiss turned to a series of sweet connections and partings. One of her hands slid below his waist. She pulled the two of them closer and his breath caught. Blood had already rushed to all the right places, and the intensity of his desire left him lightheaded. Ty turned with her in his arms, so her back was against the door frame. He leaned his hips into hers. She inhaled sharply at the pressure. She kissed his neck. He found her mouth again and teased her with kisses, waiting for an unequivocal invitation.

The extent of her permission was clear a moment later when her hand slipped between them and massaged him gently, making him groan. Ty swept an arm behind Naia's knees and lifted her. He carried her from Lamia's doorway, away from the sadness and trauma of their past few days, away from the tension and stress and danger. She pushed down on the door handle to her bedroom with her foot before he could adjust his grip to open the door. They both smiled. He set her on her feet next to the bed.

Naia removed the brooches at her shoulders and let her dress fall to the floor. Beneath it she wore an old-style strophion of linen about her breasts and a light perizoma about her loins. In his second sight they were a bra and panties, which he removed for her while he kissed her neck and explored the newly uncovered skin with his hands. She climbed into bed and slid over to make room for him.

He remembered his dream of Naia in the back of Mara's shop, and waking to find a soul-sucking creature over him. He sincerely hoped that this was no dream. Undressing, he slid beneath the covers with her.

She traced the history of his time in Erebus by the wounds stamped across his skin. The healing scratch on his cheek, his bruised shoulder, the avulsed skin at his collarbone, the injuries to his calf. Her touch was salve and spark both. Urgency built within him, but every moment deserved to be savored. When they came together again, he matched her slow and sensual touch.

Making love to her felt too intensely real to be a dream, and as acutely emotional as it was physical. If the Graeae set the whole world on fire that minute, he wouldn't have been able to stop. Naia moved with him to the smallest degree as if a part of him. Her touches, her kisses, were all so maddeningly erotic he both did and didn't want it to end.

It did end eventually, and that brought its own sweetness. They slept afterward, tangled together in an exhausted refuge from gods and demigods, politics and enemies and death.

Ty woke to moonless darkness, though he guessed it was no later than evening. He'd never seen a clock in Erebus, which didn't surprise him given the randomness of standardized units of measure here. Naia was awake also, watching him.

"Do different times have different feels here?" he asked. "Like midnight and 4:00am, for example."

"Of course," she said. "Are you only now beginning to feel it?"

"I think so."

He scooted closer, finding her in the darkness, and laid one arm across her hip, folding his other arm under his pillow. "Can't sleep?"

He felt the shake of her head.

"Bad dreams?"

"Good dreams." She brushed his chest. "But now that I'm awake, the less pleasant things come back.

"How about a bath? I'm pretty sure I could use one."

They rose and climbed together into the sunken tub. She sat between his legs, leaning against his chest.

"How does this stay warm anyway?" he asked. "For that matter, how does it stay filled, or clean?"

"I'm not only the daughter of Eros. I'm also the daughter of a water nymph."

"I'm not likely to forget anytime soon that you're Eros' daughter." Ty kissed her temple then laid his head back on the edge of the pool and closed his eyes, more content than he could ever remember feeling.

"I need to find Selia," she said.

He'd known this would come, but he'd hoped not so soon. He slid his wet hands up to her shoulders.

"You have Prometheus in your corner now. How about letting him do some of the heavy lifting for awhile? Update your followers, rally support, but let go of running point. You've been a target for too long." He massaged her neck.

"I need to make sure Selia knows the truth about the Graeae and Prometheus."

"I'm not saying you should do nothing, I'm just saying that Prometheus is a Titan. You're not. Don't think you have to match him and take on the same level of danger."

"I asked Prometheus what I could do to help. He asked me to keep others from interfering and keep enemies from his back."

"He also said not to engage Ares. If the Graeae have found Selia, she'll be hunting Ares by now. I'm sure Prometheus didn't mean for you to get in the middle of that."

"If there's something I can do, I have to try."

"Because of the message your father sent you?"

She twisted against his chest to look at him. "Because all of this is my fault."

"What?" He lifted her so she sat next to him with her legs over his. "What do you mean your fault? The Graeae started this."

"The factions. They're my fault. Enyalius was right when he called me naïve. When I heard the lie that Deino had tried to harm the gods and her sisters had killed her, I assumed all threat to the gods had been eradicated. It never occurred to me that anyone else would wish them harm. I spread the word, looking for heroes to find them, practitioners of magic to heal them. Letting too many know their plight had the opposite effect. It gave the wrong people ideas. Opposing factions sprang up because I wasn't clever enough to be discreet." Her voice was tight with restrained emotion. "My father was wrong to put his trust in someone he loved. He'd have been better off telling a scholar, or even a warrior."

He took both her hands in his. "The message and the key came to you and you've done all you could. You kept the gods and the key safe all this time."

"I've done nothing. You bringing the key into the open generated more information than I've uncovered in twenty-five years."

"And it nearly got you killed. And alerted the Graeae. What about your followers? Do you have an army somewhere? Fighters, like Selia had?"

"Some rallied to me at first, but most have scattered over time. My goal was never war, it was preservation. Some of my best warriors undertook quests to find the gods years ago—a few drifted away, some searching for clues, some not finding enough adventure to hold them. The ones who stayed close were the scholars, Aletheia and the others like her whose talents aren't martial." She looked down, sadness in her dark eyes, her face drawn. He brushed her dark hair from her cheek. "The one I relied on the most was Lamia."

"I know," he said. He found her hand again and squeezed it.

"I won't engage Ares," she said, visibly pulling her thoughts from Lamia's death, "but the least I can do is find Selia and let her know the truth. When she finds out that Prometheus is alive and has regained his memory, surely she'll call off her campaign."

"Maybe not. Ares killed her followers."

"But without his memory. And now we have Prometheus working on reversing that spell."

"How would you even go about finding her?" Ty asked. "Last time we saw her she was getting her butt kicked."

"Selia lives in a place I can't reach. But I know the location of her lieutenant's home."

He sighed and laid his head against her cheek. "I don't want to risk losing you either, you know."

She reached up and touched the side of his face. The wetness of her hand made it feel as if she was about to dissolve into the water and slip away from him.

"I love you," he said.

It felt strange speaking those words. He couldn't say how many years it had been since he'd said it to a lover, only that it felt more right now than it ever had before.

"And I love you," the daughter of Love said to him.

23

---◆---

Separate Paths

A t first light Ty and Naia made their way around the outskirts of the large village he thought of as downtown. He avoided using his surface sight as it disoriented him to see two versions of everything. They skirted the buildings and continued on out into the countryside of dried grass.

Ty felt sure they were moving faster than the last time they'd come this way, though he hurried no more than before. It felt as if they took the steps of giants, or perhaps the land rolled toward them as they walked, like a reverse escalator. He looked at Naia, wondering if she controlled it somehow, but she seemed lost in thought. Perhaps it was just some new vagary of this world.

As they approached the next village he recognized the buildings in the distance as the same village where he'd spent the night when on the run from Enyalius. Naia angled that direction and he realized Selia's lieutenant must also live in the community he thought of as his own neighborhood.

He kept a wary eye out, not only for Momus but Mara as well. Either would be able to spot him easily. Naia gave him a sidelong glance when he kept staring around, but said nothing. He followed her as she angled through the village to their right—Mountainside, he thought, with more pride at his growing familiarity with Erebus than it probably warranted.

Looking at the village in daylight with both his true sight and secondary surface-world sight, he was pretty sure he recognized at least a few of the homes. No surprise, really, but the ancient cottages in the older sections of his neighborhood—some hundreds of years old—looked fresh and new here. Newer structures there didn't exist here at all; most likely he was seeing their ancient predecessors. It seemed Erebus existed in a different age than his world on the surface, or at least a better preserved one.

Naia made her way through the village to a small and unassuming cottage—old Nick Petro's home on the surface, Ty thought. The door stood open and he laid a hand on her arm before she reached the stoop.

"Are you sure this is a good idea?"

"I've already sought help at the home of a friend who turned out to be an enemy. Maybe my enemies will turn out to be my allies." She stepped up to the threshold. "Cyrene?"

He touched Naia's shoulder and pointed to the toe of a boot hooked around the bottom of the door; someone lay prone on the other side. They both froze, listening, but he heard no sound from within. Naia stepped inside and squatted by an unconscious woman, Cyrene, he assumed. Naia shook her and the woman flopped like a cloth toy.

Ty did a quick reconnaissance and saw no sign of attackers lurking. The house looked undisturbed for the most part, but trampled—dusty booted footprints, an overturned plant stand, a chair pushed into a corner where it seemed out of place—as if it had been over-crowded in here not long ago.

Returning, he said, "I'll carry her into a bedroom."

He knelt and rolled the woman's shoulders onto his arm, slipping his other arm under her knees. She was muscular—heavier than she looked—and his bruised left shoulder protested the weight. He followed Naia into the only bedroom of the three room cottage and laid the woman on the unmade bed.

Naia explored an angry lump on Cyrene's forehead with her fingers. "Can you find a wet rag?"

Ty poked around until he discovered a bit of cloth, and looked longer before he found a pail of water out back that must've been drawn from the village well. Like the tepid light of Erebus, the water was neither warm nor cool, but it would have to do. He dipped the cloth into it and took it to Naia, who stroked the rag across the woman's forehead. Cyrene didn't wake.

"I'll look for vinegar," he said.

Using his second sight, he rummaged the pantries (shelves) near the stove (cooking hearth) and found a sealed jar with liquid the color of piss. He opened it and sniffed carefully, then returned to the bedroom. Naia poured some of the vinegar onto the rag and held it under Cyrene's nose.

The woman turned her head away from the strong smell. Her eyes opened, beating a few beats against the light, like moth's wings.

"Cyrene, what happened?" Naia asked.

She swung a fist at Naia's jaw.

Ty grabbed her wrist and Cyrene jerked back, seeming aware of him for the first time. She went slack then, apparently having expended the extent of her energy. Drips of water rained from Naia's cheek—the target of the punch—onto Cyrene's chest. The droplets floated upward again, rejoining the flesh of her face and making it whole once more.

Ty wondered if he'd ever get used to that.

"We need to share information, for all our sakes," Naia said. "Too much is happening. We can't afford to be at odds with each other any longer."

"Swear on your father's name you mean Selia no harm," Cyrene said weakly.

"I swear by all the Love in the world and all that means to me. I seek a truce. I have information important to us all which I need to pass on to Selia."

Cyrene loosed a long, resigned sigh. "She was abducted. I've never seen them before. They were uniformed. Maroon and gold. White gloves and white masks." Ty's blood ran cold before she could finish. "They had no eyes. No, that's wrong. They had terrible eyes."

Cyrene saw the recognition on their faces. She pushed herself to her elbows. Ty tried to help her into a sitting position, but she shrugged him off and swung her legs down. "Who were they?"

"Those were the Graeae's guards," Naia said. "They've taken her to the sisters. I'd hoped to reach her before the Graeae did. I imagine they'll set her on a path to find and kill Ares."

"Ares? What do you mean?"

Ty exchanged a glance with Naia. Cyrene would know nothing of Enyalius' true identity or the revelations about the Graeae and Prometheus. A breeze blew through one window and the front door thumped shut. They all turned toward the front room.

"I think it was just the wind," Ty said. "I'll check while you fill her in."

The breeze had indeed kicked up, and he saw nothing untoward at the front window. He decided to make a full circuit of the house anyway. He even checked the ground for tarantulas. The time alone gave him space to think.

Naia wanted to find Selia.

Cyrene wanted to find Selia.

Selia, by all accounts, had talked with the Graeae by now and wanted to find Ares.

Selia would have seen Momus when her small army burst into Enyalius' home, and if they lived in the same village, it stood to reason Selia might have recognized him.

The last time Ty had seen Enyalius-Ares, Momus had been with him. And Momus' apartment was here in this village.

It hadn't come up yet between him and Naia that he knew where Momus lived, and Naia would probably be looking next for Selia at Enyalius' old house.

If Naia was set on finding Selia, so be it, but Ty didn't want her running into Ares or Momus in the process. He might have a way to help her, while protecting her from one avenue of danger at the same time. He could jog over to Momus' apartment and see if Ares might be there, considering that he'd blown two walls out of his own house.

If he saw no sign of Ares at Momus', then maybe he could convince Naia to let Cyrene check out Enyalius' house on her own. Cyrene would be far more likely to reason with Selia anyway, and Naia would be protected from yet another confrontation. The only problem he could see with the plan was that if he shared it with Naia, she'd insist on going with him.

Ty opened the door and looked down the street, considering his options. He couldn't tell Naia his plan, but he didn't want to worry her by disappearing. Hurrying in case she decided to check on him, he scooped a couple of handfuls of sandy dirt from against the foundation of the house onto the stoop. Drawing with one finger, he wrote, "Be right back."

Naia brought Cyrene up to date and watched suspicion tighten the woman's mouth. It was natural that Cyrene would suspect it all to be lies, some clever twisting of words to make the Revisionists call off their campaign despite Naia's vow of truce.

At last, Cyrene nodded. Naia relaxed when she saw reason prevail over suspicion. Shoulder muscles unwound that she hadn't realized were tight. Her bet had paid off, helped no doubt by the fact that Cyrene had seen Enyalius survive an arrow to the heart, and Selia's abduction by the Graeae's guards. Cyrene, like everyone else in Erebus, knew that Ares had never been accounted for and Prometheus' body had never been found.

"Selia was so weak," Cyrene said, wincing as she stood. Naia could imagine the headache that came with that lump on her forehead and the second concussion in as many days. "She was near to death when she was taken."

"If the Graeae wanted her services, I would guess her illness is no longer an issue."

Cyrene didn't look comforted. "If so, then, she's probably hunting Ares right now, alone. A memoryless madman with the power of a god. Someone who already managed to kill a dozen of us."

"Do you think Selia would come here before setting out to find Ares?"

"I'd hope so. Without her moon, she can't even access the refuge of her own home, but I can't sit here waiting, hoping she comes to me. The Graeae could have sent her anywhere."

They both silently mulled the possible scenarios. In the sudden quiet, Naia realized she hadn't heard Ty for the past few minutes.

"Ty?" she called out.

No answer.

Fear rose from the pit of her stomach to her throat, constricting muscles along the way. She hurried from the bedroom.

"Ty?"

There was no sign of him in the front room or the kitchen. She ran out the back door, trying to look all directions at once, then around the side of the house, searching for any sign.

"Here," she heard Cyrene call.

Naia hurried to the front. Her heart skipped a beat when she read the message, knowing there was little they could do but wait or risk missing him return.

Ty felt he was getting a firmer handle on navigation. The new sight Aletheia had given him didn't stop the anfractuous Erebus from twisting like a snake, but with it, he was able to locate landmarks until the latest twist sifted through his preconceptions and settled in place. 'What should be' and 'what was' were beginning to speak the same language in some mapping center in his brain. He took each turn with more confidence, plotting a course he hoped would take him directly to Momus' and still avoid Mara's apothecary by a few blocks.

Despite his growing skill at orienting, he had to check his second sight when he arrived at what he expected to be his apartment building. Apparently, in the real Erebus, the building was only two stories tall. It sat slightly apart; a square of apartments around a large courtyard. He wondered how he'd walked up four flights to Momus' when he first arrived, and decided it might be best not to think about it too hard.

He'd hoped Momus' home, like Naia's, might have become a single dwelling. If it had, he could have circled it from a safe distance. It hadn't, though, and the only thing he could see of the apartment was a balcony and a front door he was pretty sure, but not positive, belonged to Momus. He wasn't even certain the man had survived the Revisionists' attack, but Enyalius had, and Ty thought Momus would probably be almost as hard to kill.

Knowing that Ares and Momus would have no trouble seeing him, he made a wide circle of the building, keeping at least one other building between himself and the apartment complex. The back of the apartment wall was stone. The only way to see or hear anything inside would be from the balcony. And he wasn't stupid enough to push his luck that far.

His message to Naia had said he wouldn't be gone long. Disappointed he hadn't accomplished more, he crept back toward Cyrene's.

Aello had circled the park one last time before darkness fell then flew to the nearby home where the tarantula had found Love's daughter and the mortal. The home lay empty and ransacked. Next she flew to the site where she had fought Naia's bodyguard. Nothing remained of the wraith except a patch of red grass and a couple of gnawed bones.

Aello returned to her previous spot and spent the night in a tree near the brook.

She had remained vigilant throughout the night, but when morning broke and none of the three she sought had reappeared she made one last circuit of the area. Despairing at the news she bore to her master, and fearful of the effect it might have on his Promise, she headed Mountainside.

She flew to the outskirts of the park and beyond, over the hills. The joints and muscles of her wings ached long before she came to the village. Aello spotted the two story structure with its multiple doors, courtyard, and a railing around the second floor.

As she banked sharply to lose altitude, her attention flicked to a shadowy figure darting away from the building. A man. A mortal.

The blood in her veins sang with joy.

24

Into the Breach

There was much Prometheus needed to do before leaving Aether for the palace of the Graeae, though he regretted the need to assume the form of Kalyptra again. He'd lived many years in her body and it felt as familiar to him as a second skin, but today he couldn't just wear it as a disguise as he'd been doing since recovering his memory. He had to *bury* Prometheus, as he had been buried for all those years by the Graeae's spell. Hide any hint of true self far below the surface, wrapped in multiple layers of disguise. Far too like his memoryless days for comfort.

The first time he'd taken the woman's form had been soon after the Graeae had violated his mind and Ares had attacked him on Olimbos, leaving him for dead on the side of the mountain. An eagle as large as a man had landed near him, and he thought his end had come. Instead it dragged him away to a nest where he healed enough to crawl, half dead, out of Erebus and up to the surface.

It was an unsettled time in Ellada's political history, a time between kings, when the people of one party refused to acknowledge any government set up by the other. Coups and coup attempts were the order of the day, and he emerged in the middle of one such attempt.

He hid in ditches and barns, fugitive, trusting no one. The only memories he possessed were the ones formed since the onset of amnesia. He wondered often if the others had survived, though he hadn't known their identities at that time anymore than he'd known his own. He wondered if the drugged wine had done its job, and his counterpart, the other voice of reason in the storm of confusion, had moved the others to safety.

He'd found Kalyptra dying near a refuse heap. A rebel fighter, perhaps, or a military widow—perhaps just a victim of famine or poverty. Whoever she was, the woman wakened a kindred empathy in Prometheus; she had also been lost, someone homeless and friendless. He'd found her beaten and starved and had given her what comfort he could until her spirit left her body the following day. Folding her arms across her chest, he wanted nothing more than to be her. To be someone with an identity, to continue her small and unremarkable life. He even envied her death, having come so close to it himself but not finding the release she had. When next his eyes had opened, he'd seen the world from the perspective of somewhat diminished height, lighter weight, and a body not his own. He hadn't understood the power that had changed him, nor had he been able to duplicate the magic to change back again.

Twenty-five years he'd lived as Kalyptra. In his new life on the surface he had felt drawn to politics, feeling out the various parties vying for power and listening to their arguments, but within months the queen arrived and the government stabilized. Life normalized in the cities and he found himself drawn instead to a new kind of outsider, the kind who hid what they were—non-mortals who'd come above, witches who toyed with power, seers. He moved in their circles, learned things from them, though he never gleaned how he might have stolen Kalyptra's body. Over the years he studied increasingly complex magics, using them to color his skin, winding potent spells in the patterns and colors that kept him hidden from his unremembered enemies. Over the decades he began to think of himself as Kalyptra.

And now he must do it again. Hide so deeply that even he would barely be aware of his true identity. But this time, he knew exactly what he did and how.

He descended from Aether before weaving his spells, so that magic in that realm wouldn't alert the Graeae. The first spell was complex, as was the second one, which masked the first—he knew he must leave no traces of magic that would be beyond the alchemy, parlor tricks, and witch spells that Kalyptra alone could have performed. A summoning to reach the Graeae also needed to be set, yet another layer to blend in before he submerged. That done, only one thing was left.

He hesitated on the brink of that last spell. Fear of losing himself again corroded his will. He wondered how long it would take him to break through if he went too deep, how much control he could safely retain if he needed his own greater power to fight for his life. Prometheus wished the gods had taken time to learn more about the Graeae. They had always been a part of the universe, a part of magic. The Titans had come into being, the world and the heavens had been created, but the Graeae had always been.

He bowed his head and closed his eyes, mustering his courage. All the elements were in place. Waiting longer was pointless. Resolved, he triggered the spells. He felt their weight as they layered in place, one after the other, like dominoes falling.

His body shrank by nearly half a meter, grew breasts, exchanged genitals, sprouted colors as if flowers bloomed on his skin. Kalyptra stood in his place. The real Kalyptra was long dead, of course, but this persona knew who moved her arms and legs, as a puppeteer might, though touching awareness of that true self felt elusive and slippery.

She sent the summoning the other had prepared.

Kalyptra stood steady as the lion approached while her hidden self, far below the surface, shuddered at the proximity to the sisters and their magic. The lion followed the orders of the Graeae, but the lion *was* the Graeae after a fashion, as were the guards and the servants; all manifestations of some whole large enough that even she found it difficult to comprehend.

She mounted the animal's back and clung to the mane.

The first leap nearly unseated her, and she gripped tighter as its speed steadily increased. It ran to the edge of Erebus, and the world passed her by, faster and faster, until vision became no more than a zoetrope of moving images. The edge of the land approached, and the lion bunched its muscles and leaped. Rather than looping them around to the other side of the underworld, the beast surmounted the boundary and passed into something beyond Erebus' fickle reality.

Whirling cosmoses flew past; lightning flashed in distant purple skies. Like a kaleidoscope cranked too rapidly, Kalyptra's surroundings spun through color and sensation. They traveled through environments hot and freezing, soft and harsh. The lion skimmed between darkness and light, over chasms where one could fall and never strike bottom for the rest of eternity. Kalyptra experienced realms with which even her other self was unfamiliar.

The world blurred and wind-tears filled her eyes, but the human eyes of her disguise weren't keeping up with the complexity of images anyway. Her hands cramped on the rough, burnt-orange hair of the lion's mane. Her legs grew tired, but she kept them tight around his middle. She couldn't breathe. Either the rush of air passed by too quickly or the air had vanished altogether, though it seemed she didn't need to breathe as long as she stayed seated on the beast.

At last, the dizzying vista of sound-filled color and light-filled darkness slowed and resolved into a sky full of strange stars hanging close overhead. Her arms and legs were beyond fatigued but she clung tight. If she fell, there was no telling where she might land, or what magic she would need to pull up from her depths to save herself. If she could.

A small rock appeared, floating through the heavens before her. The lion alighted and shook stardust from its coat, nearly unseating her. She slid down, relieved to have made it here. Before her loomed the shimmering gold palace that was home to the remaining Graeae. There was no turning back.

Kalyptra approached the palace. The height dwarfed her, and she felt as frail as this body looked. Guards along the path fell in with her, their eyeless stares drinking her in, delving for her secrets. The guards at the entrance swung the towering, arched wooden doors open toward her. She entered the domain of her enemy.

25

Convergence

Selia had been hurtled home to Erebus as a ray of starlight. "With your ability to travel moonbeams," the Graeae had said, "this should not harm you."

Should not.

The cold had been unbearable and the speed nearly stole her consciousness. Her previous illness, the Graeae, and her terrifying journeys to the palace and back had left her feeling untethered.

She arrived in the black of moonless night, somewhere out in the country. She assumed it to be the night of the same day she'd been abducted, and near to morning judging by the feel of the darkness. Walking a short distance in a randomly chosen direction, she realized she was near the village of Enyalius' home, not back at Cyrene's as she'd requested. Naia must have told the Graeae where Enyalius lived and, apparently, they wanted her to begin searching immediately.

The lack of moonlight made her shaky and off-balance, unable to dispel a gut-level revulsion. Nighttime was not the friend to Selia that it had been with her moon in the sky, but she regretted that morning was close, for the darkness provided cover. As for the night-dwellers, she'd always commanded their respect. The determination in her eye or the arrow in her fist maintained that respect, moon or no moon, and the few residents she encountered moved quickly out of her way.

She gripped the blood-red shaft as if choking it, swinging it as she walked. For more than a quarter century she had espoused her view that killing the gods was the only way to ensure safety for all. Now, with the means to begin at hand, she doubted. And she hated that she doubted.

Morning arrived before she reached Enyalius' house. Two walls of his home gaped open, forming a huge mouth. One listed inward, held at an impossible angle by its tenuous attachment to the back wall. The furnishings were rubble-strewn and the stacks of books had been widely scattered; one pile had toppled to the floor from a shelf to lie with pages crumpled and spines snapped like broken limbs. Selia dimly recalled her last sight of fallen comrades on this same floor. She pictured them with their bodies torn apart by the explosion that had thrown her clear. Not even gore or severed limbs remained to mark their fate. Only the bloodstains testified to the sacrifice made by warriors who had followed her and the ideals she had preached.

She could see at a glance that her quarry wasn't here and wouldn't be likely to return. Fingering the feathered fletching of the Graeae's arrow, she considered where to look next. Whatever doubt she had harbored moments ago was gone like the darkness. The death and destruction that had occurred here erased any reservations she might have held about killing Ares. Or anyone else who got in her way.

She turned from the house and took in all the surroundings, as if her next course of action would be self-evident once she spotted it. The house sat at the edge of the village, and the neighboring homes were unremarkable. Open land spread out on three sides.

Her moon shadow globe had led her to the harpy who, in turn, had led Selia to an officer of the New Order who lived in an apartment in Cyrene's village. Selia wished now that she had warned Cyrene about the cigar-smoking man, but things had moved too quickly while planning the attack on Enyalius that same night.

When the Graeae's guards had dragged her away this morning, she'd seen Cyrene's still form lying near the door. She focused on the hope that Cyrene had been unconscious, not... not anything worse. She would go first to Cyrene's home and hope to find her recovered there. They could go together to the apartment of the cigar-smoking man, and if that bore no fruit, they would start searching for the harpy. She would find the enemy she sought. Enyalius had killed her allies. Ares might kill a whole world.

Yes, once begun, there would be no going back, nor should there be.

The door opened to Aello's tentative knock. A gout of cigar smoke wafted toward her like smoke from a hearth fire lit with the chimney flue still closed.

"I have brought one that the master seeks," Aello rasped. She spoke seldom and hated her voice when she did. It came out weak as an old hag's and with the croaking catch of a bird.

The master's man looked down at her taloned feet, which held the shadow-mortal face-down on the stone, struggling beneath her nails.

He glanced over his shoulder into the dimly lit room behind. Receiving some confirmation, he opened the door wider.

Aello hesitated, unsure of entering into the unmasked presence of her master. She stepped off the mortal's back and lifted him with one claw, grabbing his arm with one of her thin hands. He surprised her by planting a foot against the doorframe and kicking back, trying to send her over the balcony. She beat her wings for balance. Her master's man gut-punched the mortal and hauled their, now unresisting, prey inside.

Aello waited a moment to be sure she was still invited, but the door remained open. She stepped gingerly over the threshold. She had always inspired fear in those beneath her and been loyal and respectful to those above her, and that was the sum of her. Initiative was not her way. She folded her wings tightly, so as not to bump anything.

"He had some troubles a few days ago," the man said to her, indicating their master with a nod toward the corner while still gripping a wad of the mortal's T-shirt with one hand. "He's, ah, not exactly been himself lately. Why don't you tell me your news, and I'll tell him. How's that then?"

The shutters were closed, the room dim, but the shadows here were not the deep shadows of her cave; she could clearly see her master, draped in blue robes, sitting in a large chair near the far wall. He stared at her silently, unnerving her more now than when he had been an enigma. She raised one of her hands to the sparse feathers on her head in a futile sweeping motion, trying to smooth them.

Addressing her master's man she said, "I stayed at the brook, like I was told. I saw who holds the item the master seeks. I caught the feel of it and flew toward it, and found the three of them. Eros' daughter, this one," she indicated the human man with her head, "and a woman I've never seen before. Her skin all stitched, her neck red as fresh blood and her face green as moss. She held the thing of power." She swallowed painfully from talking so much at once. The wounds in her throat had not yet healed from the bone the master had made her eat. "And then they were gone, like they'd never been. I was coming here to tell you about them when I saw this one creeping around outside."

"Well," the big man said, letting go of the mortal. "Well, well." He walked to the chair in the corner, stopping a few feet from the master. "Aello here says Kalyptra has your key."

Ty, finally able to draw a gasping breath after being punched in the solar plexus, sucked in the smoke that Momus puffed like a campfire in a breeze and choked back a cough. The hammering in his heart hadn't slowed since the harpy had grabbed him. She'd been surprisingly careful with him, leaving no more than scratches from her claws, but his memories of Lamia being torn to shreds had invoked a blind panic at her touch, only now slowly ebbing.

In the same way Naia's apartment had changed with his new sight, Ty noted the differences here. Like the exterior, the interior was now more in keeping with ancient styles. There was no evidence of the fine craftsmanship in Naia's home; furnishings were spare and done in rough hewn wood and stone, the walls bare of decoration. The throw rugs were mostly of single colors and without patterns in the threads. One detail remained unchanged—the place was still a mess. Clay cups and dishes covered the few surfaces, clothes lay strewn where they'd been discarded, and cigar butts filled small bowls everywhere.

"Where is Kalyptra?" Enyalius said, his deep and theatrically-pitched voice rumbling from the corner.

"Gone," Ty bluffed. "Back to the surface, I think."

"Then you're no good to me anymore."

Aello made an odd gurgle behind him, a sound of shock, or perhaps sadness.

"You're wrong," Ty said, before the harpy standing behind Momus could fly off with him, or tear his face to shreds, or whatever Enyalius might have in mind for him. "Why do you think I came here?"

With the bullshit confidence of gamblers he'd known, Ty pushed his way past the bulk of Momus and stood in front of Enyalius-Ares. The god sat on the battered recliner, one which Ty saw in his real sight as only a slightly less battered chair covered in tanned hide and probably stuffed with coarse hair. The meter of Ares' madness was clear in his eyes, which were divided horizontally across the irises—the upper halves deep brown, the lower halves gold. He seemed only slightly less fractured than when Ty had last seen him, downtown, near the park.

"Tell me then, Eutychios, why are you here?"

"Kalyptra doesn't have the key anymore. I do. And I've come to bargain."

It was pure skatá, of course. His hopes for coming here furtively had been dashed, and the best he could do now was try to buy time for Prometheus and protect Naia. If his ploy got him outside the apartment, all the better. His chances of escape would improve at least a little.

"The only bargain you can strike," Enyalius said, "is the key for your life."

"I know. That's why I didn't bring it with me."

Money into the ante.

"Then what is there to make me believe you have it and not Kalyptra?"

"Nothing." Ty shrugged. "But what are you going to do about that since you don't know where she is?"

Raise.

"I want out of here," Ty continued. "I want out of Erebus, out of your fucking politics, and out of your fucking lives. I want to go back to the surface and be left alone."

Enyalius showed no reaction, no surprise. Neither belief, nor disbelief. "And what of Eros' daughter? No bargain for her?"

Ty opened his mouth to answer, but the god suddenly addressed a corner of the ceiling. "Eros, do you stir?" He looked back, not quite at Ty, but at some middle ground between them. "They watch us even now. The others sleep, but they watch and I see the world through their eyes."

Ty felt out of his depth. His gambling streak had been nothing more than Kairos' hand up his ass, working him like a puppet. His father had been the real thing, though. Ty had always hated that heritage, but he called on it now to channel the part he needed to play. He replied to the question about Naia, as if Enyalius hadn't babbled utter nonsense.

"Naia can rot, for all I care. She manipulated me with love spells, nothing more. I stole the key from her and it wasn't so hard to take it again from Kalyptra. And now I've hidden it where even your harpy can't find it." Ty's back muscles tensed, feeling the grotesque bird-woman behind him. "I'm nothing to you, and you know it. You lose nothing by letting me go, and you gain everything you want in return."

Enyalius pushed off the couch and approached Ty. Momus, who had watched the exchange in silence, moved to his master's side in one long stride. Aello moved forward to flank Ty.

Just as the god's irises and sanity were divided, so was his disguise. He had shaved—or simply lost—the long, white beard, revealing a strong square jaw. His skin was tighter, unlined, younger. Having stood before Prometheus, Ty could see the god-like similarities.

"Take me to it. Now."

"No."

Call.

"Fine. Aello will get the information from you. It's her specialty, after all."

The harpy's feathers fluffed with what Ty interpreted to be eagerness.

"It'll take longer that way. You sure you want that? You're not the only one looking for this thing. Besides, there's no need. I'm not resisting. I'm willing to give it to you. All I need from you is a promise I can trust. Some token. A free pass."

"I think maybe he's right, you know," Momus said, speaking up at last. "No need for Aello here to bloody up my rugs."

Ty observed his opponents. Momus could see reason in taking the easiest path to the goal, but Aello shot him a baleful glance from an angle that Enyalius couldn't see. Disappointment at losing out on a little torture?

She smoothed the feathers on her head. "Whatever you wish," she croaked. "I only serve."

No, Ty thought. She wanted something, and he wished he knew what it was. The most important question, though, was what did Enyalius want most? With an intuitive leap, and maybe some innate gambler's skill after all, Ty threw all his coins in the pot.

"Ares, don't you want to turn that key and see them all again? Don't you want to remember?"

"It's been too long," Naia said.

Fear for Ty's safety had crawled up and down her skin so often, she felt like she'd been covered in ants. Every time she decided to leave and try and find him, Cyrene had countered that Ty might return while she was gone, making it harder for them all to meet up again. Naia flung back the same argument when Cyrene told her to stay put while she went to Enyalius' house to look for Selia.

The time they'd spent waiting hadn't been wasted. Naia shared with Cyrene how Ty had ended up in Erebus and what little she knew of Momus, who had been torturing Ty when the Revisionists broke in. She also told her all that Prometheus had shared about the Graeae.

Cyrene, in turn, told Naia what happened at Enyalius' after Ty and Naia escaped, including the ruthless executions and her loss of consciousness that had doubtless saved her. Also the fact that Momus had not been among the dead when she'd recovered. She couldn't say what had become of the man who had single-handedly killed a centaur, but she had recognized him from having seen him around her village. She'd only risked bringing Selia here as there'd been no other option now that Selia's moon and her road home were gone.

By the time they'd finished their stories, they were both done with waiting.

"Do you think Selia will go to Momus' apartment?" Naia asked.

Cyrene shook her head. "I don't think Selia knew him. You and I can go by his apartment first, though. It's close, and we might learn if Ares has been seen around there, disguised as Enyalius or not. If that proves fruitless, we could head for Enyalius' home next."

"And if that fails too, it'll be anyone's guess where Ty, Selia, or Ares might be found," Naia said, helping Cyrene to her feet.

Cyrene swayed less now when she stood, but still looked unwell. Her pale skin, clenched teeth, and the light sweat on her forehead said plain as words that nausea still assailed her, but Naia knew that saying she would go alone would be useless.

They left the house and started across the village. "Do you need to rest?" Naia asked, when Cyrene stopped and grabbed at a low wall for balance.

Cyrene shook her head. Naia saw her push the weakness down and stand straighter. She wondered what cost Cyrene would pay when she stopped holding herself up by sheer willpower.

The village was smaller than Naia's, and they soon neared the two-story building they sought. With their goal in sight, Cyrene staggered a second time. Naia threw an arm around her shoulder, but too late. Cyrene fell. The only purchase Naia found was a scrap of garment at her back and a handful of the woman's hair. It was enough to break her fall, if not gently. Naia lowered Cyrene to the ground.

The wind of an arrow ruffled the air across her back.

Naia threw herself flat across Cyrene's limp body. The bits of her that had reflexively turned to water at the sound of the arrow pulled back into flesh.

"Harm her at your peril!"

Selia's voice.

Naia wished she knew what the Graeae had told Selia. Lies, she felt certain, but which ones? She carefully let go of Cyrene's hair and rested the half-conscious woman's head on the ground. Remaining on her knees, she raised both hands, half in supplication, half in a gesture of yielding. She spotted Selia. She hovered at the edge of a nearby home, using the corner of the house for cover. She had a quiver at her back and a second arrow notched and drawn.

"Selia," Naia raised her voice to carry. "One of the gods has regained his memory. He is sane and he offers us his help."

"I know that Enyalius is Ares," Selia shouted back. "He is far from regaining his memory and farther still from sanity. He heads the order that seeks to destroy everything, the way he destroyed my moon. Ares is proof of all I have said would come to pass."

"I don't speak of Ares, I speak of Prometheus."

"Prometheus died," Selia shot back.

Naia doubted she could change to water more quickly than an arrow could fly, and hoped Selia gave her the chance to explain.

"The arrow you sank into Ares' heart should have killed him. So it was with Prometheus. What seemed to kill him did not. I'm certain the Graeae brought you to them, as they did me. They seek to kill all the gods, and they're using you to keep their hands clean."

Naia remained on her knees, hands elevated, giving Selia no reason to loose the arrow drawn to her cheek. Cyrene stirred against her feet.

"Enyo and Pemphredo were behind it all," she continued. "Not Deino. Prometheus remembers their attack. They want to rule in place of the gods, and we've all been pawns in their game."

She didn't dare stand, but Selia was either listening or, at the least, she was hesitating. Naia continued. "You're not like the followers of the New Order; you're not motivated by greed or power. I've always known this, even though I couldn't agree with your goals. We're the same, Selia. We've both been seeking in our own way to make things right. We've both been working to ensure the safety of the surface world as well as Erebus and Tartarus. Now we have a way."

Selia's arm held steady, bowstring at her cheek, the tip of the arrow aimed at Naia's heart. She could hold the stance with no tremor in her muscles long enough for Naia to say what she would in her defense.

Naia's words were convincing, but only this morning Selia had seen the destruction Ares had wrought, reaffirming her conviction to destroy the gods and anyone who stood in her way. Naia was right, though; they weren't so very different, only their solutions. Prometheus. The Graeae. What was true and what false? The Graeae said not to kill Naia until Ares was found, and then they would destroy them all. But why was Cyrene here with Naia? Why did Naia drag her by the hair like a doll toward the home of an enemy? Selia sought to discern truth or deceit in every line, every nuance of expression, every word.

Cyrene moved. She pushed to her hands and knees behind Naia. She tried to rise.

"Selia," she croaked. "Help—"

Selia loosed the arrow.

26

Parlay

The guards surrounded Kalyptra like wolves around an animal separated from the herd as they led her to the Graeae. Kalyptra gathered all the indifference and cool arrogance she'd hidden behind for so long. They stopped at one door of many lining the hall. A female guard depressed the ornate gold handle, pushed the door inward, and stepped back. Kalyptra entered alone, and the door closed behind her.

The two living Graeae stood back to back in a room done in multiple shades of green. They wore a green dress with gold embroidery, their heads crowned in gold diadems and mirrored circlets. They stood sideways to her, but Kalyptra knew both watched her in their mirrors.

"You have commandeered our lion to your own purpose, girl," they spoke in unison. "What have you to say before we pass our judgment?"

She wouldn't survive this on bravado. Even her other self couldn't. Her red neck went a shade deeper and the moss green of her face felt as if it glowed with the blush beneath.

"I wouldn't have done it but for the greatest urgency. My Queen, I have something to offer you." Kalyptra reached into a pocket of her pants. She proffered a closed fist and opened her fingers slowly. The glittering colors of the gryphon key winked at the sisters.

They turned, Enyo facing forward. Their excitement showed in the quickness with which they approached Kalyptra. Enyo reached for it, but Kalyptra snatched it back.

A pregnant silence filled the room.

"How did you come by this?" Enyo and Pemphredo said coldly.

"That's not all. I know how to find the sleeping gods."

Pemphredo walked forward, making the sisters seem to walk backwards from Kalyptra's perspective. They turned as one and sidestepped over one of the heavily padded benches in the room and sat. Enyo extended a hand, indicating the couch before her, and Kalyptra took a seat. The silence stretched beyond tension and into discomfort.

Kalyptra spoke first. "What I offer is beyond value. I want things in return."

The sisters said nothing.

"I've assisted the New Order for many years, but I think if the order succeeds I'll be kept as far from power as their lowest member. Besides, I've lost faith that anyone could actually control the gods once woken. I've come to believe you want to kill them." Kalyptra met Enyo's eyes steadily. "If I help you instead, I want to be the only one sitting at your side. I want to be the sister you lost."

A wild conceit, of course. But a believable one for a woman as young and arrogant as she seemed.

"To find us here, to summon our lion, to capture the key, these are not small things you have achieved. Tell us how you came by the key and how to find the hiding place of the gods."

Kalyptra stood, knowing full well it was unconscionable to stand while the sisters sat. She paced around the couch and placed her hands on the tapestried back.

"Not yet. The key you could take from me by force. The knowledge you could not. When I give you both things, you hold every card. What assurance do I have that I get anything in return?" She reached in her pocket and gripped the key, squeezing the uneven edges of metal so tightly it hurt.

"I do this for power," Kalyptra continued. "That's no secret. Give me some now. If I pledge to be your god-killer, then give me the spell that put them to sleep and kept them asleep all this time. If one wakes up and fights me I want to be able to do more than piss my pants." She finished her circuit of the couch and sat again.

"This we cannot do. The gods drugged themselves to sleep. The herbs they used channeled their inherent magic, and their source of power is different than ours. The spell of endless sleep they combined with the drug is one you could only learn from them."

Kalyptra, whose other self had known this very well, simulated a moue of frustration. "Then give me the spell that took their memories. Do that and I'll hand you the key. I also want an escape spell to get the hell out of there if things go wrong. For that spell, I'll give you the means to find them."

The sisters rose. They sidestepped the bench then sidestepped back again to stand in front of Kalyptra. Enyo reached forward and laid a finger on her chest. Kalyptra's human heart thudded in her ears. The Graeae had spelled an entire pantheon of gods at once; they could kill her for the infractions she'd dared here with no more effort than it took them to breathe—if they breathed at all.

Her heart pounded so violently, Enyo's finger should have jumped in time to the pulse. If they even suspected her deeper subterfuge, her death was certain. Or perhaps they would turn her request against her, show her how the gods lost their memories by doing it to her. By doing it to her again, her small, hidden self thought—lose it all again between one loud beat of her heart and the next. She squelched the hint of an inner self, hoping the sisters hadn't detected it.

Instead, she felt bonds form. Heavy but invisible chains ran from her chest to Enyo's finger. They wrapped about Kalyptra's heart, binding her irrevocably to her promises. Whatever happened now, there was no escape.

"Swear on your life," Enyo said. "The key and the hiding place."

"On my life," Kalyptra said weakly.

The sisters shuffled until they both stood sideways to her and each held out her nearest hand. Kalyptra stood from the couch and tentatively took their offered hands. They didn't have the feel of real skin, more like cold and finely malleable rubber with no hint of callous, wrinkle or fingerprint. Kalyptra fought down a terror previously unknown in this body or any other.

And then it was there. The spell of amnesia. So vast, so complex. "It's too difficult. I don't understand it." The words came from Kalyptra's lips—something that would have been true had this knowledge been handed to the witchy girl she pretended to be—but her other self experienced a surge of triumph.

"That is not our concern." They let go of Kalyptra's hands. "The key."

Kalyptra retrieved it from a pocket and placed it in Enyo's palm. They both stared at it intently through Enyo's eyes.

"And your strongest escape spell," Kalyptra said.

They replied in unison, "Done."

And it was there also. Inside her head, just like that. Not an escape she—her inner self—could have contrived, but the Graeae's own spell, a thing of their making that should work against them. She fought the impulse to use it this second. Breaking the pact would kill her on the spot, as would anything less than the truth. The chains about her heart would kill not only Kalyptra's body, but even the self hidden within.

"Tell us where the gods hide."

"I will tell you who knows. Eutychios Kleisos."

"The mortal?" Their faces never changed, but from their dual inflection, it seemed Kalyptra had succeeded in surprising the sisters a second time.

Her other self felt a twinge of regret at using Naia's lover yet again. "He isn't aware of it consciously, but it's there, in his childhood memories."

The Graeae remained sideways to her, but instead of watching her in their mirrors both stared straight ahead with a faraway look. Kalyptra wondered what pieces of the puzzle she had just handed them to add to their visions of past and future.

"What now?" Kalyptra asked. "I've heard rumors you seek Ares. If you want proof of my loyalty, send me to hunt him for you."

"No. We will go now to the mortal." The sisters walked across the floor to a nearby window, both staring out, Enyo forward and Pemphredo, apparently, through her sister's eyes. "First, Prometheus, tell us how you defeated your amnesia."

Panic flared through Kalyptra's human body, adrenaline numbing her lips and hands. Prometheus fought his suppression spells and struggled to surface. His body changed as his godhood emerged. He called up the escape spell they'd given him.

He had bet not only his life, but all the lives in multiple worlds, on three principles of magic. The Graeae couldn't defeat their own magic—only tie it; his god's power could overcome any inherent traps they may have laid for someone with the power of the human witch-girl he seemed to be; and, most importantly, his magic—so different from their own—in combination with their spell, would succeed against them where nothing else could.

He loomed above her, all trace of Kalyptra gone. He triggered the escape spell.

Nothing happened.

PART THREE

Tartarus Descending

27

Best Laid Plans

Prometheus dwindled, along with his hope, until he stood eye-level with the Graeae, fully himself once again.

"No," the sisters said, answering his unasked question, "your thoughts didn't give you away. You can't hide a god."

He didn't think they could actually read minds but, with their understanding of past and future, it seemed they didn't need to. When Deino lived, they must've been virtually omniscient. Prometheus harbored no regrets. The crossroads of his returned memory had demanded he choose a path, and this was the only path that might have led to the rescue of the other gods.

Enyo and Pemphredo each lifted one hand and, together, unbuttoned the high neck of their dress. The flesh above their shoulder swelled, distorted, darkened. A face pushed out from the mass like a fast-growing tumor. Their sister's grotesque head flopped forward until the nose nearly touched their shoulder. The first expression

Prometheus had seen on either of the Graeae's faces flashed; a tiny hint of tremendous relief.

"Was it worth it?" he asked them.

"Not yet, but soon."

"Would you have stopped with us? With Ellada's pantheon?"

Enyo and Pemphredo turned smoothly and walked back to him until Enyo stood only inches from him. Deino's head rolled forward when they stopped, her horrified expression aimed now at his feet. "No," they said.

He had suspected as much. If they embodied the universe, why not rule the universe? Killing his pantheon would release the power of the gods on their deaths. The laws of nature wouldn't allow the magic to disappear. It would be there for the Graeae to absorb. And if the Graeae absorbed the new and different magic of his pantheon, then gods of other nations would be that much more vulnerable to them. And if they absorbed all the magic in this world, then other worlds—if there were any—might fall to them as well. It was a plan worthy of infinity.

"There's only one problem," he said. They stared at him impassive, unblinking. "Even if you kill both Ares and me, even if you obtain the location of the other gods, you won't open their hiding place. And without them, you can go no further."

He thought he detected haste in their movements as Enyo and Pemphredo both reached into the pocket of their dress. Their two hands together fit poorly in there, and they grappled for a moment. When they pulled the key out, each of them held one half.

The Graeae looked at the broken halves of the gryphon key; the snare he had set when he laid his other spells. They watched in horror—as close to it as those frozen faces could come—as the two halves disintegrated to dust. The sisters turned their hands palms down and the multi-colored dust drifted to the floor in a cloud of metallic sparkles, not unlike the shifting walls around them.

Enyo still faced Prometheus. Her eyes darkened until they were black as the sky outside. He was glad he couldn't see both their faces at once. Unlike the guards' eyes, hers were pinpricked with tiny stars. She opened her mouth wide, and the same blackness loomed within. The multitude of reflections of Pemphredo in her mirrors showed she did the same.

Prometheus' heart wasn't human, but if it could have thundered in his chest with fear, it would have.

The Graeae's mouths continued to open, wider and wider. Above the neck they morphed into nothing but blackness filled with cold silver pinpricks. Small swirls of bright color appeared, and flashes of light, like the strange, otherworldly things he had seen on his journey here. Prometheus could never have imagined an entire universe enraged. He wished he was not seeing it now.

There were no words for what Enyo and Pemphredo felt, but there had never been a need for words between them. Had they been complete and whole still, their rage would have shaken the pillars of existence. They had laid traps within the spell they gave the god, but traps that had been within the rules of magic. If the human witch, Kalyptra, had possessed the skill to perform the escape spell, no trap would've sprung, but it had been the god within that tried to use it. The god had played the rules even closer to the edge; he had given them the key—the real key—but he had not said it would work. In their eagerness, they had missed seeing the open jaws that came with his offer.

The time of hiding was done. Two gods were loose, and between them they could be the ruination of everything. Enyo and Pemphredo couldn't wait any longer for others to do things for them. They couldn't risk this god using the knowledge they had given him to cure the others. They had to find where the amnesic gods slept and, once there, find a way in or lose everything.

This god would be needed for a while longer, and the mortal man they needed right now. They knew how to track him by the scars cut into his left wrist, and so the sisters became the universe. They found what they sought. And they moved.

"Help her," Naia heard Cyrene rasp at her back. Before she could finish, Selia had fired her bow.

Naia let go of her body with more abandon than she'd known possible and rained down to the flagstones. As if from underwater, she heard the sound of the arrow strike flesh and wondered distantly if it had hit some part of her still unchanged. She flowed downhill.

A keening cry of grief split the air, a sound so mournful it pulled Naia up off the cobbles into her body again as if drawn upright by the pressure of emotion filling the air above her. Selia hunched on her knees a few lengths away, hugging Cyrene's lifeless body. The arrow fletching poked up from under Selia's arm, making it look as if both women were pinned together, face to face, by the same arrow.

Selia's grief was unbearable to watch. Naia swayed with the memories of her own love and grief for Lamia. She wished that she could have held Lamia as she died.

Naia tore herself from the scene before her; she needed to get away while Selia was distracted, but to where? She'd had no chance to scout the apartment. She didn't know if Selia had heard Cyrene's final words in their entirety or if the woman would try again to kill her.

Naia ran toward the apartment one street away, trying to put cover between herself and Selia while she puzzled out what to do next. This close to her goal, she couldn't leave without at least trying to see if Ty was there. She could change to water to be less noticeable, but she'd have to get to that second floor balcony first. Angling toward the building, she paused near the courtyard, searching for any discreet way to approach. She scanned the area for run-off paths, aqueducts, wells, or any other water ingress or egress possibilities she could follow.

Just as she entered the courtyard, the world went crazy.

Darkness exploded, hacking the soft light into distinct edges. Pinpricks of silver dotted the blackness, sharp and lancing, and cold beyond measure surrounded Naia. Flashes of light blinked crazily. The emptiness within the dark stole her breath, sucking it out as if ripped from her lungs.

Suffocating, she spun in a circle. Though the blackness felt huge, bigger than the sky, she saw it covered only this one building. There was no doubt what caused it—who caused it. She fought to keep her feet, to breathe in and out, though the air seemed to rush past her from every quarter of Erebus, disappearing into the vacuum.

The apparition vanished as quickly as it had appeared. Nothing remained to indicate it had ever been—nothing except the residents of the building vacating quickly, whether or not they understood the source of the threat.

Naia ran heedlessly against the flow, up the exterior staircase to the second floor of the building, and down the balcony to the door Cyrene had pointed out.

28

---◆◇◆---

Arrivals and Departures

T y had named Ares and reminded him that he was a god. He
braced for any of the many responses his rashness might provoke,
but Momus reacted first. He grabbed Ty one-handed by the neck of his
T-shirt and a few unshaven chest hairs, and carried him to the nearest
wall. Slamming him against the stone between the shuttered window
and the door, he gripped his cigar in his teeth to speak.

"I've spent a fair bit of time and effort getting him back to normal,
Ty." The smoke and the words hit him in the face. "I don't appreciate
you interfering. No, I really don't appreciate it one bit."

"What you've spent time getting him back to was an invented
persona," Ty said, calmly as he could. "What he is, is a god."

"To remember," Ares said. His irises flashed entirely to gold when
light from the window caught them. "The others sleep, but I see
through their eyes. They dream of remembering."

He'd said something similar earlier, and Ty wondered if maybe it
wasn't madness after all. Momus and Aello both turned to the man

they knew as Enyalius, perhaps thinking the same. Aello's face lit with an eagerness that looked to Ty almost hopeful. Ty held his breath, waiting to see which way the wind would blow. Momus turned back to Ty and laughed. Not a jolly, belly laugh, but a dark, rumble from his smoke filled lungs. He shifted his grip from Ty's chest to his throat, apparently remembering the effect that choking had on him the last time, when he'd tried to burn his eye.

The pressure over Ty's scar evaporated all pretense of calm, and his gambler persona fell away. He thrashed and tore at Momus' large hand, more from panic of choking than knowing his one chance to reason with Ares was lost. Momus removed his cigar from his teeth with his other hand and held it between two fingers, wagging it at Ty as he spoke.

"Why don't you just tell us now where that key is, and then we'll talk bargains, eh?"

Ty reached toward the floor with his toes, scraping the tips of his boots on the rug. He clawed at Momus' meaty fist.

"Go fuck yourself." His voice pushed against the constriction, coming out uglier than Aello's. "Kill me and it's gone forever."

Momus' stubbled jaw hardened. His dirty, round face pulled into lines angrier and more serious than before. Ty had hoped the key a big enough safety net, but may have misjudged. With his master lost in delusions or visions, maybe Momus would kill him and deal with the consequences later.

Momus pulled Ty to him until they were belly to belly, then slammed him into the wall again. Ty tipped his head into the choking pressure of Momus' grip at the last moment to avoid getting his head smashed, but felt bones in his neck and back pop. Momus pulled him away from the wall again, staring into his face, seeming prepared to repeat the process until Ty gave him what he wanted or until he was nothing more than a skin sack full of broken bones and mush.

With no breath left for words, Ty spat in Momus' face.

Prometheus felt the icy floor beneath his feet fall away. The void into which he tumbled seemed larger somehow than the void through which he had traveled to the Graeae's palace. The unreal chains tied to his god's heart pulled him along by his chest, bouncing sometimes face up, sometimes face down, though he knew up and down no longer existed. He stopped amid a crash of darkness colliding with light and opened his eyes onto a small room.

The first thing he saw was Ares. His eyes shimmered gold, mad as a lunatic's. The sight of his fellow god and his open, unguided mind gave Prometheus more hope than anything had since re-discovering the key. "Brother," he said silently into that unguarded mind. "Run."

When the darkness descended, Selia wondered if she'd held Cyrene to her chest so long that night had fallen. No, that couldn't be right. Perhaps her grief had summoned some manifestation. Looking down, though, she saw Cyrene still illuminated in soft light. Perhaps her soul outshone the darkness. Selia looked up through eyes blurred with tears, confused.

So many reasons Cyrene had not needed to die. Selia had never witnessed Naia's talent for water. She'd had no idea she'd inherited such strong skill from her mother. Had she realized, she never would have fired her bow, but worse guilt than that haunted Selia.

"Her," Selia heard in her mind for the hundredth time. "Help *her*," she'd heard as the arrow released. Help Naia.

She pulled back from her grief reluctantly and turned. Darkness draped the sky nearby. Not night, but a void in the world. Utter blackness, shot through with searing silver. Squinting against the sparks and streaks, she raised a hand to shield her eyes. The void had irregular dimensions, sharp as razor cuts, and it covered only the apartment building.

Selia set Cyrene gently on the ground, placing a soft kiss on her forehead. Standing, she found the blood-red arrow of the Graeae by feel in the quiver at her back and nocked the arrow to her bowstring. The iridescent red and black feather fletching shone in the wild mix of light and dark and silver sparks. The slice of cold, black space could mean little except the Graeae, but if they had come here, that meant something more. Ares must be in there. She began walking toward the building. Someone was going to pay in blood for Cyrene's death.

The apartment was blacker than the deepest cave. The silver sparkles could have been no larger than the pointed end of his locksmith's rasp and did nothing to illuminate the room, but they were so bright that Ty couldn't look directly at them. It felt like watching shooting stars from only a few feet away. He blinked into the contradiction of dark and light and tried to orient.

Bright light unable to illuminate pitch blackness wasn't the only contradiction. The darkness held none of the claustrophobia he'd experienced in the cave under Lake Marathon; instead he felt as if he had just stepped off a cliff of impossible height and hung now, like a cartoon, for that moment before gravity realized he was there. He couldn't catch his breath, and knew the source was no longer the fact that Momus still had him by the throat. The big man's grip had loosened, and Ty's feet rested on the floor. Dizziness assaulted Ty and a whine began in his ears. He sensed others in the room with him besides Ares, Momus, and Aello. He could feel their mass taking up space not previously occupied.

Someone ran past him. He had the fleeting impression of a robe fluttering.

The disconnection and disorientation lasted only a few seconds before light, gravity, and other physical sensations of normalcy returned. The Graeae stood sideways to him in the center of the room. Prometheus, in his loincloth, stood to Ty's right of them. Ares was gone.

Ty twisted free of Momus' grip and lunged for the door that he could now see had been half-blown off its hinges. Momus grabbed him by the back of his shirt and pulled him against his belly, crooking one big arm around his neck to hold him there. Ty tensed to slam his head back into Momus' nose, but froze, registering a puddle of water on the balcony that hadn't been there before.

"You," the Graeae said, "stop." Aello froze halfway to the door. She smoothed the feathers on her head and bobbed in what Ty thought might be an awkward bow. The Graeae each lifted a hand and each hand pointed one finger at Ty. "Where do the gods sleep?"

"What?" he stammered. He tried to shrug Momus off, but the big man held him firmly.

"I can't find the door," Prometheus said to him "but you can."

Ty felt as if another concussion had just slammed him against the wall. More betrayal? And this time from Prometheus? The treachery tore open his emotional scars yet again, but it would be nothing to what Naia would feel. If that puddle of water was her, as he was sure it was, he wondered if she could understand the conversation while in that form.

"I don't know anything about the gods." He spat the words in the general direction of both Prometheus and the Graeae.

"Guide the memories," the sisters said, addressing Prometheus. The god jerked toward Ty as if he'd been tugged forward by his breastbone.

"I don't know where they are," Ty said to the god, hearing the desperation in his own voice. "It's the truth. I don't."

Momus pulled Ty backward a few awkward steps. The man said nothing, but Ty could feel the tension in his muscles. Chances were that Momus had never encountered the Graeae. He wanted to hang onto his prize and wasn't sure what fought him for it. The constriction of his hand on Ty's arm and his forearm around his throat were gone in the next instant as Momus fell away from him. Ty heard the thud of his landing.

He turned to see Momus on the floor. His face had exploded like a melon dropped onto concrete. The split ran lengthwise, exposing the red, gelatinous mess inside, and continued down to the top of his chest. Ty looked at Prometheus, who looked almost human in his sadness, then to the Graeae, who did not. He had no doubt which enemy had just removed a minor obstacle to their goal.

Prometheus laid a hand on Ty's shoulder, not sparing Momus so much as a glance. "You grew up in the neighborhood where I lived, Ty. My conscious memories had been stolen, but when I slept, I dreamed the dreams of a god. A god's dreams are tangible; they drifted."

Ty couldn't focus on the words. He couldn't stop the replay of the image of Momus' head, looking as if it'd been split open by a sword then pried apart and stepped on repeatedly.

Prometheus gripped his shoulder harder, forcing him to listen. "When I regained my memories and my power I searched, hoping against hope I might find someone nearby who had died and come back; someone near enough that their death journey might have been affected by the sub-conscious twining of my dreams with those of my fellow gods. I heard of a neighborhood boy who had died not once but twice."

Now he had Ty's full attention.

"You saw the gods, didn't you?" Prometheus asked.

Falsehood now would be pointless. "I saw them, but I have no idea where they were," Ty said.

"You will." Prometheus glanced back to the Graeae.

And then Ty was there.

He was a child again, flickering between five and seven years old. His clothes changing from swim shorts to the pajamas he had worn when he hanged. The room he stood in was enclosed in vast, gray stone, the biers stretched out in rows all around him. The smell was musty and damp, sulfurous and sweet. His heart lay unbeating inside his chest. His lungs were simultaneously filled with water and emptied of air, his skin pale from lack of blood flow.

The god on the bier closest to him had his hands folded across his chest in an aspect of death. His face was chiseled perfection and his dark hair fell in soft curls to his shoulders. His robe was pinned with a silver clasp at one shoulder, leaving half his chest bare.

The room thrummed with power. It vibrated like a stringed instrument after the last note has passed beyond hearing. Ty's small body trembled, as if moved by the vibration. He wasn't supposed to be here. The adult Ty watching the memory with Prometheus knew that his spirit should have gone to the other side of this tomb's wall. Not the fields of heroes. Not the pits of torment. But just outside this place to Asphodel, where the faithful spirits lived on, shades of their former selves. Where his mother and ancestors walked the shadowed lands. Instead he had gone to the place Prometheus had dreamed of while asleep.

"I know the place," Prometheus said, as if to himself. "Had I not fought against my fellow Titans long ago, I would have been buried there also." His voice came to Ty as if from a great distance. Ty opened eyes filled with the tears of a child, the memories of that tomb as fresh as when he first revived from his deaths.

"We know it also," the Graeae said in unison, "but you will come with us until we are sure." Ty didn't know if they addressed him or the god. "Daughter of the Moon," they said, raising their voices. "We feel you outside. Ares has fled. Follow him. As for your lover," Ty felt certain they spoke to him now, "we need her no more."

'Daughter of the Moon' must mean Selia was nearby, but more importantly, they were aware that Naia lay pooled on the balcony. The Graeae could act in the space of a thought and, like Momus, Naia would be no more. *Damn the consequences*, Ty thought. He rushed the sisters.

The strum of a bowstring and thud of an arrow beat him. The arrow knocked the sisters backward, passing through Enyo's breast and emerging from Pemphredo's. The tip of the arrow nailed them to the wall. Their fused spine and skull held them perfectly upright, like a dead bug on a pin.

Prometheus lunged out the door. "Ares," he shouted.

Ty stared from the Graeae to Selia, who stood in the doorway. He rushed out the door, past her to Naia, who was reforming into human shape. Aello shouldered him aside and leapt over the railing, wings flapping to gain elevation.

Ares stood at the corner of the balcony, Prometheus' hand on his shoulder. Things were happening too quickly for Ty to parse, but he felt a spark of hope that maybe Prometheus worked with them still and that the god had accomplished whatever he'd wanted by going to the Graeae. It certainly hadn't looked like it when he'd been yanked around by some invisible bond and done the Graeae's bidding.

"Are you okay?" he asked Naia.

She nodded, clutching him as if he might vanish. "We need to get out of here," she said.

He took her hand with a last glance back at the Graeae.

Enyo twitched. Her eyes opened and she lifted first one hand then the other to the shaft of the arrow. Pemphredo did the same, pushing her hands between her body and the wall. The arrow disintegrated and fell to the floor like ash.

Ty jerked at Naia's hand. They ran.

A noise on the balcony made Ty look back. Prometheus had been yanked off his feet. He slid now along the balcony on his back, his chest arched in pain. Ares stood where he'd been, his eyes deep brown and his aspect that of a god.

Enyo and Pemphredo each lifted an arm and Ty's world turned black.

29

The Key

One moment Naia was running hand in hand with Ty, the next, he vanished. She turned, looking down the length of balcony.

"They're all gone," Selia said. "The Graeae, Prometheus, and Ty. Ares disappeared a moment later."

Naia walked to the door, her legs unsteady at the thought of losing Ty to them again. If Ares had left after the Graeae, perhaps he had escaped. Even if Prometheus hadn't been able to heal him, 'Enyalius' might have conjured a spell borne of fear.

She looked into the empty apartment, not because she didn't believe Selia, but because she had to see for herself. The 'nearly empty' apartment, she amended. Momus was recognizable only by his size and the cigar lying near his head.

"Why?" she asked, turning to Selia.

Selia understood her question. "Seeing Prometheus convinced me. You were right. He's whole, I'm certain of it. I'll not kill any gods today."

Naia nodded. "I think I know where they've gone," she said. "I have to try and follow. Will you be all right?"

"I'm going with you," Selia said, hard and cold. "Wherever they've gone."

"I believe the Graeae will have taken Ty and Prometheus to the Tomb of the Titans."

"I thought the tomb was metaphorical," Selia said.

"In a way it is. That's why the key opens a concept more than a place."

"How do we get there, then?"

"We start with the messenger who brought my father's message to me twenty-five years ago."

Selia looked past the courtyard, into the village, to where Cyrene's body lay untended, a couple of streets away. "Let's go," she said.

When Ty traveled to Aether with Prometheus, it had been disturbing and nauseating. Traveling with the Graeae was nightmarish. Where Prometheus had cocooned him, the Graeae ripped him from Erebus, hurtling him to the deeper underworld of Tartarus.

Inky blackness surrounded him, broken only by the bright, silver sparks he'd experienced when the Graeae had arrived in the apartment. Air ripped from his lungs as if torn from him by a great fist. Cold seeped through him to his bones. Thankfully, the journey lasted only seconds. When the world stopped spinning, he gasped for air.

Prometheus stood on one side of him, and on the other was whatever the Graeae had become. The sisters had lost all hint of humanity. He stood next to a billion galaxies outlined in the form of the conjoined sisters. They radiated immeasurable coldness; they implied a vastness their form couldn't possibly contain. He looked around for Naia and relief rolled through him when he didn't find her.

Grayness surrounded him, as it had in Aether, though the feel of this place carried a heaviness Aether had not, as if he could feel the weight of other worlds above him pressing down. Even the air seemed gray and heavy as he drew it into his lungs. He rubbed at the chill on his forearms.

The ghosts of this underworld swirled around him. He could see them no more than they would be able to see him, yet he felt a tingle and a chill as something bumped his arm, perhaps even passed through it. He'd been taught as a child that the dead in Asphodel were unaware of each other, but moved constantly on their way to somewhere they felt they must be, to do something they felt compelled to do.

"Open it," the universe next to him said to Prometheus, their voices no longer two, but millions, stars winking within the blackness in their mouths.

"I can't without the key," Prometheus said.

Ty knew very well they were talking about the Tomb of the Titans, though nothing lay in front of him but gray air and gray sky and gray ground—no different than anything behind him. Yet, in the same way, he knew the place was near. He was aware that something loomed up within arm's reach, as if he could put his hands out and lean against a wall, and that behind that wall lay a place he knew well. The feeling of familiarity should have decreased his terror. It didn't. His heart thrummed as fast as a bird's to think of that tomb where the gods slept.

"Then make another," the Graeae said across him to Prometheus. "We held it in our hand. These were the elements, were they not?"

Ty felt the cold of a shade pass through his left shoulder. He flinched. This one had been different, not just cold but somehow resonating with him. A relative perhaps?

The shade moved on.

Prometheus glanced at him, but a shower of multi-colored dust drifted to his feet just then, pulling his attention away. The clink of small metal objects striking each other as they hit the ground echoed in this place where little else seemed solid.

"We have given you moon dust and blood, midnight, ocean and iron. Make another key."

"Make it yourself," Prometheus said.

Ty smiled. As much as he wanted whatever was going to happen to be over with, what he really wanted was to see the Graeae utterly fail.

"We cannot make it. Your magic sealed this door, your magic must make the key."

Apparently the Graeae weren't completely omniscient. Not only couldn't they make the key, they appeared not to have understood the god's sarcasm.

Without warning, Prometheus doubled over, hands to his chest. Ty didn't know what could make a god groan in pain, but the Graeae had some hold over him. He'd seen it when Prometheus had been dragged from Momus' apartment. This time it brought the god to his knees.

When the spasm ended, Prometheus lurched forward to his hands and knees. Panting, he nodded. "All right."

Ty winced to see him concede so quickly. "Prometheus, don't do it. Hold out if you can."

Prometheus ignored him and ran a finger through the dust. It coalesced as he drew shapes, iron pulling to iron, forming the base. The red and black elements swirled together in a tiny dust devil. They rose from the ground inches high at first, then tall as a man. Ty stepped back, confused, knowing that the dimensions of the key were nowhere near the thing that was forming.

Enyo lifted a hand. "What... "

The elements took form. Ares stood before them.

He was dressed in a short, one-shouldered robe and cross-laced sandals. He held a long spear, cocked and ready, which he launched in a single motion. It pierced both Graeae in the same way Selia's arrow had done, but the size of the spear and the strength of the wielder was far more formidable.

The sisters disintegrated. They shrank in on themselves with a whistling scream, like a teakettle the size of a house might make. The shrill sound dwindled, as if moving away from Ty and the gray of Tartarus rushed in to reclaim the space they'd occupied. As the last speck of black disappeared, Ares' spear reappeared in mid-air and fell to the ground.

"It's good to see you again, brother," Ares said over his shoulder to Prometheus.

"The sisters will recover soon," Prometheus said, speaking urgently. "The sleeping potion was belladonna, nardostachys, and toporochia. You'll recognize Eros' spell of sleep that went with it when you touch it. Wake the gods. The Graeae have me bound, so I can't give you the spell of amnesia they gave me. If I fall, you'll have to find a way to defeat them and force them to give it to you."

Prometheus turned to Ty. "Quickly. Open it."

"I don't know how," Ty said, alarmed.

"I transferred the key's properties to you." Prometheus touched Ty's right wrist over the scars Kalyptra had given him. The wrist

Prometheus had taken when he pulled Ty and Naia into Aether. "The key is yours now, not mine. You must open the tomb."

Ares retrieved his spear and watched in all directions.

"Whatever you're going to do," Ares said, "do it fast. I feel them coming."

Ares and Prometheus stood on either side of Ty, facing out as he stared at the nothing before him.

He had no fucking idea what to do. He didn't possess magic to pull the key from his scars, or a god's wisdom to divine his course of action. If Prometheus had known how to accomplish the thing, he supposed he would have told him. The gods had one magic and the Graeae had another. Whatever Prometheus had given him had now become Ty's own.

He stared at the inside of his right wrist and tried to tap into it. Nothing happened.

"Hurry," Ares barked.

"I don't know how," Ty repeated.

Sweat dotted his forehead despite the coolness. He focused harder on the scars, trying to force the shape of a key from the four lines. He tried to picture it three-dimensional, twisting into the image of the gryphon key, and opening the invisible door. Still nothing happened.

There was a great rushing of wind. It didn't blow toward him, but sucked away into some great hole in the world.

"Hurry!" Prometheus this time.

Ty didn't need the prompting. He knew as well as any of them that they needed the gods. All of them. Right now.

He felt rather than saw the Graeae appear. A swirling hole of blackness punched into the world over his shoulder. He turned to see Ares cast his spear dead center again. It vanished without a trace, having no effect.

Naia and Selia ran across the fields and hills toward Naia's village. Arriving at last at the outskirts, they cut to the right and down. Naia's home lay Oldside from here, but she wasn't headed home.

Two terraced drops later, they arrived at the river.

Charon waited for them, as he would always wait at the precise spot on his river where anyone sought him. The ferryman's sparse white hair stuck out from under his cloth cap like dandelion down. The old man reached a hand toward Naia and helped her into the narrow boat first, then Selia. He began to paddle down river angling gently across to the large homes on the other side. Naia laid a hand on his forearm.

"No, friend. This time we need to go straight across."

Charon said nothing, only nodded. His image of frailty fell away as he dug his long, wooden pole into the river bed and heaved. Swinging the prow Farside, he headed for the open field on the opposite bank. "You have never asked to go this way before," he said, lifting and swinging the pole with fluid grace, guiding them across a current she knew no other had the strength to ford.

"The message you brought me so long ago. I act on it, finally." She thought she saw his grim features draw up into a small smile. "Time is of the essence," she said. "We need to get as close as possible to the Tomb of the Titans."

He gave a short nod and struck the bottom of the river so hard a distant, deep chiming sounded below the water, as if he'd struck iron.

Aello flapped her wings and flew as fast as she was able. She had been used often in the underworld as an instrument of torture, and as such had dispensation to travel to and from all areas of Haides. She knew the way well.

She'd cared nothing for politics. If her master was set on killing gods, then she would aid him. If the twins—whoever they were—wanted him dead, she would fight them. She had believed her master's Promise because she had wanted to believe, but to know now that he was a god left no doubt in her that he possessed the power to fulfill it. Panting, she flew as fast as her wings would carry her.

30

To Die, Perchance To Dream

With a loud sucking sound, the Graeae reappeared in their human form, still gowned and wearing their crowns and mirrors. They showed no sign of harm from the arrow or the spear.

Registering more movement from the corner of his eye, Ty glanced to the side. Naia and Selia were running up from the river toward them. *Gods no,* he thought. They had to have seen the Graeae appear, yet neither of them slowed. Selia was chanting something as she ran; he thought he heard Selene's name. She had a look of battle madness about her, as if her heart had no room for fear.

Ares gave a loud war cry and launched at the sisters. Ty felt the Graeae gathering a burst of power so immense it raised the hair on his forearms.

A loud screech pulled all their gazes upward. Aello plummeted from the sky. Ty flinched back, shocked, as she struck the sisters with both taloned feet. Her wings knocked the crowns and mirrored circlets from their conjoined heads, and her claws dug into the flesh over their skulls at the topmost point where they joined. With teeth, fingernails, and claws she made an impressive start at ripping their heads apart, fused bones or no.

"Make me beautiful," Aello screamed, looking to Ares.

The harpy exploded in a burst of feathers and a spattering of flesh. The blood that flowed in rivers over the heads of the Graeae was both their own and Aello's.

Ares and Prometheus launched together. To Ty's horror, Naia ran to join them, one arm outstretched as if she could spell the Graeae with love. The only way to stop this madness was to reach the other gods while he still had Ares to wake them and Prometheus to return their memories.

Ty reached out in front of him, feeling for a wall he knew must be there, frantic to find a way into the tomb.

The need to get past a boundary he didn't understand reminded Ty of the first time he'd entered Erebus through the bowels of the cave under the lake, and had encountered a flat stone wall ahead of him. He'd found a keyhole in the blackness and picked the lock, a lock that had vanished on the other side. That had been before he'd understood the first rule of Erebus. *You see what you expect to see.* He had acted in ways that were familiar to him, and had seen what he expected. It was the same as having seen the city of Athina instead of the villages of Erebus; the strange physics of these underworlds flowed to bend around what he perceived.

If he wanted to get through a locked door, he needed to be a locksmith.

Ty felt time running out as he reached into his back pocket for the toolkit he barely noticed anymore. He risked a quick glance behind him as his fingers unzipped the pouch.

Aello's attack seemed to have slowed the Graeae more than he would have expected. It gave Selia the chance to fire three arrows from her quiver. Maybe her words had been prayers to her mother to spell the arrows. Maybe Selene's magic would do against the Graeae what the sisters' own arrow had not. Or perhaps she'd been praying because there was nothing else to be done.

The first arrow pierced the eye of one sister's head. The next pierced the area of the heart for one body and lung of the other. The third cut through their mutual abdomens. The assault took only seconds and he watched, his breath held in hope. The Graeae turned toward Selia bristling with the three arrows. Selia flew backward, and landed split from crown to crotch, suffering the same fate as Aello and Momus.

"Naia," Ty shouted. "Don't move."

She had closed the gap, reaching for one of the sisters as if she could make a universe feel love. His heart leapt into his throat as he pictured her split open like the others who had opposed the Graeae. Ares intervened, saving her, swinging at the sisters with his fists. Prometheus strained to lift a nearby boulder.

Ty turned back, hands shaking, telling himself over and over that nothing he could do would help her, help any of them, except this. Heart racing, he walked along the wall that wasn't there, willing the magic of the tattoos on his feet to lead him where he sought to go, letting it help him find what he needed. He understood at last that he didn't need to access the key; he *was* the key.

He stopped at a random patch of gray earth and air that felt somehow right, and put his hands out before him again, feeling air and telling himself it was the wall of a tomb. A vertical slit materialized under his fingers. He couldn't see it, and could only barely feel it. Keeping one finger on the tiny fracture in the air, Ty pulled his tension wrench out one handed, placing it in the not-really-there lock. It vanished into the invisible keyhole. He found his rake next, slid it in beside the wrench and felt for the pins, willing them into existence. Something clicked. A section of not-there-wall swung open and the smell of freshly turned earth wafted to him. A moist, ozone smell, musty and sulfurous.

"Prometheus!" Ty yelled.

The god had lifted the boulder. With a shout to Ares and Naia to stand clear, he thrust it at the Graeae. It circled their heads like a moon. With horror, Ty watched it gain speed to slingshot back at Prometheus with many times the original force. As the god dove to the side, Ty could make out a faint outline of chains trailing from his chest to the sisters hands. They pulled taught, jerking Prometheus back into the path of the boulder. It struck his head with an awful crunch, and he fell beneath it.

"No," Naia screamed. Ty heard her heart breaking.

A roar erupted from Ares, and a battle axe larger than Ty could have lifted appeared in his hands. Faster than even the Graeae could counter, the god swung it in an arc from his feet, over his head, and down. The axe struck directly on the split between their two skulls that Aello had started. With a scream, they divided into two bodies and fell face down.

Naia, still gripping the arm of one sister, fell to the ground with them.

With the sisters taken care of and the door to the tomb open, Ares dropped his axe and dashed past Ty.

Prometheus lay crushed beneath the boulder. Selia's body sprawled, torn and mangled, not far from him. Ty needed to get Naia out of here. He looked toward the river, but if they went that way, they would be exposed to any enemy. The tomb might not be safe for long, but sticking near Ares while he tried to help the others seemed the best option.

He ran to Naia, determined to carry her to the tomb. Halfway there he stopped. The sisters were drawing together, their two halves spilling black and silver star-stuff as they rose from the ground, peeling up in ways their bodies shouldn't have been able to move. The legs, bent at soft angles until the calves of one sister touched the calves of the other. The remainder of their bodies followed, bending like rag dolls as they joined and knitted at hips, back, neck, and, finally, head.

Naia lay on the ground, one arm and shoulder pulled upward by the grip she still held on the sister's wrist, unable somehow to let go. Ty grabbed her around the waist and jerked back. Her skin was slick— not with sweat, but with water—and Ty realized she'd been trying unsuccessfully to shift.

Her features were painted in agony. Great ravines appeared in her flesh, spreading along her arms, her legs, down her forehead. She trembled so hard she vibrated. Ty guessed her water properties were the only thing saving her from blowing apart like Selia.

Blood coursed down the bald patch of the sisters' heads where Aello had ripped at their skulls, though Ty saw no wounds from being axed in half. It made no sense, but their true injuries probably weren't something he could perceive. Regardless, it was clear that the arrow, the spear, Aello, Ares, and whatever other magic the two gods had thrown at them had taken a toll on the Graeae. They were whole again, but hadn't moved. Their eyes held blank stares full of swirling stars. Ty suspected they had more to repair from Ares blow than their costume of humanity.

"Naia," he hissed.

His skin crawled as he felt a presence above him. The Graeae had returned to their conjoined body. They couldn't look down or turn their heads, but one moved her arm and Naia's hand fell away at last.

Naia shifted instantly into water and began to flow toward the river. Ty felt a shudder beneath his feet and fought to keep his balance as a narrow pit, a couple of meters deep, appeared in the rocky ground. Naia tumbled into it as Ty watched, helpless. She didn't shift back into her body and Ty wondered if the sisters held her in water form in the same way they'd kept her in her human form before. One of the sisters pulled something from a pouch. She dangled it in front of his eyes. It was the black ribbon he had lost.

"Do not follow."

With more grace and coordination than he would have expected, they ran to the tomb. They could have killed him with a thought, but apparently, they were keeping him alive until they accomplished their goal. He had led them to this place and opened the tomb. Naia and the ribbon would be powerful collateral if they needed more from him.

If they hadn't shown him the ribbon, hadn't threatened him, he might not even have realized what they feared. Now he knew. If he could close and lock the door to the tomb with the Graeae inside, they would be trapped in there like the gods. Whatever else that tomb was, it was secure.

The Graeae ran past the invisible door and vanished into the nowhere place that existed between the molecules of Asphodel, just as Ares had done. Ty could almost feel the ribbon in their grip. Without the spell for the gods' memories, Ares had little chance of doing more than waking angry, amnesic gods. But at least it was a chance. Maybe they'd strike out at the Graeae in blind fear. But if the Graeae killed Ares, or even disabled him, all was lost.

Maybe he and Naia could live through this if he just stopped now. He'd given the sisters what they wanted—not intentionally, of course; he'd opened the tomb to help Prometheus and Ares—but if he just stepped back, walked away from this battle between powers too large to comprehend, he and Naia would be no threat. Once the Graeae succeeded, there'd be no reason not to let them go. He could take Naia to the surface. If the Graeae killed all the gods and ruled the nation— the world, the universe—did it really matter? Was it any different than the decades of political unrest and coups he'd always known?

Only one thing stopped him: Naia would never give up and run. And she would never forgive him if he did.

Gods. Anything but choking to death. Why couldn't they have just blown him apart like Selia and Momus and Aello?

"I'll be back for you," he shouted to the pool of water.

Ty tapped into every tool Prometheus had given him, all his tattoos and scars. He visualized the door, drawing it in his mind where he willed it to be, but opening outward now instead of inward. All he had to do was distract the sisters enough to give Ares a chance. If Ares could wake the other gods, maybe the lot of them could threaten the Graeae into returning their memories. Ty laid hands against solid rock he couldn't see and pushed with all his strength. As the invisible door swung shut he shouted, "Leave Ares and the gods unharmed or it stays locked." He counted on the fact they wouldn't choke him once he had it locked.

With one hand still on the invisible door, he felt frantically for the keyhole and found it when he knocked his wrench and rake, also invisible while in the door, to the dirt. "Gamoto!" he swore. He half expected the door to blow apart in his face while he scrabbled in the dirt for his tension wrench. He got a poor grip on it in his rush.

Swearing, he grabbed it again and jammed the tool into the sliver of a keyhole.

The door crashed into him, throwing him backward. The conjoined sisters stood on the threshold between Asphodel and somewhere far away. Enyo, he supposed, faced him with the ribbon in her hand. Ty crabbed backwards trying to gain his feet.

Before he could stand, she had the thing tied in a half-knot. She gave it a vicious jerk. He felt like he'd been knuckle-punched over the sensitive and prominent cartilage beneath his scar. His windpipe collapsed, crushed. The force and pain of the assault knocked him to his back. He couldn't breathe in or out.

Pemphredo, facing into the tomb, lifted one arm in a gesture.

Ty tore uselessly at his throat, trying to rip away the ribbon that wasn't there. Suffocation wasn't a quick death, he knew that too well. Air hunger, pain, and panic passed in half-time. Long moments in which to taste his defeat. He collapsed onto his side, trying to gasp in the air beyond his reach. He felt a shade touch him. A sad revenant that he would soon join.

Ty saw shadows moving within the tomb. Ares had woken the gods, but without their memories they might all just stand around or run away. Ty clawed at the ground, trying to pull himself toward Naia. He wouldn't see the end of this epic tableau, but he wanted to be near her when he died.

The water that was Naia lay multiple body lengths' distance from him. He crawled less than a handspan toward her. He caught movement at the corner of his eye. The boulder covering Prometheus' face shifted. Ty would have gasped if he could.

Gods truly didn't die easily.

The rock rolled to the side, strangely silent in the gray nothingness. Enyo was preoccupied watching Ty suffocate and Pemphredo faced off with Ares. Ty knew that Enyo couldn't turn her head, and neither of them had recovered their mirrors. And without Deino, neither of them could sense the present.

They hadn't seen Prometheus move, but he had. As anoxia stole the last of his consciousness, he smiled.

And then he died.

31

New Beginnings

Ty stood on a hillside of dry, colorless grass. He felt at his throat but there was no constriction, no pain. He couldn't even feel his fingers against the skin of his neck. No rise and fall of breath in his chest. He felt nothing but cold, and even that was distant.

The world still defined itself in monotone shadings of gray, like the fog on Lake Marathon, like the misty waterfall in Aether. This place was neither of those. He knew he was truly in Asphodel as surely as he knew he would soon lose that awareness.

He walked forward, drawn by an urge to be somewhere, though he didn't yet know where. Topping a small rise, he found himself looking down on his old neighborhood. Everything here was gray as well, except for one house near the center of the neighborhood. His childhood home; his mother's house until she died. The color was the same, unremarkable sandy tan it had always been, but in this world of gray it shone like a lighthouse beacon.

Ty hurried down the hill toward it. He passed into his neighborhood like he had passed into Erebus, moving in a single stride from grassy hills into familiar streets. People he knew—had known—stepped out of their homes or looked up from their gardens as he passed. Many were elderly, but not all—Nick Vallis, who had been hit by a train while trying to jump the tracks on a dare from the other boys. Saffi Dukas, a classmate of Ty's who had died when she was fourteen from some disease he'd never heard of before.

Some of the shades waved, lifting gray, ethereal hands in greeting. Others continued their small tasks, seemingly unaware of him. Ty wondered what menial, repetitive obsession would settle into his mind soon, occupying the rest of his eternity.

He pushed open the small, white gate and walked up the paving stones to his old front door. A vague nervousness clawed at his stomach. He didn't want to see his mother on her hands and knees, scrubbing the kitchen floor forever, but his mother opened the door before he reached it. She wasn't gray; she wore a pale yellow print dress that had been a favorite. A bright yellow cooking apron was tied at her waist. She was thin, but it relieved him to see she didn't look ill.

Wordlessly, she opened her arms to him. He climbed the last step and threw his arms around her.

"I'm so sorry," he said. "I'm so very sorry for everything. I should have been there for you when you got ill. I should have been there the day you died." Tears came, but they dried on his cheeks as they fell.

She said nothing, but he felt her forgiveness and understanding suffuse him, as if spoken through her touch.

There was something he needed to be doing, a motorcycle engine he'd been working on in the back yard. He squeezed his mother tighter while the last sparks of his living brain went out like the embers of a dying fire. He let her go and she turned for the kitchen.

His motorcycle. He needed to work on it before dark. There was something else, though. Something he needed to do first.

"I love you." he said it loudly, knowing it would be the last time.

She looked back over her shoulder and smiled at him, then walked through the archway. He headed for the back door.

"*And I love you.*"

It wasn't his mother's voice. He knew the voice well, though he couldn't place it.

Something stroked his cheek. The sensation felt different than his mother's hug; it felt visceral, lighting up sensory neurons on his skin. His real skin.

He inhaled deeply, taking a breath like a baby's first, full of need and newness and wonder. A breath of life. He coughed and his throat burned. His breath came ragged and magnificent.

Ty's eyelids fluttered, though the light he opened them to was pale and gray. He started, sitting halfway up before a massive headache stopped him. He wondered if this was just some new phase of a never-ending death dream.

The hand touched his face again and he turned his head. Naia was kneeling next to him, the black ribbon in one hand. Two men—no, two gods—were next to her, one standing, one squatting next to him with a hand on Ty's shoulder. The one standing was horribly maimed by a deep facial wound. It ran from the bridge of his nose to the inside edge of one white and blinded eye, on down to his mouth, twisted up by split and partially healed skin. Looking at the other half of his face, Ty recognized Prometheus.

The god squatting near him, Ty didn't recognize.

"Thank you, Thanatos," Naia said. She bowed her head to the God of Death. He placed his hand gently on her head in acknowledgment or blessing, then stood and moved to speak with the other gods.

Ty sat up the rest of the way, head pounding. Gods and goddesses were talking in groups or pairs, individuals were winking out like stars at dawn, probably going back to Aether. All seemed sane and hale.

"Where are the Graeae?" he asked.

"Locked in the Tomb of the Titans," Naia said. She stood and helped him to his feet. You gave Ares enough time to wake the gods and tell them the Graeae were their enemy, some were able to channel enough defensive magic to hold the sisters until Prometheus could undo the spell of amnesia. Once all the gods were restored, the Graeae were easily bound and locked inside."

"Why didn't the gods kill them?"

She took Ty's hand. He stood and they started walking toward the river. "There were some who wanted to, but Prometheus convinced them to imprison the sisters instead. No one really knows exactly what they are, or how integral they are to our world or to magic."

"And that tomb will hold them?"

"If anyplace can, that one will. Just don't go letting them out of there, now that you have the only key." She smiled.

He pulled down the neck of his T-shirt, but the tattoos below his collarbones were still invisible. "Will I keep the marks?"

She shrugged. "I'd imagine so." She swung their hands in silence a moment. "I'm proud of you, Ty. You're a hero, you know. A true hero, like those of old."

The concept seemed absurd, but saving the entire pantheon of gods couldn't very well be defined otherwise, he supposed. He'd died three times so far; twice he'd ended up in the Tomb of the Titans, and once in Asphodel. He wondered if being a hero meant that next time he'd go to Elysium.

Ty stopped suddenly, pulling Naia to a halt as well. He looked back toward the tomb. More of the gods had left, but Thanatos remained, talking with Prometheus and Ares. Ty began walking back up the slope and Naia followed.

He stopped in front of Thanatos. "I didn't get to thank you personally," Ty said.

Thanatos smiled. "Nor I, you," he said.

Ty felt a blush climb his cheeks. He had no idea how to respond to gratitude from a god.

"I... When I die next time, where will I end up?" Naia looked at him with an odd expression.

"You would go to the Elysium Fields."

"Could you send my mother there instead?" he asked, heart in his throat. Now that his hopes had been raised, he didn't want them dashed.

Thanatos considered. "Hades would be the one to decide."

"Is he still here for me to ask?" Ty looked around as if he'd be able to tell one god from another based on artist's imaginations.

"He's already returned to his throne. I'll speak to him for you if you want. I can send word of his answer to Naia through Charon, but I think there's little chance he'd say no. You saved him too, after all."

Ty thanked him again. He'd rather have his mother alive, but Prometheus had already explained that wasn't possible, no more than Thanatos could bring Lamia back for Naia's sake. But if his mother had been given the option of cleaning houses for a few more years in Ellada or dying now and spending forever in Elysium, he thought he knew what she would have answered. He felt lighter of spirit than he had in months as he and Naia headed back toward the river.

When they reached the water's edge, one of the gods was there, talking to the ferryman. Naia stopped next to him and reached out with her free hand. He took it in his.

He had dark hair that fell in soft curls to his shoulders, and a short robe clasped at one shoulder. Even with the entire pantheon of gods surrounding Ty, this man's beauty stood out from the rest. He was the god whose bier Ty had stood next to as a child. Eros. Naia's father. The god Prometheus had dreamed of when his dreams had sent Ty to the Tomb of the Titans as a child.

"I love you," Naia said to Eros.

"And I love you," he said, touching her cheek. Addressing the ferryman, he said. "Take them home safely, my friend." The old man nodded to Ty as he and Naia boarded the narrow boat.

The ferryman looked oddly familiar, though Ty couldn't remember seeing him before. He squinted and a superimposed image appeared. The man in the second image was shorter, more wizened, and wearing the red uniform and cap of an elevator operator.

Eros raised a hand in farewell and flashed a smile of pure joy at his daughter. Charon dipped his pole in the water, and the ferry moved out into the river.

Ty didn't know what would happen from here, whether he and Naia would return to Erebus or go to the surface, or split their time in two worlds like Persephone. She squeezed his hand and he leaned into the warmth of her shoulder, knowing that it didn't matter to him where fate took him, not as long as she was by his side.

OTHER BOOKS BY THIS AUTHOR

A Borrowed Hell by L. D. Colter (contemporary fantasy)

The Halfblood War by L. Deni Colter (epic fantasy)

Visit the author's website at https://www.lizcolter.com/

To get news of new releases, sales and more, straight to your inbox, sign up for L. D. Colter's newsletter at https://mailchi.mp/bc969529fd5b/4tnr6lc28f_ldcolter

Did you know?

Reviews and star ratings help readers choose books they'll enjoy.

As few as 25 reviews on Amazon will increase the visibility of a book on Amazon's website, allowing more readers to find it.

A few words are as helpful as longer reviews. What matters is the number of reviews a book gets.

Please help promote books and authors you've enjoyed by leaving a review!

ABOUT THE AUTHOR

Liz has followed her heart through a wide variety of careers, including farming with a team of draft horses, and working as a field paramedic, Outward Bound instructor, athletic trainer, and roller-skating waitress, among other curious choices. She also knows more about concrete than you might suspect.

Her novels written under the name L. D. Colter explore contemporary and dark fantasy, and ones written as L. Deni Colter venture into her epic fantasy realms. She's an active SFWA member with multiple short story publications, and her debut novel "A Borrowed Hell" was the winner of the 2018 Colorado Book Award for Science Fiction/Fantasy. Following a long interlude in Southern and Northern California, she returned some years ago to her home state of Colorado, where she spends her time with her husband, dogs, horses, and writing (according to her husband, not always in that order of priority).

Made in the USA
Lexington, KY
17 July 2019